BOOKS BY JOHN MOOERS

Pillar of Stories

J.P.

Fire in Winter: Copper Meadow

Fire in Winter: Proustian Walks

A Farewell to Windemere

A Farewell To Windemere

John Mooers

A Farewell To Windemere

Published by riverrun
16310 Sandalwood Street
Fountain Valley, CA 92708

ISBN: 978-0-9886486-8-5

First published July 8, 2014

Front cover photograph:
"Hemingway canoeing as a young man"
Courtesy of the Ernest Hemingway Collection. John F. Kennedy Presidential Library and Museum, Boston.

Back cover photograph:
"Ernest Hemingway with friends in the Walloon Lake/Petoskey area Michigan"
Accession number EH5529P
Courtesy of the Ernest Hemingway Collection. John F. Kennedy Presidential Library and Museum, Boston

www.riverrunusa.com

To Georgiana Hennessy

With love, and for all that you have done

CONTENTS

On the Piave at Fossalta

It was dark. There was no moon. Ernest felt his way along the side of the trench. It was a hot night. It was past midnight. He was sweating from his bicycle ride down from Fossalta. In the dark it was hard to find his way through the trenches. He came between two soldiers standing behind the trench. Ernest could hear men talking down in the trench. Ernest reached into his bag and pulled out some chocolates. He handed one to the soldier on his right. In the dark the man smelled it to see what it was.

"Grazie," the soldier said.

Ernest nodded and said: "Sei il Benvenuto."

A star flare burst into sparkling light down the line. It gave just enough light for Ernest to see the man next to him. The man wore his helmet and had a growth of beard. Ernest could briefly see the lay of the trench in the diminishing light from the flare. A second man stood several feet away to his left and another approached from his front.

The man to his left also wore his helmet and had his rifle slung over his shoulder. The man was looking at Ernest. The man whispered to him.

"Che cosa avete?"

Ernest reached into his bag again and whispered back.

"Cioccolatini."

Ernest looked at the third man approaching him. He was shirtless in the heat of the night.

Far off there was a metallic cough. Then from the black sky he heard a whirling chugging chugging, louder and louder. Then it hit.

In front of him there was a blinding flash and a rush of hot roaring wind. It knocked him down. Mangled dirt splattered all over him. The roar sealed his ears and he could not hear. The air melted and moved back. He could not feel anything. He could not breathe. He gasped but nothing came. The hot wind pulled him out. He floated. He was out in the wind without breathing and his body was gone. Then he gasped again until finally he breathed and he was back. The wind was gone and he was back.

Chapter One

He was breathing heavy, gasping for air. He opened his eyes. It was dark. It was hot. He moved his arms. Dirt fell off his chest and he tried to brush it away. It was all in slow motion. His hand was shaking. There was crying and then screaming. It was to his right. A star shell exploded up in the night and he was awash in silver light. In the light he turned to his right and brought his left hand up the leg of the man next to him. At his waist there was a gap. He could feel hot blood pumping onto his hand. Ernest pulled it away. It was wet and sticky. He will be dead. Ernest rolled over. Pieces of shattered wood and dirt fell away as he rolled himself up. Another flare fired and burnt bright for a moment. In the light he could see the third man in front of him face down. His body was shredded and in parts. Ernest tried to stand up but his knee was funny and did not work right. He felt it with his hand and his pants were wet and torn. His right kneecap felt strange. He heard the moaning of the man to his left. He crawled the few feet over to him. He lifted up the man's head. The man was still breathing and he was moaning and whispering something.

"Let's get you out of here," Ernest said.

Ernest pulled the man's arm up and then hoisted him up over his shoulder. The man's chest was sticky wet with thick blood. Ernest tried to stand but he had no power in his right leg, it was wobbly and shaking. He heaved up and stood, It was one hundred yards to the rear dressing station. He walked with his leg trembling and feeling as if it was going to give out at any moment. He kept walking, breathing heavily, he could barely see in the dark but he kept walking and wobbly walking.

Suddenly he was flooded with light. An Austrian searchlight combed the horizon. He heard a metallic rat a tat and bullets splattered the ground around him. It felt like a hard icy snowball slapped into his right knee and another hit his ankle. He fell forward and went down with the man draped over him. Ernest could not move for a moment. The light passed and it was dark again. Ernest pushed up with his left leg. Standing, aching, his leg trembled as if stung by a thousand hornets; he kept walking and walking blindly walking in the direction of the dressing station toward the rear.

1. Station

Ernest watched out the window as the train pulled into the station. It was a cold night. Flakes of snow crusted into ice on the outside of the windows. The train slowed as it pulled alongside the platform and Ernest tried to see everyone standing on the station. He looked at as many of the faces he could see but he did not see anyone he knew. The train came to a chugging stop. Steam billowed out into the cold night air; a whistle blast announced their arrival. People in the train were already standing as the train came to a full stop, swaying back and forth as they stood, themselves looking out the windows looking for a familiar face. He could hear the squeaking rattle as the porter pulled open the door and leapt down onto the platform. The cold snowy air whirled into the warm but stuffy cabin.

When enough people cleared the aisle Ernest stood up. He wore his khaki colored uniform, covered in part by his long knee length black cape lined with red satin that he had flung over his shoulders and fastened at the neck with a double silver buckle. His brown pants were tucked into his new high black leather boots laced tightly all the way up. As he stood he reached down into his seat, put on his brown beret cap and picked up his wooden cane. He started to struggle with his bag when the black porter came over.

"Let me help you with that, sir."

"Oh, thank you. Thank you very much."

The man smiled a wide smile

"It will be my pleasure, sir."

Ernest held the tops of the seats as he limped his way to the door leaning heavily on his cane.

"Watch your step, sir."

Ernest stepped down with care the few steps onto the platform.

"Is anyone here to meet you?" the porter asked as he put the bag down onto the platform.

Ernest, with his cane, took a few steps and glanced around at the other people coming and going. Small flakes of snow whirled about in the wake of people passing by.

"Yes, I think so. I wired my father that I would be here."

"You don't see him?"

Ernest looked up straight ahead of him. And there he was, his father: Dr. Clarence Hemingway, 47, tall, brown hair, neatly trimmed brown Van Dyke moustache and beard, he wore a heavy woolen overcoat dappled with snow. He held his hat in his hand.

5

Clarence walked up to his son, his face warming into a full glowing smile. They stood staring, smiling, at each other.

"Hello, Dad," Ernest finally said.

"Look at you," Clarence began to say as he looked his nineteen year old son up and down. His eyes stopped on the cane.

"I'm home."

Clarence nodded and held out his hand. Ernest took the cane with his left hand and held out his right hand. But Clarence stepped in toward Ernest and hugged him strong, slapping his back with his hand. Clarence tightened his embrace for a moment but then broke apart and stepped back.

They both took a deep breath.

The porter broke the silence.

"You were in the war, son?"

"Yes."

"How old are you, if you don't mind me asking?"

"Nineteen."

"That's a mighty fine thing that, you going to war an' all, fighting for us. Mighty fine thing," he mumbled as he reached down to pick up the bag.

Ernest, proud, raised an eyebrow as he smiled at his father. Clarence reached for the bag.

"Here, let me take that."

"You parked in the car lot?"

"Yes."

"I'll see that his other bags get to you there."

"Thank you. That will be fine." Clarence started to reach into his pocket.

"Oh no sir, there's no need for that. You got a mighty fine boy here."

When the porter walked off Clarence, holding the bag in one hand, put his hat onto his head with the other.

"Well, shall we go, mighty fine boy?"

They walked toward the station. Ernest limped with each step and needed the cane.

"Here, son, take my arm, let me help you."

"No, I'm fine. Really, Dad, I'm fine."

At the bottom of the stairs leading up into the station Clarence nodded up the stairs with his head.

"There's s small surprise waiting up the stairs for you."

Ernest looked up. The stairs were filled with people rushing up and down. Ernest, holding onto the railing with one hand and with his cane

6

in the other began ascending. Clarence, slow step by step, came up behind him. As Ernest reached the top of the stairs he looked around and heard a shout.

"Ernie!"

His sister Marcelline, sitting on a bench, stood up and ran over to him. She flung her arms around his neck and hugged him tightly. There was s swirl of perfume. She was a year and a half older but it had only been in the last few years that Ernest inched taller than her.

"Hello, Ivory. How's the old keed?"

They kissed each other on the cheeks. Marcelline had to wipe her eyes as she stood next to him.

"Are you," she said as she waved her hand down toward his leg and the cane, "are you all right?"

"Sure, Sure. Getting better every day. Soon I'll be as good as new."

"Listen you Old Brute," she said as she wiped her eyes. "I really missed you, and when we heard you were wounded, oh my God I was so worried."

"Hey, I'm fine. The Austrians threw everything they had at me but here I am, soon to be as good as new."

Clarence walked them toward the front entrance.

"Come on, let's get you home. We have to take Marcelline back to her school before we can get you home."

"Your school?"

"Yes, I live on campus at the Congregational Training School."

"Really?"

"I wrote you about it, but I don't think you ever got more than half of my letters."

They made their way slowly down the walk ramp to the front doors, Ernest deliberately taking steps one by one.

Clarence insisted that Ernest take his arm.

"Here, boy. Here, lean on me."

"Now Dad, I've managed all right by myself all the way over from Milano. I think I can make it okay now."

As he stepped outside again into the snow flaked night Ernest waved them forward.

"You and Marcelline go ahead to the car. I'll follow down the steps at my own pace. I'm getting pretty good with this old stick."

He took the steps one by one while holding onto the rail. They stood watching him.

"I'll get there. It may take me a little bit but I'll get there."

"Take your time son."

7

Clarence and Marcelline walked beside him in the cold snow flaked night.

The porter was at the car with the rest of his baggage. Clarence went ahead and opened the back seat of his Ford. When Ernest reached the car the porter was done loading the car.

"You know, son, I remember you."

"Me?"

"Indeed I do. It was maybe a year, year and a half ago. I remember when you and a couple others came running onto the platform swinging your bags laughing and shouting looking this way and that totally lost for which train was yours. You asked me, puffing and out of breath, which train was yours so I pointed to it and it was just about ready to pull out. You and your friend threw your bags onto the train and it started to leave while you were still on the platform. You jumped on yelling as it was starting to move, my oh my did I laugh at you then. I saw your face in the window looking out laughing and out of breath. You waved and shouted to me that you was going off to Europe for the war. I thought then that you was mighty happy about going off to war."

"You remember that?"

"Indeed I do, now that I place your face."

"We were out on a fishing trip in upper Michigan when the call for duty came. We barely had enough time to get to Chicago and then, yes, we almost missed the train."

"Well now, welcome home Mr. Hemingway."

"Thank you."

"Folks say you was the first American wounded in the war in Italy, is that so?"

"That's right."

"Well there's always got to be a first in everything, I'm awful glad you was the first one wounded and not the first one, you know."

Ernest nodded and looked down.

"Yes, well, that sad distinction went to a Lieutenant Edward McKey."

"Well bless his soul, bless his soul. But I'm mighty glad you've come back."

"Me too."

2. Party

Grace Hemingway was nervous. The house was filled with people. She had sat most of them in the music room but others were walking about. Ruth was walking around seeing that everyone had a drink and one of the cupcakes and some of the cookies she baked earlier in the day. When Grace knew for sure that her son Ernest was coming home that night she and Ruth immediately telephoned a long list of friends, family and neighbors. My boy is coming home, she said, and there will be a small welcome home party this evening. Please come.

More showed up than she had thought. It greatly pleased her. She and Ruth were seeing to everyone when fourteen year old Sunny came running into the music room.

"He's here," she yelled out. "Mom, he's here." Sunny had been given the task of lookout from the front parlor window. "Dad's car just drove up."

Grace placed her hands together in front of her.

"Oh my goodness," she said. "Now, Carol, Carol where are you?" she asked as she looked all around.

"Here, here," little Carol said as she came up with her hand raised like in school. Carol was seven years old.

"Okay, now Carol I want you to go up and wake up Leicester just like we planned and then come downstairs with him, okay?"

Carol nodded and turned to carry out her assignment.

"Now, everyone, everyone," Grace called out as she clapped her hands. She was a music teacher and knew how to pull a class into order. "I'll meet him and then bring him in here, all right?"

People nodded and laughed as Grace turned and made her way down the hall and through the parlor that served as a waiting room for her husband's medical practice. He saw his patients in the adjoining side room. She glanced out of the window toward the street and in the walkway she saw two figures approaching the house. The second one was carrying a large duffle bag. The house inside was brightly illuminated and streams of light flowed outward across the snow covered ground and into the night. Grace stood at the front door. She smoothed her dress. She then took a deep breathe.

She opened the door.

As she walked out onto the porch she could feel the chill of the cold night air. She could see the thin layer of white across the lawn and flakes of snow filtering down. She walked over to the side steps of the porch leading to the drive. Ruth came out with a shawl and tried to cover her

9

shoulders but Grace waved her off.

"Now now, my dear. Not now."

Grace watched as her son came up to the bottom of the steps. He was dressed in his uniform. A brown beret cap covered his head, a black cape draped down from his shoulders, opened in the front where she could see his khaki uniform tucked into his knee high black boots. He walked heavily with a cane, hardly putting any pressure on his right foot.

She had to gasp a little when she saw the cane.

For the first time her son looked up at her. There was a momentary pause but then he smiled that big wide full faced smile of his.

"Hello, Mom," he said.

"Oh dear," she replied, "My dear sweet boy."

Grace came down the steps to the bottom step and threw her arms completely around him.

"You are home, home at last, safe and sound. Oh how I worried so."

Ernest tried to raise his arms in order to return the hug but she enveloped his upper arms and he could not move them.

"You have no idea how worried your father and I have been. And when we heard that you were wounded, and that they might even amputate your leg, oh you just don't know how worried we were."

"Well, hey, I'm here now," he said.

"How are you, how is your leg now," she asked as she released her bear hug. She held his left hand as she looked down at his right leg. "Are you all right?"

"Yes, yes, don't worry so much. I'm fine. I've got a little bit of a limp but it's getting better everyday and soon it will be as good as new. Doctor's orders."

"Let me look at you," she said as she placed both of her open palms on either side of his face. She stared into his eyes. Small flakes of snow drifted between their eyes. His cap and cape were growing dusted with white.

"My goodness but you are so skinny. Look at all the weight that you have lost. Aren't you eating properly?"

Ernest just shrugged his shoulders.

"You look so tired, you're not rested. Aren't you sleeping well?"

"Well, as a matter of fact I do have some trouble sleeping at times."

"Really?"

"Just nerves I guess."

"Well we'll take care of that. Now that you are back home, sleeping in your own bed, your own room, we'll take care of that."

To Ernest it did not really seem that way.

"Here, let us go in. It's chilly out here."

She held his left arm to help him climb the stairs. It was no use him saying no.

Grace brought him into the parlor, holding the door open for him. Clarence came in after him carrying the duffle bag.

"Just set it down over there for now, dear. We have to meet everyone."

"Who is everyone?" Ernest whispered, nervous.

She pulled on his arm and led him across the room, down the hallway, and then finally into the well-lit music room. There, as Ernest emerged into the room, the twenty or so people all cheered and clapped their hands. There were shouts of 'Welcome home, welcome home.'

Ernest smiled. He nodded to some, winked at some, and waved at others. People came up to him and shook his hand, slapped him on the back, and patted him on the shoulder.

Sunny came up to him, shy at first, but finally rushed in and hugged him. He hugged her back. Then he saw little Carol and just behind her baby Leicester. When Leicester saw his big brother he beamed.

"Ernie," he screamed as he ran toward him. People laughed as Ernest hoisted little Leicester up onto his shoulders. Leicester, all excited, was telling his older brother of how he was awake so late at night and how all the lights were on and there was hot chocolate being served in the dining room and no one was watching how many marshmallows you took.

Then, from atop Ernest's shoulders Leicester announced to anyone who would hear that his big brother was glorious because his big brother helped make the world safe for democracy and now his big brother was home and he was a hero.

As the night wore on Ernest made the rounds around the room saying hello to everyone and thanking them for stopping by. At one point Grace took him by the hand and brought him over to Grandfather Anson Hemingway. He was Clarence's father. Anson sat in a sofa chair by the fireplace. He did not say much. At seventy four years old he did not get around as much as he once did. Balding white hair, a white full beard, he sat and watched as the world whirled around him. Grace brought Ernest over and stood in front of the Grandfather.

"Anson," she said a bit loud.

Anson looked up at her.

"Anson, this is Ernest. He has come back from the war."

Anson looked at Ernest and smiled.

"Oh, is that so."

"You two have something in common now, you were both in a war."

Anson waved her off as if a bit annoyed. "Yes, yes, I know, I know where he has been," he said. Then he turned his focus toward Ernest. He nodded, as if there was something between them that she could never understand.

"I was in the war, the big one. It's been a long time ago now."

"Yes, I know Grandpa: The Civil War."

Ernest had heard the stories more than once. His grandfather had been wounded.

But then Anson grew serious.

"I saw a lot of men die," he said, more to himself than anyone listening. "A lot of men."

Ernest, as he was growing up, had heard all of this before but, for the first time, he understood what he meant.

Grace brushed it off. "Oh Anson, we don't want to hear about that now. It is a happy occasion, don't be so negative."

Anson seemed to ignore her, lost in his own memory.

But to Ernest it was clear. There were no truer words spoken. It was a clear and clean truth. All of the words that people spoke, all of the slogans about truth and glory and democracy, they did not really mean anything. The names of places, of army units, of battles, of rivers and bridges fought and died over, only those words had any meaning. Only those words were true.

Ernest bent over and reached down and put his hand firmly on Anson's shoulder. Grandfather Anson had said those words but for the first time Ernest understood. It was as if Ernest had returned to where he had left but only now knew and understood it for the first time.

"I know Grandpa," Ernest said. "I too saw a lot of men die. I was almost one of them."

Grace, pulling on Ernest's arm, whispered in his ear, "Ernest, please don't encourage him, you know how he can get with his war stories, this is a happy occasion, it is a home coming, lets not make it depressing talking about killing and death."

Ernest straightened up.

What do they think war is? Men die. That is what war is. That is what war does, it kills people. Why do they not want that to be known?

His mother pulled Ernest away from his grandfather. As Ernest walked away he could see that his grandfather was smiling, remembering: of all the people in the room only the two of them knew the real truth. Yes, Ernest thought, it is indeed a homecoming, a homecoming to the truth.

3. Dad

When the last of the guests left, Clarence went about the house turning off the lights.

"Do you want me to take a good look at those wounds on your leg?" his father asked as he turned off one of the lamps in the front parlor where Ernest sat in the overstuffed arm chair. His father waved his hand toward the door that led into his office.

"Isn't it after hours?"

"A good doctor never has after hours."

Ernest shook his head no.

"Maybe we can do it tomorrow."

Clarence stood before him. They were down to only one small lamp lit. They were alone together.

"So, does it really hurt?"

Ernest nodded. It was easy to be more honest with his father. He was a man of science. He was a man of what was real.

"Sometimes it's pretty bad and other times it just aches." He stretched his right leg out its full length. "They operated several times taking out the larger fragments. I could tell how large they were by how loud they sounded when they dropped them into the metal pan. I was afraid for a bit that they were going to take off my leg."

Clarence nodded. "They kept it from getting infected, that's the important part."

"One of the doctors was so worried to do a good job because he knew that the great Doctor Clarence Hemingway of Oak Park was going to be inspecting his work."

Clarence laughed.

"Well, son, I have to say that doing the job that they do under the conditions they work under I'm not really the one to judge."

"I thought a lot about you while I was in the hospital wondering what you would be doing if you were there as my doctor."

"Most likely the same as they did."

Ernest nodded.

"Maybe tomorrow, then," Clarence said. "Just to be safe, as long as it feels alright now."

"It hurts a bit but I've been up on it more than usual."

"Well, get some rest. Your room is on the third floor. Why don't you sleep down here just for tonight? Save you the trip up the stairs."

"They said there were two hundred and seventy seven fragments in my legs and groin."

"Amazing."

"They got the big ones out but the smaller fragments keep working their way up to the surface of the skin. I've been digging them out with my pocket knife."

"Ouch," his father laughed.

"Yes, I know."

Ernest sat back against the soft back of the arm chair. He looked up at his father standing in front of him, overlooking him. With only the one small lamp most of the room was dark. The light glowed behind his father. His shadow stretched across the darkened room.

It was at night, in the darkness, when the thoughts came.

"You told me that once, you know."

"What was that?"

"Work past the pain, the pain is not important."

Clarence tilted his head to one side as if trying to remember.

"I was a little boy. We were out camping. They came to get you, the doctor. There was an Indian woman having a baby and she was screaming. I asked if you could make her stop. You said her screams are not important; you said you did not hear the screams because they were not important."

Clarence nodded as if he remembered.

"You have to focus on the important things, not on the distractions, you said."

"Did I?"

Ernest remembered. He was a young boy. They sang a hymn in Church about dying, 'some day the silver cord will break' they sang. He knew then that he was going to die too. That night he had to sit in the hallway under the hallway light and read and even after the maid chased him back to his room to go to sleep he came back out after she went to bed so that he could sit in the hallway under the hallway light and read his book all night long. Otherwise in the dark of his room the silver cord might break and he would be asleep and not be able to stop it.

Several days later he and his father and Uncle George were camping far out in the woods. It was night and dark and his father and Uncle George went out onto the lake to fish at night. He sat alone in the tent. The fire was going out. He could hear the night time woods outside his tent, sounds here and there. When will the silver cord break? He was afraid.

Then the two Indians came for the doctor. She was struggling, they said. She was bad off, they said. They rowed out across the lake toward

14

the Indian camp. He went in the shack with his father and held the lamp up high.

"She is going to have a baby," his father said.

He looked around at everyone.

"It is turned around backwards and is coming out wrong. I have to fix it," his father said.

"Okay, Daddy," Ernest said as he held up the lantern but was looking away.

Later, after it was over, as it was just getting light, his father rowed the boat back across the lake. Ernest sat in the stern of the boat. He watched his father's back as he rowed. Ernest trailed his hand in the water as they crossed the lake through the rising mist. In the crisp morning cold the water felt warm. A bass jumped and splashed the calm water. Ernest knew that he could never die.

Ernest noticed the way his father stood. Leaning a little forward, his eyes looking down to the floor, his hands clasped behind his back, his head bent slightly to one side as if trying to listen to something far away, or remember something far away. He seemed so distant.

"Dad," Ernest said.

Clarence, as if startled, looked to Ernest and smiled.

"Remember the Agassiz Club?"

Clarence had formed the Oak Park branch of the Louis Agassiz Club. It was devoted to the Natural Sciences for young children. They took trips out into the woods and along the Des Plaines River and went hiking and camping and fishing and Clarence pointed out the trees and the plants and the animals. He taught them how to look. They all sat around the camp fire with their science books that had the names and pictures of things and talked about what they saw that day.

Clarence smiled.

"What on earth made you think of that?"

"Oh, I don't know. Those were fun days don't you think?"

"Yes they were. Those trips were fun. All the kids were so excited."

"You taught me a lot about nature you know."

"Those were nice times."

They both remained silent for a moment.

"Have you ever thought about doing it again? Maybe reform the Club, do it for Carol and Les, why even Sunny and Ursula would like it."

Clarence shook his head.

"Oh no; not now. Time moves on, there just isn't the time."

"It's their time now, just like it was my time then. Maybe I could help you."

Clarence again shook his head no.

"Well, it is late. I put your luggage up in your room. Do you need help up the stairs?"

"No, I'm fine," Ernest said as he stood up.

"By the way," his father said as he reached down and picked up several letters sitting in a flat dish on the table. He handed Ernest the letters. "These came for you."

Ernest looked down at the letters. It was her handwriting. Both letters.

Ernest glanced back at his father. Clarence raised one eyebrow. "You'll have to tell me all about her someday."

"I will."

Clarence put his hand on Ernest's shoulder.

"Good night son. It is good to have you home."

4. Letters

Ernest made his way up the stairs to his third floor room. He took the stairs one at a time, slow. He stepped up with his left leg, then placed the cane and then brought up his right foot. Step by slow step. There had been times he ran up and down these stairs with leaps and bounds as if there were no stairs at all.

The door to his room was open and his large bags sat on the floor in the middle of the room. He put the two letters on the table next to his bed. The bed was neatly made up. The bed frame was made of iron and painted green, the bed covers white.

Ernest sat down on the bed with his right leg stretched out. He put his cane down on the floor next to the bed. He knew he would need it again. His legs hurt, ached. He looked over at the letters and wondered if he should open them and read them now or get undressed and comfortable. That way he could just doze off thinking of her.

He reached down and unlaced his boots and slipped the black boots off and placed them next to each other next to a wooden chair. He unbuttoned his shirt and carefully draped it over the back of the wooden chair. He took off his pants and folded them and put them onto the seat of the chair.

Ernest stood and opened the top drawer of the chest of drawers. There, still, neatly folded, were his pajamas. He had not worn pajamas since he left home. It was like returning to himself, returning to before the war, before he left. It was as if Italy had all been a dream, he was back to where he came from. But it felt different.

He pulled down the covers and the sheet. He opened up one of his bags on the floor and pulled out a quilt, a Red Cross quilt neatly knitted with large squares of green, red, black, yellow and white. It was a quilt that ladies had made for 'the boys' at the front. Agnes gave it to him. It was his magical quilt.

Ernest got into bed, trying not to put any pressure on his right leg. He pulled the covers up and then spread out the quilt on top, a final layer of warmth and comfort.

Settled, he reached over and pulled the lamp on the table by the bed in closer for better light. He picked up the two letters, looked at the postage and then opened the oldest letter first. As he opened the letter he could smell her. He held the paper up to his nose. It smelled vaguely of her. Her perfume. Her scent. Her warmth. Her presence.

It was in her handwriting. It made him smile.

Agnes von Kurowsky: his nurse from the Milan Hospital where he recovered from his wounds. Agnes; his love. They were going to get married soon. Soon. Being away from her he realized he loved her so much that it hurt.

"Kid dearest," he read out loud.

He laughed.

Then he read the letter.

She wrote that they all went to the Palazzo Reale to see President Wilson. Lined up, dressed in their fresh uniforms wearing white gloves and their freshly polished white shoes all of the nurses from the Milan Hospital lined up to ascend the velvet carpeted stairs leading into the crowded building. It was so crowded that it took a long time for each of them to get into the building. They were then all ushered into a stifling hot room with closed windows and the sun streaming in, and were lined up along a wall.

She stood with the others, waiting, watching flocks of people coming and going, and tried to ignore the heat.

But then there was an excitement that rippled through the crowd. Dignitaries and Generals flooded into the already crowded room and in a brief moment, in walks President Woodrow Wilson and his wife. Agnes, from where she stood, only saw the top of Mrs. Wilson hat, a flash of the Presidents face as he walked by, and hundreds of white gloved hands reaching out to wave or shake his hand. He shook a few hands, smiling, but then, seemingly in a flashing moment, he was gone again. Agnes could see almost nothing of the two of them since she was several people deep from where they rushed through.

And then it was done. She left as soon as she could in order to get out. Outside. Air. Fresh air.

Ernest lay back with his head in the pillow. He had seen Woodrow Wilson too. It was in New York, waiting to be shipped overseas. Wilson was there to launch the Red Cross War Fund Drive. Thousands of soldiers and Red Cross Volunteers were hastily lined up and marched down Fifth Avenue from 82nd to 8th Street.

The bands were playing and the crowds of people lined along the street were cheering and waving their small flags and their handkerchiefs. It was a warm day and the sun shone clear through the small sprinkle of thin white clouds. His friend Ted Brumback was marching along side of him. He could see Ted out of the corner of his eye.

But then the command was given. Eyes right.

When Ernest turned his head in perfect unison with the whole platoon he saw Woodrow Wilson and his wife sitting up upon a stand, surrounded by dignitaries and soldiers.

Wilson nodded, Ernest thought. He thought he saw him nod. He must have nodded. After all, Ernest was going to war and Wilson must be saying thank you and good bye.

Ernest propped himself back up on his elbow. He placed the letter from Agnes back into the envelope and picked up the second letter. Again, as he opened it he could smell the scent, the perfume that was his love, his Agnes.

He read, again, out loud in the quiet room: "Dear Old Man."

It made him laugh. Old Man? Agnes said she wrote it to hear what it sounded like. It was night in a new hospital where she was stationed. She sat on the side of a hospital bed with her legs propped up on a small wooden stand. She wrote the letter using a clip board in her lap. She went through a list of her new patients: a lady with pneumonia who mumbled so Agnes couldn't understand a word she said; then a cute but spoiled little baby, Assunta; a howling man with mouth sores; a man without two front teeth who likes to smile all the time; a woman who sits up in bed bent over with a white shawl draped over her head as if she were going to die at any moment; and a sweet and beautiful girl of fourteen.

During the war the hospital was in the hands of the Austrians and many had died there. There are stories of ghosts, wounded, wandering around. Since she was writing at night, and the patients were all asleep, and it was so quiet, she wondered, alone, as she peered out into the dark hallways.

It was getting very dark and the only lights were a few lanterns sitting here and there through out the hospital. In the town below there were no lights, no lanterns. The people of the town slept or stumbled around in the black of night.

Ernest rolled back and laid his head on the pillow. He stared at the ceiling of his room. How he wished she were there with him. He tried to imagine her, at night, sitting on the empty hospital bed writing to him, smiling as she wrote thinking about him. She had come to him in the night when everyone else was asleep. She came and sat on the bed beside him. It was night and dark with only the soft glow of the lanterns in the hallway. She reached up and took out the hairclips that kept her hair up and her dark brown hair tumbled down. She leaned forward and their faces almost touched and her hair draped down surrounding him like elegant lush draperies shielding him from the outside world. Small dangling strands of hair tickled his cheek. The aromatic scent of her perfume enveloped him.

"Oh, Aggie," Ernest whispered to his empty room.

19

He held the letter up into the air and continued reading. They had driven in a column of trucks from Treviso to the Hospital in Torre di Mosta. The roads were bumpy and still damaged from the war and they passed bombed villages where children played in the ruins. There was mud everywhere splattering up into the truck and bouncing in the seat of the truck she almost fell out several times. But she made it, and was now, at night, writing to him.

She signed the letter: "Suo cattiva ragazza."

Ernest reread the letter and then put it on the table by the bed. He reached over to turn off the light but then stopped because then it would be dark. Sometimes it was bad in the dark at night; he could not sleep very well in the dark. It had happened then, when it was dark, and he was afraid that it might happen again, in the dark.

5. Sleep

Ernest closed his eyes. He felt very tired. It had been a long day. His leg hurt and he tried to move it around where it did not hurt. He stared with his eyes closed at the lit lamp for a long time. It made him feel safe.

He remembered at the front. They were in a bombed out farmhouse. The roof was gone and in his cot he could see the stars. They had turned out the lanterns. Enemy star shells streaked into the sky and exploded in a shower of sparkling light. Here and there they shot up. Then, once in awhile, they could hear the distant boom of a cannon and the long whizz and a nearby explosion. They were random, here and there.

"They're on a fishing expedition," one of the solders said.

Ernest looked around in the dark room. The light from burning cigarettes was all that could be seen in the room. The soldier who spoke flicked his cigarette onto the floor and settled into his bed.

"Let's hope they're lousy fishermen," he said. Another soldier laughed and took a long drag on his cigarette.

Ernest looked up. The walls of the house blocked out the rest of the world. It was like he was in a deep tunnel looking up into the sky. The star shells had all burned out. The night sky was clear and cold. Ernest stared at the distant stars.

Ernest opened his eyes. He was breathing heavy. His heart was racing. It happened again. It had happened again. As he fell asleep it had taken over. Again he was standing next to the trench in the pitch black and pulling out some chocolates from his jacket pocket. The soldiers were coming over toward him. And then there it was, the whirling chug chug roar from the sky and the furnace hot blast of sheer blinding light and he felt himself shoved back and to the ground by an overwhelming force and dirt splattered all around him. It woke him up, the scream of the explosion, and thank God it woke him up because that meant that it was not real, it was not happening again, and he was still here and alive.

He frantically looked all around the room. It was his room: his bed, his lamp, his chest of drawers, his bookshelves, his quilt. He was safe. He tried to ease his heavy breathing and calm his racing heart.

He was angry. Why, why couldn't he sleep? Just close his eyes and quietly drift off to sleep, that was all that he wanted. Why did he have to always return, why did he always have to return to that place, that night, that moment?

He had to think about something else. That was how he got over it, he thought about something else and then just kept thinking about it and

21

thinking about it until he fell asleep. It was as if by sending his mind somewhere else it temporarily forgot about that place and that night.

He tried to picture in his mind Agnes in the truck bouncing back and forth, laughingly screaming a little, as the truck made it up and down the muddy bombed out roads. It was like that. He had been a Red Cross ambulance driver and had to drive those grey Fiat ambulances, grinding gears, up and down the hills sliding in the mud and trying not to go over into the ditch. He could hear the moans of the wounded in the back of the truck as he tried to drive as smooth as he could with the rain and the mud splashing up and the slap of the windshield wipers and the torn up barbed wire tearing along the sides and the shells coming in tearing up the land with those horrendously loud booms. It scared you every time one of those huge shells exploded but he kept on driving trying to drive as if it was a sunny day out in the beautiful countryside. You could taste the wet mud in your mouth.

On the floor of his room, standing up against the bookshelves, Ernest could see his fishing poles in their case. Yes, fishing is what he could think about. He so much wanted to get back to that now that he was home. He couldn't wait to call up his friends, maybe Bill Smith and Ted Brumback, Charles Hopkins, Howell Jenkins, and Bill Horne.

He closed his eyes and imagined a stream, cold and clear with a swift current cascading over the white rocks. Wading out into the stream with the cold swirl of the river around his legs and feeling the sun on his back he casts his line. He waits; pulling the line, then a strike and tug and the fighting give and take begins.

You pitch your tent, or make a soft bed from the pine needles and brush, and cook your catch over an open fire and share with your friends stories and tales and adventures that are true, partly true, and as well as should be true.

He was on a trip like that when the orders came. He had signed up for Red Cross Ambulance Corp with his friend Ted Brumback but they did not exactly know when they would be ordered to appear. So Ernest decided that they should go with his friends Carl Edgar and Charles Hopkins, both also waiting to be called into service, for a last fishing trip before going off to war. His father would send a telegram when the orders arrived at the house. Ernest knew of a good fishing spot on the Canadian Soo Line. It was so far out in the wilds that there was no town there but only a lone railroad station where trains only stopped when they were flagged down. Ernest told the lone telegraph operator at the station where they would be and arranged for an Indian messenger to bring them the telegraph when it came. So off they went and camped and fished.

But the message, delayed, came to the house. They were to report in just a few days. His father sent the message on to the lone telegraph operator. He in turn searched around until he found the Indian. The Indian in turn ran out into the woods in search of the group. He finally found them. They had not shaved or bathed in days but there was no time now. They had to immediately bundle up their things and run back through the woods to the station. They laughed and joked as they caught their breath waiting for the next south-bound train. The passengers on the train were not too pleased with the group of dirty ruffians who boarded at the station and everyone tried to keep their distance. They only just made the train leaving for New York as they raced onto the platform and threw their luggage onto the moving train.

Ernest now remembered the porter at the station. He stood there watching them board the train, laughing and shaking his head back and forth.

Ernest tried to focus on that memory, to think that, to be there again as he fell asleep so that he could fall asleep and stay asleep.

But his leg was hurting him. He had done too much walking and standing today, just too much for one day. He was not fully recovered and his leg hurt.

Alone in his bed, wrapped with his quilt, Ernest stared at the ceiling and began to whistle a tune.

His father had taught him that.

During the summer the family would go up to their cottage they owned on Walloon Lake in northern Michigan. It had been christened, by his mother Grace, 'Windemere.' When Ernest was old enough one of his daily chores was the 'milk run' where he got Mason jars filled with milk from the Bacon farm half a mile away and return the empties from the previous day. One day he ran off to fetch the milk carrying a stick in his hand. He stumbled as he tried to jump over a ravine and the stick jammed up into his mouth and stabbed the back of his throat gouging out parts of his tonsils. He choked on the gushing blood and ran home screaming as he spit out more and more blood. Ernest could still remember the look on his mothers face as she stood in the front yard aghast at seeing him running toward the house. But Clarence his father the doctor was there and he managed to stop the bleeding and stitch up the back of his throat.

But Ernest cried because it hurt. His father, holding him close in his arms, told him to whistle when it hurt.

"If it hurts just whistle and it won't be as bad."

23

It worked.

Ernest did a lot of whistling in the Milan Hospital.

He was proud of his father: his ability to deal with what was real; his Stoic acceptance.

They used to hunt and fish together. His father taught him about Nature. Almost everything Ernest knew about hunting and fishing he learned from his father.

Once Ernest and his sister Marcelline rowed out with their father and his friend Wesley Dilworth to the far western end of the lake to a place known as 'Crackin' in order to fish. There are big ones there, father told Wesley, and he held out his hands to show just how big. It was a long row up through the Narrows and the sky was dark grey with heavy clouds. No sooner than they put out their lines that it began to rain. Everyone glanced over at Clarence as if to ask: well, what now? He glanced back.

"Don't mind a little heavy dew."

So they continued to fish. But then a huge bolt of lightning shot across the sky and the thunder rolled across the lake and the rain came down. Clarence and Wesley pulled up the lines and they quickly rowed to shore.

"We'll make a fire and I'll have you kids dried off in no time," he said as he pulled the boat up onto the shore.

"How are you going to make a fire in the rain, Daddy," Marcelline asked.

A crack of thunder rolled the sky.

"I'll show you," Clarence shouted over the thunder. "Bring the umbrella over here." It was the black cotton umbrella that their mother Grace kept in the boat to protect her from sunburn.

Clarence bent over an old rotting log and with his knife started scraping out some of the dry wood chips. As he scraped he gave out orders. "Now Marcelline, quick go and get some loose pieces of birch bark over there at that tree, and Ernie, pick up some little twigs on the ground, and Wes, get some bits of Cedar from that tree over there. Bring them all here real quick."

He pushed some rocks together and positioned the open umbrella over the rocks while he poured the shaved parts he had cut out with his knife down between the rocks.

"Here," he said to Marcelline, "hold the umbrella and give me the stuff you got. Now," he said, holding up his finger, "now watch."

Bending over he piled some of the bark and the twigs between the rocks and then took out a flint from his pocket and struck the side of the rock. He struck several times making sparks and finally one of the sparks caught on the bark. It began to smoke. He protected it with the palm of his hand and very gently blew on it. Soon a small flame shot up and the bark began to burn.

"Feed it slowly," he said. "Just a little piece of bark, birch is best, and then small twigs of pine or cedar, they all have resin in them. Never smother it with too much all at once. Start it small and feed it slow because a fire has to breathe."

It helped to keep their cold hands warm.

Ernest remembered that time whenever he started a fire on fishing trips with his friends. Start it small and feed it slow because a fire has to breathe.

It was a philosophy of life.

Slowly, slowly, Ernest fell asleep.

Chapter Two

The two soldiers saw him coming and they ran out. They pulled the man down off of his shoulders and Ernest collapsed onto the ground. His legs were trembling with strained muscles. The sensation of a thousand hot piercing needles pricked his leg up and down. The two soldiers turned the man over and dragged him by his arms to the station. Then they came back for Ernest and dragged him over the pebbled dirt to the station. Everything went black and silent for a moment but then Ernest woke up again. There was a doctor. He was bent over the man. There was a covered light in a tent behind a grove of trees. Ernest could see the man's chest was soaking wet with blood. The Doctor turned to a man beside him and shook his head no. The second man came into Ernest's sight. He was a Priest. The Priest bent over the man and made the sign of the cross and then began mumbling something. Ernest knew him: Don Giuseppe Bianchi. Ernest looked away. But then the Doctor's face loomed up in his sight. The Doctor was looking down at Ernest's legs. He rolled Ernest's right leg back and forth at the knee. Ernest hissed from the pain. Then the Doctor looked down at Ernest's tunic. The Doctor turned to the Priest and shook his head no. The Priest came over to Ernest and leaned down. He made the sign of the cross over him.

"Avete qualcosa da confessare, figlio mio?"

"No, no, you don't understand."

The Priest continued whispering words as he bent over Ernest.

Ernest tried to sit up and look down at his chest. His tunic was soaked in blood.

"No," he whispered, but then with gaining force, "No, you don't see. Get the Doctor, this is his blood. His blood, it isn't mine."

Ernest reached down with both of his hands and tried pulling his tunic up. It was caught at the belt buckle. He pulled and pulled rolling his head back and forth in the pain until the tunic finally cleared the buckle. He pulled the bloody tunic up and the Priest looked down at his chest. There was a surprised look on his face but then he turned and called over the Doctor. The Doctor came back and pulled up Ernest's tunic even more and then looked straight into Ernest's eyes. He smiled and nodded.

The Doctor called over for a stretcher.

1. Marc

Marcelline knocked on his door.

"Who is it?"

"Hem, it's me Marc. Can I come in?"

"Okay, come on in."

She opened the door and walked into his room. He was in his bed sitting up against his pillows against the wall. Brown hair against white pillows, his Red Cross knitted bed cover across the sheets with multicolored squares of green red black yellow and white squares. His quilt was stretched across his lap. Immediately she could smell the smoke.

"Are you smoking?"

"Close the door," he said waving the door closed with his hand. She closed the door and walked over to the bed. He was smiling a big grin when he pulled out a burning cigarette. It was a very sweet smelling smoke.

"You're smoking in the house?"

He put his finger against his lips and shushed her into silence.

"Don't announce it to the world, will you." He held the cigarette up toward his open window as if trying to get the smoke to go outside.

"Marc, these are great. Smell that sweet aroma. They're from Italy. There's nothing like them over here. I hope I can find some more in Chicago, maybe in an Italian market or something."

"They smell nice."

"Want to try one?"

She squinted her face and waved her hand no.

"Sunny told me that you were all changed. She said that you were hiding booze and cigars in your room. If either Dad or Mom catches you you'll be dead. Especially if Dad catches you."

Ernest put the cigarette down onto a dish and reached down under his bed. "Here," he said as he pulled out an opened and corked bottle of Kummel. "Here, take a nipper of this, Mazaween." He poured a little into a glass and handed it to her. She smelled it and then, her eyes watching him closely, took a sip. But she did not swallow. She was afraid to swallow.

"Don't be afraid, Sis. Don't ever be afraid of trying something new just because it's new. I've learned that. Let me tell you, some of the things that the guys in the hospital with me went through, man it would knock your socks off. There is great comfort in this little bottle, it helped both them and me. Taste everything. We only half live here; in Italy they live all the way."

Finally she swallowed.

"Well?" he asked.

"Oh my," she said as she squinted her eyes. "Wow, you can feel that burn all the way down your throat."

"Exactly, imagine having a bottle of this on a cold wintery night. You wouldn't even need a fire to keep you warm anymore."

"All of this is from Italy."

"This and so much more Mazaween. I have to tell you Sis, they really know how to live over there. It makes life over here seem like a prison term in comparison. They really know how to live and enjoy every moment of their lives."

"Tell me all about it," she said as she took another sip from the glass.

"Ah, so you like it already I see. So soon I have corrupted you.

She waved her hand in the air as she squinted as she swallowed.

"I don't want to shock you."

"Oh go on, you can tell me."

"My God, Sis; there is a whole world out there that you would not believe."

"Wait, don't tell me: they smoke their cigarettes and drink their sweet wines and then they all fall in love?"

"Yes."

"And then they all make passionate love in the moonlight."

"Yes."

"So how does it feel being home?"

Ernest seemed to get very serious for a moment as though the question struck a cord deep inside of him.

"Honestly I'm beginning to feel as if I'm being stuffed into a box and the lid is being nailed down tight."

"Really?" she asked. She could sense that it was true.

Ernest nodded.

"So tell me, Hem, who is this mysterious lady who keeps writing you all these letters. Every time a letter comes you disappear into your room and we don't see you again for a long time. Who is she? You have to tell me everything."

"All right. Marc. I am in love."

They both giggled together.

"I mean, Sis, that I am really really in love."

"Tell me, tell me."

"She is really, I mean really a fine peach of a lady. She is one of the Red Cross nurses at the hospital in Milan. Agnes. Agnes von Kurowsky."

"She's Polish?"

"No, no. She's American but I think her dad was Polish, or Polish-German something."

"My, my, my. Our little all American boy goes off to war in Italy and falls in love with a Polish nurse; aren't we Mr. International now. Are you too big of a man of the world for us now?"

Ernest beamed.

"You'll love her, Sis, I know that you will."

"So you are caught hook line and sinker."

"Yes. When she's done over there she's coming back here and we are getting married."

"Married? You asked her and she said yes?"

Ernest opened the drawer of the table by his bed and pulled out a ring. He handed it to her. "She gave me that."

"Wait a minute. Aren't you suppose to give her a ring, not her give you one?"

"That will come later. She gave me that as a friendship ring."

"So are you officially engaged?"

"Well, not officially officially. Listen, don't tell anyone, okay, this is just between you and me right now. Promise."

"Yes, yes, I promise. Wow, my baby brother is in love. And this is going to be the real thing?"

"I can't tell you how happy she makes me. Just thinking about her makes me want to laugh out loud. I can hardly contain myself; I just had to tell someone."

She noticed the quilt on his bed.

"Wait, that's the quilt."

He looked down at the quilt and then back up at her, a confused look on his face.

"We saw you, we all saw you in the newsreel at the movies."

"What are you talking about?"

"Okay, listen to this. One night I went to the movies in Chicago with my friend, you know Marion Vose."

"Yeah, so?"

"Well, after the feature there was a newsreel about the work being done by the American Red Cross in Italy. They showed the new Red Cross hospital in Milan. And then right there on the movie screen was you. I was so shocked."

"Yes, there was a film crew there one day, I remember. You mean to tell me that became a newsreel?"

She laughed out loud.

31

"Yes," she screamed as she held her hands up to her cheeks.

"You mean I'm a movie star?"

"You were wearing your uniform sitting in this wheelchair on what they said was the porch and this very pretty nurse was pushing you along."

"Actually it was the balcony."

"Well across your lap was this robe or quilt or something of knitted wool squares. Then you smiled at the camera, your famous big fat smile, and you waved your crutch at the camera for a second. Well, my friend and I were so excited we waited after the regular picture but they didn't show it again."

"Wow."

"So we go to the manager and asked if we could see it again and we told him that it was you and all so he tells us that after the theatre empties out he can do a special showing for us. So we wait around and then he comes down and he shows it again."

"Did Mom or Dad get to see it?"

"Well wait. So the manager tells us at what theatre it was going to be playing next. So it was already past midnight but I phoned home from the drugstore to tell Mom and Dad."

"They were awake?"

"No silly. I woke them up. So the next night me and Dad and Mom all went to that theatre and sure enough right there on the big screen was your big fat happy grin. Oh my God did Mom cry her eyes out seeing you all wounded and in a wheel chair with a crutch wearing your military looking cap and overcoat out on the terrace. We were all so proud of you, our little Ernie up there on the big screen, in the movies, like all of the famous movie stars."

"What did Dad think?"

"Are you kidding? He told everyone he knows and he personally followed that newsreel all over Chicago and saw it over and over. I saw it once more and Mom I think saw it twice more."

The two of them sat for a moment in silence smiling at each other.

Marc sat straight up.

"Wait a minute. Was that her?"

"Who?"

"The nurse in the newsreel holding your wheelchair, is that your big romance?"

"No, I don't think so. No, she wasn't there that day."

"Well that's a good thing because if it was then I'd have to track down that newsreel again and watch it all over again just to see what she looks like."

Ernest beamed.

"Mazaween, Aggie is prettier than anybody you guys ever saw. Wait till you see her."

"Ernie, that's just the love talking."

"No," he replied. "That is the truth talking."

2. Big Brother

Four year old Leicester stared at all of the army gear on the bookshelf. There was a pistol and a bayonet, a star shell pistol and a gas mask, and propped up against the wall was a carbine. Maps of Italy were pinned to the wall. Les reached over and picked up the pistol and held it with both of his small hands.

"Did you shoot a lot of Germans?"

"No," Ernest answered. "I'm afraid not."

Les, standing by the window, stared over at Ernest as he sat on the bed.

"Why not?"

"Because I drove an ambulance. It wasn't my job to shoot people it was my job to get our boys who were shot to a hospital."

"Why?"

"So they wouldn't die. I got them to the hospital so that they would be safe and get patched up."

"They were shot by the Germans?"

"I was in Italy. There were some Germans but mostly there were Austrians. They were the enemy."

Les held up the gun with a big grin on his face and pointed the pistol at Ernest.

"Now Les, no, no, no." Ernest reached over and pointed the pistol up into the air.

"The first thing you have to learn about guns is that you never play around, and you never point the gun at anyone, and you never handle a gun that is loaded."

"Is it loaded?"

"No, that one isn't but you didn't know that when you picked it up now did you."

Les put the pistol back down on the shelf. He picked up the bayonet.

"Did you stab any Germans?"

"No, but I knew some men who did."

Les looked back at Ernest wide eyed, as if that impressed him. He put the bayonet back down. He squatted down and reached for the carbine but then stopped. He glanced back at Ernest.

"Is it loaded?"

Ernest laughed.

"No, it isn't. But that's very good to ask."

Les picked up the carbine. He had a hard time holding it.

"Here," Ernest said as he slid off of the bed. "Look at this."

Ernest picked up the gas mask and put it over his face and then started breathing very heavy. Les screamed, dropped the carbine on the floor, and backed up giggling. Ernest bent over, put out his arms, and started slowly stepping toward Les with uneven and jerky steps.

"I'm going to get you, I'm going to get you."

Les stood in one place and put his hands to his mouth as he giggled and screamed.

Ernest stopped and reaching with both of his hands yelled out: "Boo."

Les screams again and with a laughing squeal runs out the door into the hallway.

From downstairs Ruth called out.

"Is everything all right?"

Ernest took off the mask and put it back onto the shelf. "Yes," he calls out, a little annoyed. "Everything is fine."

"But what was that screaming?"

Ernest walks out into the hall next to Les and looks down the stairs.

"Nothing, Ruth. It was just Les."

Ruth, as she started to climb the stairs, came into view. There were two boys with her. They were Jack and Troy from high school.

"Ernest, these two boys are here to see you."

He watched as the three of them came up the stairs and into the hallway.

Ernest waved at the two. They both smiled and waved back.

"Well, come in guys."

The two boys entered the room and Les started to follow but Ernest stopped him.

"No, not you. Now out."

"But I wanna."

Ernest, smiling, shook his head no. Ernest leaned down to whisper into his ear. "This is big boy stuff, so bye bye."

Ernest shut the door leaving Les standing in the hallway. Les sat down and listened through the crack in the door.

Jack and Troy were all over the war souvenirs, passing them back and forth. Jack aimed the carbine out the window toward the street and then clicked the trigger.

"Pow. Another kraut in the bag."

Troy, wearing the gas mask, laughed.

"Oh. Listen to the big hero."

"Here," Ernest said as he gave each of them a cigarette. He already had one dangling out of his mouth. "Open the window Jack so the

35

smoke goes out."

He struck a match and lit each of the three cigarettes.

"These are straight from Italy, my friends. It'll be hard to find these babies over here."

Jack coughed.

Ernest smiled at him. "Good stuff, eh."

Ernest was getting dressed into his army uniform. His pants were hung neatly over the back of the chair. He stood in his undershorts and naked feet watching himself in the mirror as he buttoned his shirt. He glanced at the clock by his bed. Eleven forty five.

"Walking is good for my leg, see, but too much walking is bad."

Sunny nodded. At fifteen she adored her older brother. And now he was a war hero and dressed in his uniform.

"Why don't you get up in the morning with the rest of us?"

"Well you see, Sunny, I like to just lay here in my nice and cozy bed and read until about now. Then I can walk in town for awhile and help strengthen my leg."

"Does it still hurt?"

Ernest nodded yes.

Ernest picked up his cigar from the ash tray and took a long puff. He blew the smoke toward the open window. Sunny waved away the smoke.

Ernest helped to raise his naked foot onto the bed next to where Sunny was sitting.

"Look at this, can you do this?"

One by one he wiggled each toe separately. Sunny laughed and put both hands up to cover her mouth. She glanced to his face and then back to his individually wiggling toes.

"How do you do that?"

She stood up next to him, took off her shoe and put her foot up next to his. She tried but she could not move one toe without wiggling another at the same time.

"How do you do that?"

"I don't know. Some of the shrapnel cut some nerves or something and now I can move each toe separately. Pretty neat huh?"

Sunny touched his leg where a piece of shrapnel was just below the surface.

"Yeah, they keep coming to the surface. Hand me that knife."

Sunny handed him the knife and sat down on the bed.

Ernest cut along the edge of the sliver of iron. Blood tricked out as he cut and sucked in air as if trying to still the pain.

"Quick, the towel."

Sunny handed him the towel and he dabs the cut. Then with his fingernail and the tip of the knife he pulls on the sliver of iron and pulls it out. Sunny was watching his every move with her face quenched up as though she was in pain. While holding the wound with the towel he hands her the small sliver of iron. She puts out her hand and he drops it into her palm.

"Souvenir."

She makes a face and then smiles.

"Here," he says as he reaches over and takes his cigar from the ashtray. "You did good as my pretty nurse, you should be rewarded."

She takes the cigar and carefully takes a puff. She holds the smoke in her puffed cheeks as she hands him back the cigar.

"Sunny, there's a whole big world out there. Try this. Smoke this and we'll be friends again."

Sunny, still holding the smoke in her cheeks, nods, but then all at once blows out the smoke.

"Here, always blow toward the window so it will go out. We don't want busybody Ruth to know now do we?"

"When were we not friends?"

"Oh, it's just an expression. Here, take a puff or two."

She took another puff but then immediately blew it out toward the open window.

"If Mommy knew what you are doing you'd be in big trouble."

"Oh well, I'm afraid that may be inevitable."

"What do you mean?"

He waved it off.

But then he grew serious.

"I'm a different man now, Sunny. I wish there was some way to explain to you how different I am now from what I was before. I'm excited, I've seen things Sunny that shows me we only half live here. I want to see those things. I want to live those things."

"Take me with you."

"No, not just yet."

He slid on his boots. The right one was painful to put on.

"Where are you going?"

"I don't know yet. Just around. To the library I think. I've been reading the newspapers about the war."

"But why? You were there."

"It's for the bigger picture, Sis; the bigger picture."

Late in the afternoon of Valentine's Day two eleven year old girls, Dorothy Reynolds and her best friend Katherine De Voe, walked up onto the porch of the Hemingway house. They placed their large red valentine addressed to "Ernie Hemingway" against the door and then rang the door bell. They instantly ran away and stood on the sidewalk a half of a block down the street. They giggled as they waited. Their deepest hopes were realized.

Ernest himself opened the door and then reached down and picked up the Valentine. The two girls could barely contain themselves. But then Ernest, having read the Valentine, looked over and saw the two girls trying to not notice. He smiled his big smile and waved at them. They screamed and instantly ran away.

A week later Sunny gave a small party. Several of her friends were there and Ernest had Leicester walk over and especially invite both Dorothy and Katherine. At the party Ernest wore his uniform and told everyone stories of his adventures in 'the war.' All of the young friends of Sunny sat in silent awe of his stories.

In the early evening, just after dark, he picked up his Austrian Star Shell pistol and walked outside. Most followed. It was a cold night and they were all bundled up in jackets.

Ruth, who was supervising the party, was against it all but then said that well, if you have to go outside on such a cold night then at least be bundled up tight, I don't want anyone to get sick.

The night was cold and clear. It was moonless and the stars were out.

Ernest stood in the center of the front yard and waited until everyone gathered around him. He held up the large pistol with its foot long barrel and four gauge bore. He pointed it up into the sky.

"Are you ready?"

They all shake their heads yes and some put their hands to their ears.

He pulls the trigger and there is a loud echoing bang. A thin line arced into the sky. Five seconds later a great white light burst out in the sky and lit up the night and slowly, ever so slowly, the flaring flame drifted down over onto Grove Avenue. Several of the boys ran down several houses to the dying sizzling light in the middle of the street and stamped it out with their feet. Neighborhood dogs began barking.

"Let's see if I can improve my aim."

Ernest loaded the pistol and again held it up into the air.

He fires.

The light flies up into the night sky and then explodes into a sizzling light. The neighborhood briefly lights up and the sparkling light floats down. The light floated down into the pack of children as they all scattered giggling as the light came down onto the grass of the front yard. There was a strong scent of burnt powder. It burned the grass as Leicester stamped it out.

Ernest laughed at them all. He was the hero of the moment to all of the children of the neighborhood.

3. Speech

Frank Platt was sitting at his desk in the school's Oxford Room. When someone came into the room he looked up. For a moment he froze, and then he sat back in his chair. Standing at the doorway, nonchalantly leaning against the door, was a man dressed in uniform.

"Well I'll be," Frank gasped in amazement. "As I live and breathe if it isn't Ernest Hemingway."

"Hello Mr. Platt."

"Look at you, all decked out with your fancy uniform and boots. I heard from some of the students that you were back. Welcome, welcome, here," he said as he stood and offered Ernest one of the chairs. Frank watched as Ernest, with his cane, slightly limped over to the chair and sat down.

"How is that," he said, pointing toward the leg.

"Oh, it's stiff and hurts sometimes but its okay. Doc says I'll be as good as new here pretty quick."

"Good, good."

"How's your English class?"

Frank smiled. "Not what it was with you and your sister. How is Marcelline by the way, she's in Oberlin College now?"

"No, she was just there for one semester. She's at the Congregational Training School now."

"Really. And how about yourself, now that this war is over, what are your plans?"

"Well I really don't know yet. My Dad suggested Oberlin but if not, maybe a state university, maybe Wisconsin and study medicine."

"And do you want to follow in your father's footsteps?"

Ernest shrugged his shoulders.

"Well, there is plenty of time for that. So, how was it over there, the war?"

Out the window Ernest could see the campus green. The sun was strong and the trees across the campus were bright green, fresh with new spring growth.

"It was exciting at times, boring at others."

"You drove an ambulance with the Red Cross?"

"I brought wounded back from the front to the rear field hospitals. Most of the time there wasn't much, but some days there was a lot of action."

Frank nodded in silence, watching Ernest closely.

"It sort of changes you, you see," Ernest said not knowing why.

Frank smiled and nodded again. There was a long pause.

"Ernest, I have an idea. Tonight is the Burke Debating Club meeting. Why don't you come, see the boys, and they can see you. You can give a little talk, talk about what you experienced. The boys will love it. And maybe it will help you to talk about it. What do you say?"

Ernest smiled at the idea. "Can I bring some of my souvenirs along?"

"Yes, by all means. That will make it even better. Seven o'clock."

That night in the classroom Mr. Platt told the boys tonight would be a special night and then he introduced Ernest.

Ernest stood before them in his full Red Cross uniform. He stumbled at first, not knowing what to say, but picked up as the presentation progressed. He told of the front, the trenches, the troops, and the artillery. He told of sleeping in bombed out farmhouses watching the star flares overhead like a monster searching for prey. He held up his Austrian bayonet and his pistol, and told how fierce hand to hand combat could be; he held up his gas mask and then put it on so they could see it in action.

He told them about how he was at a forward listening post one night, July 8, 1918, and around midnight an Austrian trench mortar came chug chugging down from the sky and exploded not that far from him. There was a deafening roar and it was like a blast from a hot furnace and he was shoved back and had the wind knocked out of him. I felt as if my life was sucked out of me, I was no longer inside me and I was floating outside thinking, Hey, Ernie this is it, I am dead. But then I rushed back in, sucked back into my body and I was covered in dirt and a solder next to me was screaming. His legs had been blown off.

All of the boys in the room hung on every word he said.

I stumbled up. The soldier who stood between me and the blast was dead. The one to my right was still alive but his legs were gone and the wounds were pumping blood. The soldier to my left was still alive, barely, so I picked him over my shoulder and ran to the trench line dodging Austrian machine gun fire. Little did I know that I too was wounded. Two hundred and twenty seven shell fragments had shredded my leg.

Ernest then very slowly and very carefully pulled out the pair of pants he was wearing at the time and held them up for all to see.

"This is what is left of my pants."

There was complete silence as the whole room full of boys stared open mouthed at the shredded blood stained pants.

Ernest, for effect, walked around the room holding up the pants for

41

all of them to see.

Walking home, carrying his souvenirs in his knapsack strapped to his back, tapping his cane, breathing in the night air, Ernest kept thinking about the faces of all of the young boys. Actually they were all only a year or two younger but there was a world of difference between him and them now. He had lived something real and important. All those boys could only sit in a room and imagine what it was like while listening to someone telling them what it was like. They will never know what I know now. I actually lived it. One of the boys had said to him that he was a hero. Ernest smiled at the time and said thank you but thinking about it now what the boy said was true. I am a hero. I am a hero to them.

He remembered when the ship S. S. Giuseppe Verdi pulled into New York last January. He stood on the deck watching the seagulls circle around and hearing the ship's horn blasting out as she pulled in and then, looking down, watching the crowds of people flocking on the dock. Ernest was returning from the war. He was coming home. Struggling down the gangplank with his cane and his baggage he spotted his friend Bill Horne coming toward him. Thin, shorter than Ernest, with his glasses and his hair parted down the middle of his forehead, no sooner had Bill taken the baggage from Ernest and swung it down onto the wooden dock than a reporter with a checkered jacket and a notepad in his hand came over and tapped Ernest on the shoulder. Excuse me but are you Lieutenant Ernest Hemingway, the first American wounded on the Italian front? He was from the New York Sun and began firing off questions at Ernest, how was he, what had he done, what are his plans now, what was the war like.

Ernest answered the questions, inflating the truth a bit. The man thanked him and ran off to do his story.

Bill Horne, standing off to one side with his girlfriend Ann Sage, laughed when the reporter left.

"Well now, aren't you the big celebrity hero."

"Ah hell Bill, you saw as much action over there as I did."

Ernest, with his tall cordovan leather boots and draped with his long black broadcloth Italian officers cape, lined with red satin with a silver clasp at the neck, and resting his weight on his cane, smiled and winked at Ann.

"Yeah," Bill said, "but I didn't bring back souvenirs embedded in my body."

Ernest waved him off. The three of them went off and had tea. Ann, impressed, kept asking Ernest questions.

Thinking about it now, as Ernest walked home from his lecture to the boys, even on that day he was treated as if he were something larger than life. Why was he a hero in the eyes of so many? Why would the paper care to write a story about him, and why would the readers care to read the story? He was just himself, a young boy returning home from the war, wounded.

But I have done what is the stuff of dreams and fantasy in boys other than me.

When Ernest got home he made his way up to his room. He was tired but was glad the talk went so well. On his bed, on the neatly folded many colored quilt, was a letter. He picked it up. It was from her.

Ernest undressed and got into bed. Under the beam of his lamp he read the letter.

"We had a frightful day yesterday," she wrote. Just after dinner it was getting dark and she and the other nurses were washing dishes when they heard wailing and screaming coming up to their door. They went out to find a blood soaked oxcart with four children drenched in blood and screaming and crying. The mothers and fathers who pushed the cart up the hill to the hospital were wailing and shouting. The children were playing in the yard and they found an unexploded bomb. It went off. Two of the children were killed instantly. The other four were heaped onto the cart and pushed to the hospital. One was trying to hold her intestines inside of her and the other was bleeding from the face and eyes.

They were all scared out of their minds.

"We all worked like mad over them for about two and a half hours," she wrote. Finally Bruno got one of the Ford ambulances to work and he drove them off to the S. Stino Hospital five kilometers away where they could get better care. After it was over, and Agnes sat down by the lantern, she noticed her dress was splattered with blood.

The war is over but the killing continues.

4. Italian Party

Ernest took the trolley into downtown Chicago. He spent the morning walking the streets of the Italian neighborhood. He went into a small shop with small tables on the sidewalk in front. In the shop were stacks of shelves with different packages, foods, breads, wines, cigarettes and cigars, and behind a windowed counter fresh cut meats and sausages. He found the cigarettes and cigars he was looking for.

Ernest went to the counter and paid. The man, older, white haired with a large bushy white moustache, was friendly and smiled and nodded. He gave Ernest his change.

"Graze," Ernest said. The man's face lit up.

"Ah, parli italiano?"

Ernest shrugged his shoulders. "Si, parlo un po italiano."

"Ah, si studia a scuola?"

"No. Ho combattuto in Italia durante la Guerra."

"Ah," the man exclaimed as if he has just encountered a saint. He reached out and shook Ernest's hand. "Graze, signore, graze."

Then a man came up behind Ernest and slapped him hard on the shoulder. When he turned around he saw the smiling face of Nick Neroni.

"Tenente Ernest Hemingway," he said in a loud booming voice, "amico mio."

The two of them hugged, slapping each other on the back.

"Come," he said, "have some wine with me. Outside, we can watch the world and talk."

The shop owner brought out a bottle of wine and two glasses and they sat at a small table on the sidewalk in the shade of a tree.

At the hospital in Milan when Ernest could finally get around with crutches he used to dress in his uniform and go out to the cafes. It was there that he met Nick Neroni. Nick was a Captain in the Italian Army. He was from Abruzzi and had joined the army in 1916. He fought in the battle of Gorizia, the battle of Isonzo, the retreat of Caporetto, and the final battle of Vittorio Veneto; along the way he was wounded three times and was awarded four silver crosses and the Croce de Guerra. Ernest told him he was wounded fighting on the Piave River, where Neroni had also fought. In the cafes and bars of Milan they laughed and traded war stories like fellow soldiers, Nick's being real stories of what he actually lived and Ernest's being what he had heard.

When Ernest told Nick about his fishing and hunting back in Michigan Nick just shook his head and tapped the table with his finger.

"My friend, when you are more recovered you must visit Abruzzi, my home town. It is in the mountains. The air it is clean and crisp, you suck the air into your lungs and are reborn. Not like the heat and the dust down here. And the hunting and the fishing, it is the finest in the world. Pheasant and rabbit; and the trout in the streams, the water is crisp and clean and cold and runs swift over the rocks. It is God's land, my friend, and we are not ashamed to say it."

Sitting at the little table on the sidewalk beneath the tree drinking their wine they talked of their times together, they talked about the war. Ernest told him that after being wounded, when he was well enough, he was near Bassano and Monte Grappa with the Arditi.

Nick sat back and waved his hand. "Oh, my friend, do not get mixed up with those fellows. They come from Italian jails, murderers and thieves, and are used as shock troops in exchange for their freedom. They are tough and mean."

Nick told Ernest and the shop owner who loved to hear all of the tales of the war about one Arditi soldier who was wounded, shot in the chest, and to keep fighting he simply plugged the bullet hole with a lit cigarette cauterizing the wound. When they are being transported they throw grenades into the ditch just to see them explode and shock the truck driver following behind them.

Nick, pointing to Ernest, told the shop owner: "My friend was wounded, nearly killed. He has won medals."

"Thank God the war is done," the owner replied.

"No my friend, thank the soldiers, thank the brave soldiers who fought and died. It is because of their honor that the war is done."

Nick told Ernest that he was now working at the Italian Consulate in Chicago. And you, what are you doing now? Anything you need you come to me. Where are you living?

"Well, with my folks for now."

"Is it a big house?"

Ernest nodded yes.

"You know, lets have a party, can we give you a party at your house. I know friends who would love to honor an American who almost died protecting Italy. What will your folks think? I will send a committee to discuss it with them, no?"

When Ernest got home he told his father and mother about the party. They were confused. Why do they want to do this?

"Just let them do it, Dad. They want to bring everything, all of the food for them and us and any of our friends. And they'll bring an orchestra, Mom, and opera singers, drinks, everything."

"But the cost, son, we can't afford that."

"There's no cost to us. They love doing it and it would be a personal insult if we say no."

Clarence turned to Grace.

"Well, dear, I certainly would love the music and the singing."

So on a Sunday they came. Cars and cars full of laughing and shouting people speaking Italian started arriving in the quaint quite streets of Oak Park. They unloaded huge hampers packed with food. They took over the kitchen and dining area. Chefs from different restaurants put on their aprons and went to work. The spaghetti and dishes of meat were laid out on the dining room table. Platters of chicken and fish and salads appeared and then plates of pastries and tarts filled with meats and cheese as well as frosted cakes and long crusty loaves of bread and gallons of red and white wine all appeared as well.

Out in Grace's music room two Italians brought out their guitars, another his violin, another a mandolin, and three members of the chorus of the Chicago Grand Opera Company began playing and singing. From the upper stairs balcony they unfurrowed a large Italian flag.

The night wore on: singing, dancing, laughing, Italian and broken English filled the rooms and the Hemingway family and friends could understand almost none of it but somehow everyone seemed to be able to communicate. Little seven year old Carol and four year old Les were put to bed over protest.

At some point most of the group jammed together in the music room and a photographer set up his camera and then turned to them all: alright everyone; smile.

Snap.

It was around one in the morning when Ernest and Marc and Clarence helped the last of the party out the door. Others who had left before were still by their cars laughing and shouting. Clarence noticed that lights came on in several of the neighbors houses.

When the door was closed there was a sigh of relief.

"You've let this sort of thing go too far," Clarence snapped. "They are being a neighborhood nuisance."

But then Marc, with a smile on her face, asked: "But Daddy, did you have fun?"

He did not say anything for a moment.

"Yes, well, yes I suppose I did. But my God, just the drinking alone," he said as he shook his head.

"We will lock up and turn out the lights, Daddy, you just go on up to bed."

After they turned out the lights the two of them crept exhausted up the stairs to their rooms. But when Ernest walked into his dark room he kicked something on the floor. When he turned on the light it was a neighborhood boy sound asleep. Ernest went to Marc's room and then the two of them searched the whole house again. They found another local boy asleep behind the davenport in the music room. They guided the two drunken boys to the front door, onto the porch, and then shut the door hoping that the boys would find their way home and not be found asleep on the porch in the morning.

Wine was a new element in the small world of Oak Park.

5. Agnes

Marc was there when the mailman came. She took the mail and was sorting through it as she walked into the parlor when Ernest came up behind her. She glanced back over her shoulder into his big smiling face.

"Anything for me, perhaps?"

"Who would want to write to you?"

"Oh. . .," he said, his voice trailing off.

Marc finished sorting through the mail. There was a letter.

"Oh lover boy," she said in a sing song voice holding the letter in the air.

Ernest took the letter.

"Thank you very much; see you soon."

Marc watched as Ernest, as was his way whenever he received a letter from Agnes, went upstairs. He liked to read the letters alone. It seemed more personal that way. She knew that it would be hours before she saw him again.

But this time it was different.

She heard a muffled scream as she walked up the stairs. Something was wrong. It seemed to come from his room. She continued up the stairs toward his room.

As she came to the landing outside his door she heard him vomiting.

She listened: wondering, concerned. Afraid.

Marc walked over to the door and knocked.

"Ernie," she said. There was no reply.

"Are you alright?"

She heard shuffling and the sound of the springs on his bed.

She knocked again. "Ernie?"

"Go away."

"What's the matter?"

"Go away."

Marc opened the door. Ernest was curled up on his bed with his arms around his knees. She could see he had vomited in his trashcan.

"Are you sick? What's wrong?"

"Nothing is wrong, not a god damn thing is wrong."

"Is it Agnes, is she alright, is she sick or something?"

"No," he says in a sudden rush of words, "she's dumping me, she says it was just a boy girl thing, and to top it off she is getting married soon, and she calls me 'dear boy,' dear boy?"

Ernest reached down and briefly held the letter up but then quickly threw it to the floor.

Marc walked over and picked the letter up.

"Can I read it?"

"No," he screams at her.

He stares at her with a raging hate in his eyes. But then it melts.

"Yeah, I don't care, do what you want. How can she do this to me?"

Marc read the letter. "Ernie, dear boy... trying to convince myself it was a real love-affair... I know that I am very fond of you, but, it is more as a mother than as a sweetheart... I am now & always will be too old... you are just a boy—a kid... I expect to be married soon... Your friend, Aggie."

"Ernie, how old is she?"

"What difference does that make?"

"Apparently it makes a lot of difference."

"So, she's a little older. Twenty seven."

"But you're nineteen."

"So now you're on her side? Thanks a lot Marc."

"No, I'm not on her side. Ernest, I'm so sorry."

"Yeah, so big deal. Go away and leave me alone."

Marc put the letter on his desk and left. Once she was in the hall and closed the door behind her she heard what sounded like crying.

When Ernest came home late he went upstairs trying not to wake anyone. But at the top of the stairs, sitting just outside of his room, was Ursula. She was sitting, leaning against the wall, asleep. He bent down and held her cheeks in his hands.

"Heh, Ursula. Sweet Sixteen."

She opened her eyes and smiled.

"Ernie," she said, still half asleep.

"What are you doing?"

She stretched and seemed to pop her eyes out as if to wake them up.

"Waiting for you," she said.

"Why?"

She smiled and shrugged her shoulders.

"Because you've been so sad. I know you can't sleep good so I thought it might be because you're lonely."

"You came to keep me company?"

"Yeah, so you can sleep."

"Well, come on in."

The two of them went into his room. She sat on his bed while he undressed.

"You're a peach of a sister you know."

"I know."

"Oh, so you already know that do you?"

"Yeah," she giggled.

She looked around the room. Several large maps of Italy were pinned to the wall. One was of the entirety of Italy and one was of the Venice region, there was a small pin stuck in the map at Fossalta di Piave.

Ernest crawled into bed next to her and draped the multicolored quilt over the two of them.

"I'll keep the light on until you fall asleep," she told him.

"You're a peach."

"Ernie."

"Yes Ura."

"Do you miss her that much?"

"Yeah, I miss her a whole bunch."

"Well, another couple months and we all go to Windemere again for the summer. You'll forget about her there."

"Maybe. I hope you're right."

"I am."

His back was turned to her so she did not see him smile.

"Ernie."

"Yes Ura."

"Why are you at the library all the time and have all these maps that you are studying?"

"I'm learning about the war."

"Why? You were there."

"It's different. Things are different now. Something important happened and I want to know what. Why was I there? I need to understand it all."

"How are they different?"

"You know those talks that I give about the war to the different schools and groups?"

"Yeah."

"Well at one of them these girls were all giggling, me being the big war hero and all, and they asked me if I was coming to the school dance. And I was standing there in my uniform but with my cane. My leg was hurting a lot that day and I could not walk without my cane. So I told them that no, I wasn't coming to the dance because of my shot up leg. I couldn't walk much less dance. And they got a little annoyed and then they brushed me off like I was no longer of any importance to them. It made me think of how different things are now. I don't know. It's like things that were so important then just don't seem that important anymore."

Ernest paused for a moment. Ursula was staring across the room at the map on the wall, staring at the little pin pushed into the map, at the shadow the light of the lamp cast.

"Ura," he continued. "I saw a man's legs blown off. I carried a dying man who bled all over me as he was dying. What difference does it make who I am taking to the dance Saturday night?"

"Ernie."

"Yes Ura."

"Is that where it happened?"

Ernest turned his head and looked over at the small pin and the shadow of the pin. He turned his head back.

"Yes," he said.

"Okay, time for you to go to sleep now."

The bed was warm, the quilt, laying next to Ursula. Warm. Peaceful. He tried to sleep.

He could remember one night in the hospital. It was around one in the morning and Agnes came and woke him up. She needed his help, she said. She needed his help with an influenza patient that seemed to be dying. She handed him a small white mask to tie across his face. Dressed in his hospital pajamas and robe he followed her down the darkened hallway to another room and his leg was stiff and hurt as he walked. Sitting straight up in a brass bed against the wall was a young man breathing heavy and gasping for air. His shirt was soaked with sweat and sweat drooled down his cheeks and dripped from his nose. The room smelled strong of medicines and alcohol and vomit. The room was only lit by a small lamp covered by a towel. Two girls with cloth masks knelt by the bed quietly praying. As Agnes and he approached the bed the man fell back in the bed. Agnes said to take a hold of him. But as soon as Ernest held the man's shoulders the man shook and collapsed perfectly still. His bowels discharged a yellow slime. The stench filled the room.

Ernest remembered that he went back into his own room and washed his hands and then washed his hands again and then gargled with alcohol and washed his face. He sat on the side of his bed and could not sleep.

Agnes was cleaning and preparing the dead body.

Chapter Three

Two solders set a stretcher down next to him and then picked him up and put him on it. One picked his shoulders and the other picked up ankles. He almost passed out from the blinding pain. They picked up the stretcher and began running down a road toward the rear dressing station. On the stretcher Ernest bounced up and down as the men ran. They started across a field. The ground was uneven and blown apart so their progress was slow. When they heard the screech of a shell coming in they both let go of the stretcher and dropped to the ground. Ernest hit the ground each time with a hard thump. The shell exploded either near or far. If it was near then the spray of dirt and whiz of shrapnel flew overhead. Then, after a moment, the two men got up, picked up the stretcher and began running again toward the rear station. From his stretcher Ernest looked up at the night sky. The stars so serene and so far away were blinded by the exploding flares burning up the night sky. They hissed and sparkled as they descended leaving trails of silver smoke. The whiz of a shell came in close and they dropped him in a hole where his head was down below his body but his legs were bent at the knees at the top of the shell hole. The pain from his twisted knee rippled throughout his body. The shell threw dirt into the hole and into his mouth. They picked him up again and kept running toward the rear. They came to a barn and brought him in. There were rows and rows of stretchers on the dirt. They put him down next to a man in a stretcher bundled in blankets. The man was shivering and moaning. Ernest looked up. The roof was gone, blown away by a direct hit. The walls blocked out the surrounding world but he could see up, as if he was at the bottom of a deep tunnel, and he could see the stars way high up. The sparkle of star flares flicked here and there and the burning phosphorus crackled as they descended leaving the slight silver trails of smoke. He was closer to the artillery. When they fired the ground trembled like an earthquake. The floor was covered with straw and pine needles from the trees next to the barn. Ernest squeezed the soft covering with his hands. When he went fishing he used pine needles for a bed.

1. Katy

They drove up to the curb and stopped in their Blue Convertible Buick. They had the top down. Ernest was sitting in the parlor and watched through the white laced drapes as they drove up. A small clock on the fireplace mantle chimed just as they came into view. Ernest got up, grabbed his cane, and went to the door. Bill Smith had just gotten out of the car and was coming up the sidewalk when he saw Ernest coming outside. Bill was tall and slender with sand colored hair that he kept slicked back close to his head. He was twenty four to Ernest's nineteen. Bill stopped and opened his arms, tilting his head to the side, as if he were going to hug Ernest from that distance.

"Wemedge," he called out to Ernest.

"Bird," Ernest yelled back.

Ernest waved and walked toward him. He and Ernest embraced and tightly hugged.

"How are you doing old Hemingstein."

"Good, good."

"I haven't seen you since you went to put the old Kaiser in his place."

"Well, we put him."

"Looking good, man; a bit thinner but, wait, what's with this leg thing?" he said as he looked down at the cane.

"Nothing, it's just a prop for all of the girls."

They both laughed.

"Well, get into my lean machine."

Bill's sister Katy, twenty eight, was sitting in the front seat. She flicked her dark wind tangled hair back and smiled.

"Hello there Ernie."

She smiled and her penetrating green eyes seemed to sparkle.

"It's been awhile Katy," Ernest said, getting into the back seat. He stared into her cat-like green eyes. It did seem it was a very long time.

Bill turned on the engine.

"So we'll pick up my brother Ken and Doodles and then trolley over to your Venice Café, save me from the traffic."

"How is Ken doing, he's back okay from the sanatorium?"

"Yes, he's alright. It was the Trudeau Sanatorium in the Adirondacks. Tuberculosis. It killed mother but he said it was not going to kill him. He does not believe in this like mother like son business."

"So he beat it?"

"So they say. Time tells all things. Shall we go?"

"It sounds good to me."

"Well then," Bill announced as he gunned the pedal, "we're off." The car shot forward. The wind whisked through Ernest's hair.

The five of them sat around a large table toward the front of the restaurant. Nick Neroni had taken Ernest there: it is, he said as he kissed the tips of his fingers, the best Ristorante Italiano in the neighborhood, but, with a laugh and a slap on the back, don't tell that to any of the others because that will get me into trouble. He winked him into secrecy.

The restaurant was packed. A band off to one side played and a few couples danced. There were large parties shouting and laughing. Almost everyone spoke Italian.

Ernest and Katy had the ravioli, Bill and Doodles spaghetti, and Ken a meat dish. They passed around a bottle of red wine. And then a second one. Ernest kept watching as a steady stream of tough looking young men in suits entered into a back room. They knocked, the door opened a crack, and then opened up to let them in.

Ken was drinking and talking to Bill, drinking and talking politics. The Bolsheviks. The Revolution.

"It's a bloody mess over there," Ken was saying, "it will lead to no good."

Doodles leaned forward, a glass of wine in her hand: "Ken, I want to dance, let's dance."

"If chaos like that continues then strong arm leaders are going to come to power, just like in the French Revolution."

"You never want to dance and have fun," Doodles said as she giggled a little and took a long sip of her wine. She almost spilled it.

Ernest watched as Katy threw her arms in the air and laughed. She tossed her head back trying to shake the curls of hair away from her face. He watched her sip her wine.

Ken continued talking, Bill nodding in silence.

"Drink up," Ernest told Katy as he leaned in toward her so that she could hear over the noise of the restaurant and the band. "Drink up because it all goes away come January."

Katy shook her head no, touching her lips and then swallowing.

"Never, never will that amendment last."

She leaned in toward Ernest sitting across the table.

"Too many people love their booze, Hemingstein. Too many people like getting happy."

Katy laughed.

Ken tapped the table with his finger. "Ordinary people will not stand for it, all they want is peace and they will sacrifice everything for peace and order."

"Oh who cares about the silly old Bolsheviks," Doodles said as she carefully, with both hands, set her wine glass down. Then, loudly: "I want to dance."

A young man with slicked black hair walked over to the table and leaned down toward Doodles.

"Do you want to dance, lady?"

Doodles, a bit surprised, glanced at Ken.

"I don't think she does," Ken said.

The man stood up straight and, without taking his eyes off of Doodles, lit a cigarette and blew the smoke skyward.

"I think I was asking the lady," the man said without taking his eyes off Doodles.

Ken stood up.

"And I answered for the lady."

The man took a drag on his cigarette and then finally looked at Ken. "It seemed to me that she wanted to dance."

"Yeah, so?"

The two of them stared at each other for a silent moment. The man took the cigarette out of his mouth.

"I was just being a little friendly, that's all."

Ken nodded his head. "Okay. So, good bye."

The man looked around the table and then walked away.

Ken sat down. Ernest leaned in toward him.

"You could've taken him. Easy target. You're taller, longer arms, you could have taken him out in no time. It would have been great. Want me to be your second?"

Ken shook his head. "No, Hem, I do not. And Doodles, don't act like a fool."

"I was not."

"Come on," Ken said. "Let's get out of here."

In the trolley car on the way back to Ken's apartment Ernest asked Bill if he noticed the back room action. Yes, Bill said, he did.

"You think they're killers gathering to discuss who and when and how much?"

"Or just some card games."

"Those guys look like the Ardito shock troops I saw in Italy," Ernest said. "You want to stay clear of those guys."

"The what troops?" Katy asked.

"The Italian government released criminals on the condition that they serve in the army as shock troops instilling fear in the Austrian army."

The trolley bells dinged and it came to a stop as some people got off and others got on. Ernest and Katy were both standing holding onto the bars. The others sat around them.

"I was with an Ardito on the night before the battle of Vittoria Veneto. We were getting drunk."

"That's a noble cause," Katy said and then laughed. She threw her head back a little bit when she laughed. She was not afraid to show it.

"He taught me the secret short sword technique to kill a man."

"Show us," Doodles piped in as she leaned back heavily against Ken.

"Here," Ernest said to Katy. He took her by the shoulders and turned her around so that her back was facing him. The trolley swayed back and forth suddenly so they almost lost their balance. "I come up behind you," he said as he stabilized himself. Quickly he reached around with his right arm across her chest and grabbed her throat.

"Now," he said into her ear, their cheeks touching. With his left hand holding his cane he jabbed the handle of the cane into her back just between her left shoulder blade and spine.

"And then thrust home," he breathed as he pushed the cane handle deeper. She arched her back and he could feel her breasts against his arm. "By now the blade is in the back of your heart and you will die."

Katy turned her head and looked into his eyes.

"When the Ardito showed me he took an Austrian prisoner and did it for real. He just tossed the limp body aside."

Ernest was still pressed against her, pressing her against the side of the trolley. He could smell her hair. The bells of the trolley dinged again as the car swayed to a stop. He held her for a moment longer.

"Well then," Ken said. "That seems to have potential. Are you now effectively dead, dear sister?"

Ernest stepped back. Katy turned to face him, a strange look in her eyes. She smiled. "I'll slap you if you left a bruise."

2. Horton Bay

There are the Permanent People and then there are the Summer People: like the birds, some live and spend all of their lives in one place, but then others, flocks of migrating birds, sweep in for a little while to rest and recover only to fly out again with the changing of the seasons.

"Liz, look what the cat dragged in," Jim Dilworth said as he and Ernest stood on the porch.

Jim opened the front screen door as Ernest scrapped the bottom of his shoes on the door mat. Jim twirled his black moustache with his other hand. Ernest had hiked over from Walloon Lake village and walked into the blacksmith shop that Jim owned at the far end of town. Jim, in his black leather apron and hammering on a hot slab of iron, stood up straight and laughed that big laugh when he first saw Ernest. Ernest, with his walking cane in hand, wore his hiking outfit with a large backpack with several blankets tightly bound across the top, his leather tube for his fishing rods dangling down, and his slouch hat pushed back from his face.

"Liz will drop dead when she sees you," Jim told him as they walked over to the porch of the Pinehurst Cottage and restaurant.

There was a strong scent of fresh baked bread as Ernest entered the house. He took off his hat as he walked into the kitchen.

Liz Dilworth, her apron dusted with flour, came walking toward him as she wiped her hands on a towel. She stopped when she saw him.

"Oh, my goodness. Hemingway," she said as she came up to him and put her arms around his shoulders. "How in the world are you?"

They quickly kissed.

She looked into his eyes and smiled that huge warm smile of hers that turned any room into a warm and friendly home.

"I'm fine Aunty Beth," Ernest said. She was not his real Aunt but all of the kids over the years had come to call her 'Aunty Beth.'

"We heard you were home from the war, a natural born hero and all."

Ernest shrugged his shoulders.

"Well, then, summer is come again. I'm making some bread, and we are preparing the rooms. Soon there will be dinners and a house full of guests. The Summer People are already arriving. Has your family come yet?"

"No, it's just me. They'll come up in a month or so."

"Have you opened up Windemere?"

"No, I haven't been there yet. I just got in and came straight over here."

"Then you must stay here with us, maybe until your folks get here. Jim, that cot bed is still back in the shed isn't it?"

Jim twirled his black moustache as he talked.

"Yes, as far as I know."

"Well, Ernie, a couple blankets to take off the chill and you can sleep in the shed just like old times."

"I'd like that."

Ernest made up the bed in the shed behind the house. Horton Bay was a small town with only a few buildings along the main dirt road about half way between Charlevoix and Boyne City. The Horton Bay General Store and post office with the high false front formed the center of town. Toward Charlevoix was the Methodist Church painted all white and then the Charles house by the large apple tree orchard. Across the street from the general store was the Stroud house where the owner of the mill used to live before they closed the mill, and then the Dilworth house with the Pinehurst Cottage and Restaurant. Down the road toward Boyne City was the Red Fox Inn and then the Horton house, the Van Hoesen house, the small one room school, and across the street from the school, painted all red, was Dilworth's blacksmith shop.

The Dilworth family, Jim and Elizabeth and their son Wesley with his wife Kathy, all listened closely over a dinner of fried chicken, famous for miles around, as Ernest told them about the war, his wound, and his recovery in the Milan Hospital.

Later that night after everyone else had gone to sleep Ernest sat on his cot and smoked a cigarette. The quiet moonlight streamed in through the window and streaked the floor. He listened to the small sounds of the forest at night. He heard the distant lap of the waves from the lake.

In the summer the area of northern Michigan filled with people, the so called Summer People, camping and fishing and boating along the lakes, they came from all around to avoid the summer heat. In the cool of the lakes, in the cool of shadowed forests they found relief.

But it was the regulars, like the Dilworth's, who lived here all year. Many times Ernest wished that he too could live here all year. His father built a cabin, his mother christened it "Windemere," and the family came here every summer. Ernest grew up here. All of his best memories were from here. What was real was here. He wanted to stay every year but every year he had to go back, back to school, back to Oak Park.

But this time it was different. School was over: at the end of this summer there was no school to go back to. As a matter of fact, what was there to return to at all? The dream of a life with Agnes was done. He did not want to live with his parents. What else was there?

He wanted to write.

He brought some of his stories with him and had some ideas for other stories. He hoped that he could start writing seriously this summer. He did not think he could do it at Windemere with his mother wanting this and that and the kids running around yelling and screaming. He needed quiet. He needed time to think: time to write, and get it right. He could do that here, at Dilworth's. This was the summer he could start writing seriously.

But for Agnes he would have gotten a job and worked and saved and they would get married and have a family and bless their love with happiness. But she was gone now. It hurt to think about it but perhaps it was a good thing.

Now he was free to be what he wanted to be: a writer.

There was one time when he and his sister Sunny slept at the Dilworth's. Grace let her stay as long as Ernest watched out for her. She was barely a teenager. During the day several of his friends came by and they all played baseball in an open field, with Sunny hitting just as hard as the boys.

That night there was a big barn dance not too far away. Ernest told her that he would take her if she was not any trouble. She said she was no trouble. When they got there the music was loud and there were a lot of people laughing and dancing. Sunny danced with a few of the younger boys but she got tired. It had been a hard day of baseball. Ernest was across the barn with his friends.

Then an older boy asked her to dance. She said no, she was too tired.

Maybe we can rest and get some fresh air.

Sunny noticed that a lot of couples had left the barn and were sitting in their cars, resting.

So she said okay and she left with the boy without telling Ernest. They were just going to sit in the back seat of a car.

Soon Ernest came outside shouting out her name. He looked all around shouting out her name. Several of his friends came out with him. Then he saw them. Ernest ran to the side of the car where the boy was and yanked open the door. He pulled the boy out by his shirt and threw him to the ground. Ernest shouted at the boy as the boy struggled to stand up. He shouted at him that she was his sister, how dare you take my sister out here, you'll have to answer to me if you so much as lay a finger on her. Once the boy stood up Ernest slammed him against the car and then against another car. He was in a rage. The boy ran away.

Then Ernest told Sunny to get out of the car. On the ride back to Dilworth's Ernest lectured her in front of his friends. Everyone was quiet as he held his finger pointing at her and shouted with a rage in his eyes.

"Never go out to sit in a car with a fellow unless you want to be necked. Never let a man press you against a wall, and never lie down on the grass."

Sunny sat silently almost in tears.

Ernest crushed out the butt of the cigarette and watched as the last of the smoke floated up through the shaft of moonlight from the window. Ernest got up and went outside. The night was light with full moonlight. He walked through the trees toward the lake. He could see the sparkle of the water, the dark silhouette of The Point, and beyond toward the far side of the lake small white caps from the wind rolling down from the north. It was still a bit cold but the smell of spring was everywhere.

Through the trees and across a small meadow in some distant trees he heard an owl hooting. He could not see it but there it was. It hooted again. He whispered to the night.

"Beware little chipmunks, take heed. The silent one is on the prowl."

Ernest looked up through the tops of the trees and stared at all of the stars.

3. The Dock I

Ernest walked down the sandy path to the lake. He could hear the shouting and laughing. He could see the cars, Carl Edgar's car and Bill Smith's blue Buick, down by the warehouse and the docks. They both lived in cottages only a mile or two away so why did they need to drive down here? Ernest walked past the two cars, past the warehouse and the Bean House painted white, and out onto the wooden dock. They were all at the end of the dock. Katy Smith and Carl Edgar were sitting together on the wooden dock. Carl, as always, sat as close to her as possible and Marjorie Bump was sitting off to one side. They all sat with their legs over the side splashing in the water. Bill Smith and Georgianna Bump were swimming in the water.

Those sitting on the dock all had their backs to him and did not see him walk onto the dock. Ernest stopped and slipped off his shoes, socks, took his shirt off over his head, and then took down his trousers. His bathing suit was on underneath. His leg was wrapped tight.

As he walked he could feel the smooth wooden boards beneath his feet, the slight give of the wood, and could hear the small lapping of waves against the pilings. Those sitting on the dock did not know he was there until he was standing next to them and took a long dive into the water. He plunged down deep into the water and then came to the surface.

It was Katy who shouted to him first.

"Thanks a lot for getting me wet Wemedge."

She sat on the dock just after having been in the water herself. She was still dripping wet.

"My pleasure," he called back.

The water felt good. It was a little cold but then warm after awhile. Ernest pulled his knees up and held them with his hands. He exhaled and began to sink. His bubbles floated to the surface. When he stopped exhaling it got quiet. He floated weightless under water: quiet, still. When he resurfaced everyone was laughing at something. Ernest swam over to the ladder and pulled himself up onto the dock. Everyone noticed the tight bandages wrapped around his right knee.

"I want to see you dive, Wemedge," Katy said. "You have a beautiful dive."

Ernest, flattered, stood at the edge of the dock. His toes curled around the edge of the wood. He took a deep breath and calmed himself. Then he sprung out across the water and then slipped into the water with barely a splash. He swam underwater to the ladder and pulled himself up again.

Ernest nodded and smiled to Carl. It was the first time Ernest had seen him since he left for the war.

"Hello Odgar."

That was his nickname. Carl stood up and the two of them hugged. Carl, serious for a moment, nodded.

"Glad to hear you came back, buddy, more or less in one piece. You had me worried there at first when I heard."

"I'm back to torment you to your grave old boy."

Carl was thirty two and worked for an oil company. He and Ernest had lived together for awhile when Ernest worked at the Kansas City Star. Carl was so much in love with Katy that it hurt. And everyone knew it. And Katy knew it too. But Ernest knew that nothing was ever going to happen. It made Carl seem like a fool, a sad fool. Ernest at times wanted to tell Carl to just forget it; drop it, it was not going to happen. But things just do not work that way.

Ernest smiled down at Marge. She was looking up at him, smiling, but with her head slightly tilted away as if wanting to look but a bit afraid to look. Her red hair shined in the sun. She was now seventeen. It had been two years since he last saw her. She had grown into quite a woman.

"Hello Red," he said.

"Hi Ernie."

"Liz said that you two were down," he said as he glanced over at her sister Georgianna in the water.

"Hello there Pudge," he called out to her. She waved at him.

"Liz expects a heavy crowd this summer."

They had been helping Liz for several years now. The two came down from Petoskey each summer to stay with their uncle, Professor Ernest Ohle. He had a cottage across the way from Pinehurst. When Liz needed it they helped her out. When Ernest went overseas she wrote him letters. Marge had joined the Petoskey ladies war effort by wrapping bandages for the Red Cross. And she knitted a sweater, her first ever knitted sweater, and sent it to Ernest when she heard he was in the hospital. She secretly wondered if any of the bandages she had wrapped were used on his wounds.

"Are Helen and Connie coming down too?"

"I don't know yet. It depends if it gets busy enough."

"Well, you know," Ernest said as he winked at her, "I still have that sweater you sent me."

She giggled and tried to hide her face.

"It was the first one I ever tried to make. I made a lot of mistakes."

"Well, it doesn't matter. It's been to the war and back and I still wear it mistakes and all."

He could still remember the first time they met. He was about fifteen walking down a path and this short thirteen year old girl came along from the opposite direction holding in both of her hands a huge fish and a cane pole. She was smiling like it was the best day of her life. She had red hair, tangled up, and bright red freckles. As they got close she beamed her smile toward him.

"Look what I caught," she loudly announced.

"I see it, boy it's a peach of a fish. Where did you get it?"

"I caught it in Horton's creek. Do you know what kind of fish it is?"

"It's a speckled trout. See the markings along here," Ernest said as he showed her with his finger.

"It's a big one isn't it?"

"Yes it is; he's a real good one. Did you catch it by yourself?"

"Yes I did," she proudly said. "I was fishing all day today by myself."

"What kind of bait did you use?"

"Grasshopper."

"That's a smart thing for trout, Red. Can I call you Red because your hair is really red?"

"My name is Lucy."

"Lucy?"

She shook her head yes. "Lucy Marjorie Bump."

"How about if I call you Marge?"

She shrugged her shoulders.

"Mine's Ernest Hemingway. Do you live near by?"

"Yeah, my uncle has a cottage and we visit every summer. Do you?"

"Right now I'm visiting my friend Bill Smith. My family has a cottage over by Walloon Lake about four miles or so. We come every summer too."

"Well then we should see each other again sometimes."

"How about we go trolling for rainbow trout off The Point someday? I need an extra pair of hands."

She beamed a big smile with her freckled face.

It was a date.

4. The Dock II

Bill Smith came up the ladder and out of the water. His wet body and swimsuit drenched the wooden boards.

"Do you know, Wemedge," Katy said, "that when we first met you Bill did not really like you that much. It's true." She raised her eyebrows as if for emphasis.

"He used to see you just as this husky kid in shorts, with some sort of backpack because you were always hiking or something. We were already by then twenty something and you were still some snot nosed teenager hanging around."

"But then we fished," Bill said as he threw an imaginary line out into the water and started tugging on it.

"Yes," she said, glancing at her brother. "Odgar here fished up a storm and he got the two of you to join him and pow, best of friends. All of this over some gutted fish."

Carl laughed and then said: "Never will you understand the bonds forged among men."

"Oh don't I," she said.

Ernest sat down on the dock and then lay down facing out toward the water. He could see the sparkle of the sun on the waves. He used his hands as a pillow for his head. The sun felt good on his skin. Warm. He could feel the water already starting to dry off. Katy, still sitting, scooted around and put the flat of her foot on his back massaging his back with her toes.

"So, are you two settled in over at the Charles place?"

"Yes."

"And how is The Madam?"

Mrs. Joseph William Charles, Laura, opened up her summer cottage every year. Everyone in town called her Mrs. Charles; Liz and Ernest's mother Grace called her Laura, Bill and Katy called her Aunty, and they and Ernest, between themselves, called her The Madam because she tended to be a little bit too formal at times. Her husband, Dr. Joseph William Charles, was an optometrist in St. Joseph, Missouri. He seldom made the summer trip.

"The Madam is doing just fine, thank you very much. And we told The Madam that The Wemedge has arrived so she is waiting. She has rung her little night bell so The Wemedge must now come running."

"She wants to get started on the garden," Bill said.

For the last few summers Bill and Ernest traded off. Bill helped Ernest dig potatoes and pull beans at Longfield and then Ernest helped

Bill by picking apples and chopping wood at Aunty Charles. This year she wanted to plant a garden and harvest the vegetables in the fall before she went back home to St. Joseph.

When her sister died in 1899 of tuberculosis Laura acted as guardian of her still young children and each summer brought them with her to her cottage in Horton Bay. It was impossible for their father to raise them. Professor William B. Smith was rather eccentric. He taught Greek, mathematics, and philosophy at the University of Missouri. He was a religious scholar, writing several books on the historicity of Christ. He was constantly working on what he felt to be his greatest work: he called it The Birth of the Gospel.

Whenever he visited Horton Bay in the summer, 'for inspiration,' Laura never let him stay at the Charles cottage with the children. She felt that his eccentric neglect of his wife and family had contributed to her death. So whenever he came north he rented a room at the Dilworth's Pinehurst.

It has been said that once Katy's brother Ken and some friends were out sailing on the lake when a severe storm swept in. They did not immediately come to shore but continued sailing. In the thunder and the lightening Aunty Charles was terrified that the boat would be hit. She stormed over to the Dilworth's in the rain and burst into the Professor's room. He was sitting by the fire reading, oblivious to anything else. He put on his coat and slowly walked down the sandy path to the waters edge. In the thundering lightening and the drenching rain he raised his arms and called out across the water: "Oh, Lord, give up Thy dead."

After standing there for a moment he turned and walked back to his room to resume his reading.

Katy put both of her feet against his back and massaged him with her toes. Ernest closed his eyes.

"So, Wemedge, what does the future now hold for you, is it school this fall?"

"No."

"No?"

"No."

"Then what?"

"I am going to write."

Katy pushed her tangled hair back away from her face and laughed.

"So you still see yourself as a young budding Shakespeare?"

"Why not?"

"Because," Carl broke in, "he was a bloody genius."

"Now Odgar, don't break the boy's spirit."

"So you like my diving?" Ernest asked.

"You dive divine," Katy said.

"You really do," piped in Marge.

Ernest smiled. He liked the attention.

"So Wemedge, when are we going fishing?" Bill asked.

"Oh Bill, let us settle in first," Katy replied.

"I was thinking of a camping trip out to the Pine Barren. Fish the Black or the Sturgeon."

"Count me in," called out Carl.

"Me too," Bill said, "but can your leg take all that hiking right now?"

"No, but that's why the good Lord giveth thou a blue convertible Buick."

"The Lord giveth me nothing, I paid for that thing with my own hard earned cash."

With his eyes closed Ernest suddenly felt a trembling. It seemed the wooden dock was crumbling away. The sky screamed. The heat of the sun on his skin burned. A roaring blast and then someone was screaming and screaming.

Ernest opened his eyes.

His heart was pounding.

He sat up and looked around. He sat up with such a start that everyone looked at him and stopped laughing.

"Are you alright? What happened?" It was Bill. He knelt down next to Ernest. "You're as white as a ghost."

Ernest waved him off.

"Nothing; nothing."

It was over. He was back: the dock; the warm day; the friends. And the Lord doth taketh away, he whispered to himself.

5. Windemere

The cottage was up a slight embankment from the waters edge. Ernest walked around with his hands on his waist as he looked around at the cottage and the trees, the lake and the small wooden dock that ran out into the water. The cottage was boarded up for the winter. The ground was littered with dead branches and twigs. That would have to be cleared off. And it looked like some pilings on the dock needed repair. For all the years that Ernest could remember early each spring he and his father would come and together walk around the cottage to see what damage the winter had brought. His father would point out this or that and young Ernest would shake his head as if he too had seen and knew everything that his father saw and knew.

Ernest turned and looked up at the boarded windows of the kitchen. Clarence and Grace visited the lake on a vacation and fell in love. They bought a small acre plot of shoreline from Henry Bacon, who owned a farm just up the hill behind them. There were white birch and cedar trees along the shore, with a mix of maples, beeches, and hemlocks further back. The shore was shallow far out into the lake before it dropped off into deeper water. It was perfect for the children to play and swim.

They had a small cottage built. It had a small cozy living room with window seats on either side of a large brick fireplace; there was a dining room, a kitchen, and two small bedrooms. As the family grew the cottage grew as they eventually added an annex with several more bedrooms. It had a roofed front porch with white railing and a double hinged gate.

Murphy's point that jutted out into the lake protected the cottage from the cold northwestern winds coming across the water. The cottage was close enough to the Bacon's ranch where Ernest could go over every morning and get fresh eggs and milk, but it was far enough that, as Grace put it, 'you don't smell the pigs.'

Grace christened it Windemere after the Lake District poets. Windemere of Walloon Lake. She even wrote a waltz "Lovely Walloona" published by the E.A. Stege Company of Chicago in 1901. Each summer when they gathered at the cottage to start the summer she had all the children sing the song: "Oh, lovely Walloona, fairest of all the inland seas," while she played the tune on her out of tune piano.

Every summer of his life Ernest had come with the family to Windemere. He loved it here. His father taught him how to fish. His father taught him how to hunt. His father taught him how to shoot, he taught him all of the safety rules like point the gun down toward the ground and never at someone, never shoot unless you know exactly what you are shooting at, and never never close your eyes when you shoot because you are afraid of the blast or the kick.

And do not shoot anything that you are not going to eat. You do not shoot animals just to shoot things.

He remembered that he violated that rule once when he was fourteen when he and his friend Harold Sampson shot a porcupine. The Bacon's dog came home one day with a face full of porcupine quills. The Bacon's brought the dog over to Doctor Clarence to get them out. He had to charm the dog into letting him cut the quills off one by one and then pull out the fishhook barbed tips. It was long and painful but the dog let him do it. So Ernest and Harold hunted the porcupine in question, shot it, and brought it home as a trophy.

But Clarence was furious. The poor animal was only doing what God made him to do. So Ernest and Harold had to cook the meat and eat it. It took hours to get the meat as soft as shoe leather and it tasted horrible.

But the lesson was learned.

Ernest heard a crow cawing in the trees behind the house.

It was like Clarence. When it was time for dinner his father stood on the front porch and blew a large ram's horn. There was only one shrill note but it carried out and across the lake. All of the six kids came home from wherever their separate adventures had taken them.

Ernest smiled, but it hurt. Memories rushed in.

On fourth of July at night father shot fireworks off into the dark sky over the water and explosions of light electrified all of them into giggles and shouting laughter. They released little multi colored Japanese balloons with small candles attached and the heat lifted the balloon up over the dark water floating so silent, small dabs of colored lights suspended in the darkness.

Father hoisted him up a tree to see a small nest with little naked baby birds wobbling their heads back and forth, but don't touch them, he said, don't touch them or the Mother won't return.

Father had Ernest learn the names of the birds from his father's bird books and his father would point them out as they walked the woods.

On a cold rainy day Father pointed up and you could see the ducks and geese in perfect V formation quacking their way across the sky. Father turned and smiled down at him, a big face full smile.

And while walking together in the woods Father would stop and raise his finger and say: 'Listen.' And everyone got quiet and soon they all heard the buzz of insects, the twitter of birds, the flutter of feathers, the crow's distant caw, the woodpeckers hammering, the chatter of

70

chipmunks, the soft flow of the wind through the trees, the quiet fall of leaves twirling down through space. And the sounds were there, there, but unheard.

The wonders of the world never end.

Ernest remembered that Grandpa Hall with his balding white hair and his bushy black eyebrows and his large curly white muttonchops side whiskers that came down all the way to his chin came and stayed the summer at Windemere several times. Ernest was only about five or so but he could remember it. Grandpa Hall did not really like coming to the lake. Even though the children ran around barefoot and on occasion swam in the lake naked, and Clarence wore his boots and his patched and torn baggy pants and a large floppy straw hat to protect from the sun, Grandpa Hall always dressed in his suit with his tie and starched white collared shirts like he did on any other business day. He did not much like the lake or the swimming or the sailing or the fishing or the hunting but he did like to climb up the hill behind the cottage next to the Bacon farm, through the trees, and out onto the bare hill top to watch the sunsets. He took the children with him and Ernest could remember that he held his hand as they climbed up the wooded hill. Grandpa Hall held both Marc's and Ernest's hands as they walked up the hill together. Grandpa Hall would stand still and stare off into the sunset. When Ernest talked or made noise Grandpa Hall just knelt down next to him and put his arm around him and whispered into his ear, 'Hush now child, you have to watch such beauty quietly,' and then he would kiss Ernest on the cheek.

And Ernest watched the sunset quietly.

There was a family story that Ernest heard from his older sister Marc, that when Grandpa Hall returned from his spring 1905 visit with his son Leicester in California he was a very sick man. He was bed ridden with Bright's disease. Since the whole family lived with him in his house at that time the children all had to avoid the front parlor where he was bed ridden and come around the back of the house and be very quiet so not to disturb him in his painful sick bed. But in preparation for the end Grandpa Hall slept with a loaded pistol under his pillow so when the pain was too great he could end it. But Father, one night, took the pistol and emptied it and put it back under the pillow. But then, one night, in such pain as he had feared, Grandpa Hall reached for the pistol, cocked it, put it to his temple, and pulled the trigger.

Nothing happened.

Grandpa Hall had to suffer the pain until he died.

Ernest turned and looked out across the water to the other side of the lake. He could see the Grace cottage. It was almost complete. In 1905 there was a plot of land that was being sold for back taxes. Grace, with money she had just inherited from the death of her father Ernest Hall, bought the land. She felt that one day she would retire and end her days there.

When she saw the long fields of planted potatoes she christened the farm Longfield.

In addition to the potatoes Clarence planted fruit trees. The farm sloped up to the top of a hill where there was a lot of red grass.

Grace christened the hill as Red Top Mountain and said that she one day wanted to build a cottage there since it had a wonderful view in all directions.

It will be my place, she said: my place.

This spring, finally after all these years, she contracted to have it built.

Grace Cottage: her cottage, her place, for her.

Chapter Four

Ernest passed in and out of sleep. The artillery stopped after several hours.
Orderlies kept walking back and forth along the rows of stretchers. In the row where
Ernest was there was moaning and groaning. But in the row of stretchers across the
walkway it was silent. Those were the dead ones. The orderlies every once in awhile
stopped beside a stretcher and looked down at the man. Every once in awhile they
picked up and carried the stretcher over to the other row. Ernest watched this happen
all night long.

It must have been toward early morning. It was not as hot as it was during the
night. Ernest awoke to find two orderlies over him. They were picking up his stretcher.

"No, no," Ernest said in a sudden shock. He grabbed at the men and waving his
hands. "No, no. I am alive, alive. Non e morto, non e morto."

The orderly laughed and touched him on the chest.

"No worry, mio amico. The ambulance, we take you."

The man looked over at the silent row of stretchers and waved his hand laughing.

They carried him outside to an ambulance with the engine running. It was just
beginning to get light. The canvas flaps in the rear were up. There were two side
shelves, one on either side of the truck. Above each side shelf hung a hammock where
stretchers could be tied in. The truck was full except the left side shelf. They slid
Ernest in and then secured the stretcher. There was some shouting and then the truck
lurched forward.

Ernest closed his eyes and waited. But then he heard a dripping sound. When he
opened his eyes it was just light enough for him to make out the hammock above him.
The man was bleeding and the blood drained down onto the canvas hammock. The
blood pooled until it seeped through the canvas. It was dripping down onto his blanket.

Ernest called out to the driver. The truck came to a stop but the engine continued
running. The driver poked his head through the opening between the cabin and the bed
of the truck.

"He is bleeding," Ernest said pointing to the man.

The driver looked over at the man but then shrugged his shoulders.

"There is nothing to do," he replied in English, "We will be there soon."

The driver sat back into his seat and drove on.

1. Grace Cottage I

Ernest took the small narrow canoe tied to the Windemere dock and paddled across the lake to Longfield. It was narrow and a difficult canoe but he had done it before. A shift of weight will throw the canoe out of balance: 'You can only paddle across if your hair is parted in the middle,' he once told his sister; otherwise the weight will throw you out of balance.

As he walked around the cottage it was true, it was almost complete. The contractor had done his job. The project for the summer was to paint the cottage, and for her to move in.

"I shall do my composing there," Grace told everyone. "And I will simply rest."

"Can't we come too?"

"Yes you can at times, but by invitation only. I love you all, but I have to have a rest from you all now and then if I am to go on living."

Ernest realized that music was his mother's salvation. She grew up with music as a second language. Her entire family sang. But when Grace was seven she had scarlet fever and was left totally blind. The doctor said there was little hope she would ever see again. Blind, she learned to play the piano by ear. But then one day while the family was at church Grace was at home playing when she began to vaguely see the movement of her right hand. Excited, she continued playing as her fingers came more and more into focus. She ran to the stairs shouting but the family was away so she sat back down and played and played until her parents came home. She ran to them as they came in the front door.

"Mama, Papa, I can see. I can see you."

Grace was convinced that on some level God granted her sight because of her music.

Afterword she had bad sight but she could see and too bright a light gave her severe headaches. Many a time she had to lie down in a darkened room with a moist cloth draped across her forehead. At the cottage she wore sunglasses and huge straw hats to shade her face.

As long as Ernest could remember Grace gave music and voice lessons in their house. Many times he was told to tiptoe around so not to make noise. Some students who could not afford lessons but showed promise she taught for free.

"I love to open new windows," she said.

Grace wrote songs and music: 'If I Could Know,' 'Madonna's Prayer,' 'Serenade,' 'God Laid Me Aside to Rest Me,' and 'Lovely Walloona.' She published them with Oliver Ditson Co. in Chicago, E.A. Stege Company of Chicago and Summy Co. in New York. She sang in public whenever possible: Woman's Christian Temperance Union, Fine Arts Society, P.T.A., Nineteenth Century Club, and at local suffrage meetings. She sang with Belle Watson-Melville at the Third Congregational Church where she became chairman of the music committee and director of the choir. She gave recitals in the large music room in her home in order to advertise promising students. Ernest helped at times with the folding chairs for up to three hundred people and giving out biscuits and tea for everyone.

Many a night, in the middle of the night, Ernest heard his mother downstairs on the piano working out a tune that had just come to her. She had to let her fingers work it out on the keys or she would forget the melody.

So Ernest knew that music was her life.

She said it so herself: "Art is salvation."

So when she said she would do her composing there, alone, in Grace's Cottage, away from it all, Ernest understood what she meant.

It was the same with his writing: he needed time and peace. But something was strange about it all. It was different because she had a family. It left him uneasy. Things seemed to be changing so fast.

As Ernest walked around the cottage, stepping over some of the left over wood, he could not stop his thoughts.

He was different. He was different in many ways. He was not what he was and was not yet what he would be. He lived through the war, he lived through being wounded; that is bound to change anyone. How can anyone, after that, go home again and be again what they are not now?

Marc was a grown woman. She was in college. She spent her time with Walter, her first serious boyfriend. It made her different.

And he received a letter from Ursula, who was all of seventeen now, telling him about her new boy Marvin who is "loads of fun and has a marvelous car" who is not to be confused with her other new boy also named Marvin, and both were different from the Joe that she saw when she came up to the cottage, and Mom and Dad didn't like it but she went out anyway. Ernest feared that Ursula had a bit too much of the rebellious streak in her that he had in him. Rebellion was fine under the right cause, but it was a measured rebellion. She seemed to be running riot.

And he did not quite know what but there was something going on with Ruth, his mother's student and companion. Ernest felt a tension growing in his father over Ruth.

There was a growing distance in his father in everything. Why did he seem so confused at times? Ernest could sense it but he did not understand it. His father was just not as focused or driven as he used to be. He used to be strong and centered and steady.

One morning, years before, Ernest went hunting with his father and the large fat Indian named Simon Green. Simon owned a farm along Horton's Creek. He rolled when he walked because he was so large. And he laughed a lot. They were out by Dilworth's grist mill when they spooked a covey of ruffed grouse feeding on the ground. There was a huge flurry of large birds and flapping wings as they all took flight at once. Ernest, surprised, quickly raised his shot gun and fired twice but missed both times. But his father stood steady and sure and aimed with an old lever action Winchester pump and rapidly fired again and again and dropped five of the flying birds one after another. Simon was laughing out loud and shaking his head as he picked up the dead birds.

"Wow, Mr. Hemingway, you sure are the fastest and cleanest shot that ever there was, anywhere."

His father, with a controlled smile as he reloaded his rifle, winked at Ernest.

To this day, every summer sitting over at Dilworth's blacksmith shop sweating in the afternoon heat, Simon brought up that story just shaking his head and laughing.

To Ernest his father just knew what was right. He just knew as if without even thinking about it. And he had a courage that was bottomless.

Dilworth's son Wesley told the story about one early spring when Clarence and young Wesley and several others were on a fishing trip near Horton Bay. They were in a cabin a day or so walk from any town. Clarence had accidently caught a fishhook in his left arm and developed blood poisoning. The infected arm bothered him bad but he put hot compresses on it so that he could keep fishing. He knew he could fix his arm when he got home. But Clarence woke up early the next morning when it was still dark and his arm was severely swollen and red and rock hard and throbbing. He was a doctor and he knew what that meant. He knew he had to drain the arm of pus, right now, or he might lose the arm. He knew what he had to do.

What he did not know is whether he had the courage and strength to do what had to be done. There was only one way to find out.

He had the kerosene lamp burning bright and he held the sharp hunting knife in the flame until the blade was searing red hot. Then, as Wesley and the other men held him tight, he stabbed the knife into his own arm. He screamed and shook as they held him down and the squirt of white pus shot up and hit the ceiling. The hot blade cauterized the incision.

"Oh, Clarence," Grace shouted out shaking her head and putting her hands to her ears whenever the topic came up. "Please be quiet, be quiet, please I cannot hear anymore of it. It's too upsetting."

"Well, I can tell you right now it was no picnic. It's a real good thing that the boys held me down so tight."

Ernest turned and looked back at Windemere across the water. He could see it but it was blurred. His eyes were not the eyes of his father. He had the eyes of his mother. Once, at darkening dusk he and his father came over the hill where he now stood and his father laughed telling Ernest that there was Windemere and the flag on the pole was still flying and Carol was on the dock splashing her feet in the water.

Ernest could barely make out the cottage much less anything else.

Father was eagle eyed.

But now, from where Ernest stood, it was all fading away. Nothing was in focus anymore. Had it ever been?

2. Grace Cottage II

"Do you really approve of all this?"

Marc looked toward Ernest.

"What do you mean?" she asked.

The two of them were on the porch of Grace Cottage painting the outer wall. She was standing and he was kneeling. The paint was a reddish brown.

"I don't know if I like the whole idea."

Marc shrugged her shoulders.

"I guess it's alright. It's been a long time dream of hers to build a place here on Red Top Mountain ever since she bought the land, what, fourteen or so years ago. I think it's exciting to be able to fulfill a dream, don't you?"

Ernest stroked his paint brush back and forth across the wood without replying.

"It gives Mom her own place, her own place where she can be alone if she needs to be."

"Yeah, I get all that but what about the cost of the thing."

Marc stopped her brush stroke.

"What difference does that make? It's all her money from teaching."

"Shouldn't that be family money? That can help pay for college for all of us."

"But Ernie, this is her money that she made from teaching. So she's using it for something for her."

"But money Dad makes all goes toward the family, why doesn't hers?"

Marc stared at him for a moment as he turned and looked up at her.

"It's just different, that's all," she said.

"But getting away is the whole idea of having Windemere, isn't coming here every summer getting away?"

"Ernie," she said as she bent down and put her paint brush into the can of paint. She turned and held out her arms toward the lake. "Just look at this."

Ernest looked. He could see the open lake stretching out flat far into the distance, a sparkling blue in the afternoon sun. And at the very far end of the water, in the heat of the afternoon, shimmered the town of Walloon Lake.

"Just look at that; and in this direction too."

Ernest looked up the lake, past Eagle Island, through the narrows and up into the West Arm as far as he could see. Farms and meadows and woodlands were sprinkled along the banks of the cool blue water. He could see the white of the clouds reflected in the water.

"Now tell me, what actually can you see from Windemere? Just the part of the lake right in front of it, and we are backed into a wooded hill so you can't see out very far in any other direction."

"What does that matter, it's all the things to do that makes it fun."

"Like what, Ernie, for her, not you, for her. She doesn't like swimming, you know that, she doesn't like hiking or fishing or hunting. She likes to be alone and paint, or go out painting with Liz Dilworth."

Ernest took a deep breath. "Okay," he said, "I guess you're right."

"Do you remember those couple of times that she had Dad take her out on the boat, just the two of them, at just around sunset and they would go way out and all of us were back at the cottage wondering what they were doing and then as night closed in we could hear her voice across the water singing quiet and sad like songs?"

Ernest nodded, remembering. Neither of them spoke for a moment until finally Ernest spoke.

"Dad likes the action; Mom likes the peace."

Marc bent down, picked up her paint brush, wiped the brush against the side of the bucket, and began painting again.

"I thought she liked coming up here," Ernest said. "She's been doing it for almost forever."

"Ernie, you know what she told me? She said that Windemere was new and fresh and exciting for the first eight or nine years when it was just her and Dad and you and me as little babies. But then she had all of the kids, we all grew up, and she had that typhoid fever, and her arthritis set in so that just small regular chores became painful and a burden."

"So why does she keep coming?"

"It is for us, Ernie; for Ursula and Sunny and Carol and Les. It's for their enjoyment and excitement."

Ernest looked down at the floorboards of the porch and shook his head. Marc continued.

"When she realized that she could build this on her own it was like an answer to her prayers. She could still come and be relaxed and at peace. She said she wanted to rebuild a place of neatness and cleanness and simplicity and wholesomeness. She could do her music, and listen to the woods, and watch the sunsets just like Grandpa Hall used to do."

Ernest picked up his brush, dipped it into the bucket of paint, and began painting again stroking back and forth.

"Well," he said, "I still don't like it."

"You know, you have to be critical of her, can't you just be nice once in awhile? She's a very fine woman."

"I'm not critical; it's just she grates on me sometimes. And look at you, you know you side with her all the time no matter what it is."

"I do not."

"You are more and more becoming just like her."

"And what does that mean? Even if it is true, and it's not, is that supposed to be a bad thing?"

"Yeah, because it means now I'm surrounded by two of you."

Marc, standing over him, held her paint brush out in the air.

"How would you like a red nose for your birthday?"

He held his brush up.

"How would you like some red hair?"

Suddenly there was a voice behind them.

"Now children, how about a little more red on those walls and a little bit less on you?"

Both Ernest and Marc turned.

Standing on the pathway to the cottage were Grace and Ruth. Both carried large rugs in their arms. Grace, with her large hat shielding her face from the sun, wore a simple white blouse, black skirt, and black boots. Ruth, standing next to Grace and blinded by the glare of the sun, squinted her eyes as she looked at them.

"Hello Mother," Marc said, as she put her brush back into the can of paint.

"Can you help us dear?"

Ernest and Marc came over and took the rugs from them. The four of them went into the cottage.

"Just put them over there until I know where I want to put them."

Grace and Ruth had woven the rugs themselves from old pieces of clothing. At home, sitting on the floor of the large music room, they spent nights listening to music and weaving and talking. Marc helped a few times when she was home from school. But it was mostly Grace and Ruth. It seemed to be just Grace and Ruth all the time. Ernest used to look in and then go up to his room.

Ruth Arnold came to their house in 1907 as a thirteen year old music student. Daughter of a River Forest salesman who was seldom home, with an inattentive mother, and with two older dominating sisters, Grace took pity on her. Eventually Grace took her on as a live in student who traded lessons for chores as baby sister and cook and maid. Ernest did not think she was that bright, or had that great of a singing voice, but she cooked and cleaned and mother wanted her around. She had lived with them for so long that she seemed a part of the family.

"Ruth, dear."

"Yes, Muv." It was her pet name she called Grace. It was just between the two of them.

"Dear, can you get the other rugs from the boat?"

Ruth glanced back and forth. She was quiet. She was at Grace's side. She loved to wash and then comb out Grace's long hair. Grace would sit in a chair with her eyes closed humming a tune as Ruth combed and combed. There were times she seemed to appear out of nowhere and Ernest never heard her coming. She reminded him of a mouse, watching, waiting, quiet, and then scampering away.

"So what do you think children?" Grace asked, turning her full attention to her two children. "Doesn't the furniture look nice in here?"

The furniture, as Marc and Ernest both knew, Grace had made herself.

Grace visited the Oak Park woodworking class and admired the student's projects. She approached the teacher.

"Tell me young man," she asked the teacher who was himself barely out of high school, "could someone like me learn this?"

"I don't know why not."

"Would you give me lessons?

"I could but private lessons would be expensive, it would be cheaper for you to have a class."

"How many students would you need to make it worth your while?"

The man shrugged his shoulders, thought for a moment, and then replied: "Six."

A week later she called up the man. She had six friends who would take the class with her, when can he start.

Never having hammered a nail without bending it all out of shape she entered the world of sawing and hammering, the world of woodworking tools like a square, a level, and a carpenter's plumb line, she entered the woodworking world with intense devotion.

Before long she made a living room table of bird's eye maple with a side drawer. She made a padded davenport with a straight back that could be folded over into a table. She made a dressing table with four sliding drawers. She made a tea cart with a fitted tray for a top, a shelf below, and with wheels. She built a four poster bed with curtains.

And now, in a cottage that she designed, a cottage that she contracted to build, surrounded with furniture she herself made, with rugs she herself made, Grace, more than anyone else lived within her own created world.

3. Fishing

They drove down the road fast, the headlights seeking the way. The four of them were in Bill's Blue Buick, top down, wind roaring, darkness of the night above, their hair dancing around on their heads at the mercy of the wind. Edgar was driving with Howell Jenkins at his side. Ernest and Bill Smith sat in the back with all of their equipment (poles, canvas tents, fishing poles, back packs, blankets, pots and pans and Howell's Austrian carbine) stuffed in between them.

They were coming home. Four days of fishing and camping in the deep forest along the Pigeon River. They had not showered or shaved or changed clothes in four days. They smelled of fish and sweat and forest damp and wood smoke. Jenkins howled as the car raced through the night. He turned to Carl. He had to shout to be heard.

"So, how's lover boy doing, doing better?" he asked as he turned to look and laugh at Ernest and Bill.

Carl looked at the two in the rear view mirror. "Heh guys," he said, "I'm sorry about that little incident. I didn't mean to break down like that."

"Don't worry about it," Ernest said. "It was the booze talking, that's all."

Carl looked at Bill in the rearview mirror.

"And Bill? Please don't tell her about it will you?"

Bill waved him off.

It was early in the trip, after dinner, sitting around the fire, passing around one of the bottles of booze, now nearly empty.

"Oh man," Carl was saying, stumbling on his words, as he passed the bottle. He looked as if he was about to cry, shaking his head slowly back and forth.

"What's up with you?" Jenkins asked, taking a strong sip of booze and then licking his red moustache with his tongue.

"It's Katy, man; Katy. What else is there?"

Ernest and Bill exchanged glances.

"What am I doing wrong? Why doesn't she want me? I don't understand what I'm doing wrong. I love her, you see. You see, Jenkins, you see I love her so much it just burns me up. I have to have her, don't you see. She just has to be mine."

He seemed to fall toward Ernest but then stopped himself. Jenkins put out his arm and held Carl's shoulder.

"Watch it there, you're falling off the earth a little," Jenkins said and then laughed.

"Get a hold of yourself Odgar," Ernest said.

"Hey," Jenkins said, holding the bottle out into the air, "no more Grog for Odgar."

"But, Hem, she just has to be mine, you see. There is nothing else."

"Sometimes you don't get what you want," Ernest replied.

"No no no," Carl said as he waved his finger back and forth in the air. "I have to have her, I love her, I really need her, you don't understand, you don't understand about love. This has to happen."

Ernest spoke up: "Hey, Weak One. Don't tell me about love. Agnes was the only thing I could think about. I lost the best thing that ever happened to me, it walloped me good. It knocked me down so bad I didn't think I could get up. It hurt like hell but it's done. It's done," he said, convincing himself. Then: "I got back up and now I'm alright about it."

"Katy said you got a letter from her," Bill said.

"Yeah, I got a letter from her. It seems the guy she fell for isn't going to marry her after all. He's some count and his mother convinced him that Agnes was from the wrong class. She is beneath him, the bastard."

"Tough thing," Bill said.

"I feel sorry for the poor kid, I do. When I got that first letter dumping me I wanted her to trip and fall and knock all her front teeth out. But that was just silly hurt talk. Poor kid," he said again.

They were all quiet for a moment. The fire crackled, sending up small sparks.

"What are you going to do?" Bill finally asked.

"I tried to feel it again but it isn't there anymore. What am I going to do? Live on. Move on. Yesterday is done. Tomorrow is going to be here. The sun always rises."

The car raced on into the night, headlights seeking the road ahead.

"Hey," Carl shouted out as he turned his head toward Jenkins. "Since we are recapping the trip how about you? Forget lover boy, don't you remember that I was almost bear lunch because of you, Mr. War Hero."

Jenkins laughed. "I drove ambulance, my job wasn't to shoot it was to take the shot back to the dressing station."

"So what does that mean? After the bear had his fill you were going to take me to the hospital."

"Yeah, whatever was left over."

They all laughed.

As they were hiking deeper into the woods to find a good spot to camp Carl, walking in the lead, froze. The others, one by one, came up behind him and when they looked to see where he was staring they all froze as well. In the path way, sitting back on his rear legs, sat a large black bear. The bear was shaking its head back and forth and grumbling as it watched them approach.

No one spoke for a moment.

Finally Ernest, in a low whisper, said "Jenks, got that carbine?"

Jenkins brought his captured Austrian carbine along for hunting. It was strapped across his backpack.

"Yeah," Jenkins responds. But he does not move.

Ernest waited, but Jenkins does not move.

"Jenks, the carbine," Ernest whispered again.

"Yeah," Jenkins responded again and then again did not move.

All of them watch as the bear roars at them and then turns around and wanders away as if he has all the time in the world. They stand still until the bear is completely out of sight. Then, one by one, they each take a deep breath and turn to sit down on the ground.

"That was close," Bill said.

They all laugh shaking their heads in agreement.

Carl whistled. "He was looking me over for lunch."

Ernest turned to Jenkins. "Why didn't you get the carbine ready, he could have charged?"

"There aren't any bullets in it."

"Where are they?"

"They're in my backpack."

Ernest rolled his eyes and looked up in the sky shaking his head. "Why do you go hunting with an empty rifle?"

Jenkins gave a large grin.

As the road made a slow turn to the left the headlights of the car illuminated one by one the trees along the side of the road. Bill reached across the pile of equipment in the center of the seat and picked up the carbine. He rummaged through Jenkins back pack and pulled out some bullets.

Ernest: "What are you going to do with that?"

Jenkins "Where's the grog, is there any left?"

Ernest: "No, we hit the last of it. What are you going to do with that?"

Jenkins: "Damn."

They were coming into the town of Boyne, driving under the first of the streetlamps. Bill smiled at Ernest and then took aim with the carbine toward the lamp of an approaching street lamp. He aims and then fires. The bulb of the street lamp pops and shattered glass falls to the pavement as they drive by.

Jenkins: "What the hell?"

Bill hands the carbine to Ernest, a sly smile on his face. Ernest then aims at an approaching street lamp with his elbow steady on his up raised knee. He follows it and just as they are even with the pole he fires. The glass shatters sending sparks shooting out.

Jenkins: "Two for two."

Carl: "Are you guy's crazy?"

Ernest hands the carbine back to Bill. He again aims and then fires. But he misses. They whiz past beneath the still lit street light. Bill hands the carbine to Ernest.

Carl: "Hey guys, cut it out."

Ernest takes very careful aim. If he takes it out he wins. Ernest had to win. He sees some people walking along the opposite side of the road. They watch the approaching car on the empty road. Ernest levels and aims, pulls the trigger. The street lamp explodes and tinkling glass flies everywhere. Huge electrical sparks fly out that lights the night. The lamp crackles as they pass by it.

Jenkins: "Wow, hey."

Carl: "I don't think this is such a good idea guys. We could get in big trouble."

Ernest, now up one, hands the carbine back to Bill. He holds it and looks at it.

Bill: "Yeah your right."

Bill empties the carbine and drops the bullets back into Jenkins backpack. He puts the carbine down. Ernest watched as the buildings and trees of the town pass by, the car passing under street lamps, splashed with light again and again as it drove through the night.

Standing in the cold river, his line cast, Ernest looked out into the forest. Shafts of sunlight came down through the tree canopy. Falling leaves and buzzing grasshoppers swam through the light. A hammering woodpecker echoed the woods. Ernest slowly pulled up on his line and then relaxed. He hears a shout and splashes as Bill pulls a large trout in. Standing in a shaft of daylight, surrounded by shadow, Bill holds his pole high and reaches down with his hand to pull the trout up by its gills, the sun sparkling diamonds in the swirling water.

Some moments last forever.

From behind they all heard the siren. They all looked back. The motorcycle cop with lights flashing approached. They were beyond the town. They were in the darkness of the forest again. Carl slowed and then pulled off the side of the road at a small clearing. The motorcycle came up behind. The single beam of light from the motorcycle illuminated the car. The policeman approached, his boots crunching on the gravel along the side of the road. Ernest could see the night sky above them pulsing with stars.

The policeman flicked on his flashlight and searched the car with its beam as he came along side the car.

"Good evening gentlemen."

"Good evening officer," Carl said as nice and pleasant as he could.

The flashlight searched each face one by one with the wind blown mangled hair, the unshaven face, the smudges of dirt, the wrinkled and dirty shirts and the tired lean look. The beam searched the stack of equipment in the back seat: the poles, the backpacks, the canvas tents and the carbine. The light stopped on the carbine.

"Is there something wrong officer?" Carl asked.

The policeman hesitated. His flashlight was still on the carbine. It was otherwise dark. Ernest could not make out the features on the man's face.

"Well," the policeman began as he brought the beam of light up to Carl. "Well," he began again, "there seems to be a group of kids riding through town shooting out street lights."

"No, really?" Carl said. "How awful is that?"

"You didn't happen to see a car like that did you?"

"No, can't say as I have. Guys; anyone?"

They all shook their heads. "No, can't say as I have," Jenkins agreed.

The policeman stood for a moment before he spoke.

"Well, I'll let you be on your way. Report it if you happen to see them."

"Absolutely, officer. That we can do."

Ernest listened to the crunch of the policeman's boots on the gravel as he walked back to his motorcycle.

"Carl," Jenkins whispered. "Let's get the hell out of here."

"Ditto that," Carl replied as he started the engine, put it in gear, and then drove off. They drove on and Carl kept looking in the rear view mirror to see if the policeman was following them but he was not.

After a minute they started laughing.

"That was a close one."

"He was one scared cop."

"Poor cop, just think: along a dark road, late night, four dirty and unshaven savages with a carbine and who knows how many other guns shooting up the town, he must have been thinking to himself now exactly how important can a couple of light bulbs really be?"

Ernest felt good as he looked around at each of the others as they laughed and told and retold the cop story. Fishing with his friends, experiences, laughing and enjoying it all, it made Ernest feel good. This is what makes it worth it all.

Ernest put his head back and looked up at the starry night as they drove toward home.

4. The Code

Ernest sat at a table on the open porch of Dilworth's Pinehurst Cottage. He was writing and thinking as he stared off through the trees to the lake beyond and then returned to his paper to write some more.

Marge was inside serving the guests their lunch. Ernest occasionally glanced in to see her. At times she was glancing out the window to see him.

He was writing when she came out the screen door and stood before him. When he looked up she smiled.

"I didn't want to disturb you," she said.

"That's alright."

"Are you writing a story?"

Ernest nodded.

"Can I read it when you are done?"

"Sure you can. Maybe I can read it to you."

"That would be nice."

Ernest took a sip from his lemonade. The ice clinked in the glass.

"Katy said that you might not go home at the end of summer? You might stay around here."

"That's right. I can't write at home. It's too complicated. I can write much better around here. I thought I'd stay here as long as Liz will have me and then maybe get a place in Petoskey."

"Really?" she asked excited.

"Sure, kid. Just think; we'll be neighbors."

"That would be nice," she said. She was tracing the top of the chair in front of her with the tips of her fingers, back and forth.

"It's important for you to be where you can write, you know, I mean you need inspiration and all and if you don't get that at home then, well, you should go where it is."

Liz called out to Marge from inside the restaurant.

"Oh, well, I guess I'd better get going."

"See you," Ernest said as they both waved and she went inside.

He stared after her for a moment and then turned to return to his writing. But he was distracted and looked over. Standing on the porch some three feet away stood the big Indian Nick Boulton. A step back from him, coming up the stairs and onto the porch, was the Indian Billy Tabashaw. Nick was big and muscular and intense. Some said that he was a half breed; others thought he was white and just lived in the Indian camp in the woods near Bacon's farm with his wife Annie. Billy was short and fat and was trying to grow a moustache but after a decade only

89

had a few wisps of hair.

Ernest hated that you could never hear the Indians when they came, you never heard them approach. They were just there. The women came down to sell their woven baskets to the Summer People. Nick and Billy were sawyers at the mill.

"Hello Nick," Ernest said.

"Your father's not here this summer?"

"No. He's coming up later to close down Windemere but he's not here yet."

Nick winked.

"Your father doesn't like it anymore, now."

Ernest controlled himself. Every time Nick brought it up Ernest felt like just punching him. Punch the rotten smirk off of his face.

It was years before. Ernest was young. He was carrying his book when he came through the back gate and saw his father, Nick and his son and Billy down by the water in front of the cottage. Some logs drifted onto the beach and Clarence asked the two Indians to saw up the logs. Ernest stopped and watched. Something seemed wrong. Billy and Nick had their hooks and saws but Nick and Clarence seemed to be arguing. Ernest watched as his father seemed to wave his arms and then turned and walked away toward the cottage. His father walked like he did when he was mad.

Nick and his son laughed and then they and Billy picked up their saws and hooks and walked up the hill through the back gate. Nick stared down at Ernest as they walked by. There was a strange smirk on his face. They left the gate open.

Ernest walked over to the cottage. He could hear his father in the bedroom. He could hear his mother's voice coming from another room. She was having one of her headaches. Whenever she had one of her headaches she closed all the curtains in the room and lay very still in the semi-darkness. It was the light that hurt her eyes. Ruth was probably with her holding a cold compress on Grace's forehead.

Ernest turned and walked away. He went through the back gate and sat beneath a tree. He was going to read his book. Soon Clarence came by. He was going out into the woods. He had his hands in his pockets and his head down watching his feet walking.

When he reached Ernest he looked over at him.

"Your mother wants to see you."

"I want to go with you, Daddy."

Clarence looked away and then back at him and then nodded.

Ernest went into the woods with his father.

Nick and Billy walked past Ernest toward the door into the restaurant. Nick turned and looked back at Ernest.

"My daughter Prudence is dead," he flatly said.

"I know. I heard."

"You heard? My only daughter, pregnant at sixteen, she kills herself with strychnine. You could hear her screams across the lake until they finally went silent. Your father was not here. And you, what did she mean to you, you of all people, all you can say is 'I heard?'"

There was a long pause where no one said anything until finally Nick turned and went into the cottage, slamming the door behind him.

Of the Indians Ernest did not like Nick Boulton at all. Billy was nice and when he was away from Nick he was good. Ernest liked to hunt with fat old Simon Green who was happy and laughed. Then there was a tall thin spider of a man who carved Ernest an ash wood paddle canoe. He taught Ernest how to canoe. But then one fourth of July the man went up to Petoskey to celebrate and got drunk and on the way home he fell asleep on the Pere Marquette railway tracks.

Clarence came running into Windemere that night and grabbed his doctor's bag. There was trouble, he said. An Indian got run over by the train.

Ernest wanted to go with him but his father said no.

I went with you when that lady had her baby.

That was life, Clarence said. And that you should understand. This is death. It's different.

Ernest stayed up listening to the breeze through the trees. Waiting, he watched the sparkle of the night sky. He could not even imagine what would happen to someone run over by a train. When he came home from Petoskey with the Bacon's last Fourth of July Mr. Bacon had to stop and pull Indians out of the road otherwise he would run over them. They all went up to Petoskey; they all got drunk; then walking back they all just passed out wherever they passed out. Drunken sleeping Indians littered the way back to Walloon Lake.

It was very late, almost daylight, when Clarence finally came home. He was quiet and dignified. It was part of what he called the code. If you handled something not pleasant then you handled it but you did not let it disturb you. His dinner was still there, cold, so he heated it up in a pan and then sat down and ate it. Only he and Ernest were still awake. Ernest sat with him but knew that you could not talk about it.

"So then Ernie," his father said, "what shall we do tomorrow?"

Ernest, sitting on the porch, thought of his father, Clarence, Dr. Clarence Hemingway. He was a man of nature: he was a man of science. But he was also a man of God. In his mind there was no conflict.

But he did not like all of the spiritualism, the Christian Science of Mary Baker Eddy, (once at Windemere when he found a copy of her 'Science and Health' in a wave of disgust he threw it out the window) nor the Theosophical Society writings of Helena Blavatsky. But Grace liked to speculate and Ruth brought them all in to help Grace in her speculations. Clarence did not like it at all.

Clarence could abide by nature and he could even abide by Darwin because, after all, the entire natural world is what God created and the natural world is where we live. But this speculative spiritualist theognosis stuff was to him sheer nonsense and he wanted no part of it.

"It messes things up," Ernest once overheard his father tell someone else when his father did not know that Ernest was listening. "There you are and then there is God and you talk to him through prayer and you tell him what you feel, and that is that. It's as clear as that. There's nothing murky and mysterious about it. It is like if you take a pond where it is clear and clean and you can see right through to the bottom of the pond and then you stir it all up and make it so you can not see the bottom anymore and it is becomes hidden and all murky and mysterious. Why mess up something that is so simple and straightforward?"

The man, to whom he was speaking and did not know that Ernest was listening, nodded.

5. Seney Ghosts

When the small two car train pulled to a stop Ernest and the others stood up and got their backpacks and poles. Bill Smith and Jack Pentecost held their gear as they jumped off the back stair onto the ground. The Brakeman, standing at the back of the train, watched as Ernest came to the stairs. With cane in hand he slid his gear to the stair and then carefully started to climb down. His leg was hurting again. It hurt whenever he had to get up after sitting for a long time.

"Hold her up Mac," the Brakeman shouted out with his loud gravely voice. He spit some juice from his chewing tobacco onto the dirt. "There's a cripple and he needs time to get his stuff down."

Ernest stepped down onto the ground and reached up to get his pole and backpack. Ernest glared at the man. The man smiled. His moustache needed combing and one of his brown teeth was missing.

Ernest walked with the others toward the black iron bridge over the river. He looked back over his shoulder and watched the train pull out, black soot swirling in its wake. It was a hot day. Everything was burned. The forest fire had burned the whole area. It was a ghost town from what it was. The saloons were shut down, buildings boarded up. No one was in the street. A lone black cat sat curled up in the shade under a wagon and watched them. They walked passed the stone foundations of the hotel. The charred wood of the burnt hotel was a big pile of rubble.

"Did you hear that guy, calling me a cripple?"

Bill and Jack nodded but did not answer.

"Who the hell does he think he is calling me a cripple?"

"Don't worry about it," Bill said.

They walked on.

"I'm not a cripple."

"Well you do have a cane," Jack said.

"Better to smash you over the head with."

"Okay, okay. It's a joke. Lighten up a little."

"He shouldn't call me a cripple, certainly not to my face, how do you think that would make a real cripple feel?"

"Yeah," Jack said as he looked off at what was left of the black burnt trees. "So he's crippled in the head."

"How is your leg now?" Bill asked.

"It's all right now. It just hurts at first. Once I'm up then it gets better."

Jack piped up. "Well you're a half cripple then," he said as he moved out of range.

93

The three of them made it to the bridge. Ernest looked down into the brown sluggish water. It was hard to see into the water. There were several trout holding themselves steady in the flow of the water.

"Look at those babies," Jack said.

"It's going to be a good day," said Bill as he stared off. "We'll hike up to where the water is fresh."

A small bird flew from the bridge and up the center of the stream his tiny shadow skimming the water.

Ernest took his cane and broke it in two against the side of the bridge. He held the two broken parts over the water and let them fall into the water.

He looked at Bill who was looking at him.

"That's done," he said.

Bill nodded.

"Come on," Ernest said. "Let's go across the river and into the trees. We've got a long walk before sundown."

They walked in silence up the burnt road. Their boots kicked up black soot as they walked and it made their lower pants black. They spooked several grasshoppers that flew off. The grasshoppers were black from the soot.

The sun was hot on his back as he walked. They walked up the hill. They left Seney behind in the heat. He began to sweat. Soon the charred ground gave out where the fire had stopped.

Nature renews naturally. His father told him that. When Ernest was hurt his father said 'oh son I wouldn't worry about it. It will heal. All things in nature heal.' And he was right. Nothing is forever. Nature heals, nature renews. Always look to that.

It was good to walk across the dirt again, the earth, soil, fresh grass, brush and it felt cooler in the shade of the trees. It began to smell good again away from the stench of blackened burnt. It was fresh and clean, the trees and the breeze.

They hiked deep into the woods keeping the river to their right. They kept their bearings by the path of the sun. They stopped by a stream and ate lunch. It was a hot day. After a short nap the three hiked on deeper into the woods. It was not until the late afternoon that they crossed over to the part of the river where they were headed. There was an open meadow by the river, like a small island in a sea of trees. The sun was down into the trees, the shadows were almost horizontal. They stopped and set up camp on the edge of the meadow.

Ernest smoothed out the sandy ground with his hands. He then took pine needles and sprinkled them down. Over that he put down his blankets one by one. Then he set up the canvas tent over his little space.

They set up a campfire and ate their dinner. Ernest was tired but it was a good tired. It was an exhausted body tired so he would sleep well. They talked and laughed. Jack told some of his funny stories. He was one for telling funny stories.

Finally they all went to bed. Ernest lay in his tent, wrapped in his blanket, looking out the open flap of the tent at the night sky. He stared up through trees to the sky above. The upper branches were moving and swaying back and forth. The stars glittered the night. He remembered being on the stretcher, his leg hurting bad, in the bombed out stable without a roof staring up through the top branches of the trees swaying in the night. Small star shells sparkled in the night sky, searching. Ernest closed his eyes. He tried not to remember. He did not want to remember.

There was a loud explosion, a screaming from next to him, a heat searing blast of fire: a man was screaming.

Ernest jerked and opened his eyes. He was breathing heavy and deep. He was trembling and in a panic. He jerked his head back and forth. But he was in his small tent and wrapped in his blanket. The night air was much cooler than it had been. He turned his head to see the others. They were all still asleep.

There it was again.

Ernest closed his eyes and tried to breathe steady and deep, steady and deep, steady and deep. He relaxed and felt the tension drain out of his body. When he was relaxed and peaceful again he felt like he wanted to cry.

There it was again. How can I get rid of it?

Staring up into the cold night sky he thought about tomorrow. It was going to be good tomorrow, there was going to be good fishing tomorrow. Standing in the cold rushing water, casting out, the whizz of the reel, the warm sun on his back, the birds in the trees chattering away, yes, fishing was going to be good. The sunlight will penetrate the dark forest with shafts of bright illumination.

The swift cold river is clean and clear. You can see the small white stones and the sandy bottom. Yes, it was going to be good.

Chapter Five

When they placed him down in a row with other stretchers a doctor came over and gave him morphine and tetanus shots. From where he was he could see inside the canvas tent that was surgery. The tent flap would open as they brought in another soldier on a stretcher. Inside by the light of the hissing kerosene lamps he saw the surgeons standing with bloodied aprons like butchers at a meat market. The flap closed as they went to work.

Next to him, sitting upright on his stretcher was an older man. His hair was white and thin. His uniform was a dirty grayish green. Blood soaked white field dressing was wrapped tightly around the stump of his arm where his right hand would have been. The man sat staring at his wound. Finally he looked over at Ernest. Ernest nodded and smiled.

The man asked in English: "You are American?"

"Yes, I am. Are you a soldier?"

The man nodded.

"But you are too old for this. You should be home with your family."

"I will be fifty five next month. Why? I can die just like any young man."

The old man then turned away with his back facing Ernest.

A man came and sat down next to Ernest. Ernest recognized the man: Priest, Don Giuseppe Bianchi. You have made it to here, my son. You are on your way to recovery. Yes, Father. Thank you, thank you. Do you wish to confess? But I am not Catholic. It does not matter; we are all children of God. I am afraid, Father: I wish to be somewhere else. The Priest touched Ernest's forehead. Do not fear; God provides. I am afraid. Think of something you enjoy, a place you love perhaps, and it will help your mind to pass the time. Yes, fly fishing in a cold rushing river. Ah, my son, if you love fishing you must visit Abruzzi. In Abruzzi it is heaven; it is in the mountains where the air is fresh; the rivers are clean and clear; the waters are cold and rush down the mountain side; the fish jump high and snap at everything. In an afternoon you catch enough fish for a banquet for all. After all this you must come and visit me in Abruzzi: we will fish together and it will be like heaven.

But the morphine was taking hold. Ernest eased into sleep. I so want to Father, he said, I do.

1. Changes

It was a hot day. When Marc, with Ursula and Sunny, got out of the cab she could not wait to go up to her room where, hopefully, it would be cooler than standing on the sun drenched sidewalk. The two kids were both too tired and hot to talk. They just went through the motions in order to get home as fast as they could.

Grace stayed on at Windemere with the two small children Carol and Leicester. But both Marc and the kids had to get back. Last June Marc had graduated from the Congregational Training School and now she was starting a job at the South Church Parish House. For the two kids school was starting soon.

It had been a bad summer in Chicago. There was fear everywhere. On July 21 the Wingfoot Air Express dirigible caught fire and crashed down through the skylight of the Illinois Trust and Savings bank. Thirteen were killed.

And then on the hot afternoon of July 27 down at the lakeside Eugene William was stoned to death by some white men because even though he was still in the colored area he came too close to the white area. In the hot summer sun the race riots ravaged the city far and wide. Dozens were killed and hundreds were wounded. Houses were looted and burned to the ground. Riots broke out in other cities as well.

When they got to the porch Clarence opened the door. There were hugs and kisses all around and Sunny and Ursula went off to their rooms. It left Marc and Clarence in the kitchen together. She watched him as she drank a cool glass of water. She was apprehensive.

His mood swings had become more severe. Marc openly discussed it with her mother. He becomes upset, over tired from over work, Grace said. He has a nervous condition. He needs to rest, alone, away from us. They all decided that he should stay in Oak Park this summer, the rest of them went on to Windemere. Although it was hot in Oak Park Grace felt that the rest would do him good.

Clarence worked and wrote daily letters to them. He typed the letters with carbon paper and numbered and catalogued his copy of each letter. He complained about the weather, the heat. He complained about his patients, he was working hard with a lot of patients. The car broke down and he had to get it fixed. He was so tired his fingers could barely type. It was late but he had only just now had time for dinner. He talked about the horribleness of the war. He worried about the raging flu epidemic. He talked about the stress of Ernest being wounded. With the crash of the Wingfoot Air Express how can we be safe from the sky? And with these race riots, how are we to be safe in our own city. He heard from several parents that they would not be needing her music lessons anymore for their children. Where was the money to come from now?

Grace wrote back telling him to rest, get your mind off of work, relax, take a vacation from the day to day, do not read the papers anymore, just let the stories of the day go away.

But then there were the letters about Ruth. He said he had decided; he was putting his foot down.

As soon as Marc saw Clarence she knew that he was not better. He was sweating. His upper lip was wet. His hand shook a little. When he hugged her it was very tight, hard, it seemed desperate.

"I have something to show you," he said as they stood in the kitchen.

"Really? What's that?"

"Follow me," he said.

They went upstairs and into her room.

When she entered he smiled and said: "I did this for you."

It was completely different. He had painted the walls. Her old furniture was gone. There was a new freshly varnished bed and chest of drawers. Marc was aghast. She had no idea of what to say. She was only here for a day or two, a week at most. She was leaving for her new job and would be staying there. She had already rented her room.

She looked at him.

His proud smile for what he had done for his little girl beamed from his face. How could he not know, how could he not remember that she was going away? She realized that he was desperately trying to create something too late.

All she could do was hug him and cry. He thought it was because of the room. She could not tell him the real reason why.

It was the next day that Ruth called. Marc answered. She could see her father in the yard watering.

"Hello."

"Oh thank goodness it's you. I called before but he answered and I had to hang up."

"Ruth, you shouldn't be calling."

"But why shouldn't I call? Please tell me what is going on, Marc."

"What did he say?"

"Nothing. I called after I got back and he said that I could not come over. He said that I was no longer allowed in his house."

"Write to Mom and tell her all about it."

"But now that you're there can't I come over. Marc you are like a sister to me."

"No, I don't think you can. He's quite adamant on that."

"But what have I done? I don't understand."

Marc watched as her father walked over and turned off the water. He rolled up the hose.

"Ruth, I have to go."

Clarence would be coming in after he rolled up the hose.

"But I haven't done anything."

"It's just you and Mom, he thinks, you know."

"What do you mean?"

"You two are close, he thinks a little too close, you see. Let Mom straighten it all out."

"But in the meantime I'm banned from the house?"

"Is that what he said?"

"Yes."

Marc watched Clarence come onto the front porch.

"Ruth, I have to go."

"But wait. . ."

Marc hung up the phone as Clarence entered the house. He smiled at her and she smiled at him and then she went up to her freshly painted room.

2. Grace Cottage III

Clarence came up in September to close down Windemere. To close for the winter the doors had to be boarded shut as well as all of the windows. He and Grace went over in the canoe to see Grace Cottage. It was late in the afternoon. Grace followed him around as he inspected the place.

She designed a simple cottage of two big rooms. There was a fireplace in the living room downstairs and a large dormitory style bedroom above it. At first she only wanted a ladder between the two floors because she did not want to waste any space for stairs. But when it was pointed out how hard it would be to carry water and bedding or mattresses up and down a ladder she relented and had a small and narrow stairway put in.

He pointed out that there was no road on this side of the lake so everything had to come in across the lake.

She said there are steamers that traverse the lake.

Being up on a hill everything had to be carried up the hill. It was higher than the water table so she had to use the hand pump at the bottom of the hill and all the water carried up the hill.

She said I have children who can carry things. There are wagons.

They went inside.

She built a small bedroom off the living room on the lake side so she could over look the water. There was also a small kitchen and pantry off the bedroom with a separate door into the living room. She would live downstairs. The upstairs was simply for guests.

There is no plumbing and there are no electric lines. You will have to use kerosene for lamps and the stove.

She said so it was when I was growing up.

The kitchen is so small and there is little shelf or cupboard space.

She said as you well know I do not cook and I do not bake. There is plenty of room to make a cup of tea and slice bread for a sandwich.

You will tire going up and down the hill.

She said I want the hill top view. Saints of the past have done without food or water to have peace and quiet and beauty. Why not I?

They stood on the patio and he stared down the lake. The white clouds in the blue sky and their reflection on the blue water moved in quiet unison. They could hear, far away, the crows.

She whispered to him. "Listen to the sound of no screaming children."

Clarence smiled.

"Here," she finally said when he seemed to have run out of objections. "Please have a seat."

He eyed the chair.

"Is this one of yours?"

She smilingly nodded.

"You see, dear," she began, "this is one of the wonderful things that I love about you. You are forever the practical one, looking out for things, caring about things."

"Well, I suppose that is my nature."

She nodded. "Remember when my mother was ill? You were Dr. William Lewis's young assistant and the two of you came to treat her. Even though we lived across the street from each other I never got to know you until you started coming to look in on mother."

"Yes, well, I confess that I started coming more frequently for you than for her."

Grace shrugged up her shoulders and giggled a little bit.

"I know," she said. "And I knew that then too."

"But I didn't really know what would come of it. You had your music, your singing. Off to New York, singing lessons from the greats, singing opera on stage. How could I compete with all of that? I thought you were gone, away for a lifetime in the opera. You were one to do what you wanted."

"Yes, but I came back didn't I, I came back to you?"

"That you did."

He seemed to like looking up and down the lake as far as he could see.

"Look," he said as he pointed. "You can make out Windemere, just there in among the trees."

"You see dear, I will not be that far away."

She knew it was working.

"Any regrets for your lost singing career?"

"No not really. We have made a wonderful family, and with the music room I can teach and sing in the choirs, I love the fresh young talent and I like to think that I in some way helped create that. And who knows, someday a new famous singer may come from me."

She watched him closely. She knew the ghost of Ruth wandered in his mind.

"Clarence dear, you've allowed me a life, a separate life, to live as best I can. I gave up a career but you allowed me my identity."

"And if I had not?"

"Then we would not be sitting here together now."

Clarence nodded. "You were one to do what you wanted," he repeated.

In newspapers in Oak Park wives were known by their husband's names, such as Mrs. John Farson, Mrs. William Barton. But she was listed as Mrs. Grace Hall Hemingway. Only two other women enjoyed that privilege: Dr. Anna Blount the head of the suffragist chapter in Oak Park, and Belle Watson-Melville of the National Chautauqua Circuit.

They watched as the evening came on. The sun descended into the trees of the far hills.

"As you know it was meant to be," Grace said.

Clarence looked confused.

"Don't you remember? You had an old horse at the time named 'Old Prince.' We took rides in your buggy to get away and on one of those rides you got up the courage to ask me what both of us knew was to be asked sooner or later. But you neglected the reins so Old Prince wandered until he finally stopped. As soon as you asked me we noticed that the buggy was stopped."

Clarence, smiling and nodding his head, continued the story: "We looked up and saw a sign over the wooden building where Old Prince stopped: Justice of the Peace. Marriages Performed."

"And I shouted Yes! And we both laughed and laughed."

They sat in the glow of their own laughter.

After a while Grace spoke again: "Look dear, come with me." They walked around to the front of the cottage "I want to show you why I want to be here." She waved her arm toward the western sky.

The sun was setting. The sky blazed. The white clouds of the day flamed bright red and orange.

Together they stared in silence.

Finally: "My father loved this, coming to see this. I feel close to him now."

Clarence turned to her in the growing dusk.

"I am sorry that I am not him."

Grace waved him off with her hand. She smiled. "You are you, Clarence," she said.

He did not smile.

As they walked down to the canoe at the water's edge Clarence thought about it all.

He was the man of science and nature and of the world as it was. The sunset was beautiful because the sunlight was bent by the earth's atmosphere and split the wave lengths out and our eyes perceived the different wavelengths as different colors.

But that was nothing to her. She was a woman of art and beauty and of the world as it should be. The world was a place of eternal Truth and eternal Beauty. How on earth did he ever expect that they could be one? How on earth could the two become one?

She sat at the back of the canoe as he rowed across the water in the dark. As they came across she sang, she sang, as she told him, 'like I used to when we came here when we were young.'

In Windemere he started a fire because the night air was a bit chilly, it being the middle of September. He sat at the table in the kitchen as she prepared some hot tea. They were almost alone: Carol and Leicester were both asleep in their rooms.

Grace held him and kissed his head.

"It will be fine," she whispered. "It is what I need. We will be fine."

He did not respond.

"I so wish that you could find a little retreat like this, for your sake. Isn't this nice? The kids are gone, Carol and Lie are asleep, it is just like it was when we came here and there was just Marc and Ernie. We were happy then weren't we?"

"Yes," he said. "I think we were."

Grace held his head against her cheek.

"I don't know what we are going to do about Ursula and all of her boyfriends. I'm afraid she has a touch of Ernie in her with all of his rebellion."

"She will be alright," he said. "We taught them the good life with Christian piety and purity. Now it is up to them to decide to put it into practice. There is only so much a parent can do."

"You are so practical."

"I can feel that with Ernie. I'll have a talk with the boy; he and I are great chums."

"I'm afraid that Ernie is very much like me. But when he gets through this period of fighting himself and everyone around him and he turns his energy toward the positive he will be a fine man. My father said that himself. Remember when little Ernie said he had stopped a runaway horse all by himself?"

Clarence nodded. He has heard the story more than once.

"Grandfather Hall turned to me right then and said that with Ernie's imagination and energy he was going to be famous one day. Whether he is famous for good purposes or for bad, well, his fate lies in your hands."

She stopped for a moment.

"So, what do you think? Have we pointed him in the right direction?"

"He's been through a lot recently," Clarence replied. "He will be fine."

Clarence grew quiet and seemed to stare off. He was quiet when he was not engaged, it was as if he left and went off somewhere else.

She had seen it before. He was a man of troubles. At times it seemed so overwhelming.

"This is for us now, dear," she said. "The older children are going off. This was the whole purpose of a cabin in the woods, somewhere away from it all."

3. Petoskey

Bill Smith parked his car and got out. He stood in the street looking at the house. It was a white two story house with attic and a full front roofed porch. He looked down at the paper in his hand. 602 State Street. This was it. As he walked between the two trees in the yard up the path to the porch Bill looked up at the large second story window over the front door. Ernest was in the frame of the window smiling and waving. Bill waved back. By the time he got to the front door Ernest was already opening it.

"Bird," he called out to him as he wrapped his arms around him in a big bear hug.

"Hello, Wemedge. How you doing?"

"Good, good. Yourself?"

"Good. Man, you look like a bum."

Ernest wore his blue flannel shirt, untucked, brown dungaree's, and had not shaved for days.

"I'm a writer my friend, not a bum."

"There's a difference?"

Ernest punched him in the stomach.

"So this is your new place?"

"Yeah, I rent the room upstairs. Let me show you up."

They climbed a narrow stairway with pictures along the wall. The room was small and cramped with a slanted roof but nice. There was a wrought iron bed and a knotty pine chest of drawers and in front of the window a desk. There were piles of papers on either side of the desk and in the center sat his Corona typewriter. Bill let him borrow it as a house warming gift. He ran his finger along the side of the typewriter.

"So this is where the genius happens?"

"Absolutely, I am writing and writing I can tell you."

"And are you selling and selling?"

"Well," Ernest said as he shrugged his shoulders, "let's get one thing at a time. Listen to this: George Horace Lorimer himself from the 'Saturday Evening Post' rejected 'Wolves and Doughnuts.'"

"The Post, now I'm impressed. If you're going to get rejected you may as well be rejected by the best."

"Absolutely. And Charles McLean of 'Popular Magazine' still has 'The Woppian Way.' As I see it no hearage is good hearage so that means it's still under consideration."

"Yeah but what would be better is a big fat check."

"In time, good buddy, in time."

"In our time or after you're dead?"

"In our time, you write to make money, Bird. What's the point in doing it if not for the money? Come on, let me show you around. I've got some good places where I hang out."

For lunch Ernest took Bill to Braun's Diner down on Howard Street. It was a small place with tables and chairs and a long counter with stools. A large blackboard on the wall was the chalked menu. Their claim to fame was their beans. Ernest pointed to the sign: The Best by Test. I eat here a lot: it is good, cheap, and fun to watch the customers; it gives me ideas for characters. Under a large glass cover were piles of different donuts. They make them here and they are good, he said.

He rented the room from Eva Potter, a short dark haired woman. She had a daughter Hazel who was a waitress over in Mancelona and came home on weekends. She also had a son named Clyde.

Down the street was McCarthy's Barber Shop where there was talking and joking all day long and they carried all the newspapers so he could keep up with the world.

Then there was the Perry Hotel where you could take dinner in the plush red bar.

But mostly he sat in his room and wrote. Everyone said they could hear him typing away at all different hours.

"I'm trying to follow Balmer's advice."

"Good," Bill said. "That's good."

Edwin Balmer lived in Bay View. He had been a reporter for the Chicago Tribune and was now a writer. He had written six or seven novels. Ernest heard that he had a cottage on the lake where he summered. Liz pointed Balmer out to Ernest when he came to eat at Pinehurst. He was an older man, about thirty five. One day Ernest took some of his stories and approached him while he ate his dinner. Balmer held a piece of fried chicken in his hands and had just taken a bite when Ernest approached. Hello sir I've read some of your books and I want to be a writer myself and I have some of my stories here and if I'm not imposing and if you could be so kind I would greatly appreciate any advice you have and I thank you so much and I really want to be a writer.

Balmer continued to chew his chicken. He stared up at Ernest as Ernest talked. When Ernest finished Balmer was still chewing but after staring at Ernest he nodded his head and pointed with his head toward the table. Ernest placed the stories on the table next to the cup of coffee.

Finally, when Balmer finished chewing, still holding his piece of chicken up with both hands, he cleared his throat.

"Do you know where my cottage is?"

"Yes sir."

"Good. Come by on Friday afternoon."

"Thank you, sir."

Balmer nodded and continued with his chicken.

When Ernest went to his cabin Balmer was sitting on a small pier that went out over the water next to his boat house. He had a hopelessly tangled mass of fishing lines that he was trying to untangle, straighten and roll. Ernest helped as they talked about writing.

"I can't say what sells and what doesn't; it's kind of a mystery to me. I see stories sold that should have instead been thrown in the trash. And then I see stories circulating that I wonder why no one has picked them up. All I can really say is that eventually the good stuff does get there."

He paused as he watched a set of ducks quacking as they flew low across the water.

"More than the writing what a good writer needs more than anything else is persistence and patience. I call it the three P's. Practice makes you better, persistence gets you where you are going, and patience keeps you sane during the process."

"Well, I'm writing everyday now so I'm getting the practice down."

"Good. Good."

There was a light brown satchel sitting next to him. He reached down and slid out some papers. It was the stories.

"You seem to be writing for the slick magazines."

He turned over the first page of one of the stories and began writing the names of magazines and the editor of each.

"I know these people so try them first. You have potential, but are you writing for the money?"

It seemed to be a strange question.

"Of course," Ernest answered. Why else?

"I sense there is a bit more to it."

A motor boat went by. They waved, they waved back. The waves from the boat's wake washed against the pilings of the small pier.

"I don't understand what you mean," Ernest finally said.

"You see, there are writers and there are authors. The two are not necessarily the same. Authors are published. Some just publish for the money and that's it. It's just a job to them. If they weren't writing then they would be doing something else for the same money and it wouldn't make any difference to them. They may be authors but they are not writers. If you are a true writer then you write because that is what you do, whether you are published or not."

Balmer smiled as he watched Ernest listening.

"The ideal, for the select few, is to be both."

Ernest looked away. It was dusk and it was growing dim. He watched as a flutter of birds flew off into the trees. It seemed so quiet.

"I think you're a writer. And I think you can be an author and eventually break in. To be an author for the magazines you just write what they want to see and that is that. It is an intellectual exercise, to know what they want and then give it to them."

"And as a writer?" Ernest asked.

"You write from your own heart."

The waves lapped against the pilings. Far off there was the faint sound of a bell.

"Your mother wrote the song 'Lovely Walloona.' Wrote it and published it. She had it right, you know. What she wrote about the lake. That's because it came from her heart."

Balmer gathered up the papers and put them back into the satchel and then handed it to Ernest.

"I suggest you write about what you know about. Write about you, your family, or maybe friends like the people around here. If you can find things to say that mean something deeper than the words then you're a true writer. I wish you luck."

"Thank you."

4. Marge

Ernest sat in his room typing. When he finished a page he rolled it out and set it to his right. He grabbed a blank sheet from a stack on his left, rolled it into place, and then began typing again. He stopped and sat back and stretched his arms out. The white lace curtains on the window were pulled back. He could see outside his window the afternoon sky. It was completely coated white with clouds. A soft and very light snow was falling. He stood up and looked out. The street and yard were covered with a thin white layer of fresh snow. Patches of the ground still showed through. The bare branches of the trees were outlined in white.

His mind was in Horton Bay, summer. He was trying to write as Edwin Balmer suggested. Write of what you know, write about people you know. He was writing a different type of story a different type of story from what he had been writing before. He looked down and read what he had just typed.

'Pauline Snow was the only beautiful girl we ever had out at the Bay. She was like an Easter Lily coming up straight and lithe and beautiful out of a dung heap.'

He wondered if the image was too strong.

Standing in front of his typewriter he heard the distant metallic chimes of the grandfather clock downstairs. It reminded him. He turned to look at his clock by the bed. It was time to leave. If he left now he could make it. He pushed his chair back, grabbed his black leather jacket lined with sheep skin, his woolen cap with visor, and then left.

Outside it was cold and crisp. He pulled out his gloves from his jacket pocket as he walked. He was going to the high school to meet Marge. Ernest and Marge had become the best of friends over the years. From the moment he met the little spunky thirteen year old carrying the big speckled trout she had just caught all by herself they were friends. She and he and his sisters Ursula and Sunny hung out together and went swimming and boating and camping all summer. At night they camped out at The Point with tents and a campfire and kerosene lamps and sang and told stories. At the end of summer when everyone was leaving it was a bit sad to say goodbye.

Marge and Pudge stayed the summer with their Aunt and Uncle and played with their young cousin William in the cottage Uncle owned in Horton Bay across from Pinehurst. Ernest occasionally ate dinner there and on several occasions Ursula came along as well. He did not talk much around the Aunt and Uncle. Her Uncle was a mechanical engineer and had blueprints opened up on his desk by the window. Her Aunt tried to keep the conversation going. She hated silences.

Then, after dinner, sitting on the porch in cushioned wooden chairs that creaked when you moved, the light from inside the cottage streaking across the wooden slats of the porch, they sat and talked about things. Across the way, through the dark trees and up the hill a little, was the Pinehurst all lit up like a Christmas tree and people came and went and laughed and talked with cars coming and going. With all of the summer people vacationing around the lakes the restaurant did a good business.

Or on Saturday nights there would be dancing in the bean warehouse down on the dock over the water. The place would get crowded with all ages of people. It would be lit up and they played records and drank Coca Cola and ate chips and popcorn and danced and danced. Marge was not the only one that Ernest danced with, nor she him, but she was the one he danced with the most.

Heated in the hot summer night they walked along the shoreline of the lake. At times they walked as far as The Point. They would sit on the sandy grass with their backs against a log and, looking out across the water, watch the night. The moon rose in the summer night and reflected in the water. The stars sprinkled across the dark night sky.

It became of their place.

And this last summer out at The Point, at night, she asked him about the war. What was it like? Ernest told her about when they first arrived in Paris. The German's had this long range cannon called Big Bertha and they lobbed shells into Paris now and again. So he and his friend Ted Brumback rented a cab and went searching for where the shells were hitting. They would hear an explosion off in one direction and have the cabbie shoot off in that direction as fast as he could but then there would be another explosion off in another direction that sounded closer so they had the cabbie swerve over into that new direction until there was another explosion that seemed just down the street so they rolled around in that direction and the whole time he and Brummie were bouncing back and forth in the rear of the cab trying to hold on like a bucking bronco at the rodeo. Finally they stopped and saw where a chunk of stone had been blown off the side of a church and the cabbie drove off because he was sick of the two crazy Americans.

Marge laughed.

But then as the night progressed she asked him about being wounded. At first he described it like he was giving one of his lectures. But then he grew quiet. He began talking more slowly, more quietly. The thing about it, he said, is how scared you are the whole time. The whole time you are there you never really rest. And when the shells start coming in and coming in and you lose your hearing because of the noise and you smell the stench you don't know what's going to happen so you just lay on the ground and hug it as hard as you can hoping that it will end soon. Men were just sitting there and they were blown apart just because they were sitting there.

Ernest stopped for a moment. He almost lost it. He felt like he wanted to cry. And it would probably be okay to cry with her. No one would know but them, she would see to it. But he did not. He breathed in heavy and waited.

It passed.

Ernest got to the High School before the final bell. He stood on the sidewalk and waited. Marge and Pudge introduced Ernest to one of their friends. Grace Quinlan was fourteen. She had dark eyes and coal black hair cut short to her shoulders. She had a very pretty smile. And the way she walked reminded him of Agnes. Well, he told her when they first met, if we want to be friends then I can't call you Grace because that's the name of my mother. So a game ensued to rename Grace. Finally Ernest settled on 'Sister Luke' because she was like a sister to him and she wore around her neck a small silver Saint Christopher.

After school they gathered together at Sister Luke's house. Sitting in her room they talked, they played records, sang the songs they knew, and ate big bowls of popcorn. Ernest sat back in the center of it all surrounded by his admiring court of young ladies. This was nice. It was just like home. Ernest had four sisters so all of his life he was surrounded by young girls giggling and screaming. Their energy was like magic. Right now, if he were home in Oak Park, there would be eight year old Carol and fifteen year old Sunny and seventeen year old Ursula and it would be as grand as it was all the time. He missed that part of being home. He did not miss his mother, and he did not miss his older sister, but the three younger ones he missed a lot. But now he had recreated it and he felt at home. He felt good.

Ernest, standing on the sidewalk outside the school looked up at the second story window on the right. That was where Marge would be, her last class of the day, literature. She was the Dramatics Editor, and a member of the Girl's Literary Society. One day she was very late. The society was having a special meeting that went on into the night. Ernest stood in the cold outside below the window waiting for her. It grew dark. It grew colder. It began to snow. Ernest stomped his feet to keep them warm. Ernest stood in the snow and stared up at the lighted window above. Lucy, he called out in barely a whisper, calling her real name. Lucy, he called out. No one answered.

Once he went out walking with Sister Luke. They wanted to walk down to the lake. It was cold but they were wrapped up in jackets and gloves and each wore a scarf around their neck. Her boots sounded thunderous as she purposely stomped across the wooden bridge over Bear River, laughing at the noise she made. They walked for a while arm in arm trying to take their steps in unison. They stood on the shore and watched as the boats sailed by. But the wind picked up and they grew cold. So they came back holding hands. They both slid on a large patch of ice and tightly held hands as they made their wobbly way across the slick ice. When they came to a stop they were amazed that they were still standing.

"We didn't fall, oh my God we didn't fall," she said as she put her gloved hand to her mouth.

On the way back down State Street when they reached the church of Saint Francis Xavier Sister Luke tugged on his arm. "Come with me, just for a minute."

Ernest followed her in. At the entrance she dabbed her finger into the holy water and made the cross. Watching her, Ernest did the same. She walked down a side aisle and into a side chapel. There was a table with trays of small lit flickering candles, their shadows danced across the wall. She crossed herself again and then went up to the table. She took one of the unlit candles and with a small wick lit the candle in her hand. She held the lit candle for a moment with her eyes closed and then placed it into one of the trays. Ernest watched as she closed her fingers together touching her lips. She stood with closed eyes for a long moment. He waited in silence. Then she crossed herself and turned. She smiled at him as she left the chapel.

They walked back together in the growing coldness to her house.

Ernest developed a set routine. He ate breakfast at Braun's Diner, chatted with the guys at McCarthy's Barber Shop, and then came back to his room in order to write all day until the High School let out. Then he would hang out with them until they had to do chores or homework. Then it was dinner at either Braun's or at the Perry's Hotel Bar. Then it would be home to his room in order to write until he went to bed.

But things were changing. Marge was different. She was now eighteen and becoming a grown woman. He still liked her as a younger sister but things were changing. It made it all very complicated.

Once when he was having dinner with Marge and her family Marge's grandmother spoke up. She was a member of the Petoskey Ladies Aid Society and she thought that he should give a talk about his war experience. Ernest hesitated.

"Well, you see my dear," Grandmother said, "the Society has already booked you and we have already set the date. I think you had better take it, don't you?"

Ernest and Marge glanced at each other across the table. She tried but she could not stop herself from laughing. Grandmother glanced at her and then at him.

"Good, so it is settled."

And that was that.

5. Connable

Ernest arrived at the Petoskey Library carrying his brown suitcase filled with his souvenirs of the war. He was giving a lecture on his war experiences to the Petoskey Ladies Aid Society. As he approached the front he looked around at his audience. They were all older ladies much like his mother. He was dressed in his uniform although it fit a bit more tightly than when he gave this lecture in the past. He had to breathe in a bit to button it. He bought a new walking cane that he used extensively as he came into the library even though he did not need it anymore. From his suitcase he pulled out his cock feathered Bersaglieri hat and put it on. With his uniform and his shiny black knee high boots he attached his black velvet cape. He was ready.

When the time came and the ladies took their seats and he was introduced Ernest stood before them in his full Red Cross uniform. He spoke clearly and directly, having given the same speech several times. He told of the front, the trenches, the troops, and the artillery. He told of sleeping in bombed out farmhouses watching the star flares overhead like a monster searching for prey. He held up his Austrian bayonet and his pistol, and told how fierce hand to hand combat could be; he held up his gas mask and then put it on so they could see it in action.

He told them of how he fought side by side with the fierce Arditi troops. He told of how when shot they simply shoved a burning cigarette into the wound cauterizing it to stop the bleeding so that they could continue to fight the enemy.

The audience of older women gasped.

He told them about how he was at a forward listening post one night, July 8, 1918, and around midnight an Austrian trench mortar came chug chugging down from the sky and exploded not that far from him. There was a deafening roar and it was like a blast from a hot furnace and he was shoved back and had the wind knocked out of him. I felt as if my life was sucked out of me, I was no longer inside me and I was floating outside thinking, Hey, Ernie this is it, I am dead. But then I rushed back in, sucked back into my body and I was covered in dirt and a solder next to me was screaming. His legs had been blown off.

All of the women in the room hung on every word he said. They imagined it to be their own sons.

I stumbled up. The soldier who stood between me and the blast was dead. The one to my right was still alive but his legs were gone and the wounds were pumping blood. The soldier to my left was still alive, barely, so I picked him up over my shoulder and ran to the trench line dodging Austrian machine gun fire. Little did I know that I too was wounded. Two hundred and twenty seven shell fragments had shredded my leg.

Ernest then very slowly and very carefully pulled out the pair of pants he was wearing at the time and held them up for all to see.

"This is what is left of my pants."

There was complete silence as the whole room full of mothers stared open mouthed at the shredded blood stained pants. In their hearts it was as though he was their own son and the suffering that he must have felt.

Ernest, for effect, walked around the room holding up the pants for all of them to see.

When the lecture was over and the women dispersed Ernest came out the door of the library. He still walked with his cane. He stopped on the porch, standing next to one of the white Greek columns, and looked around. The air was cold. Although night, the sky was wiped white with low hanging clouds. Flakes of white snow fluttered lightly down. He watched what remained of the audience as they got into their cars and drove off. He closed the collar of his black jacket, picked up his suitcase with his souvenirs and started down the steps and the walkway to the sidewalk. As he turned onto the sidewalk a large black man with a heavy knee length overcoat approached him.

"Excuse me, sir?"

Ernest stopped.

"Yes."

"Harriet Gridley Connable would like a word."

"Who?"

The man waved his hand toward a car at the end of the block. It was a yellow Pierce Arrow. "Harriet Gridley Connable, sir. She wishes to have a word with you."

Ernest looked at the car and then back at the man. The man smiled.

The man began walking toward the car slightly edging Ernest on with his large hand. Ernest followed him.

At the car the man opened the back seat and then reached out for Ernest's suitcase. Ernest gave it to him and then got into the car.

Sitting inside was an older woman in her late forties. She wore a scarf over her head but her hair tumbled out around her shoulders. She wore a nice white fur lined jacket and a white dress. She smiled as he sat down next to her and gracefully extended her hand. Her perfect complexion and well mannered eyebrows, lashes, and fingernails spoke of wealth and pampering. He remembered her from the lecture, sitting on the right

117

hand side toward the back. He glanced at her more than once during the lecture. She was the best looking older woman that he had ever seen.

Ernest took her hand. He did not know if he was supposed to kiss it like a knight returning from an adventure. He did not. She pulled it away as she began to speak.

"I was greatly impressed by your talk Mr. Hemingway."

"Thank you."

"I am here in Petoskey visiting my mother which is why I was able to attend your talk. I reside up in Toronto."

"Oh, so you've come south for the winter then?"

She laughed. "You are a charming young man Mr. Hemingway; you are delightfully fresh and light hearted."

"Well," he smiled, "maybe on my good days."

"Well that brings us to the reason for our talk. My husband Ralph and I would like to take an extended vacation in Palm Beach Florida, three or four months perhaps, and we are looking for an appropriate companion for our son. We will be taking our daughter Dorothy with us on the trip however our son Ralph Jr., he is to remain in Toronto."

"How old is he?"

"Ralph Jr. is nineteen."

She paused and looked away out the window.

"It may seem strange at first that we need someone to look after our nineteen year old son, but, you see, he is slightly crippled, you understand, it is his leg and his hand."

"I see."

"And, quite frankly Mr. Hemingway, excuse me but may I call you Ernest?" she asked as she touched his knee.

"Sure, sure you can."

"Well, you see, Ernest, my son's attitude toward life leaves much to be desired and, quite frankly, we are also seeking a vacation from him. It may sound cruel to say but his attitude can, at times, spoil things."

Ernest nodded.

"Because of his infirmary he does require a bit of looking after, minor actually, but the real reason I am interested in having you is the hope that your wonderful and charming attitude toward life will have a positive effect on him. You are both of the same age and once he understands what you have suffered and have overcome I hope it will impact him in a positive manner. You are outgoing and robust and have overcome your injury. You can share your love of life with him."

"So it's a love of life that I have? I've often wondered what the problem was."

"You most certainly do, Ernest. I can see that clearly. And I hope that you can convey to my son the right slant on life, especially about sports and activity and the pleasures of an active life."

"So I live at your house and see to his needs? When I was recovering at the hospital in Milan I actually helped with some of the other wounded, some of the men crippled by their wounds."

"It is not as severe as that, but yes, you will live on the estate. Now Ralph sleeps in and actually goes to work each afternoon, he works at one of the F. W. Woolworth stores. My husband Ralph Sr., he is the Chairman of the Canadian Division of the F. W. Woolworth stores, you see."

Ernest nodded. He understood.

"So it will mostly be in the evenings that you will be helping him. Hopefully you will get him out of the house and taking part in various activities because he is a hopeless recluse. I hope you make it fun for him. Meanwhile you will have the entire day to pursue you're hopes of being a writer. I understand from Mate Bump that is what you aspire to become."

Ernest laughed.

"You know Marge's mother?"

"Why yes I do. As a matter of fact I've heard of you from several sources before this evening. I am even acquainted with your mother Grace."

"Really?"

"Yes. I purchased one of her paintings; it's hanging up on the wall back at the estate."

Ernest laughed to himself. It was hard to get away from his mother.

"And my husband, Ralph: he knows several of the editors at the 'Toronto Star' so perhaps he can introduce you, in furtherance of your writing career of course."

Ernest did not know what to say. It all seemed a dream. He watched as the tiny flakes of snow touched the rear window.

"I realize that this is all of a sudden to you so perhaps you would care to think about it for a day or two."

"It all sounds very attractive to me but, yes; maybe a day or two."

"Yes, of course, I quite understand. Now my husband does have quite a library of books and, I am sorry to say, quite a collection of different alcohols in his liquor cabinet, all of which would be available to you, in moderation of course."

"Of course," Ernest said, agreeing whole heartedly.

"Actually," he said, "at the moment I am free so perhaps I should resolve the matter quickly and accept your offer."

"Splendid. We will be leaving the middle of next month. I will forward the address and time to you. Mate Bump I understand knows where you live."

"Oh yes," he replied. "She certainly does."

"Well then, I am delighted," she said as she again held out her hand. This time he held it and lightly kissed it as if she were royalty. She sweetly smiled.

"Until then."

Chapter Six

They brought him into the tent. The canvas flap scratched against the side of the stretcher as they brought him in. There was a strong smell of antiseptic in the tent. Kerosene lamps hissed and flared. It was hot in the tent. When they put the stretcher up on the table Ernest smelled blood, fresh and wet. Two doctors stood over him. They wore white masks and red rubber gloves.

One doctor took a large scissors and cut away the bloodied bandage and ripped it away from his leg. Ernest was sweating. He felt the sweat trickle down the side of his forehead.

The doctor took a long sharp probe. Ernest felt the sharp stab into the skin of his upper leg. He jumped at the pain. He felt the probe slice across the open wound. Another doctor held Ernest and pressed down hard holding him in place. But with each stab and slice Ernest jumped. Chills ran up and down his body.

The doctor turned and dropped a piece of metal into a tin basin. It clanged as it hit the basin. Then the sharp slicing probe cut into somewhere else on his leg. Ernest closed his eyes hard and tried not to scream out. The first doctor held him down. There was another clang in the tin basin, louder than the last.

Ernest held back a wave of nausea. The probe sliced in again and again the sharp shiver of pain. Ernest started to breathe heavy. He tried to focus on his breathing. There was another clang of a metal fragment in the tin basin.

Over and over, on and on: Ernest was drenched in his own sweat.

Like a thousand hornets all at once.

He tried to whistle but it came out a scream as the probe dug in deeper in the soft flesh of his thigh. The metal clang in the tin basin was the loudest yet.

Finally Ernest felt someone stroking his hair. He opened his eyes. The doctor smiled down at him. It is done, he said. We will wrap the leg now.

"How many," Ernest asked.

The doctor looked at the tin basin.

"Twenty eight: you are a brave boy."

1. Lunch

Ernest arrived at the club. He wore his uniform with polished boots, black cape and Bersaglieri cap. When he told the maitre d Hotel who he was the man smiled and stroked his well polished pointed moustache. He took Ernest to the table.

His grandfather Anson Hemingway sat with three of his friends. Ernest recognized the two older men as friends of Anson but he did not at first recognize the middle aged man. He wore a grey coat with a Scottish Kilt waistcoat. He had short balding hair combed slick to the side and while lighting his long pipe he seemed to be the life of the party. They all stood when Ernest came up to the table.

"Gentlemen," Anson started to say but then bent and leaned toward the middle aged man, "and to some I use that term loosely." They all laughed as Anson stood and resumed his aura of dignity. "I would like to introduce to you my grandson, Ernest, back from the war."

Each, in turn, shook his hand. They sat down. Ernest recognized the middle aged man. Anson sat with a very straight back. He poured a glass of brandy from the decanter on the table.

"I feel that with his recent stint in the war, and the wounds that he suffered, he has earned the right to sit among us."

They raised their glasses for a toast and took a sip of brandy. To Ernest it burned all the way down.

Anson introduced everyone. His two older friends were Albert and Adam, both in the Civil War with Anson, and the middle aged man was Harry Lauder, the Scottish singer and entertainer. Ernest saw his show in Kansas City, it must have been two years ago now, his farewell America tour.

"Ernest has just now overcome the need for a cane, you see. How is the leg?"

"It's coming along alright," Ernest replied. "It only hurts now and again."

"That's the spirit my boy," Harry said.

"Well that is good news," his Grandfather said as his head seemed to wobble a little. "Surface wounds can be the most dramatic to look at but they are the easiest to heal."

Albert and Adam both nodded in agreement.

"You don't as easily heal the deeper wounds, what you don't see."

"Oh, no truer words be spoken my friend," Harry said through a cloud of pipe smoke. "And that brings me back to the point I was making earlier. My own only son Johnnie gave his life in this war so naturally I want to know what it is he gave his life for. And it is a rotten shame that they have let the Kaiser off the hook. What you don't do in a war is allow the king of the enemy to vacation in Elba, if you catch my drift. For Christ's sake we should have carried the war all the way to the bitter end and dragged the bloody Kaiser out before a firing squad."

Ernest sat quietly, as did Anson, as the others discussed the war. He watched his Grandfather as he sat so straight in the chair listening. Ernest remembered once when Anson smiled, that warm knowing smile, and said now don't go talking when you can listen because when you are talking you are only saying things that you already know but if you listen you may learn something that you don't know.

Ernest realized suddenly that his Grandfather was old. His hair was white, his beard was white, he had seen a lot in his life. It was strange to sit here with him, now seemingly equal to him, and strange to be his honored guest. Anson wanted to show Ernest off to his friends. It made Ernest feel proud that his Grandfather wanted to do that.

It was Anson who gave Ernest his first shot gun, a 20 Gauge single barrel. Ernest was twelve years old. He remembered the day clearly. His Grandfather gave him the shot gun and his father gave him only three shells a day. That way you will learn to make every shot count.

It was Anson who first taught Ernest the moral code that you do everything properly, you do everything right, you make no creature suffer, and you eat what you kill. Clarence, taught the same code when he was young, reinforced it. When you can no longer maintain the code then it is time to quit.

Looking around at all of them at the table Ernest thought that on the surface these men seemed normal old fellows. But what had they experienced?

Ernest remembered that every Fourth of July and every Memorial Day Anson dressed up and he and his war friends would stand at attention and march down the street alongside the bands. What did they carry around in their hearts?

To Ernest growing up it was just a fun dress up day with bands and fireworks. But to them it was heart-felt, it had a deep meaning, and it touched them deeplt in their soul. Now he was a part of them, now he understood in a way that he could not explain. It was just there.

Ernest thought it was like an iceberg. The part of the iceberg that you see is only a small part of the whole. The part under the water that you do not see is enormous. And the way it is shaped and molded determines what the iceberg above the water looks like. They were each like that. What had they seen, lived, laughed over, cried over, what had they experienced and how do they carry all of that in their hearts? How can you know by only seeing the tip of the iceberg?

After the meal was over Harry turned to Ernest. As he held a match to the bowl and puffed on his pipe he eyed Ernest.

"So, dear Ernest, what are your plans now? And as handsome a young man as you are is there a wee lassie in your life or are there so many that it is hard to choose?"

Albert and Adam raised their eyebrows: "Tell us the truth now," Albert said.

Harry held up his finger and sang: "When the sun has gone to rest, that's the time we love the best. O, it's lovely roamin' in the gloamin' on the bonnie banks o' Clyde."

"My boy is going to be a writer," Anson spoke out, putting an end to things.

"So, a writer then it is?"

Ernest was surprised. He had never discussed it with his Grandfather. How would he know? Clarence and Grace thought him silly for wanting to be a writer and wanted him to settle down and get a real job somewhere and start planning for a real career. Why would Grandfather say this? Ernest began to understand that Grandfather knew Ernest better than he knew his Grandfather.

"He's already worked at the Kansas City Star before the war and wrote some mighty fine pieces. And now he is off to Toronto to work for Ralph Connable. You know, the Woolworth man. Ralph knows them at the Toronto Star so Ernest will be working there now."

"Really."

"Well," Ernest said as he felt he needed to correct things a little, "that is a possibility but then nothing is for sure."

"Of course it is," Anson spoke up with a sharp matter of factness. "You just have to make it that way."

"Of course," Harry said as he winked at Ernest.

2. Toronto

Ernest could not believe his eyes when he saw the Connable Mansion from the car window. They pulled off the main icy road and drove into the circular gravel driveway now covered in fresh snow. As the car drove in closer to the main house Ernest thought that it must be the largest house he had ever seen. It was like a fancy hotel. And this is where he was going to stay for the next several months.

The driver told Ernest to ring the bell while he got his bags. The snow on the steps was icy and Ernest slipped a step as he approached the door. As he stood at the door he felt a little ashamed. He felt that he should be helping the driver with his suitcases. It was beginning to snow again.

But then the door opened. A middle aged man stepped out, full head of white hair, parted on the right, a large nose with a nice wide smile.

"You must be the Ernest Hemingway Harriet's been telling me about."

"Mr. Connable."

"Please, if you're going to be living in my home at least call me Ralph. George, take those upstairs to little Ralph's room. Please, Ernest, follow me."

The entranceway was large, polished, sparkled. There seemed to be rooms going off in every direction. The floors were polished wood with enormous thick rugs.

"So your father is Clarence, the doctor?"

"Yes he is," Ernest said as he looked all around following Ralph through the house. Off into a dining room there was a maid polishing some silverware.

"He's a very good man. I know him, actually. We've met more than once."

As they passed through another room Ernest noticed a large pipe organ along one wall. There was an assortment of musical instruments sitting around the room. The room was twice the size of his mother's music room at home. He thought of how the acoustics might be.

"Do you play?" Ernest asked.

Ralph glanced over at the organ.

"Oh no, my wife does mostly; and my daughter, Dorothy."

Then they entered a small and more intimate room. In the very center of the room was a large beautiful billiard table with a low hanging chandelier just above it.

Ernest stopped and looked all around.

"Wow, this is nice. This is very nice."

"Yes, indeed. Do you play?"

Ernest nodded.

"Well, then, I know what we shall be doing from now until we leave for Florida."

"I used to play billiards with the Count Giuseppe Greppi when I was staying at The Gran Hotel Stresa on Lago Maggiore in Italy. This reminds me of that."

Ralph was quiet as he watched Ernest looking all around the room. He smiled.

"I am actually looking for Harriet, I thought she was back here," he said as he started to walk back the way they had come. "I have to leave for work so she can show you the rest of the house."

As they walked through the music room again Ernest looked off into another room. It was lined floor to ceiling with books.

Back at the entranceway they stopped before a large carpeted stairway. The brown oak banister was highly polished. Large framed paintings lined the wall going up.

"Harriet," Ralph called out up the stairs.

"Yes," a distant voice from above answered.

Ralph shook his head and laughed. "Mr. Hemingway is here, I have to leave, should I show him up?"

"Yes, of course."

"Please, at the top of the stairs just call out her name and then walk toward the sound. George," he said to the driver who stood by the door. "We have to leave."

"I'm ready when you are sir."

Ralph stepped in close to Ernest, put his hand on his shoulder, and spoke in a low whisper.

"My son is, well," he said as he searched for the right word. "I hope you can show him sports and pleasures that would be sane and sensible."

Ralph nodded Ernest up the stairs and then left out the front door. Ernest started up the stairs. There was a young woman descending at the same time. She was very nice looking; about twenty six, elegant, poised, brown hair and dark eyes, and she stepped down the stairs with a sweeping grace.

They stopped when they were several steps from each other.

"Hello," she said, tilting her head to one side and smiling.

"Hello. I'm Ernest Hemingway."

"Yes, I know. I'm Dorothy Connable. I'm the daughter."

Ernest smiled, nodded.

They stood on the stairs and talked. She asked him about his service in the Red Cross. He told her about it. She too worked for the Red Cross in France; she helped establish a YMCA for the Sixth Division. She asked him about being wounded. He told her about it. She spent time in Germany to help establish a YMCA there as well. They say you want to be a writer, she said. Yes, he said. He told her about some of his stories. She had graduated from Wellesley College and loved to read.

"Will you let me read some of your work?"

Ernest beamed.

But then Harriet appeared at the top of the stairs.

"There you are," she said. "I see that you have met my daughter."

"Yes, mother, we have."

Ernest apologized as he climbed up the stairs leaving Dorothy still standing on the stair as she watched him climb.

When he reached the top of the stairs Harriet placed her hand on his shoulder.

"Well, Ernest, I am so happy that you have come. Welcome to our home and I hope your stay will be rewarding and productive."

"Thank you for having me. I never dreamed that it was like this."

She walked down the carpeted hallway.

"I would like you to meet Ralph Jr."

They walked into a spacious bedroom. There were windows all around with reddish brown draperies pulled back. The floor was wooden with large rugs. There were two beds, one on either side of the room, as well as chest of drawers, night stands, and in front of one large window by one of the beds was a wooden desk. Ernest noticed his bags on the floor between the bed and the table.

"This is Ralph's room. His bed is over there and I wanted you to have the bed over there. I hope you don't mind." She leaned in toward Ernest and whispered: "It's for Ralph's sake."

As they walked over to his bed she pointed out the desk.

"Here is where you can do your writing. There is plenty of sunlight."

She pointed out the window. "There below you can see the tennis court but in the winter we freeze it over and make a small ice skating rink. Beyond, over there, are the stables. If it is not too cold you can go riding up the hill."

There was a creak of the floorboards at the doorway. They both looked over. Standing in the door way was a short boy in a black suit. His hair was slicked down, heavily greased. He stood a little hunched over at the shoulders. He held his hands in front of himself as if he did not know what to do with them. His head was tilted down and he glanced up at Ernest at an angle.

"Ralph," Harriet called out as she walked over to the boy. Ernest knew the boy was nineteen but he looked more like fifteen. His suit looked freshly ironed as if he had just put it on.

"Ralph darling this is Ernest, he's the boy that's going to stay here with you."

Ernest put out his hand. "Hello Ralph."

Ralph stared at Ernest's hand for a moment before he reached up and shook his hand. "Hello," he said in a weak voice. To Ernest it felt like he was shaking hands with water.

3. Dorothy

Hemingway moved into the Connable mansion two weeks before they left for their vacation. In that time Ernest and Ralph Connable played billiards almost every night. Ralph always suggested that they put a little wager on the table, 'just to make it interesting.'

"That's your way of getting back what you pay me," Ernest said.

Ralph, chalking the tip of his cue, said: "Of course."

Ernest liked the older man. Ralph was a practical joker. And Ernest laughed at each of the adventures Ralph told him about, and his laughter made Ralph want to tell him another. In his past he was not as wealthy as he is now, he said. When he was a boy he grew up living next to the vast Chicago stockyards.

"I have yet to get the stench of cows out of my nose."

Usually when guests arrived he answered the door wearing a set of huge buck teeth.

Once he was entertaining the Eaton family, they owned the largest department store in Toronto. Ralph excused himself from the table and then returned as one of the servants, a butler wearing a long black beard. No one really noticed. When he returned with the second course he was wearing an even longer blue beard. Again, no one really noticed. For the third course he arrived as a servant with an even longer flaming red beard. Finally Lady Eaton took note.

"Red, as it turns out, is her favorite color."

His favorite escapade, which he performed more than once, was to dress as a woman and enter the locker room of the Lambton Golf Club. As the men scurried from the showers trying to hide themselves he came up to them and whispered in a high voice 'I'm looking for my gentleman friend.'

"It works every time," Ralph said as he took aim for his next shot.

Ernest spent time with Dorothy as well. They talked up in her room about books and stories and their war experiences.

"You and I are both very young old soldiers."

She liked that. It made her laugh.

They ice skated together in the tennis courts turned ice rink. She introduced him to her friends and they played friendly games of hockey. There would be Ernest and Dorothy, and then the chauffeur's son who was just learning how to skate, her tall friend Bonnie Bonnelle, Ernest's friend Dutch Pailthrop from Petoskey who now worked at one of the Woolworth stores and lived at the local YMCA, and then her friend

Ernest Smith, a Scotsman from Nova Scotia who had served in the Canadian army during the war. Smith told them all that he would handicap himself since he had played collegiate hockey at the University of Toronto. He played with a broom and his regular shoes.

What Ernest lacked in skating skills he made up for in enthusiasm. To get the puck from another he simple skated straight at them. Smith learned to just dodge at the last minute and Ernest went plowing into the waist high snow embankment that surrounded the court. But Ernest got up and came again. And again.

Ralph Jr. watched bundled in heavy coats while sitting on a bench in front of a small cabin. It was built next to the rink and inside there was a fireplace, and hot chocolate was served to warm them up from the winter chill. All the skates were hung on the walls. Laughing with all of them Ernest ran his finger along the blades of the skates. They were as dull as a dull kitchen knife.

Each morning before breakfast Ernest would skate the rink alone. He thought it strengthened his leg. Ralph Jr. watched from his upstairs window.

Late one afternoon two days before they were to leave a man walked over from a neighbor's house. When Dorothy came over to him the man introduced himself as an Englishman, 'from London,' and said that so far he found the Canadians were so ignorant of sport and sportsmanship that he hoped, as a last resort he might find some here. The man then yawned: perhaps not.

Ernest, smiling to the others, asked if the man, in honor of sportsmanship, would care to partake in a bit of a skating match. He agreed.

Even though his leg was hurting Ernest raced the man and won; and then again. The man went over to the bench to sit down, breathing heavily.

"Tired?" Ernest asked. "Don't tell me you are stopping already."

They raced another ten laps. Ernest again won. The man sat down. It took all of his energy to take off his skates.

"I'd say it was about time to go upstairs and put on the boxing gloves, what do you say?" Ernest asked the others who quickly agreed. "A bit of pugilist sportsmanship perhaps?"

The man pulled on his shoes and, wheezing as he stumbled away, mumbled something about it being an odd hour for boxing. It was only then that Ernest sat down. His leg hurt bad and would probably hurt all night. But the others were cheering him.

"No one beats Ernest Hemingway," he said. "No one."

After the family left for Florida Dorothy's friend Bonnie Bonnelle kept coming over to see Ernest. She stood a good six feet tall, short brown hair, slender and, as Ernest confessed to his friend Dutch Pailthrop, 'rather striking.' When they first met she smiled at him with a raised eyebrow.

"My name is Bonnie," she said as she held out her hand. "Bonnie Bonnelle. Wonderful name don't you think, it just rolls off the tongue."

Ernest, shaking her hand, said: "It has a ring to it."

When he first asked Dorothy about who Bonnie was Dorothy said, 'oh, she's a socialite,' as if that were an occupation. 'She's related to the wealthy Massey's, of Massey Hall fame.' Ernest nodded as if it were the natural thing of the world.

They went horse back riding up the steep ravines behind the estate and at times up Bathurst Street toward Armour Heights. Ernest could not bend his leg into the stirrups of the English saddle so he rode like an Indian with his legs straight down. Bonnie said she found it 'charming,' but only in someone 'cute enough to carry it off.'

"You and I are the Bathurst Street Hunting Club," she once shouted to him as their horses raced along, "with a total membership of two."

Just before he left, Ralph Senior telephoned his friend Arthur Donaldson, advertising chief at the Toronto Star, telling him Hemingway would come by. So, one day after Ralph left, Ernest dressed in his red flannel shirt and black jacket, went down to 20 King Street West to the four story brick building that housed the Toronto Star.

There was no elevator so Ernest walked up the stairs to the third floor. It was hot inside the building. It was winter cold outside but inside with the furnaces blazing and the windows shut tight it was hotter and stuffier than if it was summer. Ernest did not know why people did that. If it was cold outside then they heated the interior hot as if it somehow compensated it being cold outside. As he climbed the stairs his leg hurt and he was hot and he started to sweat but he refused to use a cane anymore. At times it seemed his leg was not getting any better. But then other times it seemed that it was almost normal.

Was it ever going to heal completely?

On the third floor there were long hallways and small over cramped offices. It smelled of dust and disinfectant and printer's ink and the air was thick with tobacco smoke.

He asked one of the men rushing down the hall who directed him to Arthur Donaldson's office.

Donaldson took him directly down a flight of stairs and through a maze of hallways and small cubicles. They entered a small room where two men were sitting, one in a chair at a desk and one on a tall stool before an angled drawing table.

"Are you busy, boys?" Arthur asked. The two men looked up from their work.

"This is Ernest Hemingway. He's an American newspaper man, worked on the Kansas City Star. He's up here visiting Ralph Connable, Ralph asked me to show him around."

The short man at the desk stood up. He had short chopped hair like he just had a bad haircut. He had a tiny moustache. He was just over five feet tall. Ernest towered over him.

"Greg Clark, Features Editor," the man said as he shook Ernest's hand. Greg noticed the perspiration on Ernest's upper lip and around his forehead. "This here is Jimmy Frise, Cartoonist." The second man was taller, darker completion, short crew cut that shot straight up, with large eyeglasses. A cigarette dangled from his mouth.

"Well," Arthur said, "I've got to go so see what you can see." It was unclear who he was talking too.

The two men returned to their work. Frise was drawing something and Clark was typing something. Ernest stood for a moment and then walked over to the stand up radiator and sat down on it. He took off his jacket. It was the only place in the cramped room where he could sit down.

They spent the rest of the day working and Ernest spent the rest of the day sitting on the radiator asking question after question trying to make conversation. Yes: I worked at the Kansas City Star; worked under Pete Wellington; worked the short stop run covering Union Station, the Police department and the hospital; published some articles and they liked them, they wanted me to stay. But then I was in the war, yes: on the Italian front; yes a Lieutenant; fought with the Arditi; blown up by a mortar shell; won the Croce de Guerra and the Medaglia d'Argento al Valore, the highest award for honor. I like to trout fish, I'm really good at that, fish all the good rivers in upper Michigan every summer.

It did not seem that Greg believed a word of it, not a word. He told Ernest that they too were in the war. We took it heavy at Vimy Ridge.

"Jimmy, show him your medal you got at Vimy Ridge."

Jimmy put down his sketching pencil and then rose up a hand fanning out his fingers. The tip of one of his fingers was missing.

"That's the medal that he got," Greg said with a touch of bitterness. "Me I was promoted to major because everyone above me in rank was killed off. You get promoted by surviving. They gave me the Military Cross because after thousands were slaughtered I managed to keep my unit together."

At the end of the day, that first day, Ernest stepped out into the hallway to leave. He stopped to put on his black jacket. He could hear them talking in the room. Greg was talking.

"Don't get too chummy with this kid. Kansas City Star for Pete's sake. That paper is the beau ideal of every newspaperman in America. Maybe he was an office boy. And Italian Army? Him in the Arditi? He probably never was in the war."

"Well, he does have a limp?"

"Ah, he probably stubbed his toe."

"Don't be so suspicious. Maybe he's telling the truth."

Ernest left before they came out of the office.

That night Ernest wrote to his father. He asked him to ship him his medals. The next day Ernest showed up at the office and again sat on the radiator. It was going to be a waiting game so Ernest would wait. When you are standing in a cold stream with your line out waiting for the trout to bite then you wait for the trout to bite. The next day was the same.

Then one morning Ernest arrived with a small cardboard box. He waited until Jimmy asked him what was in the box.

"These are my medals," he said as he opened the box. "I thought you might like to see them. The first I got while still in hospital in Milan and the other was mailed to me."

Greg took the first one out of the box. It was the Croce de Guerra.

"This is like the Military Cross I have."

"Yes," Ernest said. "But this," he said as he carefully took the second medal out of the small cardboard box, "this is the highest Italian award, the gold medal for valor." He handed it to Greg.

"Oh, boy," Greg said. He turned it on its side. The real person to whom it really belonged would be written along the edge. He carefully read: Tenente Ernesto Hemingway.

He froze. He could not move. He could not speak. Lieutenant Ernest Hemingway. Greg was totally wrong. It was true. All of it was true.

Greg stared at Ernest for a long moment.

"For Christ sake, Hemingway," he finally said in astonishment, "do you want a job?"

5. Kansas City Star

Ernest could not help but remember how different his experience was at the Kansas City Star.

October 15, 1917. Ernest was eighteen year old.

He and his father stood on the train platform. His bags were already loaded. He was off to Kansas City for a possible job as a reporter with the Star. Clarence spoke with his brother Tyler, who knew some of the staff at the Star. 'I'll see what I can do,' Tyler told him.

High school was done. To Clarence's way of thinking that meant college was next. But Ernest had this notion he wanted to be a reporter. He wanted to be a writer. A few published stories in the high school paper and suddenly he thinks he's born to be a writer. Clarence shook his head and as he explained to Grace, let him have his way and try it out. Give it a year and he'll get back on the right track.

As they stood on the platform a cold wind came up. Autumn wind. Change was in the air. The whistle blew, it was time. As Ernest turned to board the train Clarence put his hand on his son's shoulder.

"Son," Clarence said. "Good bye."

Ernest smiled and nodded. "Good bye, Dad."

Clarence pulled him into his arms and hugged him tight. He kissed Ernest on the cheek. He spoke with a breaking voice.

"May the Lord watch between me and thee while we are absent the one from the other."

The conductor reached down to take away the steps up into the train. Ernest climbed up leaving his father behind on the platform.

His uncle Tyler Hemingway, his father's younger brother, met him at the station. Tyler wore his three piece suit with his white handkerchief in his pocket. They greeted, they shook hands, and then Tyler said: "Well, then. Let's be off. Follow me."

He walked to his carriage as Ernest followed carrying his two suitcases. It was a black carriage, boxed, with black lace trim. The horse seemed a bit nervous.

At dinner that night in the pink wallpapered dining room Aunt Arabella went on and on about the family, how was Clarence, how was Grace, my what a handsome young boy you have grown into, you're eighteen now, my word you were just a young boy when we last saw you, why Tyler has already talked with his friend Harry Haskell, the chief editorial writer over at the Kansas City Star, and he said they can use a young talent like you, Tyler has an ever widening circle of important friends now that he is an executive over at Daddy's lumber company, don't you Tyler, and of course you can stay here with us for as long as you like, and here have some more mashed potatoes, do you like the gravy?

Ernest liked Aunt Arabella. She was plump, chatty, and loved to laugh.

Tyler sat eating his meatloaf in silence.

The next day Tyler took Ernest to the Kansas Star office. It was a large block long red brick three story building.

On the elevator up to the second floor Uncle Tyler leaned in toward Ernest.

"This building was built not long ago to honor the founder of the paper, William Rockhill Nelson. But I find it a bit strange that it faces south away from the heart of the city."

Ernest waited for more. But that was that. Tyler was done.

When the door of the elevator opened Ernest was amazed at what he saw. It opened into an enormous high ceiling room. The noise was overwhelming. Desks lined up row after row butted against each other with filing cabinets lined along one whole wall. There were no inner walls or partitions; it was just one huge office. People were walking about. Men sat at their desks with long black ties and opened collars and the sleeves of their white shirts rolled up shouting into telephones or banging on typewriters. It seemed that everyone was talking or shouting at everyone and there were telephones ringing and a constant clatter of typewriters banging away. Ernest followed Tyler as he walked along one wall all the way down to the center of the room. At the desk at the end of one row Tyler stopped. The man sitting there looked up.

"Tyler," the man said as he stood.

Uncle Tyler introduced the man as Harry Haskell, Chief Editorial Writer. They shook hands. Harry stopped another man as he walked by.

"George, this is Tyler Hemingway's nephew I told you about. Ernest, this is George Logan, he's our City Editor. George, take him over to Pete and get him set up."

George nodded and waved at Ernest to follow him as he started down one of the long walkways between the rows and rows of desks. Ernest followed him looking back and forth. He had never seen anywhere so alive with activity. They approached the far wall. There were long open windows and here and there the blinds were broken. The sun flooded through the open areas. The windows were in need of washing.

George introduced Ernest to a tall thin pale man of about thirty years old. He was Pete Wellington. They shook hands.

"So you're the new kid."

"Yes, I'm the new kid."

"Well you'll work the day shift, eight to five six days a week for fifteen dollars a week. Any questions?"

Ernest nodded and then said no.

Pete handed him a piece of paper.

"Here, this is the style sheet for the paper. Read it, learn it, use it."

Ernest started reading the sheet: "Use short sentences. Use short first paragraphs. Use vigorous English. Be positive, not negative."

"If you have any questions then read it again. Use short declarative sentences and I've yet to meet an adjective that I like."

Ernest did not know if he was serious or he was joking. Nothing in his face or the tone of his voice gave it away.

"Every cub reporter has a thirty day trial. No exceptions. If I don't like you then you're gone. Now, sit here. You'll share this desk with the movie critic but he works at night, so don't leave the desk a mess."

Ernest sat in the dark brown hardwood swivel chair. It creaked when he sat down. Rays of sunlight streaked his desk. There were two telephones at the head of the desk.

"You see two phones on the desk," Pete said as he pointed to them. "When they ring answer them. Any questions?"

Ernest looked up into the man's face. It was void of emotion. Ernest thought that he would make a killer of a poker player.

Pete walked away and left Ernest sitting in the chair at the desk. Ernest looked around. His career as a newspaper reporter had begun; his life as a writer had begun; his life had begun.

Chapter Seven

He was asleep when they first picked up the stretcher. They swooped it up and then he was immediately awake. The pain in his leg came back. It was sharp pain up and down his leg like deep stabs of a knife. He watched as they passed the other stretchers on the ground. Some of the men on the stretchers on the ground looked up at him as he passed them. Each man was waiting, each man was hurting, and several of them were dying.

Ernest watched from his stretcher as they approached the rear of the ambulance. The back of it was full of other stretchers. Men were moaning. Only the swing on the left side was open. They carried his stretcher into the rear of the ambulance and secured him to the swing tied to the side and top. There was a strong smell of sweat and stale vomit.

Ernest closed his eyes. The swing was the worst. He knew from driving the Fiat ambulances. On the trays secured against the side of the truck you were stationary and moved with the truck. But in the swings you swayed. You hung down and swayed as the truck moved.

The truck started up. There was a smell of gasoline and exhaust fumes. The truck bumped along the road. He could not see outside. The stretcher swayed and rocked. It felt like being in the smelly deep bowels of a rocking ship on an unsettled sea. He grew dizzy and unsettled as the truck lumbered on down the uneven road. Suspended in air, rocking and swaying, Ernest tried to hold back. Closing his eyes only made the dizziness worse.

He could not stop it. He vomited. On his back he tried to turn his head to one side. The vomit spewed out of his mouth and all over himself. He heard some splat on the floor of the truck below him. He tried spitting it out but he started to choke and gag. He could not breathe. He choked and his throat was filled with fluid. He frantically turned to his side to spit it out and to breathe but the pain ribbed up and down his leg. Some of the vomit came out of his nose.

The truck drove on.

1. Boxing

It was a crowded night. Ernest and Dutch and Ralph Jr. gave the ticket taker their tickets and walked into the Arena. The hallways were packed with men walking around. Ernest was in the lead and made his way through the crowd.

"Keep up," he called back to Dutch and Ralph. They walked fast. Ralph walked with a noticeable limp. They could hear the roar of the crowds in the main arena.

That afternoon Ernest walked in and waved three tickets in front of Ralph's face as he sat on the sofa leafing through a magazine. Dutch followed him in.

"Dutch got them, we are going. Tonight."

Ralph, bored, looked up.

"What are you talking about?"

"Tonight, I told you. We are all going to the fights at the Arena."

"Fights?"

"Yes, there's boxing tonight, four sets: Rocky Kansas against Frankie Bull, Atkins and Lisner, and two others. Dutch got the tickets."

"I don't like boxing."

"With my expert commentary how can you not. Be ready."

Ernest wove through the crowd right up to the ring. He made it to the ring itself and rested his elbows on the outside of the mat. He stared up at the fighters as they pranced around each other. Ernest turned to Ralph standing next to him. He had to shout to be heard over the crowd.

"That's Rocky Kansas, the other is Frankie Bull. Bull is favored because he's the Canadian."

The two fighters were sweating heavily and the lights glistened on their bodies.

The fighters came near where Ernest stood and then Kansas landed a full punch to Bull's jaw. His head flung to the left. Ernest felt a sprinkle of sweat splash on his face. Ralph pulled away with a squeal, his hands wiping his face.

"Ugh, what is that?"

Ernest and Dutch looked at each other and laughed. When he wiped the sprinkled sweat from his face Ernest noticed that there were drops of blood as well.

"I'm leaving," Ralph shouted.

"Come on," Ernest said as he put his arm around Ralph's shoulders. "Maybe we won't stand so close." But he and Dutch could not help but laugh.

"What are you laughing at, that was disgusting."

"Come on, we can stand over there."

"What about our seats?"

"Nah, they're too far away. You can't see anything. You've got to be where the action is."

There was a roar from the crowd as Bull landed a heavy punch.

Ernest noticed up in the seats a man with a long overcoat. Everyone seemed to come over to him to shake his hand.

"Ralph, is that who I think it is?"

Ralph looked where he was pointing.

"Yeah, that's Mayor Tommy Church. They say he's a big sports fan."

"He sure likes to shake hands with everybody."

"Voters. Vote for me and you'll get to shake my hand."

Dutch spoke up. "I hear he's popular with returning soldiers."

"Why?" Ernest asked as he watched the mayor smile and greet people. Ernest noticed as the mayor cheered when the crowd cheered and booed when the crowd booed without even looking at the ring.

"He's not a sports fan; I bet he doesn't know the first thing about boxing let alone this fight. If cootie fighting or Swedish pinochle or Australian boomerang hurling were taken up by his potential voters he'd be right there cheering them on as though he was the greatest fan there was."

The entire time Ernest watched him the mayor did not once look at the ring.

"I bet if they lowered the voting age to where everybody who plays marbles or leap frog or tic-tac-toe could vote he'd be the first one there shaking hands."

Ralph stared at Ernest.

"You don't really like him do you."

"Why wasn't he in the war, an unmarried man of his age, instead of shaking the hands of the wounded solders older than he is returning from the war?"

"Lucky break I guess."

Ernest laughed. "Lucky break my ass. I hate politicians; all of them are sons of bitches."

After several bouts Ralph said he wanted to leave. In the backseat of the car he leaned forward to the chauffeur.

"Take us to Ella Bell's."

The man nodded and started the car engine.

It had started to rain. The man turned on the wipers.

"What's Ella Bell's," Ernest asked.

"You'll see. You took me where you wanted to go so now I'll take you to where I want to go."

The car pulled up to a night club. The lettering on the sign flashed on and off, men where standing around on the pavement. The sidewalk glistened with rain.

The chauffeur got out of the car and went over to the two large men standing at the entrance.

Ernest turned to Ralph. "This is a strip joint."

Ralph smiled and got out of the car. Ernest and Dutch followed him past the two men who just nodded as they walked through the door.

It was hot inside, hot and stuffy. It was packed with men. The tobacco smoke hung in the thick air.

Two women on the stage moved around. They were half naked. Two drunken sailors in the front room shouted and waved. Ernest watched as Ralph limped over to a man standing behind the bar. They talked. The man disappeared behind a dark red curtain and then came back out with a small package. Ralph handed the man some money and the man handed Ralph the package. It was a brown paper bag. Ralph rolled it up and put it into his jacket pocket. It looked like pictures or magazines.

Back in the car on the drive home no one spoke for a long time. The rain increased. Ernest listened to the slap of the windshield wipers and the tires on the wet road. He turned to look at Ralph. Ralph was staring out the window at the rain. He ran his finger back and forth across the cold glass of the window.

Ernest cleared his throat.

"What do you want to see that stuff for?"

Ralph stared directly at Ernest.

"Do you have a girlfriend?"

Ernest shrugged his shoulders. "Yeah, I guess. Why?"

"And can you get a new girl friend if you need too?"

Ernest paused but then answered. "Yeah."

"Well, you see, I don't and I can't, so leave me be with what I've got."

They drove home in the rain.

2. Hat Trick

It was Greg Clark who took Ernest in to see Mr. J. H. Cranston, the Editor in Chief of the Toronto Star Weekly. The older man sitting behind his neat desk, reading some copy, had white hair, parted down the middle, round eyeglasses with see through frames, and a perfectly placed bow tie. He had a pleasant smile, like a grandfather who was happy you came to see him.

Cranston looked Ernest up and down. Ernest was tall, slim, young, with red flushed cheeks, black eyes, ruffled black hair with a woolen peaked cap, black leather coat short in the arms, tight gray trousers short in the legs, and a big wide child like smile that could charm anyone.

"Kid says he can write, should we put him to the test?"

"Well now, have a seat and let's talk."

They talked.

Cranston told him to send in articles. If I like it then I will print it. If I do not like it then I will give it back to you. Printed articles are half a cent a word.

He wanted human interest stories, interesting, funny, and most of all 'written in good plain Anglo-Saxon.'

Ernest walked back into Greg and Jimmy's small office.

"Well?"

Ernest stood in the doorway, clenched both fists in the air and said: "I've got a job." All three of them cheered.

Back in his room, sitting at his desk, he rolled a piece of paper and carbon into the typewriter. He thought for a moment and then typed: "Mind you, I do not call Mayor Tommy Church a slacker." He stopped for a moment more and then pounded out the story on his typewriter without stopping. It was on Mayor Tommy Church.

Cranston rejected it. It was promising but too hard hitting.

Ernest was furious. Greg reached out and held Ernest's shoulder as he sat on the radiator. I'll give you some advice kid: human interest, funny, a humorous slant on all the little things of life, something they read around the breakfast table with the whole family. Know who you're writing to and why. For example, it was really hot one day, I mean really hot, so I went out and on the steps of the City Hall I cracked a couple eggs there on the sidewalk and damned if I didn't cook scrambled eggs right there in front of everyone. It made a story: it was funny and it made the point that everyone could attest to; it was hot.

"Tell him about the hat trick," Jimmy said.

Yes: the famous Clark hat trick.

It was on the sidewalk in front of the King Edward Hotel. He pretended to see something and with a loud fearful shout captured the thing under his hat. As customers from the hotel gathered to watch the thing under the hat tried to escape several times but with the utmost effort Greg kept it trapped under the hat. It kept running forward and Greg had to follow it as it made its way down the sidewalk. More and more people gathered to watch in fear what was going on. Greg tried to peek under the hat several times but reacted in horror at the thing and almost lost the fight to keep it trapped under his hat. After a little while so many people had gathered to see the horror under the hat that Greg could not count them all. Finally, slowly, ever so carefully and slowly he looked under the hat.

It was gone. Greg shrugged his shoulders, put his hat back on his head, and then whistled as he walked away down the street.

"It made a good article in the Weekly."

"People talked about that one for weeks," Jimmy added.

"You see, Ernest, at times what you make up is better than what is out there for real. So make your made up real."

Something everyone knows. Something everyone understands. Direct experience is the best experience. Report it. Ernest walked into a barber college. The sign on the window said that shaves and haircuts were free. The students had to learn somehow.

It was free, but you had to be brave.

Ernest walked in and asked for a haircut, free like it says in the window. Sure, Buddy, the man said. The man told him that upstairs was what the man so casually called 'the beginner's department.' The other real barbers stared at him as he climbed the stairs.

There was a line of barber chairs and behind each one stood a very young man dressed in a white coat. Ernest went over to one and sat down. The boy spread out a sheet and tied it tightly around his throat.

"Shave?" the boy asked.

"No," Ernest quickly said. "I think maybe just a haircut."

"Okay."

He grabbed scissors and combs.

Ernest looked up into his ever so young eyes.

"You do know, I mean, I mean you do know what your doing don't you?"

"I'm learning," the boy replied.

"Well, learning fast are we?"

The boy shrugged his shoulders. "I guess we'll find out soon enough won't we."

The boy smiled. He was missing one of his front teeth.

"Don't worry," the boy added. "Your hair will grow back."

Ernest laughed.

"That's why I'm not getting a shave."

When it was all over Ernest walked home. He wore his woolen cap pulled down low. In his upstairs room he typed out an article about the free barber college: 'A Free Shave.'

Standing outside Cranston's closed door he heard him laughing inside. Ernest walked away with a smile on his face. Yes.

Greg Clark asked Ernest if he wanted to go fishing. Clark liked to fish and Ernest said he was good. It was one last test. It was one last test of the kid who claimed so much. Clark was surprised when each claim came true.

They sat by the fire, the two of them, that evening. It was after a day of fly fishing for trout, sitting by the tents Ernest set up, sitting by the fire that Ernest made, eating their freshly fried trout that Ernest just cooked, that Clark laughed to himself.

"What are you laughing about?" Ernest asked.

Clark stared at Ernest with a smile.

"You know, kid, you're alright. At first I thought you were a pure phony. How could anyone your age have experienced so much, being in the war, wounded, with medals, writing for one of the best papers in the country, and claiming to be an expert fisherman? It was all too much. But one by one I have to say you've proved it all to be true."

Ernest smiled his big wide smile and poked at the fire.

They sat by the fire.

"I think we grow up fast these days with all the stuff we've got now that our parents didn't have."

Ernest nodded.

"We grow up way too fast these days. I sometimes feel that my youth just got sucked away, especially living through the war. It was only a couple years but it seems like a lifetime. I'd like to be twelve for a few years."

"Be like Huck Finn, free and easy?"

"Yeah, something like that."

Ernest watched the upper branches of the trees as they swayed.

"I was disappointed by the Mississippi River," Ernest said. "I crossed it by train when I went to Kansas City and it was just this muddy slow moving strip of swampland. I imagined it with cliffs on either side, cliffs with caves where you could set up camp but you had to be careful because Injun Joe might be hid out in one of them."

"Books make you dream about things, you know, but then sometimes when you learn about those things in real life then you realize the books all lied."

"I don't know if they lied as much as they didn't give you the whole truth; or maybe the right truth. But don't you think some books are true even though they are made up?"

"I don't know, I don't read too many books anymore."

"No?" Ernest asked.

"No. I just report what I see and make up a bit to make it more pleasant than it is."

"You sound like you're not twelve anymore."

Greg laughed.

"And you are?"

"Yes I am. Look all around us, here we are in an enchanted forest, free and easy, at least for a few days, away from it all doing what we love to do. That's being more twelve than twelve year olds are."

Greg looked around at the camp, the trees, the river, the night sky. He nodded as if agreeing but then stopped.

"We are away from everything except ourselves."

The fire popped and small sparks flew up into the air.

"But that's where you pretend to be twelve and if you do then you will be more true to yourself than if you did not."

They were silent for a moment. Ernest did not know if Greg understood what he just said.

"I for one," Ernest finally said. "I for one am going to live this, this, forever."

Greg just shook his head. "Good luck with that one."

3. Typewriter

Sitting at his desk Ernest read the letter again. It was from his father. "The Free Shave story etc. was very good indeed. I am sure you will succeed."

Ernest stared at the letter for a long time. He put it down and looked out the window. The snow had melted off. There was only a small patch here and there in the shade. He sat before his typewriter but the story was not there. He hated when it did not work, when the ideas did not come.

He wrote and sold a lot of articles but they were small stories about this and that. There was nothing of any long lasting importance, nothing real, nothing that spoke about the deep truth of life.

It was nothing like the excitement of working the Kansas City Star. He was reporting the news, the actual events as they happened, and not little anecdotal human interest articles.

Flashes of memory came and went.

There was the fire.

It was a barn on fire. He rushed up and with an axe helped the firemen tear down the door. He grabbed the hose and helped them carry it up the stairs to the roof. The heat was intense and sparks flew up. It burnt small holes in his new brown jacket. After he called the story in he asked for compensation for his jacket. It was refused.

That night sitting on the floor with Carl Edgar in the small attic room they rented he summed it up: "Never risk anything unless you're prepared to lose it completely, remember that," Ernest said as he rose in the air a glass of red wine in his hand.

He had moved in with Carl Edgar. It was an attic, it was small, and their beds were two dormer windows where he curled up fully dressed and with blankets against the cold coming through the glass of the window. Late at night he watched the snow coming down by the streetlamps.

Ernest remembered the day at the office he was typing and typing madly and the keys kept sticking and piling up and he had to reach in and unclear them with his fingers and then keep typing. Finally he rolled the paper out of the carriage and called for the copy boy. A new man was standing behind him.

"That's rotten copy. When I get excited the damn thing goes haywire. I hope they can read it. Sometimes they can't read it but they print it all the same."

"You're thoughts are faster than your fingers," the man said.

Ernest stood up and put out his hand. "Something like that. My name's Hemingway, Ernest Hemingway. You're a new man aren't you?"

They shook hands. "Ted Brumback. My first day."

Ted was the son of Judge Herman Brumbach of Jackson County Circuit Court. Ted was four years older than Ernest. He attended Princeton for two years but then left. While on the links he whacked his golf ball that hit a nearby tree that smacked him square in his open eye. The eyeball popped into bloody goo that drooled down his cheek. He wore a fake eye ever since.

Ernest once invited Ted over to stay the night at his "lodgings." After the long trolley trip in the cold misty rain they sat on the floor with pillows as cushions.

"Like poetry?" Ernest asked.

"Sure," Ted answered but waved his hand toward the clock. It was after one in the morning. They had to be back in the office in a few short hours.

"Aw, come on. I got a jug of dago red, two glasses, and look, I've got a book of Browning. What do you say? I'll start."

He started reading out loud. It was not long before Ted was asleep. It was after four when Ted woke up. Ernest was still reading aloud.

"For the love of Mike, Ernie, you must be nuts."

Ernest looked up and smiled that beaming whole face of a smile that was his.

"It's still good even if it's just me listening," Ernest said.

There was the man on the floor of the Union Station. A crowd gathered at a distance. The man was bundled in blankets on a stretcher on the stone floor.

"What's the trouble here?" Ernest asked as he walked up to the man. Someone in the crowd spoke.

"Two men just took him off the train and left him there. He's real sick. Someone called for an ambulance."

"How long ago?" Ernest asked.

"About a half an hour."

Ernest looked around at the crowd.

"What's the matter with you people? The Hospital is just up the hill not two miles. Put him in a cab to the hospital. He would have already been there by now."

"The man's real bad sick."

149

"Ernest nodded. "Of course, the man's got smallpox, you can tell by looking at him. Help me get him up."

But the word smallpox seemed to push the crowd even further back.

"For Christ's sake, are you going to let him die?" Ernest said as he pulls off the blankets, bends down upon one knee, and then pulls the man up over his shoulder. Ernest stood up with the man over his shoulder. Ernest shouted to a cabbie who opened his back door. Ernest put the man in the back seat and then went around to the other side.

"Hospital," Ernest said.

At the hospital Ernest went inside and brought out a wheelchair and two attendants. To the Cabbie he motioned to the backseat.

"You better fumigate your car, and bill it to the Kansas City Star."

One night at the hospital the police brought in a black man cut up with a razor. A part of his heart was even cut. The surgeons stitched it up but were not sure he would live. Next day the police wanted to know who did it. The man did not say. "Just a friend of mine," was all that he said. After repeated attempts the police left him to die. But he lived. And outside of two weeks he was released from the hospital. That night the police found his assailant. He was in the street cut open by a razor. By the time they found the body he did not need the hospital.

When Ernest told Carl about it Carl just whistled as he shook his head back and forth. "I guess the lesson is do what you came to do but make sure you do it."

One night around Christmas a young kid came in, sixteen, a handsome kid. Earlier that day he came in asking if the doctor can do something, pleading if they could do something. Do what? Fix these lustful urges. The doctor told him it was natural. A boy your age, it is quite normal. No, the boy said, it is a sin against purity. It is a biological sin against the spirit. The doctor tried to calm the boy down. It is perfectly natural, perfectly normal. No, the boy said as he cried, no. That night they brought him back in. He had taken a razor to himself and now he was bleeding to death.

Ernest still sat in his chair at the desk by the window. The snow was mostly melted off. Ernest still had the blank sheet of paper rolled into the typewriter. He still had a story to write. But none of that could go into this story. None of that would fit into the human interest story he had to write.

Ernest realized that it was in Kansas City as a reporter, and not in the war, that he first understood there was more to life than Oak Park. There was more to life than either Oak Park or Windemere had to offer. The war just deepened what he already knew. It just deepened and darkened and hardened what he already had glimpsed.

He watched some birds fly across the sky. They all disappeared into the trees up the hill. He wondered what that meant, if it meant anything.

Winter is done: Spring has come.

Write what you know, write what you understand. Balmer told him that. What I know and understand is fishing. So, why not fishing? Why not trout fishing? Why not? There were many Toronto residents who liked fishing.

Ernest rubbed his hands together as if a delicious meal had appeared, as if by rubbing his palms together they would spring into action and type.

He began to type.

4. Moise

Ernest sat at his desk in front of his typewriter. He wanted to write a story but he did not know where to start. He stared out the window to the hills behind the house. There were pure white clouds in the blue sky.

Where do you begin?

He finished a piece for the Toronto Star and he had an idea for another article that he would write later. But now he wanted to write a story. Ralph was at work and would not be back for hours. Ernest had time to himself. But where do you begin?

Where does what is in your heart begin?

There were several letters sitting on the desk. He picked one up and began to read it. It was from his mother Grace.

For Easter he wired her a Lily. She was joyed.

He read: "My eyes are just brimming over with joyous tears to think that you thought of me. . . Walloon—it seemed only yesterday that I was there with you (just five years old) you know the picture of you that hangs in your room, 'Cozy Curls' you called yourself."

Ernest put the letter down. He thought of the photograph on the wall. Grace had always wanted twins. His sister Marcelline was only a year older and his mother dressed the two of them in matching clothes. With his hair grown out with bangs, dressed in a small white gingham dress with lace and a wide white bonnet with pink and white flowers, his mother paraded the two of them as if they were twin sisters. She kept the illusion for as long as she could. In a scrap book she wrote that on the sunny summer day he was born "The Robins sang their sweetest songs to welcome the little stranger into this beautiful world."

But then, in the forest of Walloon lake with his play gun and his naked feet and his oversized straw hat when asked what he was afraid of he shouted out with great gusto that he was 'fraid a nothing.' She knew then that he was now 'my little man.'

Ernest had a memory of his mother.

It was in Oak Park, he was about seven years old, the local Y.M.C.A. organized for the first time a gymnasium class for women and Grace was one of the first to join. The outfit they wore to the class was a navy blue flannel blouse with a sailor collar and full pleated bloomers. The short sleeves were trimmed with white braid. She wore cotton stockings and tennis shoes, both black. She liked to bounce a little when she walked when she wore the tennis shoes.

Grace came back from her class and told the children sitting in the kitchen that she could kick higher than her head. No one believed her.

But then she smiled and raised her eyebrow and said, watch me.

She asked Lily the maid to stand on one of the wooden kitchen chairs and hold out a pillow. Lily wobbled on the creaking chair and held out the pillow a little higher than Grace's head. Grace stepped back, stared at the pillow for a moment, bounced a little up and down, and then in one swoop her foot went up and kicked the pillow with ease.

The children stared in disbelief at each other. Now, Grace said to the children, do you really want to see something? They all shouted out yes. I'll turn on the gas jet in the ceiling with my foot.

Lily stood by the gas jet with the lighter. Grace stepped back and swayed back and forth for a moment concentrating on the gas jet valve. Everyone was quiet. Then, in a rush, Grace stepped forward, swept her foot up into the air above her head and kicked the valve. They could smell the gas and Lily clicked the lighter and the flame fired.

Ernest sat back in his chair. He smiled remembering. Grace certainly was a hero that day.

She could be athletic when she wanted to be. There was a family story about Grace when she was twelve years old. Her brother Leicester got a high wheeled bicycle. The front wheel was as tall as a man and the rear wheel was small. It was dangerous and wobbly to ride. Only men and boys rode bicycles back then. But she was determined to show them. One day Grace put on a pair of Leicester's trousers, something women then just did not do, and then she mounted her brother's high cycle, something women then just did not do, and after several tries she rode the thing around the block. Then she kept riding the thing down through town. Family legend said that people came to the window or stood on the sidewalk and watched in wonder. 'Come and look, quick,' they called out, 'there's a girl on a bicycle.'

Shouting boys and girls and barking dogs followed her down the street: the first girl in Chicago to ride a bicycle.

Yes, Ernest thought to himself: that is my mother.

Ernest pushed the letters aside. He wanted to write his story. He had to focus. It was on an incident he saw in Kansas City. It was during the war. Soldiers were upstairs in a brick building on the second floor at the local chapter of the Y.M.C.A. There was music and food and punch. There were local girls dancing with the soldiers. The soldiers would be going away soon to the war. It was raining and the streets were wet. Cars came by with their wheels splashing the streets. There was a lone woman walking back and forth on the street looking up at the lighted window where the music floated out into the wet night. She was bundled in her coat walking back and forth and looking up.

He wondered if her boyfriend was up there, dancing with the sweet local girls laughing and eating cookies. They were lovers but she was not allowed up because she was not of their kind. But when her boyfriend needed her she was there for him. But now she walked back and forth waiting for him to come down and then they would be together again.

Or maybe she was a prostitute walking her beat wondering when the soldier boys would come down and she could give them what they really wanted after the punch and the cookies and she would be able to go home with at least a little bit of money in her purse rather than nothing.

The image was there in his head. A picture. But what did it mean and where would it take him?

Ernest stared at the blank white sheet of paper rolled in his typewriter.

Ernest thought of Lionel Calhoun Moise, one of the reporters with the Kansas City Star. He was a volcano of a man with a vitality that Ernest envied. He showered sparks of creative insight everywhere when he was focused, but he was undisciplined and most of the time wasted his talent.

If only Ernest had that energy and talent.

But when Lionel drank heavy, as he did all the time, then his vitality overflowed into violence. Bartenders did not like to see him come in because there could be a fight later. He had a badly bent nose from a fight somewhere. He was tall and had long arms and huge hands. It would not be good to be slugged by those fists. He did time for slugging a policeman.

Lionel worked at different papers and got top dollar for his work but then he got fired for one thing or another. Once when he got mad he threw his typewriter out the window of the second story office. Ernest watched with envy when Moise worked on four different stories at once and then in the middle of it phoned in a fifth. He typed faster than anyone Ernest had ever seen. And his articles were good, they flowed, they were direct. 'You have to organize this chaos into a pattern,' he once said. 'That's your job.'

And he loved the women. The booze and the women, combined they tore him down. He drove around in a fancy car and it was said that a woman gave it to him, in thanks. Many of the younger reporters envied him for that.

But then one night it was raining and they were drinking and the same woman stabbed him in the front seat of the car out on the Lincoln Highway halfway to Jefferson City. He pulled the car to the side of the road and then grabbed the knife away from her. She screamed and opened the door to get out and he grabbed her heel as she got out and it made her trip onto the wet muddy grass as she got out. He threw the knife out the window onto the wet highway. He slid across the front seat and got out just as she was standing up with her dress all muddy. He grabbed her and pulled her back hard against the side of the car with his large hand around her throat. She was choking. His chest where the knife went in hurt bad and blood drained down his side staining his shirt a bright red. Then with all his strength and anger he made a fist and slugged her hard on the side of her face. She slid limp down the side of the car. He held her up and held her in place against the car with one hand while he opened the door of the backseat with the other hand. They were both wet from the rain. She was unconscious and her lower jaw was twisted into a strange angle. It hung down like it was loose and not attached. He threw her into the backseat of the car and then shoved her in further so he could slam the door shut. He stood for moment with his hand on the side of the car. The wound hurt him bad and he felt a little dizzy.

Lionel walked around the side of the car and got into the drivers seat. He felt for the wound and his hand came back all red. He drove all the way back to Kansas City in the rain and drove up to the emergency at the hospital. When he popped open the door he almost fell out but he stopped himself. Then he slid out and stood up. He could not move very fast and he had to breathe with long heavy breaths. It was still raining. He walked out around the side of the car, bracing himself against the car as he walked, and then opened the back door. She was inside moaning and crying out. Two orderlies came rushing up to him. He looked at them and then waved toward the backseat.

"The lady is in need of attendance," he said. He laughed. "She would tell you herself but, alas, for once in her life she is quiet."

He fell back against the side of the car laughing at his joke. He watched as they helped her out onto a stretcher. He looked down at himself as another orderly came up to him with a stretcher. The whole left side of his shirt and his pant leg was soaked in blood.

"Oh my," he sighed. "It appears it is not a good night."

Ernest remembered one night Lionel sitting across from him and Lionel was slightly drunk and sucking on his half burnt cigarette with one eye closed because of the smoke saying that the only thing that he cared about, the only thing real, was "pure objective writing," and then he leaned in only inches from Ernest's face and said with the strong force of a powerful punch, "No tricks."

5. Crossroad

Bill was under his car. The car was in the street in front of Ernest's house. Bill's tools were spread out around on the ground next to him. Both Ernest and Ted Brumback sat on the curb watching Bill work.

"How long do you think this will take," Ted asked.

"I don't know, however long."

Ernest laughed. "And with you as the mechanic are we sure we want to drive in this thing?"

"Look," Bill said as he scooted out from under the car. "How could I know I'd burn out my bearing on the way up here?"

Marc came over to the three of them with a small box filled with fried chicken.

"Lunch is served," she said as she sat down on the curb next to them.

Ernest grabbed the first piece and handed it to Ted. Bill wiped his greasy hands with his dirty towel.

"So what are your plans?" Marc asked.

"For Bill to fix his damn car so we can get out of here," Ernest said as he chewed on his chicken.

Ted spoke up: "We are going up to Walloon Lake for the summer."

"Yes, I know that," Marc said, "I actually meant longer term, after summer."

The three of them looked at her as they chewed their chicken.

"Ernie, have you decided what college you want to go to?"

"Hell no, kid, I'm going to travel."

"Travel? Where? Does Mom know about this?"

"Well, sort of. I need to get from her the seed to pay for a passport and to get out to San Francisco."

"San Francisco?"

"Yeah. I haven't told you yet. Jack Pentecost already has his passport. We're going to book passage on a steamer to the orient, maybe Yokohama."

"The orient? But what about college?"

Marc reached for a piece of chicken and held it over the napkin in her lap.

"Sis, I want to be a writer. You don't become a writer by going to college. That is no longer a roadmap into writing."

"I have to agree with him there, Marcelline." It was Ted Brumback. "I'm a Princeton boy and they don't teach you anything about real life and that's what you need to be a writer these days. All the Realists and the Naturalists, they did not learn to write about that from college."

157

"I'm afraid he's right," Bill said as he reached for another piece of fried chicken.

Ernest held up a drumstick. "This is pretty good but nothing compared to dear old Liz's chicken at the Pinehurst. She is the queen of fried chicken."

Everyone nodded in agreement.

"Which we could be eating instead of this if you get your damn car fixed."

"You're welcome to fix it hot shot if you want."

Marc set her half eaten piece of chicken on the napkin on her lap. "So, Bill, how is he right?"

"Well, most of the more recent writers have all worked in newspapers." He started to list them by holding up his fingers one at a time. "London, Norris, Dreiser, Crane."

Ted continued: "Howe, Lardner."

"Twain," said Ernest.

"Yes, Twain, who else?"

"Kipling," Ernest said. "And they went to sea: Conrad, Stevenson, London. When you travel, Sis, you see the world, the whole world that's out there and not just the tiny little closed circle of Oak Park. I experienced that from being in the war in Italy. It completely changed me."

"Right there was your college education, Wemedge," Ted said. "The war. The war was a better education about how life really is than anything you'll learn at Princeton."

"So you are sending your stories out to the magazines?"

"Yes, Sis."

"And, anything yet?"

Bill answered for Ernest: "Nothing yet, they have yet to recognize his talent."

"Rejection," Ernest said as he held up his half eaten piece of chicken in the air, "is paying the writers dues."

"Speaking of that, have you tried any of the Crossroad stories yet?
Ernest shook his head no.

"What are those stories?" Marc asked.

"They are going to be his best," Bill said. "Ernie showed some stuff to the writer Edwin Balmer."

"Yes, I remember that."

"Now Balmer himself writes pot boilers but he gave Ernie some sound advice. Do what I say and not as I do. He told him to write stories about things and people that he knew. Forget all of the action adventure in foreign lands stuff and focus on people and emotions that he knows."

"But that's what sells and makes the money," Ernest said.

"Forget that," said Bill. "That's a trap into the cliché and besides you're having zero success."

"Just wait until I break in."

"Marc, I keep telling him that his stuff is like redone Kipling through the lens of Ring Lardner. It's been done. It's good for Ring Lardner but it's not Ernie. He writes well but his subject matter has to change. So he and I started writing some stories we call 'Crossroads: An Anthology.'"

"It's about the people up in Horton Bay," Ted told Marc.

"Really?"

"Did you read the short sketches recently in the Saturday Evening Post by E. W. Howe called 'The Anthology of Another Town.'"

"Yes, yes, I did. They were pretty good."

"See, he wrote 'The Story of a Country Town' some thirty something years ago about just ordinary people in an ordinary town and all that they lived and felt. That's what Balmer is talking about. It was a top selling book and now Sherwood Anderson has come out with 'Winesburg Ohio' which is similar and is really good. And Master's did 'Spoon River Anthology,' they were all successful story cycles doing exactly what Balmer suggested."

Ted shook his head. "Spoon River, that one makes me uneasy. I mean, talking graves." He shivered and then laughed.

"So you're doing the same thing only about the people up in Horton Bay?" Marc asked.

"Exactly," said Bill.

"But what is the action," Ernest said, "what is the plot? People want, I don't know, excitement and adventure in order to escape their lives."

"So why does a big slick magazine like Saturday Evening Post publish Howe's Anthology? The action is life. The plot is everyday folk. Who knows what people carry around in their hearts? Disappointment. The death of a child they never got over. Or they come to realize they are not going to be anything different like they once thought they were going to be."

"All of that is depressing," said Ernest. "Who wants to read depressing things like that?"

Bill laughed.

"It's called Tragedy, my friend. Have you ever heard of Hamlet, King Lear, Agamemnon?"

"The slick magazines don't give you that," Marc said. "They don't really give you literature."

"But I want to live as a full time writer so I need the money, the seeds, you don't understand."

"Yes we do Ernie. I for one would be perfectly happy living off the royalties of Shakespeare, wouldn't you?"

Ernest shook his head and threw the bones of his last piece of fried chicken back into the box.

"Okay, okay, maybe you're right. All I know right now is that damn car is not getting fixed by us going on and on."

Bill smiled and looked at Marc.

"He does not like being wrong."

"Oh you can say that again," she replied.

"Okay. Enough is enough. Now, what's going on with the car? Do you know what the hell you are doing?"

Bill held up his wrench. "It is all in the wrench, my man, I am Archimedes so give me a wrench and I will make the world."

"I don't care about the world; just get it fixed so we can get out of here."

Chapter Eight

It was his first time in a bed with sheets and covers. It was hot. The springs squeaked when he moved. A long board served as a cast and his entire leg was wrapped in bandages. The walls were white rough plaster. The floor was made of smooth tiles.

It was hot. The orderly came by in the heat of the day and poured water up and down his bandaged leg to cool him down. The orderly gave him a rolled piece of paper as a fly swatter. The flies came in through the open window.

His bed was by the window. If he pushed himself up enough he could see down into a part of the courtyard two stories below. Along the outer wall workmen were digging graves. They dug them deep and set two wooden coffins down on top of each other.

"When die we bury right away," the young orderly told him in his broken English. The young orderly had a chipped front tooth. The orderly learned his English in school. "When we know where then dig up and ship. But bury right away, for now."

Ernest knew that in the heat a dead body would start to rot fast.

Ernest had been there for days. The doctor said they were watching for infection. If there was a bad infection then he might lose his leg. The Doctor said the fragments were sterilized by the heat of the blast. It should be fine, the Doctor said. But we wait and watch just in case.

And each day the bed springs squeaked when he pushed himself up just enough to look down and see what fresh graves were dug.

He sweat in the heat and swatted at the flies.

He waited.

1. Clarence

Clarence was standing on the beach as Ernest guided the canoe up onto the packed sand. Clarence came over and helped pull the canoe up. He brushed the dirt off of his hands as he nodded at Ernest.

"Hello, Dad."

"Hello son."

It had been more than a month since they last saw each other. And almost as soon as Ernest got home to Oak Park from Toronto Bill arrived and then Ted and they both stayed at the house. Time was spent planning trips. There was no time for his father. And his father seemed to be at the office or on his rounds all the time. There was no time for his son.

"Just arrive?"

"Yes, son, I arrived early today."

"Are you going to stay the summer?"

"No. I can't. I'll stay a week or two, maybe."

Each of them pulled a box from the canoe. It was food from The General Store in Horton Bay.

"Mom said she needed this stuff."

The two of them walked together as they climbed the small rise toward the cottage porch.

Ernest felt a certain need for talk, for discussion. The last time he really talked to his father was before he left for Toronto, before he left for Petoskey, before last summer. He could not really remember when.

"So you don't want to stay at least until my birthday?"

"No, I am afraid not," his father said.

"How about Carol's birthday?"

"I do not think so."

Ernest stood at the base of the stairs holding his box as his father climbed up onto the porch. Ernest watched as he climbed.

"Why not?"

His father turned toward him still holding the box.

"It is a busy time I am afraid. There was a car accident and several were killed and several are injured. And I have several cases of pneumonia."

"There are other doctors and you used to have them take your work load when you came up here."

His father shrugged.

"That is not possible this time."

"And taking care of them is more important than being here with

163

your family?"

Clarence did not reply. He stood staring down at Ernest and then turned and opened the screen door and went inside.

Ernest stood for a long time. It was not right. Things were all wrong. He felt like sliding the box up onto the porch and then turning and walking away. He felt like doing that but he did not.

Ernest climbed the stairs, opened the screen door and walked through the front room and into the kitchen. The light in the kitchen was on. Grace was no where to be seen. She might be in her room with the blinds drawn. Clarence was putting the groceries away into the cupboard. His back was turned. Ernest put his box on the table next to the other one. He looked at his father's back. Was there a chance? Was it worth a try?

"How was your fishing trip?" Ernest asked.

His father stopped and turned his head slightly.

"Last May," Ernest reminded him.

"Good," his father replied. "It was very good. It was so nice to get away for awhile," he said as he stared off.

"You wrote me a letter about it; you sounded very excited about it."

His father turned around. He nodded. He smiled. He pulled several other items from the box and turned to put them into the cupboard. "I was very excited," he said.

Ernest remembered the letter. He was sitting at his desk in his upstairs room in Toronto. Reading the letter made him smile. It made him feel good, good for his father. 'Say, I renewed my youth ten years at least,' his father wrote him. 'I had the best trouting by far since the trip I made across the Plains several years ago.' His father's excitement trembled through the words.

His father once told Ernest that you had to get away every once in awhile. You had to get away from it all, from civilization, from what we think is life, in order to really be alive.

When Clarence was a young man he went on extended hunting and fishing trips. He did archeological digs in the Potawatomi Indian mounds along the Des Plaines River. He had a whole assortment of arrowheads, chippers, stone axes, stone skinning knives, and pottery and woven baskets. He hunted and stuffed the animals and set them up in glass frames. There was an owl, some chipmunks, a squirrel, and several other types of birds. He made jars of snakes and things preserved in alcohol.

Even though he was a small boy Ernest could remember when they lived with Grandpa Hall in his house, Clarence had his office and waiting

164

room. In both he proudly displayed his various specimens in the glass jars and glass cases. But then over the years they were removed up to the attic. The alcohol seeped out and where the snakes were exposed they turned a hardened white. The cases grew dusty. Ernest could remember in the attic his parents wedding cake preserved in a tin box hanging from one of the rafters.

Then they moved. Grandfather Hall died and Grace used her inheritance to build another house, a house of her design. But before they moved she had to clean out the old so they did not bring it all with them into the new house.

Ernest remembered. He was seven years old. Things not to be moved were thrown onto the fire in the yard. The jars in the attic were thrown on the fire and the glass jars would pop loud and the fire would flare up from the alcohol.

Clarence got home and got down from the buggy and hitched the horse. He walked over to the fire.

"What's this?"

Grace stood on the porch. "I've been cleaning out the basement and attic, dear."

Clarence bent down and flicked something out of the fire with his hand.

"Get a rake, Ernie."

Ernest got a rake from the basement. Clarence began carefully raking out the ashes. He gently spread out burnt stone axes, stone skinning knives, chippers, pieces of pottery and many arrowheads. He knelt down and spread them out in the grass burning the tips of his fingers from the hot stones. Most of them were burnt black, chipped, broken apart.

"The best arrow heads went all to pieces," he quietly said.

Ernest, standing next to his father kneeling down on the grass, looked over at his mother on the porch. She was not there.

2. Clams

They sat together on the wooden dock, Ernest and his sister Carol. She was nine. They swished their feet in the water and waved at boats as they went by. It was late afternoon. The shade from the trees stretched across the water.

Carol looked over her shoulder toward the gate at the back of the cottage. Ernest quickly glanced back and then looked at her.

"I thought I heard something coming."

"Something? Are you afraid?"

"No."

"There's nothing in the woods that can hurt you."

"Bears."

"Maybe, but they aren't around here. Bears are further to the north. They don't like being where people are."

"Neither do I," she said.

"That's not true."

"Yeah. Sometimes."

"Yeah, well sometimes nobody likes being with other people."

"What would you do if a bear came down through the back gate all big and scary?"

"I'd say hello there Mr. Bear, what can I do for you?"

"You would not," she said.

"What would you do?"

"I'd skedaddle."

They both laughed.

The waves of the lake lapped against the pilings of the small dock. From across the water, coming from Grace Cottage, they could hear their mother on the piano. Her voice sang out across the water.

When Ernest came by early in the day it was to chop some firewood. He was going to chop some wood and dig a trash hole in the back and then walk back to Horton Bay but his mother came out to the boat.

Ernie, she said, Ernie will you watch Carol and Les for awhile. I'm going across. That was how she phrased it whenever she crossed the lake to Grace Cottage.

But where's Sunny or Ursula?

She shook her head as she tied on her hat to shade her from the sun. They are off with their boys; heaven knows they are going to be the death of me yet.

But I have to get back.

It will be just a few hours, dear. And they are to be back by sunset.

166

Sunset? That's the whole day.

Surely you can do this small favor for your mother.

And that was that.

It was just last week that his father told him he was not helping out enough around the place. You are grown now and need to take more responsibilities. There are chores to do, and you need to be friendlier toward mother.

Ernest stood on the dock with his hands on his hips watching Grace motor across the lake. This is why, he thought to himself, this is why I don't stay here anymore.

Now it was hours later. The sun was down behind the trees. He and Carol sat on the wooden planks. Les was over under the trees. He had fallen asleep under the swing wrapped in the cool shade of the trees.

Ernest moved close to Carol and smelled her hair.

"What?" she asked.

"You smell good."

"Do I smell the best of everyone?"

"Yes."

She waited, thinking.

"I want to cut my hair short," she finally said.

"Why?"

"Like yours."

"Why?"

"So I can be like you."

"Why do you want to be like me?"

"Cause you're the best person I most want to be like," she said as if it were the most obvious thing in the world.

"But I'm a boy and you're a girl."

"But that doesn't matter. Miss Stevens says that what's important is how we are inside."

"That's true."

"So everything else is like putting on clothes. If I put on a dress then I'm a girl but if I put on trousers then I'm a boy."

"Well, it's not quite that easy."

"Besides, all the girls are getting a Bob haircut."

"Dad won't let that happen."

"But if we all do it then how can he stop us?"

"Well, you'd look good with short hair."

"Mom doesn't like being with us anymore. She wants to be over there."

Ernest was a little taken back with the statement.

167

"Don't think that," he said. "She takes you with her sometimes."

"Yeah but it's not the same. I like it when we are all here and when you and Dad are here too."

"Well Beefie, things change."

"Why do they have to change?"

As they sat on the dock three ducks in a row flew across the lake quacking. They watched as the ducks flew by low over the water.

"They're funny," she said.

Ernest looked straight up into the clear sky. It was getting dark. The sun was below the horizon now.

"I don't want things to change, I was born here you know."

Ernest rubbed his hand through her hair.

"I know that Beefie, I was here when it happened. You were my birthday present."

Summer of 1911. They were at Windemere and Grace was expecting and everyday Clarence silently asked her with an upturned eyebrow and Grace quietly shook her head. They were prepared. Clarence himself was going to deliver his own child. A nurse, Miss Daubey, was there. He had it planned and went over with each child what they were to do all that day when the time came. Then the day, they were all having breakfast the early morning of July 19. Suddenly Grace held her stomach and said 'Oh, dear.' The tone in her voice made everyone freeze. Everyone looked at everyone and everyone knew. Clarence stood up dabbing his mouth with his napkin and his unfinished breakfast still on the table. 'Okay kids, finish your breakfast quickly, kids, and then make yourselves scarce, quickly.' Ruth took the two little ones, Sunny and Ursula, by the hand and went to the Bacon's farm over the hill. Marcelline grabbed her prepared picnic lunch and a book and a sketch pad and made it to Murphy's Point. Ernest, not quite twelve, grabbed his fishing poles and was to spend the whole day fishing by himself.

It turned out to be a grand day. Toward the end of the day Ernest sat by the back gate for a long time wondering when it would be safe to go in. Since it was only two days before his own birthday he thought of her as his present.

"Why did Daddy leave? He wasn't here for my birthday and he won't be here for your birthday?"

Ernest looked out toward Grace Cottage. He could still hear the music coming over the darkening waters.

"He had to get back. He has a lot of work."

"No," she said sharply. "You two had an argument and then he left. I heard you so don't lie."

"Yes, well don't you worry about that."

His father was angry. He was digging the garbage ditch he had asked Ernest to do. 'I do hope you will think more of what others have done for you and try to be charitable and kind and gentle,' he said. He was wearing his big floppy hat with the sweat stains around the rim to shield him from the sun. 'I want you to represent all that is good and noble and brave and courteous in Manhood, and fear God and respect Women,' he said. He stood resting his arms on the shovel. 'And especially your own Mother,' he said. His moustache was wet with sweat from his upper lip. 'You are not in school and you do not have a job and you sponge off of your mother and expect for her to wait on you and you cannot even do simple chores, even when specially asked,' he said. There was a small breeze but it was still a hot summer afternoon and the ground was only partly shaded. 'I feel that it is best you move out and live separately so you will no longer be a burden upon your mother, she does not deserve your disrespect.' Ernest heard someone in the cottage moving around. It must he her. She put him up to it. 'Your mother and I both love and respect you but until you chose to take your appropriate place in the family then you leave us no choice but to ask you, maybe you and your friend Ted can get a job down Traverse City way and earn some money and cut down your expenses,' he said.

Ernest stared at his father sweating in the heat, wearing his big ridiculous sweat stained hat and bent over his shovel digging holes to bury the garbage and talking and talking while she was in the cool of the cottage with the blinds drawn shut waiting until evening so she could cross the lake to her personal little haven in the woods.

Ernest somehow did not recognize him. They had arguments in the past. Ernest remembered as a boy sitting in his large tent behind the cottage after his father yelled at him for something and Ernest watched his father through the slit in the canvas where the flap dropped down and he held up his shot gun and took aim at his father and had him in his sights and how easy it would be to just pull the trigger and then 'bang' he would not be angry anymore and it would all be done.

It was almost dark. Stars, one by one, began appearing in the sky.

"Mom said the two girls were to be home now," Ernest said.

Carol laughed. "Yeah, sure, are you going to bet on that one?"

Ernest smiled.

"I heard Mom tell Daddy that they were getting to be just like you. You are a bad influence."

"Is that so?"

"Yeah. Birthdays used to be fun. We'd go out and cut a tree and you and Daddy carried the tree back with me riding it like a horse and then we'd dance around it and then burn it and roast marshmallows in the fire with a stick. Now birthdays aren't that much."

"I know what you mean Sis."

They sat for a while in silence in the ever growing dark.

"Know what I like to do?" Carol finally asked.

"I don't know, what?"

"I like to go out to Murphy's point and wade out and gather clams and pile them on the sand near the water. And then I watch them slowly edge out into the water again."

Ernest laughed.

"Sounds like an exciting day."

"No, but you see, you can't really see them move. If you watch them then they don't move. But if you look away for awhile and come back then they have all moved a little toward the water. And then if you go away again and come back then they are all moved even farther toward the water. Finally they all go back into the water. But if you sit there and watch them they move so slow that you can't really see it."

"I'd rather go fishing," Ernest said as he stood up and stretched. "Because you see it and you feel it. Come on, let's go in and see what Les is doing."

"But you know, thinking about it, it's like us."

Ernest, standing over her, looked down at his sister.

"How is it like us?"

"It's like you said, we change. Things aren't like they were. But you don't see the change until one day suddenly you look and you realize everything is changed and you wonder what happened."

She splashed her feet one last time in the water and then stood up. He watched her in the darkness as she walked in front of him toward the house.

"You know Beefie, you're a little too smart for your britches."

170

3. Moron

When Ernest and Ted Brumback came into Windemere it was already nine o'clock at night. Grace peeked out from the kitchen when she heard them come in.

"Oh, boys, you are just in time. Have you eaten yet?"

"No," Ernest said as he came into the kitchen.

"I was just reheating the meatloaf for myself. The kids all ate earlier but now's the first chance that I have had to get some myself."

"Hello Mrs. Hemingway," Ted said as he too entered the kitchen.

"Please, sit down, sit down. It's just about ready."

As Grace stirred the mashed potatoes Ursula poked her head in from the hall.

"I thought I heard you," she said to Ernest and then giggled. Ernest put his finger to his mouth to shhh her. He then winked.

"What are you so giddy about young lady?" Grace asked.

"Nothing. It's just that Ernie's here."

"Well you go on, we have to eat supper."

She dished out the meatloaf and the mashed potatoes and handed Ted the bowl of hot, thick brown gravy.

"Looks wonderful," Ted said. Grace smiled at him.

Ernest had already started eating.

She sat for a moment watching the two of them.

"I'm so tired I didn't know if I should eat or go straight to bed."

Ernest noticed some pamphlets and several books on the table. They were on spiritualism. Ruth arrived yesterday; they must belong to her. Ernest did not like the influence that Ruth was having on his mother.

"Ernie, I do hope you can help me out a little more around here. Your father is gone and I am not feeling that well lately."

"Ruth is here now," Ernest said.

"She just arrived yesterday and besides there are a great many more difficult chores that she cannot do."

"Like what?" he said as he rapidly ate his food.

"What do you mean, like what? I need more chopped wood for the stove and the fireplace. The front needs raking and I will need some supplies brought over from Horton."

"What are the girls doing?"

"Ernie, they have their chores, these are things your father specifically asked for you to do. You need to help out a bit more, step into your father's shoes since he is not here."

"He was here, why did he leave?"

171

"He had to get back for work. We are a little short of money at the moment. You were in Toronto so you may not have noticed but I've been often ill this winter, my headaches are much worse and my arthritis has become quite painful, so I've taken on fewer music students this past year. So money is a little tight."

Ernest kept eating forkful after forkful.

"So then why did you build the cottage for yourself last year?"

"Last year was last year, this year things have changed. I was not planning on being ill. And besides, young man, I built it for my health if you must know."

There was a long pause as Ernest again looked over the pamphlets on the side of the table.

"Ruth is here now, thank God, and I hope she can be a calming influence on the girls."

Grace turned to Ted. "They are at that age where everything is boys boys boys and I cannot keep up with them. I only hope Ruth can instill a degree of control on them. Correct behavior of a girl at that age is so much more important than with a boy."

Ted nodded in agreement.

"It is more than I can manage on my own."

Ernest leafed through the pamphlets and magazines. He held up a copy of Atlantic Magazine.

"So Ernie, my dear, can you mend the pier? The planks are wobbly walking out to the boat. I'm afraid that I might fall."

Ernest continued reading the table of contents of the magazine. There was a frown on his face.

"Have you two looked into the possibility of work down toward Traverse Bay like your father mentioned?"

"Mother," Ernest finally said, dropping the magazine down onto the table. "Why do you read all this trash?"

"What is that, dear?"

"Really? Atlantic Magazine with articles by Dr. Frank Crane on Maurice Maeterlinck. Crane is a hack."

"Crane writes glorious helpful articles on keeping up your positive faith."

"Mother, all you read is moron literature. Crane is nothing but a superficial and commercialized version of Maeterlinck. At least Maeterlinck tries to present this oh so happy we are all so happy stuff into a story. So, are you The Blue Bird today?"

"Ernest, really; Maurice Maeterlinck won the Nobel Prize for Literature."

"Yes he did, but so what? That doesn't make him good."

"Ruth and I find both of them very pleasing."

"You two would with all of your spiritualistic mumbo jumbo. Crane is nothing more than a Moron's Maeterlinck."

Grace turned to Ted.

"I don't know why my own son is so mean to me."

Grace ate her meal in silence.

Ted ate without looking up.

Ernest was done eating and waiting for Ted. He tapped his fingers on the side of the table.

"Look," he said. "We are staying here tonight back in the tent. Maybe tomorrow we can do some chores."

Grace waited a moment before she replied.

"That would be very nice."

4. Grace

There was a heavy banging on the door. Grace woke up trying to understand what was going on. She had been sound asleep. The banging came again. Grace sat up. It was pitch black in the bedroom. She reached over and fumbled for the lantern. She slid the glass up and it screeched against the metal prongs. She reached over and felt for the box of matches, lit one, and the hissing match illuminated the room. She held the match against the wick until it flared. She looked around the room. She was alone. When she stood up with the lantern in her hand the door opened. It was Ruth in her nightgown, her hair combed out long against her shoulders.

"What is it?" Grace asked as she reached for her robe.

"There's someone at the door."

"What time is it?"

"It's just after three in the morning."

"For goodness sake," Grace mumbled under her breath as she left her room for the living room. A few small embers in the fireplace glowed. She held the lantern in her left hand as she put her right hand on the door.

"Who is it?" She shouted out.

"This is Mrs. Loomis. Open the door."

Grace and Ruth looked at each other then Grace opened the door. Mrs. Abigail Loomis and her older daughter Mary stood at the door. They were fully dressed and holding a lantern up high. The lantern hissed as they stood in the doorway.

"Where is my daughter Elizabeth and her friend Jean?" Mrs. Loomis demanded.

Grace stood for a moment as if collecting her thoughts. She was still not fully awake.

"How should I know?"

"They are not here?"

"No, they are not."

"I have reason to believe that they have gone off with your daughters. Are Ursula and Sunny here?"

"They are in their rooms sleeping."

"Then wake them," she demanded as she swept past Grace and entered the living room. "And where is your son?"

"See here," Grace said. "You do not barge into my house in the middle of the night. You stay right here and I will fetch them."

The two women stood close staring into each others eyes. A moment

174

passed but then Mrs. Loomis nodded.

Grace went into the back bedrooms. Ruth followed close behind. Grace held the lantern high as she entered the back bedroom where Ursula and Sunny slept. The two beds were empty; the sheets were still tucked in.

"Muv," Ruth whispered.

"Where are they?"

"Muv, they are gone."

"Gone? What do you mean?"

"I am so sorry I did not tell you but they swore me to secrecy," she said, still whispering.

"So tell me now."

"They and the Loomis girls went for a midnight picnic. They thought they would be back before you found out."

"Who is in this?"

"Ursula and Sunny, and Bob and Elizabeth Loomis, and their friends Beverly Hugle and Jean Reynolds, they all went."

"Where?"

"They would not tell me for fear I would tell you. I swear to you it is nothing more than a simple childhood prank."

Grace stood in the room, lantern raised, breathing deeply.

"I will deal with your betrayal later. Ruth, the Loomis girls are but thirteen. Out in the middle of the night?"

"But Ernest and Ted went with them. They are the chaperones."

Grace rolled her eyes. So that was it. Ernest was behind all of this. Grace instantly walked down the hall to the back door and walked out to the tent in the back where Ernest and Ted slept. She pulled back the canvas flap. The tent was empty.

Grace went back into the house and into the living room. Mrs. Loomis was waiting with glaring eyes.

"Well, are they here or not?"

Grace tried to speak very calmly.

"Both Ursula and Sunny are absent. It seems that they and your daughter are on a midnight picnic."

"And whose nefarious plot was that?"

"I am sure there is a perfectly reasonable explanation and we will wait and see what that is when they come back."

"Your son is involved in this isn't he?"

"We will wait and see when they return."

"All he does is walk around in his army boots and uniform as if he was trying to impress everyone, especially the young girls. Who is he trying to fool?"

Grace stretched herself out to her full height. She took the time to compose herself.

"My son was wounded in the war in his legs and suffered two hundred and twenty seven shell fragments and the high boots he wears help with the pain he suffers when he walks. Pain, Mrs. Loomis, is why he wears what he wears."

There was a moment of silence between them.

"And furthermore what he wears should be no concern of yours."

"Grace, my daughter's friend Jean Reynolds is staying with us; she is only thirteen for heaven sake. Thirteen. And it seems she has a crush on your twenty year old son. And now they are out together in the middle of the night only God knows where and to what purpose."

"Mrs. Loomis I suggest that you may want to hold your tongue. What thirteen year old girl does not have a crush on some boy somewhere? And I assure you, Mrs. Loomis, that whatever the involvement of my son in this affair his intentions are most honorable."

"I have half a mind to pack up and go back to Oak Park. It is no longer safe to be here with young girls with those two grown men loafing around."

"Like I just said, you have my assurances that the intentions of both my son and his friend, and my friend, Ted Brumbach are in all manner honorable."

Mrs. Loomis laughed.

"Ah, your assurance to me of propriety what with her here and your husband not, surely you are aware of the rumors?"

Grace stood for a long time and did not reply. She stared, she stared intensely. She stared steady into the eyes of Mrs. Loomis without blinking. Finally Mrs. Loomis looked away.

Grace then spoke.

"Ruth."

"Yes, Grace," Ruth said, standing behind her.

"Go into my husband's room and get his shotgun. I think it is behind the dresser."

Ruth did not move.

"What?" she asked.

"You heard me. It may be loaded so be careful. Please fetch it right now."

Ruth left the room.

"Now, Mrs. Loomis, you barge into my home in the middle of the night and insult my son, my friend, my family, myself. You are to leave my home immediately."

"Not without my daughter."

"I am sure your daughter will come home when she is good and ready and you can deal with her then. But right now you are to leave my home immediately."

Ruth returned with the shot gun. She held it up by the barrel. Grace placed the lantern down on the table and picked up the shotgun. She opened the breech. There was a shell in each barrel. Everyone saw there was a shell in each barrel. She snapped the gun closed and held it in her hands.

"Ruth," she said.

"Yes."

"It is the middle of the night and there are intruders who have broken into my home. I am going to dispatch them. Do you understand?"

"Yes," Ruth responded feebly.

"Grace," said Mrs. Loomis, "you are out of your mind."

"And you are trespassing. I tell you one last time. Leave my home immediately."

"Grace, this is ridiculous."

"It was the middle of the night, it was dark, there were intruders, they broke in, I fired, how did I know who they were?"

Mrs. Loomis turned to her daughter and waved her toward the door. The two of them left.

Grace locked the door behind them. She put the shotgun down on the floor. She looked over at Ruth.

"Oh Muv, are you alright?"

Grace nodded and took a deep breath.

"No one insults my family, no one."

5. Overdrawn

Ernest woke up. A shaft of sunlight was in his face. He had to squint as he sat up in his cot. He looked over at Ted who was still asleep. They were in the tent behind Windemere. Ernest sat for a moment. He looked out the open flap of the tent. The sun was up and bright.

He thought about last night. It was the midnight picnic on Ryan's Point. At first he did not want to go but Ursula pleaded with him so he went. It was fun. They built a bonfire in the sand on the shore, cooked some food, Ted played his mandolin, they all sang what songs they knew. There was Ursula and Sunny, their friends Bob and Elizabeth Loomis, their friends Beverly Hugle and Jean Reynolds. At one point Jean got the giggles and could not stop for a long time. Everyone was giggling by the time she stopped.

Ernest pulled on his shoes.

They stayed until after three o'clock in the morning. The others went home. He and Ted rowed Ursula and Sunny back to Windemere. When they paddled the boat along the shore toward home Ernest could see that the lights were on in Windemere.

"We're in trouble now," he said to the others as they approached. They were found out. Someone with a lantern stood on the dock. As they neared he could make out that it was Grace.

"It's Mom," Sunny said, confirming their worse fears.

When Ernest came up to the dock he threw out the rope and tied it around the piling. The two girls jumped out.

"You two get to your rooms right now," Grace said in a low strong voice. She turned her attention to Ernest still sitting in the boat. "I will deal with you later," she said. She turned and walked away. Ernest and Ted unloaded the boat and went back behind the cottage and into the tent. They were both tired and they would handle it in the morning.

Ernest stood up and left the tent. He went in through the back door to the kitchen. Ruth was at the sink washing some dishes. She did not say anything when Ernest came in. She just dried off her hands on a towel and walked past him into the hallway. Ernest went over and poured himself a cup of coffee from the pot on the stove. It was lukewarm.

Soon Grace came into the kitchen. She stood silent for a moment. Ernest looked over at her.

"Good morning," he said.

"Mrs. Loomis came by and woke me up in the middle of the night demanding where her thirteen year old daughter and friend were. She

178

wanted to know what two grown men were doing with two thirteen year old girls."

"Aw come on, it wasn't anything. There were five of them. We had a bonfire and cooked sausages and had hot chocolate and marshmallows, and Ted played his mandolin and we all sang songs. It was all innocent fun."

"Staying out all night is innocent fun?"

"Nothing bad happened. It was all just a lark."

Grace controlled her anger.

"Ernest, I realize that your intentions and behavior toward the young girls were honorable but son you have to understand what other people will think. It is your reputation that you are putting at risk here."

Ernest sipped his coffee. There were two slices of cooked bacon on a plate next to the stove. He picked up one and began eating it.

"Ernest, Clarence and I have been very patient with you, because of your recent experiences, but the time has come for you to take responsibility for your actions, and to take control of your place within the community. Your father has already written to you and spoke to you that if you have postponed going to college for now that perhaps it is time for you to seek employment elsewhere and move out on your own, and to make your own way in the world."

Ernest sipped his coffee again and took another bite of the bacon.

Grace pulled a folded piece of paper from her skirt pocket. "Please read this when you are in the correct frame of mind to understand its intent."

She handed Ernest the paper and then walked out into the living room.

Ernest opened up the paper. It was letter addressed to 'My Dear Son Ernest' in her handwriting. He started to read it but skipped around.

'For three years, since you decided, at the age of eighteen years, that you did not need any further advise or guidance from your parents, I have tried to keep silence and let you work out your own salvation. . . A mother's love seems to me like a bank. Each child that is born to her, enters the world with a large and prosperous bank account. . . he draws and draws—physical labor and pain—loss of sleep—watching and soothing, waiting upon, bathing, dressing, feeding, amusing. . . the account needs deposits, . . . flowers, fruits, candy, or something pretty to wear, brought home to Mother, with a kiss and a squeeze. . . to praise her cooking, back up her little schemes; a real interest in hearing her sing, or play the piano. . . celebration of her birthday and Mother's day. . . these are merely a few of the deposits which keep the account in good standing. . . unless you, my son, Ernest, come to yourself, cease your lazy loafing, and pleasure seeking—borrowing with no thought of returning. . . there is nothing before you but bankruptcy: You have over drawn.'

Ernest looked up and around the kitchen. He could hear little Carol and Les shouting outside as they ran toward the lake. He read the last of the letter.

'Do not come back until your tongue has learned not to insult and shame your mother.'

Ernest walked into the living room. Grace stood by the opened front door staring out. When he came in she turned toward him.

"What does all this mean: I'm overdrawn?"

"I want you and Ted to leave. You have refused to do your chores, you have refused to help, you refuse to take responsibility, all I get from you is more and more heartache. I want you to pack up your things and leave this morning. I do not wish to see you for the rest of the summer."

"You're kicking me out?"

"And do not return until you have changed your ways. When you show respect for me and your father then we will welcome you back with open arms but until that day I no longer wish to have you in this house."

"You're kicking me out."

The two of them stood and did not speak. Through the open door they could hear the children splashing in the water. They could hear the buzz of the flies on the porch.

Ernest turned and walked out.

Chapter Nine

"They will take you to Milano by train. There is a brand new American hospital there. Matter of fact it is so new I don't think it's even open yet."

"It will be nice to have a change," Ernest said.

Captain James Gamble sat on the wooden chair he had pulled up next to the bed. He was Ernest's commanding officer.

"I hate like hell to lose you, Ernie, but this new hospital should be tip top. They'll have you patched up in no time."

"Sounds good, sir."

"I can't wait until you're back at the front."

"Yes sir."

James walked over to the open window and looked down into the courtyard. He looked at the grass and the torn up dirt. There was a stack of coffins off to one side. Some looked as if they had been dug up.

"We lost McKay, you know."

"I know sir."

"We were good friends, fellow painters as a matter of fact. He painted small portraits."

There was a pause before he spoke again.

"I was so relieved when I heard you were going to be all right."

"So was I," Ernest replied.

James looked over at Ernest and chuckled.

"You know, you're alright kid."

The orderly came by with a bed pan.

"I'll come and see you in Milano. I think we could be friends."

"I would like that sir."

1. Africa

"So Ernie, how was Toronto?"

It was Howell Jenkins who asked. The four of them were all sitting around the campfire under the canopy of trees. They spent the day fishing. They had dinner, the catch of the day, (Ernest cooked the trout rolled in cornmeal fried in Crisco and basted with bacon slices) and were sitting around the fire to keep warm. A bottle of wine was circulating. A chill in the forest had risen as the sun went down.

"It was great. It was a peach of a job."

"So the family was gone on vacation except for the son?"

"Yeah, I had to take care of him. We didn't get along that well because we are so different it's like night and day."

"In what way?"

It was Ted Brumbach who answered.

"Little Ralph had a little bit too much five fingered fun with his old mother to be healthy."

Howell laughed.

"And he introduced our Wemedge to Havelock on sex and transgender," Brumbach said.

"What the hell is that?" Jack Pentecost asked.

"You don't want to know, dear boy," Brumbach replied.

"Yeah but it did open my eyes a bit," Ernest said. "I've been realizing lately that there is a lot more to life than what Oak Park has to offer."

"Well, I wouldn't tell your mother about that, and the big question is how much of that 'more to life' do you even want to know?"

"All of it," said Jack as he took a gulp of wine and wiped his mouth with his shirt sleeve.

They all laughed.

Ernest glanced around the camp. The car and trailer they rented for the trip was parked behind them. Each of their canvas tents were set up in a semi-circle on the opposite side of the fire.

"Actually the whole Connable family is like an unfolding Henry James novel. Ralph the father is a total rich successful businessman consumed by his business affairs and associates; his wife Harriet is a graceful attractive middle aged woman wanting more from her life which she lives through her attractive idealistic daughter Dorothy, Red Cross volunteer, spends some time in France and Germany helping the wounded during the war; and finally locked away in his room with his miserable self hatred is their crippled son."

"And in their extensive liquor cabinet in the basement sits the young frustrated writer sipping away his dreams," adds Brumback.

"Why don't you write the thing then," said Jenkins.

Ernest thought for a moment.

"I'm not at Henry James's level yet. I don't have that depth of insight."

Jenkins shook his head. "How do you know unless you try?"

"Even though they were paying me well and I had a lot of free time it was a trap. I couldn't write; it was too soft. You know, in Italy there was this guy, James Gamble, Ted, you remember him, he wanted me to pal around with him, all expenses paid. I considered it too because, just think, all the time in the world to see the world and all the time in the world to write."

"Sounds good, so what happened?" Jack asked.

"Well, actually Agnes talked me out of it. She said it was a trap and I would become just a bum living off the kindness of others. They will suck you dry, she said; They will just keep you for themselves, she said. In the long run I think that may be why she said that she'd marry me if I came back home. It was all a plot to save me."

"Do you believe that?"

"Well, now that I've had a taste of it I must say that she was right."

Jenkins threw some more branches onto the fire. "Well what about the newspaper work, that's good isn't it, and at least you're writing."

"Yeah that's true but you become kind of a newspaper hack, you can't write the real stuff. The money is good but it sucks you dry. Is that the fate of everyone? You spend so much of your time making money to live day to day that there is nothing left over?"

"Yes, that's pretty much it," Jenkins said.

Jack, taking another long drink from the wine bottle, then said: "Not you, me; that's why I'm going to ship out to the Orient. Are you coming with me?"

Ernest shook his head.

"Oh how I want to Jack but I can't get my mother to put up the Seeds for the trip. Everything in this world seems to reduce itself to money."

"Well," Jack went on, "the solution to escape all this is simple: lead a life of adventure without consequences. It's worrying about the consequence that stalls any action."

"Here here," Brumbach said as he reached over and took the bottle of wine from Jack and took a drink himself.

"Ernie, speaking of living life without consequences, I hear you got kicked out?"

184

"Yeah, the Hemingstein is now homeless, ejected from the bosom of his family."

"Well that could be tough."

Ernest shook his head no.

"It was time to end it. After I came home from the war I was finished here. It's time to end it and move on. Everything comes to an end sooner or later; you just have to know when it is."

"How do you know that?"

"You just know it. Everything has an end. Going beyond the end is a waste. You just have to know when it is."

"So what are you going to do?"

"Well," Ernest started but then hesitated before he continued. "The Kansas City Star calls for the Hemingstein, I can go back there, they loved me. Maybe continue working for the Toronto Star. Maybe travel, but mostly I want to write. I don't ever want anything coming between me and writing again."

"So," Jenkins asked, "what are you writing these days?"

"I'm preparing. I'm trying to write about real people I know."

"You mean biography?"

"No, the fiction of a thing can be truer than the reality of the thing. It's like the saying you can't see the forest because of the trees. If you write too close then you are trying to get it as it happened and spend all your time in the trees trying to make them exactly right, like a biography. But if you fictionalize it then it is as true as it really is and can be seen as a whole forest. It doesn't matter that each particular tree is just like it happened. You write how it should have happened and that makes it truer."

"So what is it, a novel about Oak Park?"

"Oh I could write stories about Oak Park that will make your head spin if I wanted to."

"Why don't you?"

"I'd never be able to show my face there again. The best is to wait until they are all dead, then you can write it."

Brumbach stood up and stretched his arms out.

"Of course we will all be dead by then too," he said.

Brumbach walked over to his tent.

"Forget shipping to the Orient," Jack said sitting back against a log.

"How about us all going to Africa, you know, like Teddy Roosevelt. We can hunt wild game, what do you say? Wemedge, do you think you'll ever hunt in Africa?"

From his tent Brumbach called out. "Jack, I think you are too far

185

gone. You had just one sip too many of the grape juice."

But Ernest grew quiet. He remembered as a small boy standing in the natural history museum in Chicago. He and Marc and his father were standing at the exhibits. There were displays of stuffed animals as if they were in their natural habitat. They stood looking at several Zebras eating the grass and off to one side a lion stood watching. The painted background was of the Serengeti plains.

It was quiet in the museum and the lights were dimmed so the displays stood out. Several people were over looking at the brown bears catching fish but Ernest turned his gaze back to the Serengeti. He followed as his father walked over to another display. His father had his hands clasped together behind his back as he walked. In the display a tall giraffe ate some leaves from a tree and two elephants stood with intertwined trunks.

'Dad,' young Ernest whispered so not to disturb the silence or frighten away the animals.

His father bends down close, 'What was that son?' and Ernest feels his father's hand on his shoulder.

Ernest stares up at the two elephants and above them the head of the giraffe.

'They sure are big,' he whispers.

He hears his father chuckle. 'Yes they are, son; they certainly are.'

His father shot small animals and birds and had them stuffed and put into small glass cases. They were small displays like at the museum. They were in his office and in the waiting room outside his office. Ernest climbed up on the chairs and sofa in order to look in at them whenever he was in the room.

But then they disappeared. Some were burned when Mom moved into the new house. Others his father gave to the school and library. It was raining the day he gave them to the school. His father looked different. It was raining that day and his father was wet, his hair was wet and he was wet and in disarray. He did not comb his hair when it got wet and in disarray, it was not in control. His father looked different that day for the first time.

Ted Brumbach came back and sat down by the fire. He had his mandolin.

"Heh, Wemedge, read us a little from that book of fairy tales by Lord Dunsany that you're reading."

Brumbach strummed his mandolin a few times and then started to play. The others were quiet. The flames of the fire popped.

Ernest remembered the jars of snakes and lizards preserved in alcohol that his father had in his rooms. They sat next to the glass cases of birds and animals. They popped when his mother threw them into the fire, they popped loud and the fire flamed from the alcohol.

As a boy he sat in his father's waiting room. The sun streamed in through the window in the late afternoon and across the wooden floor. He sat on the smooth wooden floor between the throw rugs. He felt the grain of the wood and he felt the twirl of the woven rugs. It was silent. He felt the grain of the wood and looked up at the animals in the glass cases. A large white owl was by the door. They were silent. When a shaft of sunlight moved across him he felt the warmth on his skin. He looked at the shadow he made across the floor. It was silent.

He remembered his mother told him once: listen to the silence of things, she said. He did not know why she said it or what brought on her saying it but she said it once and it confused him. Why, he asked. Because that is the level where God thinks, she said.

Ernest heard the wind pick up and he listened as it passed through the trees over his head. The night sky sparkled. The moon shined bright and clear. There is something in that, he thought; there is something there, he thought. If I can capture that then life itself would be the trees and his one true sentence would be the forest.

2. Katy II

"Look, look," Katy said pointing out the window. She turned as what she was pointing at passed by. "Wait, wait. Turn around."

"Turn around?" Bill asked. He slowed the car down.

"Yes, Bird, turn around, back to the church. I want to go in the church."

"What?" Ernest asked.

"The Church."

"What for?" Bill asked.

Katy turned and leaned in toward her brother.

"I want to light a candle, for mother."

Bill thought about it and then nodded.

The three of them were sitting in the front seat of the car. It was raining a little bit. The streets were beginning to get wet. Bill, looking up and down the street, turned the car into the other lane and drove back. He turned on the windshield wipers as he pulled into the parking lot. Ernest opened the door and got out. Katy, sitting in the center, slid out and stood next to him. The sprinkle of rain tapped their face.

Katy led the way. Ernest and Bill followed. They walked up the stone steps and into the Church. Katy crossed herself with the holy water in a basin by the door and then kissed her fingers, hands closed together. She slowly walked down a side aisle. There were several people kneeling in the pews. Ernest tried to walk as quiet as he could. There was wet gravel on the bottoms of his shoes and it crunched with each step. Katy walked down the aisle and into a side chapel. There was a large flat tray lined with rows and rows of burning candles in small glass jars.

She stopped at the entrance to the side chapel and again brought her two hands up together touching her lips with her forefingers. She stood silent for a moment staring at the candles. She glanced over at Ernest. He could see the sparkle of the lights dancing in her eyes. She did not smile.

Ernest watched as Katy approached the tray of candles. She picked up an unlit candle and then a puck and held it in the flame of another candle. The puck flared and she lit her own candle with the flame. She blew out the puck and placed it back onto the tray. She held the candle in both her hands for a moment and closed her eyes.

In the quiet of the room Ernest could hear the small hissing and crackle of some of the candles. There were footsteps on the cement floor at the other end of the Church. Someone stood up in the pews. There was a tiny bell far off. There was the soft sound of cars on the street outside their tires getting wet from the rain.

Katy opened her eyes, kissed the glass jar in her hands and placed it on the tray with all of the others. Ernest glanced toward Bill, who stood off to the side, and then stepped up to the tray of lights. He picked up a candle, the puck, and then lit the candle. He placed it down onto the tray. He and Katy stood beside each other without looking at each other for several moments.

Then Katy turned and walked out. They walked in the rain to the car. Once they were back on the road again Katy, sitting in the center of the front seat, turned to her brother and said: "I prayed for her." Bill nodded and grunted.

As they drove on the rain increased. They talked. They talked about a lot of things. She told Ernest about when her mother died. Bill was silent when she talked about their mother. Katy was cold and nestled up against Ernest. I didn't know you were religious, Ernest said. Yeah, well, she said, shrugging her shoulders. She talked about their father. He was a professor of mathematics and philosophy. He was writing what he hoped would be the final say about the life of Christ.

"To him the world is nice and neat," she said with a smile on her face.

"And to you," Ernest asked. He looked at her with her hair falling into her face. Her tangled hair was damp and frosted with small droplets of rain.

"Not so much, maybe," she said. "And so why did you light a candle?" she asked.

Ernest looked off. "In the war I knew this Priest. He was a very nice man and I liked him a lot. On the night I was blown up he was there and he blessed me."

Ernest stopped for a moment. Katy watched him. She had never seen this side of him. Finally he turned and looked at her and smiled.

"It was a rather intense moment."

She nodded.

"Actually," he then said, "I lit a candle and prayed for all the things I want and will never get. That's why it took so long."

"Why do you have to ruin everything?"

"What? Actually I went with Red once and she lit a candle."

"Marjorie Bump?"

"Yeah. Why, are you jealous that you weren't the first?"

Katy rolled her eyes.

"Dream on Wemedge."

As the day wore on the rain increased. The windshield wipers flapped back and forth. They talked but it diminished. She leaned in against Ernest and buried her head against his chest. He had his arm around her shoulder. She gradually fell asleep.

Ernest watched as the wet trees and fields passed by. She stirred and he looked down at her. But she was asleep: dreamland. He watched her for a long time.

I could love this woman, he thought.

She felt warm against him. He watched the slapping back and forth of the windshield wipers as Bill drove on towards home. Outside the rain rained; but inside he held her in his arms.

I could love this woman, Ernest thought: forever.

3. Rooftop

Clarence walked up into the orchard. He could see Ernest up ahead. Ernest was picking apples and putting them into bushels on the ground as Warren, Mrs. Charles's hired worker, was loading them onto the wagon. Bill Smith, with bandages wrapped around his ankle, sat on the bed of the wagon. It was Bill who saw him first.

"Hello Mr. Hemingway," he shouted out as Clarence approached.

Clarence waved as Ernest stopped to watch him approach.

"Hello Bill, what happened to you?"

"Aw nothing really, I just twisted my ankle a little."

"Want me to take a look?"

"That's okay. Doc said to stay off it and it'll be fine in a day or two. Great luck that it happened right when we needed to harvest."

Clarence smiled.

"Sure you didn't plan it that way?"

"I'll never tell."

Clarence looked over at Ernest. He nodded.

"Hello son."

"Hello Dad. When did you get in?"

"I got here just yesterday; came to close down Windemere for the winter."

"Good," Ernest said.

Clarence nodded.

"I thought that perhaps you'd like to help me this time."

Ernest stood silent for a moment. He then looked over at Bill, then back at his father.

"Today?" he asked.

"Yes, I was going to leave by the six o'clock ferry."

"But I have to finish here, and Bill can't work and Mrs. Charles needed it done today."

Bill started to say something but Clarence cut him off.

"Well that will be fine, I can see I interrupted. You do have to finish what you've started here, I can see that."

"Maybe if I finish here in time," Ernest said as he shrugged his shoulders.

"Sure, if you can come on by. It's been a while since I've seen you. I was wondering what are your plans?"

"Well, I'm staying here. And then Bill's brother Kenley has a place in Chicago and he's looking for a roommate so I thought I'd go there."

"Well that sounds good, get a job in Chicago. Your brother works in advertising, is that right?"

"Yes he does," Bill answered.

"Well, son, that sounds promising. You know I was looking into the medical program at the University of Wisconsin for you. I know that we've discussed before you and your old Scout chum Dad sharing a practice. We can discuss it, perhaps."

Ernest nodded but did not reply.

"Well then, I suppose I should be off," Clarence said.

He walked back through the town of Horton Bay and then through the woods to Walloon Lake. He rowed his boat across to the pier at Windemere. Clarence kept the piles of wood by the boat house all summer. Each fall he took the same sheets of wood and boarded up the windows. Each window had to be boarded. He held up a board and nailed it into place, again and again, until a window was sealed. Then he went on to the next window. One after one.

The day progressed. He tried to not think. He tried to just work. Just get the job done. There was satisfaction in just getting the thing done.

After he boarded up all the windows and the back door he once again carefully walked through the house to see if anything important was left behind. In the bedroom he opened the top chest of drawer.

He smiled.

Once when Ernest was very young the family carefully packed up their things, crated up all the equipment they brought up for the summer, and loaded it onto the ferry that would take them to Walloon Village. From there they would unload everything and load it up again onto the train. It in turn would take them up to Petoskey where again they unloaded their baggage and awaited a steamship where they would reload all of their baggage for the trip to Chicago. Then a trolley ride home to Oak Park.

That day they were all the way at the Petoskey steamship dock awaiting the boat. Little Ernest turned to his father and said that his crow was going to be even safer now. What do you mean? Ernest had befriended a crow whom he fed bread crumbs. But one morning just before they left he found the crow dead on the ground. His father helped dig a hole and he placed the crow in the hole wrapped in a hand cloth. He will be safe now, Clarence told him.

What do you mean he will be safer now? Clarence asked. Ernest explained that as his father was boarding up the house Ernest had dug up the crow and took him inside and wrapped him up and put him in the top drawer of the chest in his room. He will be safer in the house all winter than buried outside in the cold.

Clarence grabbed the first train back to Walloon Lake and, watching the time, hired the first cab he could and paid the fare all the way to Windemere. He had to ply open the front door and go into the bedroom. Sure enough, there was the dead crow neatly wrapped in the drawer for his winter sleep. Clarence barely made it back to the Petoskey Pier in time to board the steamship as one of the last passengers on board.

Clarence closed the drawer. There was no crow there now. He walked around the house but then finally walked outside. He boarded up the front door. The sound of his hammer echoed through the trees. He walked to the boat house and came back with the ladder. There was one thing left to do. He had to seal the chimney so squirrels and chipmunks would not come down into the house.

He was a little afraid each time he climbed up onto the roof. It was not so much a fear of heights but rather a fear of falling off. He crawled his way to the chimney and wrapped a tarp over it and secured it with rope. When he was done he sat back on the top ridge of the sloping roof.

He let Ernest tie the chimney one year when Ernest was young enough to be still interested in doing chores around the cottage. Clarence let him go up and then waited for a few minutes. Then Clarence climbed up the ladder.

"Did you do okay?" he asked.

"Yes, look," Ernest proudly said.

Clarence crawled up and inspected his work.

"That's very good son," he said as he ran his fingers through Ernest's hair. "Very good."

They sat together on the roof looking out across the water. You could see much further up the lake from the roof. It was a warm day. The roof was dappled in sunlight and shade from the trees. The sun and shade floated back and forth as the breeze came in off of the lake.

They used to go hunting more. They used to go fishing together more. There seemed to be less time. Other things got in the way. He worked more and spent less time up here in the woods. There just seemed to be less time for everything.

Clarence looked over towards the chimney. He was alone on the roof. The Ernest of years ago who sat here with him was now a ghost. Gone.

The past is lost and consumed by the present. The now becomes the only thing. Then simply surviving the now becomes all encompassing. How is that a way to live?

There was a sailboat far out on the lake. A thin trail of smoke rose from Ryan's point and whirled away into the day.

"Have I been a good father?"

He spoke the words even though he was the only one there to hear.

"Have I shown my children the path of truth and goodness?"

Marc was away at school and her new job. Now Ernest was gone. Ursula and Sunny were lost into their world of boys. Soon they too would leave.

It did not seem to be the same between him and Grace. There was Ruth but it was much more than that, it was much larger than that. There were days that he did not want to get up out of bed in the morning. He wanted to just lay there and lay there and lay there and listen to all the sounds of the day come and pass over him, distant and untouched.

"Have I been a good husband?"

He was being overwhelmed by the thoughts as he watched the clouds cross the sky.

Where did I go wrong, what have I done wrong. I used to love life so. Where did we go astray?

He tapped the tile of the roof with his finger again and again.

There is nothing but darkness wherever I look.

He tried but he could not stop it. He could not. Pain swelled up through his chest and eyes and sitting alone on the roof in the floating dappled sun and shade, Clarence cried.

4. Party

Bill parked his car on the street in downtown Chicago. It was just getting dark and the street lamps were turning on. He and Ernest pulled their duffel bags out of the car. Ernest wore his Italian black cape with the clasp at the neck. Bill had driven down from Horton Bay with Ernest, Katy and Mrs. Charles. They dropped Katy off here, at Ken's apartment, and then drove on to the railroad station to drop off Mrs. Charles for her trip back to St Louis. Now he and Ernest came back to Ken's apartment.

On their way up the elevator Ernest remembered what Katy said on the drive down.

"Now Wemedge, when we get there I want you to be nice to my friend."

"What friend is that?"

"I've invited an old friend of mine from school up for a few weeks. Hadley Richardson. She's staying with Ken."

"Aren't I always nice to your friends?"

"Well, see, she's had a hard few years. Her mother just died a month or two ago after a long illness. So I told her to come up and get away from it all."

"Sure."

"No, I mean it," Katy said with intensity in her voice.

A party was already in progress when Bill and Ernest came in. There were two bottles of wine open on the table and glasses all around. There was Ken and his wife Doodles; there was Donald Wright and Bobby Rouse; there was Bill Horne; there was Katy and then next to her sat a woman in a blue dress and red hair. Everyone was talking and laughing at something. There was music coming from records on the Victrola in the dark wooden cabinet.

Ernest put his duffel bag down by the door and came into the room.

From her overstuffed chair Doodles, holding her glass of wine in one hand, watched as Ernest entered the room.

"Hello there Hemingstein," she said in a long slow drawl as she fluttered her eyes.

"Hello there Doodle dear," he replied imitating her drawl.

He started to unbuckle the clasp on his cape but then stopped. He looked at the woman sitting next to Katy. Katy was looking at him and smiling.

"Wemedge," Katy called out to him, "you've made it."

Ken stood up and reached over to shake his hand.

"Heh good buddy, welcome to my simple little castle."

Ernest shook his hand and nodded but then looked back at the woman sitting next to Katy.

"Wemedge, this is my friend Hadley Richardson."

Hadley smiled up at the young man standing before her in his long black cape. He had flushed red cheeks and brown eyes and a wide dimpled smile that lit up his face.

"Hello," she said.

"Hello."

Her long hair was loosely coiled at the back of her head. It was a shiny golden red. From the light of the lamp her hair seemed to sparkle. Her rounded freckled face wore a small smile as naturally as a cloud across the sky.

Ken hands Ernest a glass of wine.

"So Nesto, how's the writing game going? Have you published anything yet?"

"No," Ernest said as he took a sip from his glass. "As of yet the score is zero."

Holding his wine glass in one hand he unbuckles his cape with the other and swirls it off like a matador.

"Well, you can wallpaper your room with your rejection slips."

Doodles, sitting back in her chair with her glass of wine in her hand, giggled.

"Bill tells me that your stuff reads like Ring Lardner, is that true? Are you stealing from Ring Lardner?"

"Steal?" Ernest asked. "You don't steal, you borrow and then perfect. Haven't you heard that imitation is the best form of flattery? Besides, that's how you grow as a writer."

"You steal?" she asked.

"No, dear, you imitate until you're better than they are and then you move on."

"And so that's how you climb the ladder, dear Hem? Today it's Lardner and then tomorrow it's, who, Sherwood Anderson?"

"And then Shakespeare," added Bill Smith as he came over to the sofa to sit down.

"That ladder is pretty far up there," said Bill Horne as he adjusted his horn rimmed glasses.

"I'm not afraid of heights," Ernest said as he smiled his wide smile. He noticed that Hadley was following the conversation.

"Yes, well," said Ken as he sat back down on the sofa. "Maybe not this month but then, again, who knows?"

"You were the first one to call him genius," Bill said. "Now look at the Frankenstein you've created."

"It is true that I was a first in recognizing his ability, but genius? You are putting words into my mouth dear brother."

"Perhaps maybe someday," Ernest said.

"Doodles," Ken called out as he opened his arms to the whole room, "call in the carpenters to raise high the roof beams for we need to widen the door frames for Nesto's ego to pass through."

Ernest tipped Ken with his glass of wine.

"Jealousy my friend is a rather unattractive characteristic in an otherwise handsome person."

As the evening went on Ken and Don Wright spent most of the time sitting and chatting with Hadley. She laughed at Ken's remarks and he, seeing her response, tried to be even more clever.

Hadley asked about the apartment. They were renting it from Dorothy Keeley, grand patron of the arts, who was traveling in Europe for the winter. I have extra rooms so friends can stay over. It creates a swirl of motion that I enjoy. But she's coming home in January so we have to be out by then.

"Oh, that's a shame," Hadley replied.

Ernest walked around behind Bill Horne and put his chin down on Bill's shoulder and whispered into his ear.

"Mr. Horne, cast your gaze toward the red headed girl over yon. That is the woman I am going to marry."

"Ernie, you've only just met her."

"It does not matter my friend. She has trapped my soul. Mark my words."

They watched as Hadley sat very poised.

Hadley asked Doodles how she and Ken met.

"In the sanatorium," Doodles said.

Hadley leaned forward. "What was that?"

Doodles giggled.

"It's true. We were both in the Trudeau Sanatorium for tuberculosis and we found each other between treatments. We held hands walking across the grass between the Cure Cottages; yes it was ever so romantic."

"I can see that," Hadley said as Doodles giggled again as she drank her wine.

Ken poured Hadley another glass of wine.

"Katy tells me that you play the piano?"

"Yes I do."

"Well, perhaps later. Doodles plays, as a matter of fact she wants to be a concert pianist. She has an amazing talent to sight read any piece almost perfectly."

"Which practice then seems to diminish," added Bill.

Doodles frowned and stuck out her tongue toward Bill, who then replied in kind.

"Come," Katy said to Hadley as Katy stood up. "Let me show you the Twins."

"Twins?"

Katy led Hadley into the next room. In one corner was a grand piano.

"This is Doodles, it's a Mason and Hamlin so she calls it 'Twins,' as in 'oh I think I'll go and play the Twins now.'"

They both laughed.

Katy stood in very close to Hadley and whispered. "As you can see, dear little Doodles is not a wonderful housekeeper." Katy took her finger and wrote out 'Doodles' in the dust on the top of piano.

"You are so bad," Hadley laughed as she looked into the other room to see if anyone else had seen.

"Well, it's true."

Hadley touched the keys.

"So tell me," Katy said. "Are you having fun?"

"Yes, everyone seems so nice. I think I'll enjoy it here."

"Well a small word of advice. Watch out for Donald the Don Juan want to be. We call him Dirty Don."

"He seems quite attentive."

"Yeah, well, believe me it's not your charming personality that's on his mind."

"What about the young writer?"

"Wemedge?"

"I don't know his real name, he seems to have so many nicknames."

"Yeah he's clever; he started the whole nicknaming thing. Ernest Hemingway is his real name."

"He has a nice smile."

"Yes, that he does. That he does indeed."

Katy glanced out into the other room and noticed that Ernest was standing behind Bill Horne looking their way.

"I believe he is smitten by you," Katy said.

"Oh, go on. He's very young."

"He's some six or seven years younger than we are. And at times he is very young, but then again at other times he's, well, mature."

"He seems to be a center of attention for everyone."

"Yes he is; people are just attracted to him in that way: both men as well as women. And you?" Katy asked.

"He's young and charming, that's all."

"Really?"

"Well," Hadley began but then laughed an embarrassed laugh.

"I thought so," Katy then said, glancing again across the room at Ernest. "He has a way about him."

5. Hadley

Hadley spent the week. She loved the swirl of people around the Smith's apartment. People were coming and going and the conversations covered everything.

And Ernest came by everyday to see her.

They took long walks down to Lincoln Park and through the trees and across the grass and down to the water's edge. They sat on a park bench looking out across the lake. They watched the sailboats as they tacked across the waves and further out the steamers across the horizon. They threw bread to the pigeons and watched as they cooed back and forth. A bold one landed on the bench right next to him and he hand fed him a piece of bread. When the bird tried to climb up into his lap Ernest had to laughingly shoo him away.

At night was drinking and dancing back at the apartment. There was a young Russian revolutionary from Moscow and he told everyone the events that were unfolding over there. Debate was heated but Hadley listened to it all.

Ernest took her to work with him and showed her his desk and his typewriter and his tray full of freshly sharpened pencils. Hadley sat in the outer office and watched him through the partition glass as he worked. They had lunch at Kitso's Restaurant. Ernest introduced her to Jeremiah the large black cook in the kitchen.

One night they went to the show. They sat in the back and ate popcorn and drank Coca-Cola and watched the movie on the screen and whispered throughout about everything else besides the movie.

One day they walked to the library and both went through the books they had read and which was best and which was not and oh my you really need to read this one, and you need to read this one as well and what do you mean you've never heard of him.

One morning she sprained her ankle and it swelled so much she could not wear her shoes. She had to wear one shoe and on the sprained foot she had to wear a red bedroom slipper. They had plans to see the University of Chicago football game and Ernest was going to give away the tickets but she said no, we are going; I'll just wear my slipper. So they went and she limped along.

"Boy, you've got spunk girl, anyone else would be embarrassed. You're a real sport."

Ernest was so impressed that he wrote his sister Marc a letter telling her all about it. This girl is a real sport, he wrote.

Ernest and Hadley spent the day walking the galleries of the Art Institute. They found that they both liked art. They both liked painting. They both liked representational paintings. There was a display of the watercolors of Winslow Homer. They had a collection of his Gulf Stream watercolors.

Ernest and Hadley stood before the watercolors for a long time. The Gulf Stream: the broken boat awash in the waves; the single black man on the wooden deck; the circling sharks.

"I like that," Ernest finally said.

"But it seems so sad; so hopeless."

"It is a lone man against the sea. It is a lone man fighting against his fate."

"But it will end with him being eaten by the sharks."

He looked at her.

"Every story if you tell it true ends in death. Everyone will be eaten alive by sharks, if not real sharks then the sharks of old age and loneliness."

"You make it all sound so grim."

"No, it's not grim. What is noble is how you fight the sharks. You fight, knowing it is useless, but you fight."

"Would you ever want to go to the Gulf Stream?" Hadley asked, changing the subject a little bit.

"Oh yes. I think that would be grand. Just look at it. The place is washed with light."

"Yes, well, not on a little boat like that; a large ocean liner perhaps."

Ernest smiled at her and she smiled back at him smiling at her. He pointed to another of the watercolors.

"I love Winslow Homer. Just look how he catches the light on the water and fixes the moment, just that moment, but now that moment is forever. That is true art."

Ernest and Hadley had dinner with Katy Smith and Bill Horne. Bill reserved a table at the Victor House Restaurant. There was a nice full meal and drinks all around. There was a lot of drinking. And Hadley took it in. She had drink after drink the same as everyone. Ernest liked that.

"You like to drink and you find pleasure in it. You are a regular Falstaff."

He laughed at her and she laughed at him. He liked a woman who could keep up.

From there they went dancing at the College Inn. It was packed with people. Ernest noticed that Katy was not her regular happy self. She was alright at the restaurant but now there was something bothering her. When Hadley and Katy went off to the restroom Ernest asked Bill.

"Is there something wrong with Katy? Have you noticed that she doesn't seem like herself?"

"You didn't hear?"

"No: what?"

Bill glanced back and forth as if seeing who might overhear what he had to say.

"It's Carl Edgar. I hear he tried to kill himself."

Ernest blinked in shock.

"What?"

"Yeah, I don't know the details but it didn't work."

Two dancing girls with their short black bobbed hair accidently bumped against Bill and Ernest, giggling. Ernest smiled them on.

"What would have caused J. C. Odgar to attempt self mortage?"

"What do you think?"

"Don't tell me it was Katy."

Bill shrugged his shoulders.

"Oh, God," Ernest said as he closed his eyes and then opened them. He shook his head.

"Bill, I once told him, 'get a hold of yourself. Look, I said, I had the absolute love of my life stab a knife into my heart and then several months later, oh I'm sorry can we be friends. It hurt like hell but it's not worth it. There is an after, there is a time after when things heal and repair and you go on. But not this."

"I know. Just think how it makes Katy feel."

"Bill," Ernest said getting angrier. "You don't try to kill yourself. You either do it or you don't do it and if you don't do it then you didn't really want to do it to begin with."

"I don't know, do you think it was just a show?"

"You're damn right it was; and you're damn right about Katy too."

"Here they come," Bill quickly said.

Katy and Hadley retuned from the restroom. It looked like Katy had been crying and Hadley seemed much more serious than before.

Ernest took a long full drink from his glass and then stood up as he slammed the empty glass down on the table.

"Come on Butstein, we are going to dance."

Ernest took Katy by hand and pulled her up. She followed him onto the dance floor.

When the week was done Ernest drove Hadley to the station. They stood on the platform with hundreds of others but neither noticed. The large billboard announcing the coming and going of the trains was lit up. The whole platform was shinning bright from the lights.

He held her close to him. He held her hands up in his hands pressed against his chest.

"It has been a wonderful week," she said.

"Absolutely the best."

"I'm afraid to say it but I feel cockeyed in love."

He kissed her hand. "I do too."

"I feel as if my life has only now begun."

"I can't wait to live the rest of the story."

"We must write and keep in touch."

"I will post one tonight and it will race your train to your doorstep."

She took her hand and touched his nose with her finger.

"As Chaucer put it," she said, "you are my 'very parfit, gentil knight.'"

"There are no windmills in the way I hope."

Hadley smiled.

"Don't mix up your writers."

"Never, dear Beatrice of mine, never."

Chapter Ten

The train to Milano was slow. It stopped several times and sat on sidings. It was hot. Ernest was on a bed with his leg wrapped tight and he could not sit up. The window above him was propped open but it was too high for him to see out. He watched the roofs of buildings go by.

The orderly said that Venice was just over there but Ernest could see nothing.

The train started and jerked forward. It ran for awhile, Ernest lost track of time as he dozed. But then the train stopped again.

"When will we reach Milano?" Ernest asked the orderly.

The orderly shrugged his shoulders. He had bright blue eyes. His skin was dark in color and his hair was black but he had bright blue eyes.

They sat for hours. The air was hot and thick and still. Ernest swatted the flies with a rolled up newspaper. He watched as they came in the open window above him. It smelled like the train was stopped next to a sewer.

The orderly said the train would be moving soon but it did not.

Ernest watched the sun crawl across the floor of the car as the day passed. Night came on but it did not seem to affect the heat. He stared at the dark ceiling of the car and tried to imagine the cool night sky back home.

He woke up with a sudden clang of the car as it started moving. Jerking and swaying the car stopped again and then clanged into motion again. There was a loud squeal of the iron wheels against the track.

The sun was just beginning to rise.

1. Horne

It was Bill Horne who came up with the plan. He got a job with the Eaton Axle Company and would be positioned in Chicago. He approached Ernest with his plan. He could get a place for the two of them.

"It will be just you and me, my friend, together. We can be together until either an act of God or some woman tears us apart."

"May that not be too soon."

"With the new seeds I'm getting from this job I can grubstake you until you're on your feet."

"You'd do that for me?"

"Ernie, you mean the world to me. You are by far my best friend. I need you. I'll do anything to be a part of your life."

Ernest watched as Bill took a deep breath. Ernest smiled and slapped him on the back and then gave him a quick hard hug.

"Don't go soft on me. I'd love to room with you."

"I tell you it's going to be just like back at the Schio Country Club in Italy. I was hoping that you would say yes because I already found a place, I rented it from Mrs. Seymour, it's at 1230 North State Street so it is just two blocks down from Ken and Doodles place, and not that far from Katy over at the Arts Club."

"It sounds like it is perfect."

"Yeah, except it is a little small and you'll have to sleep on a cot."

"It will be like I'm camping out only it will be indoors."

They both laughed.

The small one room was on the fourth floor. There was a bed, a cot, two chairs and a table. The bathroom was at the end of the hall and serviced the entire hallway.

A block down the street around the corner was the small Greek lunchroom "Kitso's" where they ate breakfast, and sometimes lunch. They sat on the stools at the long counter and talked with the black cook when he poked his head out the serving window. Steak and fries with coffee was their main meal.

The restaurant was named after the owner who proudly wore his thick long twirled moustache, who in turn was named after Kitsos Tzavelas of the Greek War of Independence, and later General and later Prime Minister. Pictures of Kitsos Tzavelas where hanging on the walls. One of the regulars, Ole Anderson, before he stopped coming around, pointed him out and one day told Ernest the story.

For dinner they ate at the Venice Café and liked to watch who came in and came out of the back room. Whomever went in or out of the back room was dressed elegant and expensive. Freshly polished shoes were a must. But they all looked as tough as nails. Once when Bill looked over one of the men standing by the door glared straight at him and Bill quickly turned his head back and put his head down.

"Ernie," he whispered.

Ernest looked down at him. Bill pushed his eyeglasses up his nose. "Whatever you do don't mess with those guys."

At night after dinner they would talk. They would read. Ernest liked to read out loud highlighting the dialogue with different voices. They shared bottles of wine. One night by a bare candlelight they sat by the window and watched the snow drift down over the city.

They talked about the past. After their station at Schio they enlisted to do canteen duty on the front lines. Ernest was stationed at Fossalta and Horne up further to San Pedro Norello. Horne set up his cot on the second floor of an old broken building. The owner of the building raised silkworms. There were racks and racks of thousands of silkworms gnawing and chewing on mulberry leaves. Ernest rode his bicycle over and spent the night. They sat in the semi darkness of the hot night talking and swatting at an occasional buzz of mosquito and then they tried to sleep. But in the silence of the night there was the gnawing and the chewing of the leaves and the dropping sound of worms falling off the branches. They could not sleep so they talked, they talked about life and all manner of things as the thousands of silkworms chewed up the time. And from all of this, Horne asked, what silk kimono will adorn what bored Italian housewife bloated with too many childbirths.

And sitting by the window of their small room they talked about the future. Bill said Ernest should try the advertising game. You get to write, you get to learn a lot of different things, and you get some time off so you can keep writing your stories. Kenley Smith was in the game, Don Wright was in the game, they both worked at the Critchfield advertising agency. Kenley could get you set up with an interview.

Ernest nodded and passed the time.

But when Ernest sat at the small table and tried to write then Bill sat on his bed as far away as he could and was as silent as he could be.

Bill knew. When Ernest was writing you left him alone.

Bill knew. He was a small part of something that was going to become big.

But when Bill got a call from Eaton Axle Company headquarters asking him to come into the home office he was nervous.

"You don't think they are going to fire me do you?"

"I don't know. Go and find out."

But Bill was afraid.

Bill wrote Ernest from Cleveland. He had to stay there for awhile. The company was in danger of a takeover so he had to stay to help fight the proxy war.

"I'll send you some money to keep the wolf and Mrs. Seymour from the door."

2. Kiss

Ernest met Hadley at the station. It was Saturday, December 3. He watched from the platform, his coat buttoned and the belt flap tightened, as the train pulled into the station. He stood with his hands in his pockets. It was a cold crisp night. The large clock over the arrival and departure board showed eight o'clock. He wore his leather cap. He looked back and forth searching until finally she was there, on the steps, descending onto the platform holding her small suitcase. He walked over to her. She too was searching, looking back and forth until finally their eyes met. She stood and waited until he came up to her.

"Hello," he said.

"Hello."

Ernest did not say anything for a moment. He looked around at the other people on the platform walking back and forth, and then finally his eyes returned to her.

She shrugged her shoulders.

"Well, then," she said. "I'm here."

Ernest laughed. Then he quickly hugged her and kissed her on the cheek.

He picked up her small bag and they walked off the station. She followed him as he briskly walked away from the station. She looked around but they did not go to a cab. Ernest did not flag down a cab. He walked with her bag and with his other hand deep in his coat pocket. She followed. They walked all the way to his apartment, all sixteen blocks. They did not talk much, just normal general conversation, as they walked and walked. It was a cold clear night. The stars were out. She breathed in the cold crisp air.

Finally when they approached the door of his apartment he whispered to her.

"You go first, up the stairs on the left to the first landing. The landlady might come out."

Hadley passed by the first apartment and went up the stairs. Ernest closed the front door behind him. Just as Hadley reached the first landing she heard the first apartment door open.

There was a woman's voice. "Oh, Ernest. I thought I heard two of you. I thought perhaps Bill got home."

"No, Mrs. Seymour, just me. Bill's not home yet."

"Well, it's just that it's the third of December already."

"I know, I will tell him just as soon as he gets home again. Good night Mrs. Seymour."

"Well, good night then," she said slowly closing her door.

Ernest went up the stairs and shushed Hadley with his fingers. They walked up to his fourth story apartment. Once they were inside Ernest took off his coat, helped her with her coat, and came out from the kitchen with two glasses of wine.

"Now," he said as he handed her glass. "Hello."

He leaned in and kissed her. She watched his eyes as he pulled away. They were warm. That large smile of his that she so loved to see sparkled across his face.

She looked around the apartment. It was small and cramped but kept clean. There was a bed, she knew to be Bill's, and a cot, she knew to be Ernest's, and two chairs and a dinner table.

They talked and talked and passed the evening away.

"So tell me about this new job. It's a writing job?"

"Well, yes. It's advertising copy mostly. Ken got me the interview and they liked my Toronto Star stuff."

"So, let me see it."

Ernest handed her a copy of the paper. 'The Cooperative Commonwealth.'

"'The Weekly Magazine of Mutual Help,'" she read.

"It's put out by the Co-operative Society of America, founded by one Harrison Parker on Feb 20 1919. It is to allow people," he said as he reached for the paper, opened it up and then began reading, "'to avail themselves of the advantages of co-operation as a welcome escape from the unconscionable profiteering of rapacious tradesmen.'"

Hadley laughed. "Rapacious tradesmen? My they sound rather evil don't they?"

Ernest too laughed.

"Well, it has its point of view. If you're a tradesman then for a small fee you can join their business directory and members then shop your place because you'll be fair and square."

"And not rapacious?"

Ernest took a sip of wine.

"Look, Hash, it's a paying job. What can I say?"

"Oh Ernest, I don't mean to be critical. Of course, it's a paying job and that's nice. But there does sound like there's something of a con in it don't you think?"

He shrugged his shoulder.

"Actually I suspect there's something going on. But I just write copy they tell me too, I'm not in upper management or anything."

"I'm sorry," she said, reaching out to touch his knee. "I think it will be fine for now."

But then Ernest smiled.

"But I have to say, my boss Richard Loper is definitely a save the world do gooder type of guy. He's a big guy with big suspenders with this loud deep voice and he struts around with his booming voice almost like he's Moses leading us all into the promised land of cooperative commonwealth."

They both laughed a good hard laugh.

The evening passed and it was late.

"Well," she said. "I should go. Ken and Doodles place is how far?"

They both stood up.

"No more than a block away. I'll walk you over."

Hadley looked around the apartment.

"Bill is still on his business trip back east?"

"Yeah, another week or so he said."

They stood without moving.

"Is that so?" she asked.

Ernest did not reply. Hadley watched as he blushed.

Finally, it was Hadley who spoke.

"Well, we have tomorrow and Monday. I'm leaving on the last train Monday night."

Ernest nodded. "I'll walk you over to Ken's place."

Ernest and Hadley sat at the table. Dinner. Kitsos Restaurant. Moussaka, Tiropita, Wine, and Baklava with coffee. There were only a few hours before her train. The restaurant was almost empty.

Ernest kept fingering his fork as he talked.

"The advertising game is getting really tight. Don Wright says things aren't good and he's afraid that he's going to be fired."

"Really?"

Ernest nodded as he took a sip of wine. He stared off.

"But you have your job," Hadley said.

"Yeah, but it's not the start of any career that I want. I'm getting a little desperate."

"Well, no. It's not a great place to begin. But you can work on your writing in your spare time."

"You see," Ernest said as he continued playing with his fork. "My pension that I was getting for my war wound, well that's run out. And the little I get from Toronto isn't much, I write and write but in the last few months they've only taken a few pieces."

"I'm sure things will turn around. The life of any writer is difficult in the beginning."

"Well I'm rooming with Bill but he, bless his little heart, he pays way more than his share of the rent. And he even spotted me some so I owe him the National Debt."

The waiter came over to the table.

"Will there be anything more?"

Ernest nodded to Hadley but she shook her head no.

"Just the check," Ernest said.

The waiter placed the check on the table and held out a pen. Ernest took the pen and signed the check. The waiter bowed and left with the check.

Hadley, watching the whole transaction, reached out and touched Ernest's hand.

"Do you have an account here?"

"Yeah, Bill and I. We eat here a lot. Bill pays them when he's in town."

Hadley shook her head.

"Bill treats me like royalty. He wants to support me while I write but I can't do that to him. I have to do something. Don Wright is worried, Bill is worried. This merger is going on and he thinks he might lose his job too."

"Well, Bill will be alright. He can go back to New York. He has friends and family there."

"Bill still sends me the money for the rent even though he hasn't been there. It was just wired but I haven't given it to Mrs. Seymour yet."

"But can you afford the place if he moves back to New York?"

"No, see that's the thing. But see, Doodles is leaving for New York to study piano so her room is going to be free and Ken already said I can stay there until she gets back."

"See, things work out."

Ernest glanced at the clock on the wall.

"Well, best that we get back if you have to catch the last train."

Hadley made a frown with her lips.

"Must I?"

At the station Ernest stood with her until she had to board the train. She waited. He finally briefly hugged her and said good bye. As she watched him from the train window as it pulled out of the station all she could think was that there was no kiss good bye.

Why.

3. Letters

Ernest and Hadley wrote letters back and forth: lots of letters. There was hardly a day that passed where they did not write to each other. It was as if they were never away from each other but just in the other room for a moment.

They wrote about their families. Ernest asked her about her father, telling her a little about his.

Hadley was only thirteen when her father died.

She was sorry to confess that at the time she did not feel a great loss. He was aloof from the children, she explained. He loved his children, yes; he was proud of them at times, yes; and at times they bicycled together and held hands when walking through the trees in the White Mountains, and he smiled to see them with their freshly washed hair combed out and wearing fresh pressed dresses.

And at night she fell asleep listening to her mother downstairs playing the piano and her father singing songs. Hadley fell asleep many a night to his voice.

But he seemed doomed from the beginning.

"How was that?" Ernest wrote back.

His father, James Richardson Sr., was a determined man with endless energy and drive. In New Hampshire he started his career as a school teacher. Then, at twenty eight, in 1845, he moved to Pittsburgh where he managed a grocery store for twelve years. Then, not happy with that, he moved to St. Louis where he founded the Richardson Drug Company. It was there that his success exploded. He became a founder of the St. Louis Public Library where a picture of him is still hanging on the wall.

James Sr. had two daughters and two sons. The eldest son, James Jr., proved not to be what the father expected of a son of his. The younger son, Clifford, did. Clifford graduated from Washington University at seventeen and went to work at the family business where in five years he became a partner.

James Jr. now lived in the shadow of both of them.

He met Florence Wyman at the First Presbyterian Church where she played the organ for the Sunday service. She had studied at the Mary Institute and excelled in music. She got the job playing at the church. Teachers told her she should study in Europe and seek a professional career in music. But then she met James.

It did not seem right. But her suitors were few for she was a very strong and dominating woman. And he was a weak man. The marriage did not go well right from the start. She was a strong feminist and suffragist writing articles and forming groups and became quite open about her hated of men and her loathing of sex. Family rumor was that as a child she had been sexually abused by an Uncle but no evidence ever came to light. Even though she had six children she thought women were prisoners of male desire and thought intercourse drained away vital bodily fluids which should be retained and used for noble and humanitarian causes.

"But she had children, I mean, you are here," Ernest wrote to her. Yes, six children in all. There were two who died as infants and then Jamie and Dorothea were born a year apart followed by nine years before Fonnie and then I were born.

James Richardson moved into a large red brick house on Cabanne Place in the West End. The streets were wide and the houses were set back on the lots so there was a lot of front yard grass. He was 'invited' by his rich business associates to live in the exclusive Kingsbury Place but he said no. They 'were too stuck up' for his taste. Hadley could remember as a very young child sitting on a stool on the corner of the yard watching the day go by, the horses, the delivery wagons, the neighbors walking by, and the large oak trees that lined the street.

Inside the house the parlor walls were lined with cherry red panels. One of them opened into a small secret compartment inside the wall. 'If you are bad I'll lock you up in there and you don't want to know what might happen to you in there,' her nurse Mary told her. But there was the red stained glass over the window seat and the afternoon sun painted the room with its colored light.

Up the stairs there was a lamp decorated with standing skeletons intertwined. That was enough of a fright to pass by on the way up to bed but at the top of the stairs on the wall was a painting of Judith holding in her hand the freshly severed head of Holofernes.

Hadley adored her older sister Dorothea but, eleven years older, when Dorothea married Dudley Bragdon and moved out Hadley had only Fonnie to play with. But Fonnie was much like her mother. Hadley was more like her father. So Fonnie was her mother's favorite.

In addition to music Florence spent her days reading and attending Theosophy meetings. Although raised a Presbyterian, Florence took Hadley and Fonnie out of Sunday school when she became involved in the spiritualism of theosophy. She became enamored with different Swami leaders and once invited one tall and handsome blond Swami with a small grey beard to stay with them for a few days. He brought along two of his male companions.

"Papa almost went crazy," Hadley wrote, "with 'that' going on in his own house."

When Fonnie was ten years old she announced at dinner that she had decided to become a vegetarian in keeping with the theosophy ways. They were having pot roast that night. Florence said that was fine, proud perhaps at her commitment. But James slammed his hand down on the table.

"You'll eat what's on the table," he said. Fonnie refused. He took her across his knee and spanked her. She in turn kicked him in the face and then ran up the stairs.

"So how did it work out?" Ernest wrote back.

There was a fire in the St. Louis warehouse of the Richardson Drug Company where father worked. After the fire the company decided to close that warehouse and James, being the manager of the warehouse, was out of his job. The company, under the leadership of his father and his brother, was successful enough that James did not have to work. So he did not. But to keep up appearances he rented an office with the J. H. McLean Medicine Company and there, every day, he went to work. He did some consulting work for different clients but he mostly invested in the stock market. He was not successful in his investments.

And he began to drink.

Much to his wife's loathing.

But he drank never the less.

He loved to ride his bicycle around town even in bad weather. It did not bother him. Even if he had nowhere to go he rode around up and down. When Jaime and Dorothea where little he attached a small carriage to his bicycle and could be seen riding around town with the two little children in tow dressed in hats and bonnets to protect them from the sun. By the time Jaime and Dorothea were old enough to have their own bicycles the younger children, Hadley and Fonnie, became the two little ones in the carriage dressed in hats and bonnets.

Florence did not think that bicycling was worthy of her attention.

Neighbors waved and stopped James when he bicycled by and they would chit chat the day away. Neighbors liked James. He was gentle and kind and soft spoken. And he loved to laugh. He used to say that the purpose of it all was to smile and laugh.

"What's the point of life if not to enjoy it?" he used to ask.

"How did he die?"

On the morning of February 7, 1905 James Richardson went to his office at the J.H. McLean Medicine Company and worked all day as was his usual routine. That evening he went home and ate dinner with the family. He then retired early to bed. I am a bit tired, he said. He undressed and then in bed he lay awake. He stared at the ceiling. He heard each hour pass when the clock on the dresser chimed.

The night passed away slowly but steadily.

Finally, when the clock chimed five thirty, he pulled the covers away and sat up on the side of the bed. He sat for a moment and then clicked on the light by the bed. He reached into the top drawer of his bedside table and pulled out the revolver that was kept there for safety.

It was loaded.

After a moment he stood in front of the large dressing mirror. He was wearing his long nightshirt that fell down to his knees. He looked into the mirror as if he wanted to watch. He placed the barrel of the revolver behind his right ear and then he pulled the trigger.

The noise shook the house. Florence sat up in bed. She was fully awake instantly. But she sat sitting up in bed for a long time not knowing what the loud noise could be. She got out of bed and slipped on her slippers and wrapped her robe around her night clothes. She walked down the hall to her husband's room. She tapped and called out his name. When he did not respond she opened the door and went in. He was on the floor with the revolver still in his hand. Blood was slowly staining the carpet.

4. Letters II

"And your mother? She sounds like my mother," Ernest wrote. "There's no room for my Dad to survive."

From her letters a picture emerged.

After James died Florence increased all of her social and intellectual pursuits. She needed fulfillment. She helped to found the city Artist's Guild, and the Piano Club, and the Symphony Orchestra and the Woman's Trade Union League.

But her deepest passion was the movement for women's rights. Fonnie too became an intense supporter. One cold snowy day in February of 1910 Florence answered the door bell. A young woman with a long fur coat, her hands in her fur lined muff, introduced herself as Laura Gregg of the National Headquarters of the Women's Suffrage League in New York. Without her mother knowing Fonnie had written a letter asking how to organize a group here in St. Louis. The three of them spent the afternoon over hot tea and biscuits discussing what needed to be done.

At their first meeting on April 13, 1910 eighty women showed up and elected Florence as the president. But it was Fonnie who became the 'suffragist heroine' when she showed up at one of the early rallies at the Odeon Opera House slim and graceful with brown hair and blue eyes dressed in a satin gown and plumed hat, and gave a speech they all remembered.

Both Fonnie and Hadley took piano lessons from two ancient spinsters. Hadley showed promise. Fonnie did not. Once, when Fonnie was not there, the teachers, Miss Miller and Miss Schaefer, both encouraged Hadley to study piano in Germany. She was ready, they told her, to advance to better teachers.

"But of course I never went," she wrote to Ernest.

"And what about Fonnie?" Ernest wrote.

"My mother was crazy about Fonnie," Hadley replied. Florence picked out a husband for her. And for all of her suffragist passion Fonnie got married.

His name was Roland Usher. He was a young history professor at Washington University in St. Louis. A Harvard Ph.D. he had just published his first book: The Reconstruction of the Church of England. He was also an amateur composer and violinist. Florence met him at the Artist's Guild and immediately invited him to meet her daughter.

He was slightly crippled from childhood polio but that was overlooked.

Florence decided that Fonnie should be exposed to European culture and manners before her wedding so Florence and Fonnie, with Hadley, took a quick trip to Europe. On the way over they met a couple Otto and Anne Simon. She was a gifted professional pianist and music teacher. After listening to Hadley play Anne insisted to Florence that Hadley should come to Washington D.C. where Anne could teach her and groom her as a professional pianist. But she is a student at the Mary Institute; I don't want her to drop out from that. No, Anne said: college is wrong for her, she can do anything she wants in music, and it is in music that she can become successful and flower. You should let her have her chance.

But Florence said no.

They returned from Europe and Fonnie married Roland Usher on June 9, 1910. Nine months later she gave birth to a girl and named it Florence after her mother, and nicknamed it Fonchen.

The next summer they all went to Annisquam, near Gloucester, Massachusetts, for the summer. Florence had built a shingle house on the sand dunes overlooking the ocean. It was just down from a lighthouse.

Hadley spent her days on the porch reading.

But then in August one day she answered the telephone. It was her brother-in-law Dudley Bragdon. When she heard the news she had to sit down.

Her sister Dorothea was eight months pregnant. She was sitting on their porch in the early morning playing with her two little boys, ages seven and five, when she noticed that somehow a brush fire had started in the empty field next to the house. Dorothea was afraid that it would flare up and come toward the house. So she got up and went over to the fire and kicked dirt on the flames to smother it. But it continued to flare up in the dry weeds. But then her long bathrobe caught fire and then her elastic stockings caught fire. The fire scorched up her legs. She fell to the dirt screaming as her whole lower body burned. Her two little boys came running over screaming and screaming.

Her legs and abdomen were scorched and blistered. The next day, through the pain of that, she gave birth to a little girl. It was born dead.

We are hopeful that she will survive, Dudley said, crying over the phone. But I fear the worse.

When Hadley placed the phone back into its cradle she could not move. She just could not move.

Days passed and Hadley just sat all day staring off. Everyday the phone rang and it was Dudley. She was still alive. Florence sat quiet and rocked back and forth and chanted one of her theosophic hymns in a long low hum. It was eight days before the call came through.

Dorothea was gone.

It was several weeks later that Hadley took a boat out. She did not know how to swim. A storm was coming on. But she rowed the boat out into the waves. It began to rain. The waves built up and jerked the little boat about. Florence and the captain from the lighthouse stood on the shore shouting for her to come in. But she did not.

"Even now I can still smell the cold salt water splashing up, wet against my skin. I don't know what I wanted. I didn't do anything but sit. It did not matter. It was the waves that pushed me into shore. I was just lost."

"So what happened?" Ernest wrote back.

It broke Florence. After the death of her two infants, and then her husband, and now her elder daughter, she withdrew from most of her clubs and meetings. There hardly seemed a point to it anymore. She sat around the house and slept a lot. She increased her spiritualism activities. She tried harder to convince Hadley.

She held séances in their living room. She held sessions with Ouija boards. A woman down the street, Pearl Curran, discovered she had a talent for the Ouija board when she started getting messages from a woman named Patience Worth who had died in 1694. Pearl and her husband chronicled the life of Patience Worth. People from all around flocked to their house in order to be there when the messages came through. Florence and Fonnie and Hadley attended and once there was a poem that Pearl said was for Hadley.

But then, once, when Hadley was not there, Fonnie said that Pearl contacted Dorothea.

"Mother and I were there and saw it," she said.

"What did she say?" Hadley asked.

"We asked her about you," Fonnie said. "She didn't display any interest at all. She's not interested in you."

Hadley could not believe it. If it were truly Dorothea she would have said something.

Hadley wrote Ernest: I didn't believe in Ouija boards and automatic writing after that.

"What happened to your mother?" Ernest wrote.

220

For many years Florence suffered from diabetes but in 1920 she developed Bright's disease. It is a disease of the kidneys that at times develops from diabetes. She was not well. For three months Hadley was awake most nights caring for her mother, 'rubbing, pleading, cajoling and pitying' her dying mother. In the final months Hadley was exhausted and hired a nurse.

"All of a sudden I had beaus," wrote Hadley to Ernest. Her mother, as always, objected, but the nurse, who saw how drained Hadley was, took her side. When a young man arrived to take Hadley to dinner or to a dance or to a movie the nurse almost shoved her out the door. 'Don't you worry now; I will look after your mother. You just go right ahead and make real good friends with him.'

But on the night of August 19 Hadley sat on a wooden chair beside the bed of her mother and held her hand and wiped her forehead with a cold damp cloth. It was a hot night and she had the windows open. She could hear the crickets outside chirping the night away. Everyone else in the house below was asleep. Just after midnight Florence gasped. Hadley was holding her hand. Her mother stopped breathing. Hadley continued to hold her hand as her mother slipped into absolute silence.

In spite of their differences, and in spite of her mother's love for Fonnie over her, Hadley still loved her mother.

"She is my mother, and in spite of everything, she is my mother, my only mother. No matter the faults, how can you not love she who gave you life?"

But Hadley also felt release. She was twenty eight years old and felt that she had been dead for the last eight years. Her life opened up in front of her. It was finally time for her to find someone who 'hit my soul's center.'

It was then she got the letter from Katy. Come and stay with my brother: get away.

"It was then that I met you," Hadley wrote to Ernest.

5. Christmas

Ernest was on his way home for Christmas. As the cab drove through the streets toward the house he felt a growing excitement. On the seat next to him were the presents. He stretched what money he had to buy everyone at least something.

He had a lot of good memories surrounding Christmas. For them it actually began in October. Clarence canned and preserved the fruits and vegetables they grew on their farm over the summer. It was also when Clarence bought a large slab of beef and cured it in the fruit cellar. Almost everyday he walked down the stairs into the cellar and vigorously rubbed the slab of beef down with salt and saltpeter.

As December came on Clarence made his 'hockies,' enjoyed by many of his patients, boiling heavily spiced pork hocks and setting them outside on the back porch to cure and freeze in the winter weather. Then, closer to Christmas, he baked trays of mince pies and stacked them out on the back porch to be frozen as well.

Then, on Christmas Eve, the entire day was spent cooking the evening meal. Clarence and the cook would be wrapped in their aprons slicing and stirring and shooing the children away as they cooked all day. Clarence brought up some of his preserved fruits and vegetables and his homemade pickles. They heated up the hockies and recooked the mince pies and he carefully sliced the beef into long thin slices.

With the wind and the snow and the cold outside the house became a warm swirling soup of fragrances. Clarence carried up the slab of beef from the cellar. To slice the beef as thin as he could Clarence sharpened his best knife again and again with the sharp sliding sound of blade against steel.

The children set the large oak table in the dining room and when he brought in the food on plate after plate, and after he said grace, the feast began.

After dinner Mother played the piano and everyone sang Christmas songs until it was time for bed.

Ernest paid the cab driver and with his arms full of presents walked across the snow to the front door. It was Marc who greeted him at the door. She helped him put the presents under the Christmas tree. Then the two of them hugged. She took his leather jacket and put it on the coat rack by the door.

"Where is everyone?"

"Well, Dad's in the kitchen and Sunny and Carol are upstairs. Ursula is at her boyfriend's house but promises to be home for supper."

"And what about Mom."

Marc shrugged her shoulders.

"She's not here."

"What do you mean she's not here?"

"She took Les and went to visit her brother Leicester in California. Surely you knew that."

"Yeah but I thought she'd be home for Christmas."

Marc shook her head.

Ernest stood for a moment without speaking. Marc again shrugged her shoulders and then walked toward the kitchen. Ernest followed her.

In the kitchen Clarence stood by the stove stirring a soup in a pan. He wore his long apron.

"Ernie," he shouted out as Ernest entered the room.

They hugged and talked.

Ernest and Marc set the table as Clarence finished cooking. There were only a small handful of mince pies and hockies. The beef he bought from the butcher just yesterday.

When it was ready Marc called Sunny and Carol down. Clarence said grace and the feast began. Soon Ursula got home and joined them. They ate mostly in silence. They all asked Ernest what it was like living in Chicago.

After dinner Marc and Sunny cleared the table while Ernest and his father went into his waiting room. His father was sweating. He looked like he had lost weight. He talked about summers in the past when they "chummed" together. Some of those times were the best in my life, he said. Remember this time, that time: Ernest remembered and watched as his father remembered. It brightened him up.

Finally Ernest had to ask.

"Why did Mom go to California?"

Clarence hesitated a moment.

"Her father used to go there for Christmas, I don't know if you remember that. She said she wanted to revive the tradition."

"But why?"

"Well, she said it makes her feel closer to him."

"Closer to him, but she's never left him."

Clarence nodded and looked away.

"He's dead: we aren't. Where do you think her allegiance should lie?"

Clarence watched the wall clock as its hands moved across its face.

"You know son," Clarence then said, "life is not what it was and I do not know that it will ever be again."

Clarence looked over at his son and then smiled.

"Do you want some apple pie?" he asked. "I made an apple pie; I could make some coffee."

"Maybe later. What else did she say?"

Clarence, who had begun to stand up, sat back down.

"She said that it was nice to visit her brother because he was a successful lawyer. She said it was refreshing to be in the atmosphere of success."

Ernest sat silent.

Finally Clarence slapped the palms of his hands on the arms of the chair and stood up.

"Who's for pie? Go round everybody up."

Clarence cut a piece of pie for everyone and poured out glasses of milk. Around the table Ernest and the girls sang Christmas songs. Clarence went into the other room. Ernest sang as out of key as he could. The girls all laughed. It was good to have their older brother home.

Finally Ursula said good night and went upstairs. Sunny asked Ernest if he was staying the night and he said yes. She kissed his forehead and then Carol kissed his forehead and the two of them left for bed as well.

Marc cleared the plates from the table.

"So, how is living in Chicago?"

"Good. I'm living with Bill Horne, you know."

"Yes, I heard. Good old Horne, he likes his job?"

"Yeah, it pays him some pretty good seed so, yeah."

"And you?"

Ernest smiled.

"I found someone."

"Oh my, like in a girlfriend?"

"I think it's a bit more than that."

"Really? You're blushing Ernie."

"Katy introduced us. Her name is Hadley Richardson."

"Is she the first major girl after Agnes?"

Ernest nodded.

"So, tell me tell me."

"I think I'm going to ask her to marry me."

"Oh my God, are you really?"

Ernest nodded and then laughed.

Marc walked over to him and the two of them hugged in the empty kitchen.

"My little baby brother is all grown up now."

Ernest noticed that there were tears in her eyes.

Marc and Ernest went around and shut off the downstairs lights and walked up the stairs. They both lived away but for now, for tonight, they were both home. The door to his father's bedroom was open. Ernest walked in. His father sat on the bed. He had Grandfather Anson's old Civil War revolver all broken apart and strewn across the quilt. He held a white rag in his hand and was wiping down the chamber.

"Dad, what are you doing?"

Clarence looked up and smiled.

"I just thought I'd give this a good old cleaning."

He looked down at the pieces on the bed.

"It belonged to my father; he used it in the Civil War."

Ernest already knew that. And he knew that his father already knew that he knew that.

"Dad, are you alright?"

"Of course son," he said as he kept wiping down the chamber. "Merry Christmas son, it's good to have you here."

"Merry Christmas Dad."

Chapter Eleven

They carried him out of the train and into the back of an ambulance. They said they were taking him to the American Red Cross Hospital. It was early morning. Shadows stretched long. Ernest could just barely see out the window. They passed a fruit and vegetable market. They were stacking the fruit for the day. They rolled up the canvas canopies. Someone was washing down the sidewalks. It smelled like a fresh morning.

They stopped and pulled Ernest out. The building was tall, brick, with large rectangular windows. They set the stretcher down. The porter came out of the building. He said the hospital was on the fourth floor. It is new. There are no patients there yet. They discussed if they should take the elevator or the stairs. In the elevator the stretcher would not fit. They would have to stand him up and hold him up. The stairs had narrow turns. It would be hard. They said the elevator. The porter opened the iron gate of the cage. They pulled Ernest up off the stretcher and held him up. The pain in his leg was immediate. One held him up with his arms around his chest and the other held his leg. They shuffled in holding him up. The porter crowded into the cage with the stretcher held up right.

The sharp pain increased.

They pressed the button and the elevator moved up. It was slow. It clanged each time it passed a floor. Ernest watched as the floors went by. The breath of the one holding him up smelled of wine and garlic. The pain was getting severe. Ernest breathed heavy.

Finally the elevator clanged and came to a stop. The porter got out. They shuffled him out. His leg was shooting with pain. There were three doors. They rang the bell. No one came. They rang the bell. No one came. The porter said they slept on the floor below. He went down the stairs. Ernest's leg was shivering from the pain.

A door opened and the porter and a nurse came out. Please put me in a room now, Ernest said. We don't expect any patients. We are not ready. Any room, it does not matter, just do it now please. Ernest was sweating. The man tried to hold Ernest's leg from shivering. Take me in, Ernest said and they took him inside. Anywhere, anywhere just put me down. There was a large room with a large window. There were no sheets on the bed. Please put me down he shouted over the sharp pain.

227

1. Green eyes

Ernest dragged his duffel bag into the small room. Ken walked in after him. They were in Doodles' room.

"She will be a couple months, so you can use the room until then."

Ernest stood and looked around. There was a small single bed, a chest of drawers, a small vanity table with mirror, and white lace curtains. He took a deep breath and then looked at Ken.

"She's still here," he said.

"What are you talking about," Ken asked.

"Her perfume, that heavy gardenia smell; I always know when she's around or was just around by the gardenia perfume smell. Now we know for sure that it does saturate everything."

"Don't be silly. She added a touch of feminine sanity to our lives. Now that we are just a bunch of guys we'll descend into a tribe of boozing whoring brutes."

"And what is wrong with that?"

It was Don Wright, standing in the hallway just outside the bedroom door.

"Heh, Hem; welcome back to The Men's Club," Don said.

"Thanks."

"And I've been able to retain Della from the other place to cook for us."

Ernest placed the palms of his hands together.

"Glory be, I swear that woman cooks Manna from the heavens. I'm definitely going to gain weight living here with her cooking for us."

"Well," Don Wright piped up, "I know how you can exercise that off," and then he laughed.

It was Ken: "Back to your den you brute, back to your den."

As soon as he could Ernest wrote Hadley a letter. He explained the whole situation. There was Kenley Smith, himself, Don Wright, Bobby Rouse, a boy he did not know named Saltzenbach, and then Nicco Philes. He had gotten a letter from Jim Gamble wanting Ernest to come with him to Rome, all expenses paid. They could travel Europe together and he could write. He so wanted to go.

'You cannot understand how much I want to go back to Italy,' he wrote. It all began there. Oh Hash, he wrote, I love you so much. Why don't we get married as soon as possible and then why don't we make a mad penniless dash to Wopland and live happy ever after? Am I being too much a Romantic?

Hopelessly so, Hadley wrote back. But I love you for it. Maybe in the fall, maybe we can get married in September or October. A romantic dash for Italy sounds nice, my sweet, but maybe not totally penniless.

It began to sink in. He had asked her to marry him. He began to realize that their relationship had crossed a bridge. Where was this going to take him?

Katy walked into the room. Ernest, on his bed, was reading. He put the book down as soon as she entered.

"What are we reading?" Katy asked as she picked up the book. "Ah, Sinclair Lewis, "Main Street," are we into reading best sellers now?"

"He's good and it's good, the fact that it's a bestseller is all the more power to him."

She put the book down.

"So, how did she take it?"

Ernest seemed to not understand.

"Wemedge, you saw Marge. You wrote her about Hadley and now you saw her. Of course the fact that she is going to the University in St. Louis, and the fact that she knows Mrs. Charles and Bill and me and has dinner with Mrs. Charles every once in awhile, she is bound to find out sooner or later."

"Yeah," he said, as if trapped.

"Are you sure about Hadley?"

"I don't know, Katy. I just don't know. I think I love her but then again, I don't know for sure."

"So what about Marge?"

"Well, I think that it's Hadley over Marge."

"So, don't keep me in suspense. Tell me what happened. Did you tell her?"

Ernest nodded. He did not look at Katy.

"So how did Marge take it?"

"Not too well. There was a sort of outburst."

She tapped him on the top of his head with her middle finger: "Elaborate."

"Well, there was something about my abominable conceit or something. It did not work out well."

"What did you say?"

"I said I was sorry but be a sport, 'You know everything, you learned everything from me, I have nothing left to teach you,' I said it wasn't fun anymore, for me, but it's alright because in the long run I was good for you. I was good for you."

"You said that?"

Ernest for the first time looked up at her.

"Yeah, I was good for her. There is a phase in every girl's life where she has her first boyfriend, and it ends, and then you move on."

Katy paced the floor in the small room. She had to step over the dirty clothes on the floor.

"You know, for having grown up surrounded by sisters sometimes you are so stupid when it comes to women. You can be so cold and so cruel."

"What?"

"You were good for her, is that what she wants to hear now that she's hurt? She a young girl, she cared deeply about you, you were her first big boyfriend and she gave you her heart, her most precious possession and all you can come up with is 'oh it was good but now I'm bored so bye bye.' Ernie, you broke her heart."

Ernest did not reply.

"Look you moron, teaching her all that stuff about camping and fishing she didn't learn all that because she wanted to be a boy scout. She cared for you and she wanted to be a part of your world so she could be with you."

"There were all of the moonlight swims and the fishing for rainbow off the point and the dances at the Bean house. It was fun. So I told her 'cheer up Red, it was good.'"

Katy stared at him for a long time shaking her head.

"Ernie, with all due honesty and respect: you can be the most wonderful guy in the world but then you can be the stupidest idiot there ever was."

They stared at each other in silence for a long time, he sitting on the side of his bed and she standing by the door.

Finally he shrugged his shoulders.

"Maybe you're right. Can you teach me?"

"Teach you what?"

"About women."

Katy laughed.

"I can't teach calculus to someone who doesn't understand arithmetic."

"I don't want to make the same mistake."

"With whom? Hadley?"

"No, with you."

There was dead silence in the room.

"No Wemedge, don't do this to me. I'm off men for awhile after what Carl did to me. Imagine the guilt he put me through. What if he had killed himself, would I spend the rest of my life feeling guilty because I didn't go to bed with him? And even if I did how would that change anything, and how would that make me a better person?"

She turned as if she were going to leave.

"Katy, please."

"What he did to me was vile and selfish. No, I'm off men for a while. What he tried to pull on me stained the whole thing."

"I'm sorry."

Katy turned toward him. She smiled at him.

"Look here Wemedge, as I see it you and me, we have this little something between us that transcends all of it. The normal boy girl thing would disgrace what we have. We have something bigger than that."

"But wouldn't the normal boy girl thing enhance and enrich what we have?"

"Nice try you horny little devil but no, it would cheapen it and destroy it. Call me a crazy romantic but sex isn't all it is cracked up to be when it comes to loving someone. So I'll just say it straight out. I love you. I do. But I love you in a way that would be ruined by sex; there is more to true loving affection than physical sex. You see, Ernie, when that is introduced into the equation then the act itself becomes the center of attention and not the emotion and feeling behind it."

Ernest sat on the side of his bed staring down at the floor.

"Do you understand? Love to me is, like, it is androgynous. We are not boys to girls and girls to boys, we are all one, we are all souls together and it is as souls that we truly love. All of the rest just gets in the way."

Ernest did not know exactly what to say.

"So, then, with me and Hadley? You're okay with that?"

Katy reached out and ran her fingers through his hair.

"Wemedge, you and I will always be something. That doesn't go away. Whether you're with Hadley or not, that does not really matter. It really doesn't change anything does it?"

He looked up into her green eyes. It was easy to lose yourself in her green eyes, like Carl a passing ship crashing on the siren rocks.

2. Anderson

Ernest came into the apartment. There was a group of people sitting in the living room talking. He tried to close the door as quietly as he could. Ken sat across the room and had his hand in the air waving Ernest in.

"Excuse me," he said to the group and then "Ernest, come over I have someone for you to meet."

"This is Ernest Hemingway, the young lad I was telling you about. Ernest, this is Sherwood Anderson."

The man sitting next to Ken was an older man, mid forties, with dark ruffled hair and brown eyes. He wore a bright yellow shirt. He had a sad face but a nice smile. Ernest reached down and shook his hand.

"This is 'the' Sherwood Anderson?"

"Yes, Hemmy, this is 'the' Sherwood Anderson, the writer, you know, "Winesburg, Ohio" and all of that. He works with Don and I at Critchfield. I invited him over to meet the gang."

"Ken tells me that you are a writer."

"Well, I'm not published or anything."

"That is alright. Being published doesn't make you a writer. Writing makes you a writer."

"So Hemmy, take a seat and join in on the conversation."

Ernest sat in an empty chair across the room and carefully watched.

"So," Ken said, "you were saying about Mark Twain."

"Yes. Well, as I said I have been discussing with my friend Van Wyck Brooks, whose recent book "The Ordeal of Mark Twain" I recommend to everyone, about the man's spirit. Well I was just pointing out that with Mark Twain and Walt Whitman they have opened up the Midwest to American Literature. And although there were predecessors like Cooper or Hawthorne, I feel that it is with Twain and Whitman that we truly have an American Literature to rival any other. We have a distinctive American voice and vision."

"To rival English Literature?" someone asked.

"Yes. Now the English have been at it much longer, of course, but they have not had our history and they have not had our wide open vision. Our literature truly emerges out of the soul of the people."

"Chicago certainly has had a Renaissance in literature of late," someone said.

"Well yes, but it is more of a birth than a rebirth. Twain was the crude frontier river man who speaks truths of the human spirit but when he went East the barren academics did their best to mold him into themselves and thus crush his creative spirit. His frustrating career is a cautionary tale for all of the writers of today. Beware the industrialization of life and, in academia, the industrialization of art. The massive spirit of Twain and Whitman has passed into the smaller controlled and contrived masters of prose that are Henry James or William Dean Howells. Follow that path too far and you end up in the emptiness of neat slick writing of the popular magazines. There is a major difference between popular fiction and literature. You must decide now which path you wish to follow because they take you to different places."

"But what do you suggest?"

"Speak the voice of the people; speak to the frustrations of the people. The true voice of America, the childlike open hearted optimism, came from a noisy and crude swaggering raftsman and a hairy breasted woodsman. Fear not to tread there. I think it is true that a man cannot be a pessimist if he lives near a flowing river or a golden cornfield for when the moon comes up and sparkles the chattering river and paints a haunting silver the wind splashing through the corn stalks then how can that man not hear and feel the whispering of the gods."

"But we can't all live next to a cornfield."

"But you can in your heart and you can in your imagination; imagination is the most powerful force that a writer possesses so why not imagine the environment where creative energy can flow. The moon shines equally everywhere so all you have to do is decide that you want to see it. I have the notion that nothing from my pen should be published that could not be read aloud in the presence of a field of corn. Mark Twain reached that point once, when he heard the whispering of the gods, and that was when he wrote Huck Finn, one of the greatest novels ever and certainly the creative center of American Literature. Twain forgot about James and Howell and slick writing and listened instead to the flow of the river and he listened instead to the child within him in his conscious innocence."

Ernest listened and watched the others listening.

"Where did Twain write this, I do not mean physically but in his heart? I believe it was in a little hut on top of a hill surrounded by sun splashed farmland where he could write and write undisturbed. And at night he came down filled with the creative energy of playing all day with rivers and men riding the broad Mississippi down through the heart of the land watching and keeping a safe distance from the corrupt industrialized towns and corrupt industrialized people who lived along the banks."

Ken spoke.

"I think we all wish we had a little hut on a hill away from it all."

"But you can Ken. I still work at Critchfield Advertising where I still write advertising copy. But when I write for real then in my mind I am in my little hut on the hill."

"Even if your hut is in the slums of a city and the water pipe is broken," someone said.

Sherwood smiled a big smile.

"I know. It is not easy to do at times, I understand that quite well, and this is the eternal struggle that we scribblers are all engaged in but what do you have if you do not try? All you will have is to sit in your hut in the slums with the broken water pipe and have nothing else. At least if you try then you will have a dream and that dream can be more powerful than all of the things holding you back."

"Can I ask you," someone asked, "all of your books have come out with mixed reviews, some very harsh, how do you handle that, does it bother you?"

Sherwood again smiled as he sat in his chair.

"There are those who like my books and then there are those who do not like my books. But I find the ones who do like my books are ordinary people because I am speaking to them about their lives. That means that what I write speaks the truth. The ones who do not like my books are the college entrapped industrialized academia types who dictate from their towers what everyone should like if they were only smart enough to like it. To those critics I say what do they and what they say matter if what I write is true and speaks to the voice of the people. When you think of critics such as these be Rabelaisian. Fart at the moon."

Ernest watched as everyone laughed.

"That brings up a point that is as old as the hills. The self proclaimed academia guardians of literature have all the time thought that they and only they can understand literature and by implication they and only they can write literature. But life proves them wrong again and again. Charles Dickens had to abandon school and work when his father was forced into debtor's prison. As a result he wrote the voice of the people, the voice of life living. What do the high placed professors know of that? And the supreme example of them all is the beloved William Shakespeare. He was not a high born nobleman but rather a commoner, and he suffered through a limited education and was married at a very young age but yet what he wrote is considered the greatest of the great. And so there are those who say that it is simply impossible for someone of his commoner status to have written what he did for only a high nobleman of good breeding could feel that deeply and think that broadly and have such a fine knack with the language. Never underestimate the passion of the human heart regardless of social standing. Well, to his detractors I say it is simply academic arrogance, to them I say it is poppycock I say."

3. Eleventh of March

March 11, 1921. The train pulled into St. Louis. It came to a slow and slightly jerking stop. Ernest got off the train. Hadley saw him standing looking around. Her heart jumped. He wore his new three piece Brooks Brothers suit, his black Italian cape, and held a large scrapbook in his hand. His duffel bag was at his feet.

"My, my," Helen Breaker whispered to her as if he could overhear. "Doesn't he look dashing."

"Yes, and he is all mine, all mine."

When she and Helen Breaker walked over to him and he saw them he beamed.

"Hello Hem," Hadley said.

"Hello Hash," said Ernest.

As they walked toward Helen's car Ernest carried his duffel bag and Hadley carried his scrapbook. It was filled with cuttings of the published articles. 'I want to show them all to you,' he told her. She was delighted, however she noticed that he limped a little and he had dark circles under his eyes. He was not sleeping and his wound must be acting up again.

Helen drove her electric car to the house on Cates Avenue, Hadley and Ernest sat in the backseat. A lot had changed since they last saw each other. Her sister and husband had separated. Fonnie lived with the two children in the first floor of the house. Hadley lived on the second floor and taken in two boarders who lived upstairs with her. First there was Ruth Bradfield, a twenty three year old advertising copywriter for the downtown department store Grand Leader, and then Bertha Doan, a forty year old librarian and friend of Florence Richardson.

That evening was a round of introductions: Fonnie and the children Fronchen and Roddy; Ruth; Bertha. Around dinner they asked him about Chicago, what was it like living in such a big city, and they asked about his war experience, what was that like?

In front of the fireplace, when Hadley and Ernest were alone, they talked about literature and the books they were reading together: Strindberg, Lewis's "Main Street," and Chesterton's "Life of Browning."

That night he slept in her room. It was 'frilly feminine' he told her, and smelled nicely of lilac. Everything was perfect, 'like a decorated cake.' Hadley slept on the downstairs sofa. She spent a great deal of the night unable to sleep knowing that he was upstairs asleep in her bed. She stared in the dark at the print on the wall of Michelangelo's "Creation."

Part of the reason for his trip was to make their engagement known. "I am tired of keeping it a secret, and why should we keep it a secret anyway? I sit with Mrs. Charles and cannot say a thing when she tells me how much in love you are with Katy and that Mrs. Charles needs to have a serious talk with Katy in order to dissuade her from your affections. 'They are just not right for each other,' she says. But I cannot then shout out to the rooftops that you are right for me."

So they made the rounds. Ernest sat in his new three piece suit as they explained to Mrs. Charles that it was Hadley to whom Ernest's affections were directed. Not Katy. Mrs. Charles seemed surprised, and relieved.

Hadley's sister seemed to like Ernest at first. That, Hadley carefully explained, was her good side. She flips moods in an instant so let us hope she stays with her good side the whole time you are here.

I'm for that, Ernest nodded in agreement.

But then there was dinner.

"So, Mr. Hemingway, might I inquire as to your intentions?"

With a piece of pot roast in his upraised fork Ernest stopped and looked over at Fonnie.

"My intentions?" he asked.

"Yes, toward my younger sister," she replied.

"Fonnie," Hadley said, "what a question to be asking, here and now of all places."

"Well, Hadley, someone has to be the responsible one. Neither father or mother are here any longer to look out for you so as the eldest the responsibility naturally falls on me."

Hadley looked confused. "The responsibility for what?"

"Why, Hadley my dear; to determine this young man's intent and suitability. There is nothing wrong in that."

"But isn't that for me to decide?"

"But Hadley, you know how frail and at times confused you can be. So we need an objective and mature assessment of something this important. I am only trying to protect you."

Fonnie turned her attention to Ernest. He could almost feel her eyes boring into him. He put his fork down and wiped his mouth with his napkin.

"Well," he began. "I know that my intentions are completely honorable and my intentions are to explore the friendship that is growing up between us."

"I see," Fonnie said as she glanced back and forth quickly between the two of them.

"And you work at an advertising company I understand."

"I write copy at the "Co-operative Commonwealth in Chicago."

"And is this a permanent career?"

"Is it a permanent career? I would have to say no but it is alright for now.

"What are your future intentions as far as employment is concerned."

"Well, I intend to be a writer."

"You wish to be a writer of fiction?"

"Yes."

Ernest did not like the way that she moved her head and rolled her eyes.

"And exactly how do you intend to support a family by being such a writer. Are they not notorious for living off others while they chase their fanciful dreams?"

"Fonnie, this is ridiculous," Hadley said, stabbing at her food with her fork.

Ernest sat for a moment. If it were anyone else he would insult them right back. But this was Hadley's sister. He tried to remain calm. He cleared his throat.

"There are many good writers who make quite a comfortable living by writing. There is Edwin Balmer for one, and then there was Francis Marion Crawford, Harold Bell Wright makes a huge amount of money writing, and then there was Charles Dickens who became one of the richest men alive. So there is quite a financial reward for successful writers."

"Yes, indeed, but are you to be as famous as Charles Dickens?"

Ernest smiled his wide and charming boyish grin.

"I will be some day," he said.

"Fonnie, please," Hadley again said.

It was then that Ruth loudly cleared her throat. She glanced from Hadley to Fonnie.

"Perhaps a small change of subject would be best, don't you think? So, Ernest, Hadley tells me you are taken with fly fishing. I can't say that I have ever tried it myself but it does sound like a fascinating sport."

4. Seventeenth of March

Hadley and Ruth Bradfield got off the train together. She had just seen Ernest in St. Louis last week but she had to see him again. She was worried. As she explained to Ruth on the train ride from St. Louis to Chicago, she was worried that it was too much. Maybe he feels he's being smothered. Is it all going too fast? Even though it seems like an eternity and they have been friends forever still they only just met last October. It has been five months and we are talking about getting married. And now I'm pressuring him because I'm impatient and we made it all public last week and we went over to Mrs. Charles and told her. He has known her from Horton Bay for years. Am I making a mistake?

Ruth listened and nodded and here and there commented. But she mostly listened.

I don't know, Hadley continued. There was just this look in his eye, and his change of manner, it frightened me. I just had to see him again as soon as possible to make sure. I need to know that everything is alright.

They rode a cab over to the apartment. Ken answered the door. He was surprised. He gracefully hugged them both. Come in, he said. Try to overlook the bachelorness of the place. The foyer was tile. There was a sweeping circular marble staircase up to the upper rooms.

"My, this place looks so elegant," Hadley said.

"It's beautiful," Ruth said as she looked all around.

Hadley could see Don Wright and another boy she did not recognize coming out from the kitchen. But then Bill Horne followed them out.

"Bill, what a pleasant surprise to see you here, I thought you were in New York."

Bill walked over to her and they hugged.

"I was in New York but I just got back. I'm staying here for a little bit."

"My my, it's just like old times then. This is my friend Ruth Bradfield. Ruth, this is a good friend Bill Horne."

They nodded and smiled and shook hands.

Then Hadley heard someone on the stairs.

She turned her head and there he was.

With his hands in his pockets and a slightly mischievous smile on his face he almost skipped down the stairs. She smiled watching him descend. Everything was suddenly normal and sweet.

It was all right. Everything troubling her just disappeared. Her fears vanished with the touch of his presence.

Ernest boldly came up to her and wrapped his arms around her waist

240

and right there in front of everyone he bent down and kissed her. It was a long slow kiss and their lips finally parted but he held her close, their faces barely separated.

"Hello there my Hash," he said.

"Hello there my Hem," said she.

She glanced around at all of the others in the foyer. They were all standing and watching them. She was slightly embarrassed but it was a far cry from the train station when, with others on the platform, he was too embarrassed himself to even hold her much less kiss her. Everything was fine.

They sat on the floor in his room Indian style. They were drinking hot tea. The pot sat between them.

"Fonnie took you aside when you were down here didn't she."

"Well, yes she did."

"She told you things about me, didn't she."

"Yes, well, yes."

"What things? You have to tell me what she said."

"Are you sure you want to hear this?"

"Yes."

"But I defended you rigorously, I did."

"You have to tell me."

"Why?"

"Because if you ever want to get any rest ever again you have to tell me."

"She said you were weak and frail. She said that you fell out of a window and were crippled."

"Yes, well, that part is true. I was six years old and the nursery was on the second story. I was sick and home from school when I saw Mike the local handyman pass by. I was terribly fascinated with Mike. He used to clean out the gutter spouts and rake leaves. So I shouted out for him and we were talking and I leaned out too far. I fell out of the window and fell flat on my back on the brick wall."

"My God, that could have killed you."

"Yes, and it hurt like the dickens too. It injured my back and for a long time afterwards I couldn't walk and they had to push me around in a carriage. I healed eventually but both my mother and sister treat me as if I had been permanently crippled."

"Here, do you want some more hot water."

"Yes, please. So, go on, what else?"

"Well she said that you were prone to headaches and cramps and

241

other things of that nature."

"And what woman is not during her monthly time? You have sisters."

"Yes, that I do."

"So what else did she say about me? Give me the worst."

"Well, probably the worst was that you occasionally have epileptic seizures."

"I have what?"

He nodded. He did not think he had to repeat it.

"Epilepsy? She told you that I have epilepsy?"

He nodded again.

"I can't believe this. I can't believe that she would lie like that just to hurt me."

"So you're saying you don't have them?"

She stared at him but a trickle of a smile flickered across his face. She tightened one side of her face and turned her head sideways and then brought her fingers up in a clawing fashion.

"Only on Sundays," she slurred out of the side of her mouth.

"Here," he said as he handed her a cookie from a tray of oatmeal cookies, "have a cookie."

She took a bite and chewed it as she stared at the floor.

"It sounds to me," Ernest said, "that she wants to sabotage your happiness for some reason."

"But why, I don't understand her hatred of me."

"Because she loathes herself is what I think. I read some psychology books when I was up in Toronto. It makes a lot of sense."

"Do you think so?"

"Look, you said that she takes strongly after your mother. Both of them hate men, they hate sex. You said that she stopped completely having any sex with her husband. And now he's gone, right? And I'll bet that to her all of it is his fault."

Hadley shook her head yes.

"See, she thinks that driving me away and hurting you is her way of loving you and making sure that you don't get hurt. She's all messed up. Hate and love, sometimes it's hard to know the difference."

"Did she say anything else?"

"Well, she did say that there is some Mr. Hyde in your Dr. Jekyll that emerges every once in awhile."

Hadley leaned in close to him and opened her eyes wide.

"Only when I don't get my way, my good man."

"Well then," Ernest said as he took a deep breath, "I'm glad that we have that squared away."

She laughed and then with the palms of her hands against his cheeks she kissed him. They rubbed their noses back and forth. She then gave him a quick kiss again.

"And don't you forget it," she whispered into his mouth.

"You need to get ready; we're going out to dinner. Katy will be here any minute. Sure you don't want to invite Ruth?"

"No, she's out with the Breakers. It's okay."

Ernest and Hadley, and Bill Horne and Katy Smith, drove to the Victor House on Grand Avenue. Hadley wore her new dress. It was a black satin dress with Bulgarian embroidery around the neckline. She felt elegant and important holding onto Ernest's arm as they walked into the restaurant. They ate spaghetti and drank red wine and they danced to the band.

Ernest told Hadley that his old friend Nick Neroni from Italy comes by and they go up onto the roof of the building and box. 'He's quite good but not quite good enough to beat me.'

Katy leaned in and tapped Hadley on the shoulder.

"Picture the wonderful scene, Hash, all the boys together. Kenley sits in the living room discussing literature while Wright comes home with strange women for the night and Wemedge goes up onto the roof in order to box. It's all very frightfully manly I suppose."

They all drank and they all laughed and they all sang and they all danced.

"This is so wonderful," Hadley said at one point to the whole group. She took Ernest's arm. "Allah be praised that we are living at the same time and know each other."

5. Parents

They visited his parents.

"Don't worry," Ernest told Hadley on the trolley to Oak Park. "My Dad likes everyone and my Mom will like you because you are so good with your music. And my sisters will automatically like you because you're their big brothers girl."

"Well, I will try to be on my best behavior."

Clarence met them at the door. He was dressed in a new three piece suit. His oiled hair was slicked back.

As Hadley played the piano and Grace stood ready to sing Ernest watched his father cross the room toward his office. Clarence motioned to him to follow. Once Grace began to sing Ernest got up and followed his father into his office. His father closed the door.

"Shouldn't we be listening?" Ernest asked.

His father waved it off. He was breathing heavily and there was perspiration on his forehead.

"I wanted to have a small talk with you and now is the best time."

"Sure, Dad, what did you want to talk about?"

Clarence took a deep breath.

"You know that I am diabetic?"

"Yes."

"Well, it has advanced and I am now in the clutches of angina pectoris."

Ernest did not say anything.

"It is a restriction of blood flow to the heart that brings on chest pains. I feel it whenever I climb the stairs. The chest pain from the exertion of climbing the stairs is so great at times that I don't know if I will be able to finish climbing. Even getting in and out of the car can bring on an attack."

"Does Mom know about this?"

"No, no, heavens no. I don't want her to worry."

"Are you seeing another doctor?"

"Yes and he concurs with me. There are different conditions that a diabetic is prone to. I fear that Bright's disease may be next."

"We can't possibly know that."

"No, you are correct. But the possibility is there nevertheless. I do not want you to worry, I have arranged for the bulk of my estate to come to you."

"Dad, I don't want to hear about that. You've got lots of years ahead of you so don't talk about that."

"It is merely preparation. But please, son, I do not want anyone else in the family to know about this."

Ernest nodded in agreement.

"But why are you telling me?"

Clarence stood staring out the window for a moment. He glanced at Ernest and weakly smiled then looked away.

"I don't know. I just felt the need to share it with someone. To be close. In the past we have shared so many things. I guess I miss that time."

Ernest did not know what to say.

Grace's singing stopped. The piano music stopped.

"Well," Clarence said as he took a deep breath, "I suppose we should get back."

They both turned toward the door.

"I just wanted to say, son, that I like Hadley. I do. I think you have made a wonderful choice."

"Thank you. I think so too."

Clarence drove them to the trolley station. Ernest got out of the car.

"Stay here, Dad. You don't need to get out."

Ernest stood and rested his hands on the door. He leaned his head into the car.

"Don't do what you don't have to do."

"Good bye son."

"Are you sure you're alright?"

"Yes, yes. For now I'm fine. I only told you so you'll know, just in case."

"Well, I don't like you talking like that."

Clarence reached up and put his hand on Ernest's hand.

"We must be real, son."

Ernest nodded.

Clarence called out to Hadley, standing behind Ernest.

"It was so nice to meet you."

"Yes, Mr. Hemingway, it was a wonderful pleasure."

"Please; Clarence."

"Clarence."

"Well, we'd best get going. We don't want to miss the last trolley."

"But I could drive you home."

"No," Ernest insisted. "You need to get back. We'll both be fine."

Ernest and Hadley started walking toward the station. They waved and said good night as they walked away. Clarence, alone in the car, waved and watched as Ernest and Hadley walked toward the station, emerging from the dark of the parking lot and into the light from the platform lamps. Ernest put his arm around her shoulder. She put her arm around his waist.

Clarence remembered when he used to walk with Grace, back when they were young. As they walked toward twilight under the rows of trees with the wind above them making a chorus of the branches and the leaves Clarence carefully reached out and held her hand in his. She reached over with her other hand and held his hand holding hers. She rested her head against his shoulder. And they walked the tree lined road and the breeze brought the leaves down like a shower of rain. Through the descending whirling leaves they walked together down the street and into the twilight.

On the trolley on the way home Ernest and Hadley talked about his parents. Your mother is a lot like my mother, actually, Hadley said. Then I pity you, he said. I don't know if we are going to be great friends but I think she's willing to try, she said. We don't have to worry, he said. Why, she said. Because, he said, when we get married and make our penniless dash off to Italy we aren't going to look back, he said. About that, she said. I wasn't going to tell you until later, and if Fonnie had her way I shouldn't ever tell you, but when we dash off to Italy it won't be penniless, she said.

"How do you mean?" he asked.

"Well I have a small trust fund and it pays me every month. I've been calculating and if we are very careful we can almost live off of the fund."

"Really?" He could barely believe what he was hearing.

"And if you can sell some pieces to the Toronto Star here and there then I think we can make it."

"Hash, that is great news."

"So you can write and write until you break in big."

Ernest hugged her tightly.

"Oh Ernie, isn't it grand? Isn't loving each other so very very wonderful."

Ernest shouted and the others on the trolley looked over at him. While they were watching he kissed her.

"I so love you," he whispered to her.

"Dear," she said holding his cheek in her hands, "the world's a jail and we're going to break it together."

Chapter Twelve

He was the first patient there. But soon the hospital was filled with patients. The metal bed was in the middle of the room with the head of the bed against the wall. Out one side of the bed he could see into the hall; see everyone as they passed by. On the other side was the large window. He could see out onto the terrace where those who could walk gathered. He could talk to them through the open window. He could hear but not see the shouts from the street and the traffic. As days passed he watched the sun coming through the window across his room, disappear, and then pass the same path the next day.

The surgeon said he will wait for the right knee to heal cleanly so the bullet will be encysted and he can make a clean cut under the knee cap and take the bullet out without danger of infection. He will remove the bullet in the right ankle at the same time. We have to wait, he said. We have to wait for your body to heal.

As days passed visitors came.

There was a Henry Villard in the next room who came in to talk. American. New York. Driver with Section One.

There was Coles Van Brunt Seeley down the hall that came in to talk. American. New Jersey. Driver with Section One.

Theodore Brumback came to visit.

Captain James Gamble came to visit.

Captain Meade Detweiler came to visit.

Brumback wrote a letter to Clarence and Grace explaining all that happened. Eventually they removed the bandages from his hands so Ernest could write his own letters.

Agnes von Kurowsky was one of the nurses who treated him. She was tall and slender with chestnut colored hair and with blue or grey eyes depending on the light. Her white uniform, with buttons down the middle, open at the neck, was loose fitting and rustled like the breeze when she walked. She smelled fresh and clean. She tried to keep her hair tied up under her small starched white hat. She was six or seven years older.

She smiled at his charm and laughed at his jokes and she held his hand with a light touch as she took his pulse.

247

1. Anderson II

Ernest and Sherwood Anderson got off the trolley in Palos Park. They walked up the hill. It was a beautiful spring day. They walked and talked passing under the trees walking from shade into sunlight and then back into shade.

Sherwood explained that his good friend the literary critic Paul Rosenfeld invited Sherwood on a trip to Europe, all expenses paid. Sherwood said yes, of course he would go.

"I've never seen Europe, have you?"

"Yes I have but only during the war. I was in Italy mostly."

"There are many exciting things happening in the arts in Europe right now. I cannot miss this chance."

They walked along the rolling hills and mostly open fields. He called his house "The Box" since it was so small. He lived there and tried to write.

"A writer needs a place where no one bothers you."

His wife Tennessee came only once in awhile. But being gone in Europe for so long he decided to sublet it to Don Wright. He needed to get a few things, he said, and then Don would move in on April the first.

"Do you want to come along, we can talk."

"I would love to."

They entered a development of houses. The houses were set back from the street. There were large green grassed lawns well trimmed with manicured bushes and trees. A lawn sprinkler waved back and forth across the grass.

"Everything is so tidy here," Sherwood said. "Why do you think that everything is kept so tidy? What does that say of the people?"

Ernest looked around. It was not that different than Oak Park.

"Did you know that I thanked Kenley for introducing me to you? I think that you are going to go someplace. Now from the stories that you have shown me you seem to have been influenced and have mastered Kipling and O. Henry. That is good, that is very good, because as a writer we must struggle with all who have come before us and imitate and master all of them because why should we write if we do not have something to say in a better way."

"I really like your idea of there being a distinctive American Literature growing up. Most of what you learn in school is British."

"That is all fine but you have to move on. There is a whole world out there and there are many writers we must struggle with in order to create our own. I recommend the Russians, absolutely: there is Turgenev, a must, and Chekhov, and of course Dostoyevsky. Ah yes, he is a master. There is nothing like "Brothers Karamazov" anywhere else in literature, it is a bible. I have felt for a long time he is the one writer I could go down on my knees to."

Ernest laughed.

"Well I guess I have a lot of reading to do."

"Yes, read everything but especially read the good stuff. And also read all of the new stuff coming out now that is equally good as the old. There is "Sons and Lovers" by Lawrence, and "Dubliners" by Joyce, and then there is "Tender Buttons" by Gertrude Stein. She is amazing with words, and even words separated from their meaning. She is one I have to meet when I am in Paris on my trip."

There were different stories about Sherwood Anderson and a certain episode in his life. The turning point. The point of no return. Ernest asked him.

"Oh yes, you mean the day I exited to Elsinore? The crazy day."

"It changed you forever?"

"It was when I realized that you cannot bow to two masters. You must follow the path to one."

The story of what happened that day has become legend. Anderson was the president of a paint factory in Elyria, Ohio. He was married but he was not very happy in his marriage. He did not see how he could escape it. He had a degree of success in business but was completely disillusioned by the ways of business. He did not see how he could escape it. He lived in Elyria but was bored and repulsed by the petite shallowness of the townsmen. He did not see how he could escape it.

He set aside a room upstairs for himself toward the back of the house. It was barely furnished with a cot, two chairs and a flat top desk. On the table were paper, a pen, and a few books. He had a locksmith put a lock on the door and he kept the key in his pocket.

His room was where he could go to be with himself. He needed to know who he was. The outward things of his life, his marriage, his children, his business, none of then gave him pleasure or fulfillment. He was not happy and did not know why. He wanted to understand.

He began to write. He wrote about himself, about his childhood, about all the things and the people that he could remember. He wrote about what happened during the day, whom he saw, what had happened, and why.

He started to write stories. He made up stories to try and explain what was in his heart. He wrote stories to understand himself.

Anderson worked all day at his business and then came home and went up into his room to write. He wrote all evening and at times deep into the night. His wife Cornelia asked him to come down and play with the children. Sometimes he did come down but he was not happy when he was not writing and other times he just did not come down.

But he was at work at the paint factory by eight o'clock whether he got any sleep or not.

He wrote his first novel called "Windy McPherson's Son." He had his secretary Frances Shute correct his spelling and type the manuscript. He liked his secretary. He once told her that she was strong and full of virility and honest. She had worked for him for four years and was loyal and dedicated. She was a tom boy who, during her lunch break, might wrestle some of the younger male workers in the warehouse.

Frances stayed after hours in order to type his stories and his novel. When they both finally left the office they walked down the railroad tracks that ran alongside the building. She could see the strain in him. She knew that he was not getting any sleep. He was working day and night and was unhappy. Once, as they walked along the tracks in the dark, she touched his arm and when he turned to look at her she said: "It would be wonderful if you could get clear of all this."

Anderson hesitated but then they walked on.

It was on November 28, 1912, Thanksgiving Day, that Anderson went to work as usual. His secretary, Frances Shute, was there. She noticed that he 'acted queerly.' He sat at his desk opening the mail and noted that it contained very little money. He started to dictate a letter but stared out the window. Across the railroad tracks he could see the Black River. He stood up. He stood next to the gas heater for a moment.

"I feel as though my feet were wet, and they keep getting wetter," he told Frances.

She nodded in reply, not knowing what to say.

Anderson picked up a pen and wrote a note:

Cornelia:
There is a bridge over a river with cross-ties before it. When I come to that I'll be all right. I'll write all day in the sun and the wind will blow through my hair.
Sherwood.

Anderson folded the note and then stepped over to Frances and handed the paper to her.

"This is a note for my wife. I think I am going out for a walk. I do not know if I will come back."

With that Anderson walked out the door. Frances watched from the window as he waked east down the railroad tracks.

Three days passed.

It was a little after five in the afternoon of December 1, 1912 when a man entered the J.H. Robinson Drugstore at East 152nd Street and Aspinwall Avenue in eastern Cleveland, Ohio. Fred Ward, the store pharmacist, watched the man as he came into the store. The man was unshaven and his dark grey business suit was rumbled and creased, his trousers were mud stained and his shoes were crusted with dry mud. The man stood as if in a daze. Fred walked over to the man.

"Can I help you?"

The man gazed at him. He looked ill. Fred pulled up a chair.

"Here, sit down."

The man sat down. He sat for a moment in silence before he finally spoke.

"I am lost. Where am I?"

"You are in Collinwood, Cleveland."

"Collinwood in Cleveland," the man said as he held his hand to his forehead.

"Where are you from?"

"Up over there, up north I think. I don't really know from where, and I can't tell you who I am either."

"Are you alright?"

"No, I don't think so." He reached into his jacket pocket and pulled out a notebook and handed it to Fred.

"Here, see if you can find out who I am. Is there anyone in there who lives in Cleveland?"

Fred thumbed through the notebook. It listed names and numbers. Finally he saw a name he recognized, Edwin Baxter of the Elyria Chamber of Commerce.

"You stay right here while I call someone."

The man nodded his head.

2. Twenty eighth of May

The dark night flew by the window as the train made its way to St. Louis. Ernest and Bill Horne sat together unable to sleep. His back was hurting him and he walked the empty aisle back and forth trying to stretch it out.

"I have to admit I'm a little scared about my lack of jobage."

"Bill, you're looking, just because those clowns let you go doesn't mean there aren't others who want you."

"Where are they? I'm getting depressed about my prospects here. I might have to go back to Yonkers. My family might find me something there."

"It's not the end of the world."

"It's crap, Ernie. I'm twenty nine, a graduate of Princeton, unmarried, and I have to go home to Mommy and Daddy so they can take care of me? It's crap."

"You said that twice in the same sentence."

Horne glared at Ernest who then shrugged his shoulder. Horne looked away.

"Look old buddy we are whizzing to St. Louis where we'll meet up with two beautiful girls and have a wonderful and happy time. No room for a sourpuss here is there?"

Horne nodded.

"You're right. It just gets me down, everything just gets me down."

"Now just so you understand, Hadley is for me and Ruth is for you, we understand that?"

Horne laughed.

"What if we make it the other way around?"

"Heh, Mr. Horney, I've seen you box, who do you think will win that round?"

"Well, I'll settle for B.L.G. Just like I named her: Beautiful Little Girl."

The train raced on in the night. The wheels clacked on the rails. Ernest turned to Horne.

"Seriously, pal: about the National Debt I owe you."

Horne shook his head.

"Go to hell with your talk about seeds. If I can't grubstake my best and bosom buddy for a while without making him feel he owes me money, then I'm a weed and it's time for the Supreme Lawnmower."

"I'm just saying. . ."

"Like I told you Ernie, I'm backing you for the marathon not just a

253

quick sprint."

Ernest nodded. "Thanks buddy."

It was early in the morning when Hadley answered the doorbell. Ernest and Bill stood on the porch unshaved with wrinkled slept in clothes.

It was hot and humid. Hadley called down Ruth and then cooked a large breakfast for the four of them. Eggs sunny side up, Canadian Bacon, orange juice she had squeezed herself, and homemade toasted bread with hot butter and jam.

They sweat while they ate but it was grand.

After they freshened up they went to the tennis courts in the park. Hadley held her own against Ernest's onslaught. But whenever Ernest missed a shot he "sizzled." They had to sit and wait until he finished "sizzling."

On their way back from the tennis courts they walked by Hadley's neighbor sitting on her front porch. Hadley waved to her and brought the group up to meet her.

She was a very old woman.

"Mrs. Offenclause, these are my friends from Chicago I told you about. This is Bill Horne, and this is Ernest."

"So you are the young man in question?"

"I suppose," Ernest answered, flashing his wide sparkling smile.

Back in Hadley's house Ernest had to comment.

"Boy, she was wrinkled up like a prune or an apple gone bad."

Hadley slapped him on the shoulder.

"Shame on you. She is a very nice and healthy minded old lady scarred by living a long long time."

"She's still wrinkled like a prune."

That afternoon, letting Bill and Ruth be alone together, Hadley took Ernest to meet Marguerite Schullyer. Hadley wrote to Ernest about her. You have given me such confidence in myself, she wrote him, that I have been daring in many ways. She had a friend Marguerite, who was a sculptress, and she was sculpting a work on the three Graces. But through out Life class all winter the models were all men. How can you create the three Graces with male models?

I long for the female form, she said.

So, Hadley wrote to Ernest, several times a week now I go out to her place and I pose nude for her. I am the middle Grace holding up a big bowl.

Ernest did not like the idea.

So Hadley brought Ernest out to meet Marguerite. They sat on the front porch in wicker chairs and sipped lemonade. They discussed art and beauty. In her studio Hadley was amused watching Ernest eyeing the statue of the three Graces, especially the central Grace.

On Sunday they ate another large breakfast and then packed a picnic lunch. They drove to the Meramec River and rented canoes. They spent the day canoeing up and down the river. Bill Horne, reading a local guide, read out load to Ernest and Hadley in the other canoe.

"It says that the first European who navigated the river was a French Jesuit Priest by the name of Jacques Gravier in 1699."

Horne laughed.

"Here's the best part, Ernie this is for you. It says that the name of the river in the local Indian Algonquian language means 'River of the Ugly Fish.'"

"Well I guess there will be no fly fishing here," Ernest called out across the water as two ducks quacked by. "I'd be too afraid of what I might pull up."

They stopped to climb some white cliffs and then picnic in the shade and the grass. Hadley and Ernest walked along the shore of the river.

"Let's leave them together again," Hadley said. She giggled a little bit.

"What," Ernest asked.

"Horney is a very fine fellow but he's a little too eager. 'A girl, a girl, my kingdom for a girl.'"

They both laughed.

"He's jealous," Ernest said.

"But isn't it so sad that our happiness can be so cruel to others?"

They talked as they walked.

They planned for a September wedding but they did not know where, either St. Louis or Chicago. And they did not want a big fuss. By November Hadley figured they would have enough money for Italy.

And then the world, she said throwing her arms up into the air.

Ernest said he had "a peach" of a letter from Grace. She offered Windemere for their honeymoon. Just let me know when, she wrote. It's a beautiful and romantic spot, he said, and it won't cost us anything.

"Why not." Hadley said.

But it was that night before they left that Fonnie had her rampage. They argued over dinner, as before, but Ernest noticed something desperate in her manner, her eyes sparkled fear and hatred. Hadley said that Fonnie was depressed. Her husband Roland was still in a sanatorium back east. She had a hard time earning any money and she was afraid for the welfare of her children.

Fonnie's lips trembled when she talked.

She asked Ernest why he wanted to marry Hadley since she was lazy and too frail for anything. And you, how many women have you slept with, and is it true that you have a venereal disease?

Fonnie said she had consulted Dr. Schwab, a psychologist, who was one of Hadley's doctors, and he said she should not marry, but if she insisted then she was too frail for childbirth for at least six or seven years.

Hadley fumed. She demanded to know everyone that she had said this to and do not ever share my intimate secrets with anyone again.

Fonnie shouted back for Hadley to control herself, I am only doing what Mama would have done if she were here.

It is none of your business, Hadley said trying to gain control over her outburst. Fonnie was crying and started to leave the room. Hadley called out to her that she was never to speak to her again about Ernest or their marriage plans.

When Hadley took Ernest and Horne to the station she apologized.

"Don't worry about it," Horne said. "Family, you know, you can't live with them but then again they're family."

Hadley turned to Ernest.

"We cannot have the wedding here. I cannot allow her to take over and ruin everything for me."

"Then St. Louis is a no. I was thinking anyway that if Mom wants us in Windemere for the honeymoon maybe I can convince them to swing a wedding right there in Horton Bay. There's a Methodist church there. Why not there? It will be small and cozy, intimate, and just across the lake from Windemere. What do you say?"

"I say yes."

3. Munitions Factory

"I'm writing a novel now. A whole novel is just busting loose in my brain," Ernest wrote in his letter to Hadley.

"After months of frustration where I have not written anything worth saving I'm finally on the right track. I've done a couple of chapters. My friend Nick comes over and we box on the roof and he tells me all kinds of war stories. He was there through most of it. I think that first got me going on it."

When she heard the news Hadley was excited and immediately wrote him back.

"My goodness a whole novel is rattling around in that lovely brain of yours, I am so impressed with you. That is so much different than writing a short story. A whole novel can be such a labyrinth it is hard not to get lost."

Ernest wrote back.

"So far I am not lost. I'm writing different parts of my experience in the war. I have to bring all of the parts together and make it one whole. That will be the challenge. It will be on the experiences of a boy in the war wounded on the Italian front and his recovery in the hospital. I'm following Anderson's marvelous advice to write what I know and understand, and only write what I know and understand. I was there so I know. Ken says to focus on the boy recovering in the hospital and make the war part background. It could be a love story with the war as background. But can that be? What do you think?"

Hadley returned a reply.

"Love can flower anywhere. Pour your heart into it my sweet and make me so proud."

Ernest stood in front of the chest of drawers. He was typing. But the keys kept sticking and bunching up. He grew more and more angry. The ideas were there and were flowing out but they were getting jumbled up because the stupid typewriter keys could not keep up.

"I almost threw the thing out the window," he wrote to Hadley.

"Let me buy you a new Corona for your birthday," Hadley wrote back. "I would love to be the one who gave you the Corona that you wrote your novel on. Please send me the parts you've written. I want to experience it with you."

Ernest, standing facing his typewriter with a clean sheet of paper in the roller, thought about what to write.

It was a bright clear day. The truck was full of Red Cross men. The canvas covering was pulled off. Ernest sat and watched as they drove down the road. Ultimately they were being driven to their different stations at the front but there was something to do before they went.

He held his arm up to shade his eyes from the sun. There were tall trees along the road that gave some shade. He watched the dust from the truck swirl in the air in the wake of their passing. There was a stream that ran alongside the road. The water was fresh and clear but not very deep. He could see the water rushing over the stones as it swept down the hillside. Beyond, through the trees, he could see the grapevines stretching out into the distance in neat parallel rows.

A farmer stood on the side of the road as they passed and waved. Ernest and several of the men waved back. The truck turned up a hill and Ernest held the side of the truck as they angled up the road. Birds swooped through the trees chattering as they flew. Ernest followed their flight. He looked up into the blue of the day and the soft billowing clouds.

Finally the truck came to a stop. There was the smell of fire but from where Ernest sat all he could see was the valley grape vined below.

Someone shouted: "Everyone out."

Ernest waited for the men in front of him to jump down from the truck before he jumped down. When he turned around the side of the truck and walked toward the front he saw it. A large factory-like building was blown apart and on fire. A field beyond was also burning. There was a barbed wire fence that separated the road from another open field of grass. There were things clinging to the barbed wire, dangling down.

They separated the men into teams. One team was told to put out the fire in the building. There was a water well and they were pumping out the water. Another team was told to put out the fire in the far field.

Ernest was in the near team. The Captain explained. It is a munitions factory and it blew up and started the fire. We have to collect the bodies. They were blown by the force of the blast into the field.

But it was not until Ernest got to the barbed wire fence that he realized what he was looking at. The grass all around was splattered red. Chunks of flesh and small parts of bodies clung to the barbed wire. The blast blew the people apart and shoved the parts through the barbed wire shredding everything like a meat grinder.

Ernest walked through a small gate into the field. His boots slipped on the red wet grass. Pieces of flesh and parts of bodies were everywhere. He had to hold his hand up to his nose because of the stench. Flies buzzed about.

"Pick up the bodies first and take them over to the stretchers by the truck."

They were handing out blankets to serve as slings to carry the bodies. Farther away from the factory the bodies were more intact as though the blast shot them up and over the shredding fence.

There was the body of a naked woman. The blast tore her clothes off. She was headless and one arm was torn out. She was spread out on the grass. Ernest and Milford Baker spread out the blanket next to her. It took a moment before they touched the body. It was warm. They rolled the body onto the blanket. They wrapped it over to cover her and then one at each end they picked it up.

All of the bodies were women. They worked in the factory. Stripped naked by the blast, dismembered, they were strewn out across the field like thrown dice. Ernest could not believe that they were dead women. You don't see dead women like this in a war. Only stacks of dead men. There was something wrong in that.

They worked all day. They carried body after body until there were only parts of bodies left. At first it was sickening and two of the soldiers vomited into the grass. But after awhile it became mechanical. They were just picking up slabs of meat and fat as if they were in a butcher shop moving slabs of meat from one tray to another. They were not living animals anymore. They had to shoo away the ever increasing number of flies. Ernest was picking up arms and legs and placing them into the bloodied blanket. Last in the clean up were the shreds of flesh and organs hanging on the barbed wire.

4. Switzerland

As the weather warmed Ernest slept up on the roof. With enough dirt as a foundation it was as if camping out in the woods. He could fall asleep watching the night sky. It reminded him of Windemere. It reminded him of fishing trips and camping out.

He wrote to Bill Smith.

He was having second thoughts about the whole marriage thing. In your life you come to love two or three streams better than anything, the Sturgeon, the Pigeon, the Black. And to camp and fish them with your friends: there was nothing better. But then along comes a woman and the streams could all go to hell because now there was nothing but her.

Why does it have to be that way?

Sleeping under the stars he thought of James Gamble (come away with me and be free) and he thought of a vacation he took to Stresa on the Lago Maggiore.

September, 1918.

The two of them sat on the porch of the hotel. They were shaded by the veranda awning. They both had drinks sitting on white napkins on the table. They looked out across the tiled plaza to the docks. The sky was heavenly blue and the sun was bright.

The summer season was winding down. The hotel was less than half full. Some of the other smaller hotels were shut down completely. Tables and chairs were stacked up in the corner of the porch ready to be put downstairs, stored for the winter. There were only a small handful of people left. They were the regulars. There was an older Countess who referred to them as those 'dear boys.'

Ernest was strong enough to vacation for a week in Stresa. His leg still hurt at times and he still could not walk without his cane, but he decided to come and see the sights. Back at the Milano Hospital Agnes wrote him that his empty room haunted her, please come back soon.

"The war seems so far away."

It was John Miller who spoke. They came on their vacation together. John was in Milano Hospital for pneumonia but he had recovered. He was a Section Two driver for the Red Cross. He was originally from Minnesota. 'I miss the big sky,' he told Ernest. They were both in the Red Cross, they both had come over on the same ship, they were both in Milano Hospital, they were both given awards for saving a wounded soldier under fire, they both loved drinking Asti Spumante and they were both in love with one of their nurses, Ernest, Agnes, and John, Ruth Brooks. So they thought they had a lot in common.

"It's like it doesn't exist any more," Ernest replied as he reached for his drink. The ice clinked in the glass as he took a sip.

"I hear that Pier Vincenzo Bellia is one of the richest men in Italy," John said.

"Really."

"And the way Bianca was with us, who knows what might come of it."

"You are dreaming beyond your means my friend."

Seeing the two of them dressed in their uniforms, and Ernest walking with a cane, Pier Vincenzo Bellia one morning had come over to them and introduced himself. He was a robust man with a full beard and dressed in a fine three piece suit. He was glad to see Americans fighting for Italy. Please, he said, let me treat you. My family and I are taking the cog train up Mattarone. The view is wonderful. Please, come along.

So Ernest and John joined the Bellia family, Vincenzo and his wife and their three daughters, Ceda, Deonisia and Bianca. They were from Torino on vacation. They boarded the small train that swayed and rattled as it slowly climbed the mountain. It was cold at the top station. The wind was firm and cold. But Ernest could not believe the view. He stood and turned around and around. Everywhere was snow capped mountains and clinging white misty clouds and below stretched the blue of the lake.

Ernest took John by the arm.

"Look at this. This is wonderful. This beats paradise all to hell."

Vincenzo invited them to dinner back at the hotel. Bianca asked question after question about America and laughed in a rich contralto voice and her black eyes flashed between them sparkling with curiosity. Vincenzo gave them his card. They were to visit them any time. Maybe for Christmas?

"I'm just pointing out," John said, "that hooking up with pretty Bianca, daughter of one of the richest men in Italy, would be very nice."

They sat in the shade of the porch or the trees near the water and read or listened to the music from the bar. Boats were tied along the piers. Some were still open and used but many were closed up for the winter and covered with white canvas. As small waves came in the small boats quietly bumped against the wooden pier. The bartender let them troll in his boat. Ernest, his stiff leg stretched out at an awkward angle, usually rowed out. Then John rowed as Ernest set the lines. They rowed out to the small island Isola Bella where there was a fisherman's café right on the water.

Sitting on the pier they watched the twilight of the day descend. The lights from Isola Bella sparkled across the darkening water. They could see straight up the lake toward the distant purple mountains caught in the last rays of sunlight.

"The other end of the lake is in Switzerland," John said as he pointed to the distant peaks.

Ernest, watching it all, absorbing it all, shook his head.

"Jesus," he said, "who couldn't recuperate up here, both body and spirit."

John tapped Ernest on the arm.

"What do you say we snatch one of these dinghies and row up into Switzerland and sit up there for the duration of the war?"

"Sounds like a good idea."

They stayed up late. They sat on the patio outside the bar. They sat in the light of the bar. Now in the off season there were not many who sat in the bar late at night. There were only a few. The bartender spent his time wiping down the bar with his white cloth. He liked to keep a clean bar.

They did not like going to bed. It took a long time for them to get to sleep. And once asleep they woke up many times during the night. So they sat in the bar in the light for as long as they could.

John talked about his war experiences. The swampland by the river that he drove through smelled like the peat moss back home. There was a stretch of the road he drove that was open to Austrian snipers. He used to gun the truck and drive fast so to not be shot. But a bullet would clink against the cabin of the truck each time. He used to shout out at the snipers to 'kiss my royal ass' but he was relieved each time he made the run. He was scared. It was like he was reborn each day that he did not die.

Just how many of those days can you have?

Ernest talked about his experiences.

He said that when the shell exploded in front of him that the man in front of him took the brunt of the shrapnel. He was shredded. But if he was not standing there then I would have been shredded. He saved my life but I don't even know his name.

And when the shell exploded I felt my life pull out of my body. It was like a handkerchief being pulled out of a coat pocket. And I remember floating there and thinking how strange to think that I had just died. But then I finally took a deep breath and suddenly I rushed back in and I was alive.

John told him that there were a lot of reasons that could explain what you felt. You don't think that you died and came back do you?

I don't know, Ernest said. I just don't know. Something happened but I don't know what it is.

John, sitting in the arc of the bar light, leaned in further. I think that we just die and that's it. You die and then you're dead.

The bartender came over with their two last drinks.

"Closing time gentlemen," he said. "This is the last for the night."

5. Switzerland II

September, 1918.

Stresa, on the Lago Maggiore, in the Grand Hotel Des Iles Borromees, Room 106, Ernest and John Miller slept in late each morning and then with the drapes pulled back looked out across the shimmering waters of the lake to the Clouded Mystical and Delectable mountains of Switzerland.

The war was still real but it was so far away.

Ernest became intrigued by an old gentleman staying at the hotel. He usually spotted the man in the bar playing billiards. He was very old but agile. He had a full well trimmed moustache. Both his moustache and hair were white. He walked with straight perfect posture. He played billiards with grace and ease.

Ernest walked by the table and stopped. The man looked over and, bending forward slightly, smiled.

"Voi siete dalla Croce Rossa, vedo," the man said waving his hand toward Ernest's uniform.

"Yes, I'm an American in the Red Cross."

"Ah, an American. And you were wounded in the war?" The man replied in perfect English.

"Yes," Ernest said.

"And would the brave American hero care for a game of billiards perhaps?"

"That would be very nice, but do you handicap an inferior player?"

The man waved his head back and forth as well as one finger as if a professor telling a student that he had given the wrong answer to the question.

"Please," he said. "A friendly game is a friendly game."

The man held out his hand. Ernest noticed his large golden rings. "Allow me, I am Count Giuseppe Greppi, and to whom do I owe the honor of meeting?"

"Ernest Hemingway," he said as he shook the man's hand.

They played billiards and sat at the bar with drinks talking into the night.

The Count told him of his life. He was a diplomat and had served at different times both the Italian and the Austrian governments. He had served with Metternich.

"If you do not mind me asking, how old are you?"

The Count laughed with enjoyment.

"I shall be one hundred years old in March."

"Wow, I am amazed."

"No more than I, my young man."

"And what has kept you so young?"

"I drink champagne and I never go to bed before midnight. But the real reason you ask?"

The Count leaned in close to Ernest as if giving away a secret he only wanted Ernest to hear.

"Beautiful women," he whispered and then sat back.

He touched Ernest on his sleeve.

"Ah, they keep your heart beating and your mind alert. In my youth I once dinned with Marie Louise, the Empress of France, this was after her marriage to Napoleon. She was a beautiful and elegant woman."

"Were you ever married?"

"Oh no, there are simply far too many women for that. Follow your heart, I say, but temper it with the practical."

Ernest told the Count that he would be returning to the front when he is well. The Count said that he did not think that would happen.

"Why is that?"

"The war will be over soon. It has been too long. It will end soon."

"Well they said that a year ago."

"Yes but the Americans have now come. They will be in full force. The Germans cannot last much longer. They simply do not have enough men to last much longer."

The Count shook his head.

"This war is a disgrace."

Ernest sipped his drink.

"So what does the future hold for you?"

The Count sipped his champagne before he answered.

"Ernest, at my age the now is the future. There is no distinction."

"Do you think about dying?"

"Yes, but what is the use of that? To me, at my age, every day alive is a sacred blessing. I just take each day as it comes and go to sleep at night wondering if there will be another. In that way I am surprised and happy when another day comes.

"That sounds nice."

"You should think that way my friend. You do not have to be one hundred to think that way. You can begin right now. It will make you happier."

December, 1918.

The war ended in November.

It was done.

Christmas came. Ernest, back in Milano, got a letter from James Gamble. Come, he wrote, come and stay with me in Sicily. It will be so grand.

Gamble was thirty six, a graduate of Yale, and lived in Florence Italy as a painter. His family had money. Now that the war was over he rented a small villa with a garden from an English artist friend of his in Taormina, Sicily. We are just to keep it occupied while he is gone, James wrote.

With Agnes gone on assignment Ernest did not want to sit in the hospital in Milano. So he wrote James: Yes.

Ernest took the train down into southern Italy and then the ferry across to Sicily. James picked him up at the dock and drove to the Villa in Taormina.

There for a week Ernest experienced what it would be like. James offered to pay his way. He would hire him as his secretary but that did not mean anything. When James traveled Europe Ernest would come with him. He would meet interesting people, artists. But Ernest could write and write and write.

"I want to do this for you," James said.

He had one of his own paintings on a easel in the front room. He was painting the sea shore.

"How can you make it more beautiful than it is?" Ernest asked.

"But isn't that what art is about? It captures the beauty and keeps it forever? The world is a better place because of art."

"Art did not stop the war from happening."

"But maybe it will stop the next."

"I don't think so."

"But without that hope, Ernest, what else do we have?"

Ernest did not reply.

The outside balcony of the Villa was made of tile. It was up high on the hill. There was a iron railing so you did not fall. The view was the sea and below the crystal clear waters of the bay. Ernest wore white robes and slippers. In the evening in the front room overlooking the balcony the breeze came in through the open doors and the long white curtains fluttered and waved as the fresh sea breeze came in.

They drank but never got drunk, only a pleasant tipsy. Ernest learned that there was a sophisticated way to drink. They turned off the lights and sat in the Mediterranean moonlight and watched the orange glow from the top of Mount Aetna as the volcano fumed away.

They walked the narrow ancient streets and toured the ancient Greek ruins, and they walked around the Greek Temple in the moonlight walking in and out of the stark dark shadows the moon made from the ruined columns.

James invited guests over for dinner. There were two English painters named Woods and Kitson; there was a British Colonel Bartlett who was short and fat and had a huge walrus moustache, and 'Bartie's' beautiful wife Louise with the long eyelashes; and there was an old Duke of Bronte who claimed Admiral Nelson as an ancestor and who, when asked his employment, answered that he was a perfect gentleman.

"Stay with me Ernest," James said when it was time to return. "I want to be surrounded by art and beauty, forever."

Chapter Thirteen

Agnes prepared him for his surgery. She gave him a sponge bath.

He told her about his sisters. He told her all of the different nicknames he had for them.

"It all sounds so wonderful."

"You would like them, all of them."

"I'm sure that I would."

"And they would like you, I'm sure of it."

She took some pillows from behind his back. It made him flat on the bed.

"When this is all done and we are both back home will you visit me?"

"It will be some time before all of this is done. But maybe, maybe I could stop in and see these wonderful sisters of yours."

Two orderlies came in with a gurney. They slid him across from the bed to the gurney. They started to wheel him out of the room.

"Wait," he said.

Agnes came over to him. She held his hands in hers. She smiled down at him.

"You'll be here when I get out?"

She bent down and kissed him on the forehead.

"Yes, you sweet boy."

They wheeled the gurney out into the hallway and down toward the surgery. It squeaked when the wheels turned. There was a slight bump each time the wheels turned as if something was stuck on the bottom of the wheel. They wheeled him into surgery. The doctors were waiting.

He woke up back in his bed. He looked down and felt his legs. They were still there.

She was not there.

He waited but she did not come.

1. Doodles

Doodles returned from New York. Ernest had to officially move out of her room and share a room with Bill Horne but Ernest was sleeping on the roof almost every night. In the spring and summer that would be fine. But come fall there had to be a change: that change was Hadley. The wedding was set for September the third.

Ernest walked down the hall toward his room when the door to Doodles bedroom opened. He could hear talking and laughing. As he came closer Don Wright stepped out of the room. His hair was not combed. Doodles stood in the doorway. Don, seeing Ernest, looked at Doodles and mouthed the words 'oh no.' Doodles looked at Ernest as he came up to them. She wore a thin silk nightgown and ran her fingers through her hair. When Ernest stopped she giggled and shrugged her shoulders.

"Well, I'm off," Don said and then he walked down the hall toward the front door.

Ernest watched him leave and then turned back to Doodles. She smiled a wide mischievous smile.

"Hemmy, you look like you've seen a ghost."

Doodles giggled again and then turned around and took a step into her room, glancing back over her shoulder. It was obvious she wore nothing under the thin nightgown.

Ernest walked down the hall and out the front door. He saw Don near the stairs.

"Hey, Don."

Don stopped and waited for Ernest to catch up to him.

"What's going on Buddy?"

"Nothing, I'm just on my way back to my place."

"But you and Doodles; are you two doing something?"

"Doing something? What's it to you?"

Ernest was taken aback. He did not expect the hostility in his voice.

"What's it to me? Don, that's Doodles, that's Ken's wife."

"Well gee Hemmy, thanks for pointing that out, you're a real swell guy. Now if you don't mind I need to get home."

"But why are you having an affair with your best friend's wife? That's not right."

"That's not right? Who made you the king of morality? What is between me and Ken and between me and Doodles, frankly, is none of your goddamn business."

"Don, we're all friends here, we were all roommates, I'm just shocked is all. It's not right."

"Look Hemmy, don't stick your nose in where it doesn't belong."

"Ken is my friend and I don't want him hurt."

"He's old enough to take care of himself."

"So stab him in the back."

"Fuck off. Like I said keep your nose out of what you don't know."

"Well here's this, jerk, don't come around here anymore or else I'll rearrange your face."

Ernest glared at him, his eyes like piercing daggers.

Don turned and started down the stairs.

"Don't worry I won't."

Ernest wrote to Hadley explaining what happened. She was not shocked. She already sensed that something was going on between Doodles and Don right from the beginning. There were small signs, she wrote. And then one day when she was staying there she came upon the two of them in the dining room in a delicate embrace while Ken was in the other room. Don left the room stuttering with terror and laughing hysterically when I came in, Hadley wrote. Doodles was as nonchalant as she could be about the whole thing.

Is it any wonder, Hadley continued. With all male roommates the place is dirty and unkept and with Howie bringing different girls home to spend the night why is it that only Bill Horne understands the poor environment of the place.

It was several days later that Ken came up to Ernest sitting in the kitchen eating a bowl of wheat flakes.

"Ernie, Doodles tells me that you and Don had some sort of argument."

Ernest was careful. He did not know what Ken knew.

"Yeah, we did."

"So Don doesn't want to come around anymore."

"Good, what's wrong with that?"

"Look Buddy, I didn't want to have to say this but you're out of line."

Ernest looked at him with surprise.

"I'm out of line? I'm out of line for giving him what he deserves?"

"Look, both of you live here under my roof, and both of you are free to come and go as you please. Now I don't know what the problem between the two of you is and it doesn't really matter. But it's not your place to scare off anybody that I allow to come here."

272

"But I'm doing it for you," Ernest said but then instantly was sorry he had said it. Ken looked confused. It was obvious to Ernest that Ken did not know. And he didn't want to be the one to break the news.

"I don't know how that helps me but believe me, you don't understand. You don't understand what he means to Doodles so for her sake, and for my sake, just set aside your differences with Don and keep them to yourself, for the peaceful balance of things. If you hate him that bad then just don't be here when he comes by."

It took everything in Ernest to not say something. He truly must not know what is going on under his own roof. But Ernest did not say anything. He did not know what to do.

When Bill Smith came by Ernest explained the situation to him. Bill said that he loved his brother but he was certainly no fan of Doodles.

"She came back from New York where she supposedly took these great piano lessons, but from what I've heard of her playing, it doesn't seem that she improved all that much."

"So what was she doing in New York all this time?" Bill asked.

"Exactly my point."

Bill chuckled.

"Did you know that Doodles is just a pet name? Her real name is Genevieve but for the longest time I thought it was Guinevere, I don't know why. My brother likes to surround himself with artists and intelligent creative people so I built up in my mind this vision of them as King Arthur and Guinevere with their surrounding court."

"So does that make Dirty Don a Lancelot?"

"Hardly; he's not exactly a knight in shinning white armor."

Ernest grinned.

"No, but apparently he does lance her a lot."

2. Boxing

Hadley set the box on the table in the living room. Ernest watched as she set it down, a smile on his face. Bill Horne, Nick Neroni, Katy and Bill Smith, Ken and Doodles all stood around him.

"Well, open it," Doodles said, poking him with her finger.

Ernest opened the box and reached in and pulled out the new Corona typewriter. The typewriter was black with gold colored keys and across the front in gold lettering was the name 'Corona.'

"Wow, fancy," Ken said.

Hadley pointed to the ribbon. "I've already put the ribbon in so it's ready to go."

"Go on, type something," Doodles said.

Ernest took a sheet of paper and rolled it into the typewriter. He then typed: "Thank you Hash."

Hadley embraced him. "Happy birthday darling."

Ernest kissed her.

"Since you've started writing a novel I thought you should write your first novel on a brand new typewriter."

"Now he can really write instead of pretending to write," Ken said.

"Now it will type every letter and not just every other one," Horne added.

That evening everyone went up to the roof. With Doodles back, and to avoid the cramped space in the apartment below he shared with Bill Horne, Ernest built a small makeshift room in one corner of the roof against the brick parapet. With a small thin mattress, sheets, blankets and pillows, he had a bed. Then with a kerosene lamp and a small makeshift wooden wall he had light and some degree of privacy. With a stretched thick tent canvas attached to the parapet and the wooden wall he had some shelter from the rain. On clear nights he rolled away the canvas and fell asleep staring up into the stars.

Up on the roof Hadley, Katy and Doodles sat down on the mattress bed while Bill Smith and Bill Horne sat in the chairs they brought up with them. Ken sat on the brick parapet. There was a boxing match to be watched.

Ken spoke up in a loud voice.

"And in this corner we have Ernie the birthday boy fighting against Nicky the Italian warrior."

Horne finished tying on Ernest's gloves while Bill Smith finished with Nick.

"Okay guys," Ken continued as he held up his stopwatch. "One round, ten minutes, are we ready?"

They both nodded.

"Go."

Ernest and Nick, in fighter stance, began circulating around each other.

Hadley watched. Katy turned to her.

"Nick is crazy about Wemedge. They spend a lot of time together."

"That's good for him and Nick seems like a nice man."

"Yes, but be careful because he does love the women, if you know what I mean."

Ernest took the first punch but missed. Nick dodged away.

"He says he met him in the war."

"Yeah, Nick's a big hero too, he's got a bunch of metals and he fought in a lot of different battles. Wemedge loves it when Nick tells his war stories, he eats it up."

Nick landed a punch on Ernest but Ernest returned with a double punch. Several shouted out.

"He says he's going to use some of the stories in his novel," Hadley said.

"Is that right? He's using Nick's experience instead of his own?"

"Well, as I understand it the book is about both love and war. The hero fights but is wounded and he finds love with the nurse taking care of him."

"Well gee, who does that sound like?"

Nick landed a heavy punch and Ernest seemed to stagger back a step. A flicker of pain crossed Hadley's face.

"Why do men do this?" Katy asked.

"I don't know."

"I think it's very masculine," Doodles said.

"I think it's silly if you ask me," Katy said.

They watched the match as Ernest and Nick danced back and forth. Hadley glanced at Katy. Hadley considered Katy one of her best friends. She knew Katy liked Ernest. She knew Katy liked Ernest a great deal. Hadley felt sad for her.

"Was he really hurt when Agnes broke up with him?"

"Yeah," Katy replied, "He was pretty broken up over it."

"Why would he want to relive it in his book do you suppose?"

"That's what writers do. They write about what happens to them, over and over again. It's like going to a psychologist."

"He wants to go to Italy and show me all of the places and where he was wounded."

"Why?"

"To relive it I suppose."

Katy shook her head.

Ernest landed a strong hit to Nick who staggered back a few steps shaking his head. Doodles squealed and put her hands to her face. Ernest looked over at Hadley with a smile on his face.

"I think he's showing off for you," Katy said.

There was something in her voice that made Hadley concerned. There was a hint of jealousy, a hint of anger. It made her feel strange. The man of her life might be the cause of her losing her best friend.

Hadley looked over at Bill Horne sitting and watching. She knew that Bill adored Ernest. He worshipped him. Ernest was more than just his best friend. He was what Bill wanted to be, he was the part of Bill that was missing. When Ernest and Bill came down to St. Louis she thought for sure that Bill and Ruth hit it off. Ruth said they did and she said she liked him. But then they seemed to drift apart. Ruth never wanted to talk about it so Hadley stopped asking.

It dawned on her that they were all in the wedding party. Her wedding was bringing together those who had painfully split apart. Ruth and Bill would have to talk and be friendly regardless of what they were feeling toward each other. And Katy, she deeply cared for Ernest but had to watch her best friend take him away.

It all felt wrong.

Ken called out: "Time."

Both Ernest and Nick were panting heavily.

Doodles stood up and went over and stood next to Ken. Hadley wanted to know. She leaned in close to Katy and whispered so no one else could hear.

"Katy, I was just wondering, did you and Ernie ever, you know."

Katy looked confused. Hadley lifted her eyebrows forming the silent question. Katy smiled. She understood.

"I don't know what you've heard but let me put it this way. Wemedge is a writer, you know, as in fiction."

"Yes."

"You get my meaning?"

3. Yes.

After everyone filed downstairs Ernest and Hadley were left alone.
They sat on the brick parapet and looked out over the city lights.
"Is it strange living with Doodles now that you know?"
"Yeah. I just try and avoid her as best I can."
"I do the same with my sister, but for different reasons."
They watched the city sparkle beneath them.
"You know, your sister said some harsh things about you."
"What now?"
Ernest hesitated.
"What?"
"Well, she said that you had an affair with a woman, and you actually
preferred women to men."
Hadley laughed out loud. She shook her head.
"Hah, my oh my, what that woman won't do."
"Was that with Katy?"
"Katy? No, no way. Oh you would like that if it were true wouldn't
you?"
"Well," he smiled.
"Seriously, I was twenty when I went to Bryn Mawr and I had a
roommate named Edna Rapallo. We became very close friends. We had a
smash on each other but it was all very normal girl stuff. She was pretty,
thin, with dark hair and dark complexion. She lived alone with her
divorced mother Constance. When I met Constance she was quite taken
by me, I think she saw me as a helpless little something she needed to
adore and take care of. Whenever we met there were very strong kisses
and embraces. She was a little bit of an artist and they had a summer
home in Windsor, Vermont. They invited me so that summer I went
with them. It was all very beautiful and we played tennis all the time and
drove around the hills and country in this black fringed Surry. We were
quite the team to all of the neighbors. And with the mother we would
cross over the river into Cornish, New Hampshire, where there was this
artist's colony. I met some nice artists, Maxfield Parrish was there, and
many times we visited an artist friend of Constance named Lucia
Fairchild Fuller. She was nice, dark tightly braided hair, divorced with
two children, she lived in this large stucco house with a swimming pool
and she set up an outdoor studio where she painted miniature portraits.
She was into the occult and hypnotism and was awfully intrigued by
something in me, I don't know what."
"So what happened?"

"Well, nothing really, Constance was very attached to me and mothered me and showed me how pleasanter life with her and Edna would be than the situation I was in. I wrote letters home to my mother about all that was happening and, without ever having met them, my mother accused them of being lesbian and trying to turn me to their ways. I was shocked and this rotten suggestion of them being evil turned me against them for no reason. I began to imagine I had all this low sex feeling toward Constance and she toward me. My mother suggested, as she did again and again, that I was so frail and mentally weak and suggestible that I may be persuaded down that path. My mother had such sway over me that I left. I am sure that I hurt them. I was so humiliated that I dropped out of Bryn Mawr and never returned."

"So that is all that happened?"

"Yes, that is all. But both my mother and my sister have kept that over my head as if they saved me from my own weak fall into evil."

"Have you ever had those feelings?"

"No, I've never, not now and not even then. It was only her suggestion that made me even think of it. When it comes to that department I prefer men and always have. I think that the intensity and hatred of my mother's reaction toward me was actually a misplaced anger toward her."

"The more I learn about you and your family the more complicated it gets."

"It makes me mysterious."

Ernest kissed her and then stood up and stretched.

"Ouch," he said.

"Are you alright?"

"Yeah, I just took some hits in my chest and it's a little sore."

"Why don't we get in your bed, it's more comfortable?"

Ernest stretched himself out on his bed. She crawled in next to him and their arms surrounded each other.

"You, sweetheart, are my hulky, bulky something masculine."

They stared up into the sky and looked at the stars. There was a quarter of a moon.

"Do you like your typewriter?"

"Yes I absolutely do. Believe me I am going to use it. You know the more I get into writing and the more I read other writers with that in mind I can see what they are doing and how they are doing it. I know I can do it better. When we get to Italy I am going to write and write. My goal has been changing."

"How is that?"

"I have wanted to be a writer since I can remember. I just wanted to be published and make a living writing."

"And you will."

"Yes, but I don't think it's enough now just to be a writer. I want to be good. I want to be famous. I want to be the best and the most famous writer there ever was."

"But Ernie, that is a lot to ask."

"I know, but I want it. That is what I want, nothing else matters."

Hadley traced her finger along his chin as he looked out into the sky above dreaming his dreams. She remembered a talk she had with Helen Breaker one day not too long ago.

"So, is this what you want?" Helen asked.

They were in the kitchen of her home cutting carrots and celery and onions for a pot roast.

"What do you mean?"

"Is this romance what you want, this wedding, this man, the life that he will provide you?"

"What life is that?"

"Well I think we should be honest, you know, I mean as friends."

"Of course."

"He wants to be a famous writer doesn't he?"

"Yes he does."

"Well then, which does he love more, you, or becoming a famous writer?"

"What do you mean?"

"You must realize dear that the two may prove incompatible. When he gets to be adored will he still come home to you?"

"I think so."

"And what if there is a baby, will he be willing to get a regular job in order to support a child and set his writing aside as something he will do when he can?"

"He loves me and I love him. I think that will guide any decisions we have to make."

"Well, I am just saying that I'm not so sure that he isn't in love with himself a bit more."

Ernest reached over and held Hadley's fingers in his. He brought them up and kissed them and then kissed her forehead.

"How's the beat up boxer?"

"The winning boxer is fine."

"Tell me, deep down, are you alright?"

"How do you mean?"

"In your letters lately you seem blue and depressed. Are you happy?"

"When you're with me."

She ran her fingers along his arm.

"When I see you and we're together you're so fun and buoyant and funny and talking and you make me feel beautiful and young and so filled with hope. But in your letters, when I'm not there with you, you sound at times so lonely and depressed. Don't you think the future is bright?"

She ran her fingers along his leg. He kissed her lips and whispered. "With you the future is brighter than the sun." She cuddled her head in his arms, her cheek against his chest.

"Doesn't the boxing hurt your leg?"

"Sometimes."

"Do your wounds hurt any more?"

"Sometimes."

"Let me see them, you have never shown them to me."

He pulled his pant leg up to his knee. She sat up and looked down at his leg. She ran her fingers across his flesh and carefully over his scars. She smiled down at him.

"It must have hurt so."

"I was lucky. They could have amputated the leg."

"There were some a lot worse."

Ernest nodded.

"There was one kid, I'll remember him forever. He was wounded like I was. A bomb hit and he ended up with shrapnel wounds all up and down. But one piece of shrapnel sheered off his penis. His testicles were okay but he lost his penis. The kid said he was a virgin. He's still going to have all that passion and desire that everyone does but there's nothing he can do but suffer it. What kind of life does that leave him?"

Hadley bent down over him and kissed his lips. Her hair tumbled down. He pulled her into him.

"Let's not think about that now," she whispered.

Her hair was like a tent over his face. Her lips whispered into his mouth again.

"All of your parts work right don't they?"

"I think so."

"Maybe we should find out," she whispered as their lips once again touched.

"Are you sure?"

"Yes."

4. Doodles II

Ernest was on the roof in his makeshift room. He lay on his bed reading. The kerosene lamp on the floor next to him burned bright. It had been hot during the day and the coolness of the evening felt good. He had the canvas pulled back so the sky was his roof.

When he heard the footsteps he looked up and saw Doodles coming across the roof toward him. It was dark on the roof outside the circle of his light but he could tell it was her by her walk. No one walked like Doodles walked. The way she swayed men could not help but watch.

Ernest sat up as she approached.

"Hello there Hemmy."

"Hello Doodles"

"Can I sit down?"

Ernest waved her to his bed. She sat down.

"What brings you up here?"

"Nothing, I just wanted your advice on something."

"Okay."

She smiled at him as he waited for her. Ernest could smell her gardenia perfume strong. She glanced at the lamp.

"Doesn't that hurt your eyes, it's so bright."

Ernest reached over and turned the crank. The intensity of the light diminished. He turned it down to a light glow.

"How's that?"

"Fine," she said.

Ernest waited for what she wanted to ask him. She looked up at the night sky.

"Wow, you can really see the stars out. It's such a clear night."

"Yes it is."

She leaned back on the bed resting against several pillows.

"I can see why you brought Hadley up here. It's all very romantic isn't it? Was it romantic for her?"

"She said she liked it."

"I'll bet she did. Why Hemmy, you crafty little boy, almost any girl would fall for you up here under these stars."

She giggled a little bit.

"Doodles, what is it you wanted to talk to me about?"

"Well, it's Kenny."

"What about him?"

"You know, Hemmy, I want to apologize about that Don Wright business. Maybe I shouldn't have told Ken but it's just that you made me

281

so mad. Do you forgive me?"

"What am I to forgive you for, for having an affair behind Ken's back?"

"Oh don't be so dramatic. You know I like to flirt, I flirt with everyone, it's just fun. I mean I even flirt with you, don't I?"

"But it was more than flirting."

"Oh no, Don just likes to pretend that there's something and, okay, I will admit, I sort of play along, I flirt with his fantasy. It's all part of the fun. But I don't really want Don, heavens no."

"So the other night was just heavy flirting and there's nothing between you two?"

"There's nothing of anything serious. There are others who are way more attractive than Don."

Ernest did not say anything.

"Actually, Hemmy, I find you very attractive. You are devilishly cute."

Ernest shook his head.

"Doodles, look . . ."

Doodles sat up and placed her finger onto his lips.

"Shhh, don't say anything. We can keep a secret can't we?"

"A secret about what?"

"Kenny's out with some friends, he won't be back until late."

Ernest pulled away.

"Doodles, no; stop. This is not going to happen."

"But why not Hemmy?"

"First of all I'm getting married in a couple weeks."

"But you're not married now are you?"

"What a thing to say. And second of all you're Ken's wife."

Doodles sat unbelieving. She started to get angry.

"You don't really understand the Bohemian style of life do you? Too prudish to understand is what I think. Let me give you a quick lesson in life. Ken and I are free to be who we want to be, and to be with whom we want, and that applies to me as well as him, or maybe you've only noticed my side of the arrangement and not his side. Do you want a list?"

"So you're married but not really."

"Listen, Hemmy, don't be such a Puritan."

"And you listen, Doodles, don't be such a slut."

Doodles sat glaring at Ernest. She finally stood up and stared down at him.

"You think you are so high and mighty and you've got your little sweet and innocent sweetie pie of a future wife well let me tell you buster. She's not all that sweet and innocent. And you think I'm bad with Don why don't you ask her about Mr. Donald Wright, go on I dare you to ask her. Ask her about the times she was here and you were out and she was here with Don, go on and ask her. Do you think she's going to be honest and tell you the real truth? I don't think so. She knows that if you knew the real truth about her and Don and what they did when you weren't around that you'd go over and beat him up within an inch of his life. I don't think she would want you to do that."

"What are you saying?"

"Why don't you clean your own house before you accuse someone else of being dirty?"

"I think you should leave."

"I think that I will do just that."

Doodles turned and walked away. Ernest, sitting on his bed in the soft glow of the shallow light, watched her walk away. He did not know what to think.

The next day Hadley received his letter. He asked: what is this all about?

Hadley wrote back.

It is nothing: do not listen to a woman scorned.

There was a time coming home from a bookstore we were happy and we zipped along arm in arm feeling jolly and congenial and he says to me 'Well, you and I are getting nearer marrying every day, Hash.' I brushed it off.

But there was a lot of familiarity he daily attempted and he asked to kiss me and I let him do so on the cheek but he went for my mouth instead. So I ended any kissing.

And I assumed he was joking when he invited me to come to Chicago for two weeks in a hotel without anyone knowing and he would show me a good time. Do you for a moment think that I would have done anything such as that?

And one night at dinner when you were not there he kept suggesting that on my first visit I had said something, don't I remember when walking down State Street he had said something and don't I remember the something that I replied? To be quite honest I do not remember what he said I said or what he said he had said for I apparently had brushed them off as the nothing that they were. But to him they seemed to be small pearls in the necklace of a growing romance dancing in his head.

Jolly and fun to be around, yes I do confess to him being that, but there it ends.

Pausing for a moment in her writing, tapping the pen on her lips, she continued.

I do think that he was quite taken with me but not I with him. So when I was there he was attentive to me and I could feel Doodles darting glances.

It is nothing: do not listen to a woman scorned.

So there you have the crime: it is the crime of loving you too much for there to be anyone else.

5. Trips

In August Hadley was invited by her friends Helen and George Breaker to spend several weeks with them camping in a log cabin at the Charles A. Brent Home Camp near State Line in Wisconsin.

"If we are to stay at Windemere for our honeymoon then I need to practice living in the wilderness," she wrote Ernest. Or at least, she thought to herself as she looked around at the other cabins, close to wilderness.

It was a log cabin in the woods near a lake. There was a fireplace and the porch was screened to keep the bugs out. Hadley and Helen liked to take walks through the woods. Sunlight dappled the ground as shafts of light fingered their way down through the canopy of trees. Hadley listened and watched as they walked: the chatter of birds overhead; the silent twirling decent of a falling leaf; a distant woodpecker hammering a tree; a squirrel scampering up the side of a pine; the crunch of dried leaves beneath her feet; the afternoon breeze waltzing through the trees; and nearby the buzz of a fly.

She closed her eyes as she walked. She could smell the pine trees and the soil and the water of the lake.

She wrote to Ernest: "I am trying as best I can to get in touch with the infinite, and there are brief moments, but then there are bugs."

They rowed a small rowboat out to an island in the water and on a spread out tablecloth of blue and white checkerboard they sat and opened their wicker picnic basket and ate sandwiches. They watched as the clouds of the day overhead darkened and then gathered up their things and threw them into the boat willy-nilly because suddenly there was no time left before it began to rain. They were soaked by the time they got back and the sun decided to shine again.

On another day when the sun shone clear and bright they played baseball with a flock of children from neighboring cabins. A homerun put the ball into the lake and one of the children had to run home to get another.

Hadley got a sore throat and rested and gargled everyday. She took naps and sat on the screened porch working on wedding invitations.

Without a father she hoped that her brother Jamie in California would be the one to give her away but he wrote back that he was in a clinic for tuberculosis and could not make it. She wrote to her mother's brother Arthur Wyman in hopes that he could arrange it but he wrote back that he could not break away from work.

She wrote to Ernest: "I will NOT walk up that aisle alone." It was

Helen that night by the crackling fireplace who suggested that her husband George could fill in for Jamie. "I would be most delighted" George beamed as he poked the logs in the fireplace.

Mrs. Charles wrote that she discovered the organist at Horton Bay could only play "Throw Out the Lifeline" which, Mrs. Charles wrote, seems hardly appropriate, so do you want me to get another organist from Petoskey? By all means yes, Hadley wrote back.

They still did not have a minister. Hadley wrote to Ernest that it was up to him to get one.

Hadley sat in the cushioned chair on the screened in porch trying to read her book. The cool breeze from the lake came in through the screen. She looked out. Evening was coming on. She looked out across the meadow and across the lake. As the sun descended through the trees the western sky glowed. It was growing dark in the patio. If she wanted to read she would need a light. But she waited. She took the book from her lap and set it on the small table by her chair. It was by Fitzgerald: "This Side of Paradise."

Hadley listened to the sounds of the dying day. A screen door slammed in a cabin across the meadow; shouts of children and then giggling laughter; a row of quacking ducks flying low across the lake; the quiet squeak of her chair when she moved. She watched smoke curling up into the air from the cabins.

She thought of the wedding, but she thought most of what would come after. Her friend Georgia Riddle had asked her if being engaged wasn't the best and most exciting part and the actual marriage never proved to be as good. Hadley said no.

"It seems to me," she said, "that everything lovely and wonderful is yet to come. It's like looking at the sun through astronomical instruments and simply and joyously living in a country saturated with sunlight."

The coming of night was almost complete. She watched the flashing fireflies sprinkle through the cool night air.

Ernest crawled out of his tent and stood up and stretched. It was still dark but there was a hint of light in the eastern sky. The air was crisp. A thin mist crawled across the meadow. He could smell the pine trees and the brush. He looked around the camp. Howie Jenkins, his friend from the war, was in the tent to the right of him. He snored away. Charlie Hopkins, his friend from the Kansas Star, was in the other tent still asleep as well. They were two friends who represented the two most important centers in Ernest's life so far; the war and Kansas City.

It was his last fishing trip; his last fishing trip before the wedding. In less than a week he would be married. Ernest walked over to the campfire and knelt down. The logs were burned down, mostly grey ash. He felt the blackened wood of the logs but they were cold. He rearranged the logs and took twigs and leaves sitting in a pile by the fire and stuffed them in among the logs. He could smell strong the blackened charcoal, burnt wood, and he stirred up the smell of smoke.

Taking a flint from his pocket he struck several times against a handful of moss. It finally caught and a small spark of fire sizzled in the moss. He carefully placed the moss under the leaves and bent further down to gently blow at the flame.

Ernest sat back and crossed his legs underneath. He looked around. The eastern sky was growing light. As if the night were fleeing a breeze came up through the trees above him. He looked up and saw the stars. The sky seemed to pulse. But soon they would be gone, outshined by the sun.

All of his cooking tools were set next to the fire. Ernest took an elevated grate and placed it over the growing flame: his stove. Ernest opened a bag and poured out some coffee grounds into a dented metal coffee pot. He stood up and walked down to the river and held the coffee pot in the water. When the swirling cold water filled the pot he walked back to the fire and sat down. He put the coffee pot on the grate. The fire underneath caught on good. There would be coffee soon; he had some bacon and he had some buckwheat to fry some cakes.

Ernest sat and watched the Sturgeon River flow by while he waited for the coffee to boil. He felt the stubble of a beard on his face. He would be married in mere days. What fishing trips would there be then? And what of his friends, Smith and Horne, Brumbach and Hopkins, Jenkins and Edgar, when would they ever fish together like this again?

Most of his friends told him not to do it.

"Like I told you," Hopkins said, "don't let anyone ever say that you were taught writing. It was born in you. So you need to focus on that one hundred percent and a wife will just drag you down. Don't get hitched if you know what's good for you."

Carl Edgar: "When you came home from the war you were figuratively as well as literally shot to pieces and you had an intense need to write and get all of those experiences out of you. College is of damn little use because you have to live what you write, and writing itself is very hard, in fact you'll be doing good if you're anywhere in five years.

But dragging along a wife; is she going to live that tough life?"

Bill Smith: "Nah, marriage ruins a man; it cuts him off from his friends. When you're married you're bitched."

It bothered Ernest.

His response to them all: what if I really love her?

Only Bill Horne was for it. "A woman fleshes a man out. You need someone who wants to stand by you otherwise you'll just get bitter or kill yourself from loneliness."

Ernest watched the mist over the river dissolve as the day came into view. He heard the birds; they were awake. He listened to the splash of the fast moving water over the rocks. Soon he would wake the others and cook breakfast. Then he would walk through the knee high grass and scoop up the grasshoppers still wet and clinging to the glass blades and slide them one by one into his jar where he kept them for bait. And then they would all stream out into the icy cold water and begin to cast.

It will be another day of fishing; one last day of fishing. Ernest watched the morning unfold.

Chapter Fourteen

Ernest got better on his crutches. They were too long for him and when he walked he had to set them out very wide. He got around. He could get out onto the terrace with the others. There was fresh air and fresh sunlight. The terrace ran around two sides of the building. There were striped awnings which could be rolled up or down depending on the attitude of the sun. Patients in wheelchairs or crutches or under their own power could sit in wicker chairs or chaise lounges and have their meals brought to them while they relaxed among the potted plants chatting with fellow patients about this or that. There were magazines and newspapers. Multicolored flower boxes lined the balustrade. Over the railing, far below, were the streets and the hustle and bustle of the city below.

His friend Bill Horne, Red Cross ambulance driver from Section Four, arrived with a mysterious stomach ailment, the doctors said sub-acute enteritis. He watched Ernest flirt with Agnes, and watched Agnes flirt with Ernest, and told Henry Villard that their budding romance, like a blooming flower unfolding its petals to the sun, was truly a beautiful thing to watch.

Agnes giggled with Ernest about Bill Horne. He seems so very jolly and so helpful, she said, but very early each morning he fixes his hair with water slicking it down and then gets back into bed with his cap on and with his sheets covering up to his chin and with his big glasses above that he looks a picture for Puck.

They laughed and she held his cheeks in her hands.

And then one day she stared down into his smiling and charm filled and youthful face and she bent over him and kissed him lips to lips.

1. Wedding I

It was the night before the wedding. Ernest and Bill Horne and Katy Smith were all in Ernest's room at Pinehurst Cottage. The three of them sat on the large bed.

Katy asked. "Are you getting nervous?"

"Me? No."

"The whole world is going to change tomorrow, good buddy. Nothing will be the same again."

"Horney, you make it sound like a funeral."

Katy laughed.

"What makes you think that it isn't? Matter of fact, I haven't told Hash yet but I was thinking about dressing half in mourning, like the black color of typewriter ribbon. Dear writer friend, how is that for symbolism?"

"That's pretty good," said Horne.

Ernest leaned in toward Katy.

"The knot is not yet tied," he whispered even though Horne could hear him. "You and me, run away, elope, set the tongues wagging."

Katy stared into his eyes for a moment, a long quiet moment. She put her fingers against his chest and pushed him back.

"Not so fast lover boy; like I told you before, only in your dreams."

A large smile came across his face.

"Butstein, you're never going to get hitched. No one is good enough for you, and here you are as old as Hadley, pushing the big thirty years old, time is flying by, youth is dissolving away."

"Oh yeah, so why are you hitching up with one old lady and not the other?"

"Because she loves me and she's not afraid to show it."

No one spoke for a moment. Their stares were interlocked. Horne glanced from one to the other. Finally it was Ernest who broke the silence.

"You know as well as I do that I was the best thing that ever happened to you and you let it pass."

"Horney," Katy said as she turned her gaze toward him. "Could you please open the window a jar, the ego in here is a bit suffocating."

Horne smiled.

"Sure, maybe I'll open two."

"Okay, okay," Ernest said as he walked over to the chest of drawers. "Peace and bygones."

"Don't worry," Katy said, "I'll try and act like there's nothing and its

Hadley's wedding and not mine. But I have to say. . ."

"Do you have too?"

Katy made a face at Ernest.

"I have to say that I woke up the other night and realized that the syrupy way you love her cannot last. I almost called you on the phone right then and there to tell you. I give you two a year or so and she'll be off from you and I'll have to come and live with you two in order to hold the home together."

Horne shook his head.

"Heh, Katy, don't say things like that just for spite. That's cruel."

"No, Bill, honesty is not cruelty."

Ernest, standing at the chest of drawers, picked up several photographs.

"Want to see some recent photographs of us?"

"Sure," Horne said.

Ernest handed the photographs to Katy.

"Oh my God, who is this man standing next to Hadley? He looks like such a sweet, sweet little boy. Surely this cannot be you."

"That's me, Butstein. Do you need to get some glasses?"

"No, this cannot be you; this cannot be the great Hemingstein that I know. The great man that I know is a large, solid, rough, Rabelaisian, cosmic force of nature. That is who I know as Hemingstein. But this, this is a slim and frail overwhelmed young Flemish poet."

"Let me see," Horne said as he moved over closer to Katy. She handed him the pictures.

"So tell me," Katy continued, "tell me what it is that Hadley has done to make you into this dear sweet boy."

Ernest made a face at her and she then made a face back at him.

But then they both broke into laughter. Horne joined them.

After a few moments Ernest became quiet and distant. Both Katy and Horne noticed the sudden shift in his mood. They were used to his mood changes.

"Wemedge, what's the matter?" Katy asked.

Ernest started to brush it off but then stopped.

"My father wrote me a letter asking me if I wanted him to be at the wedding. He said he heard I did not want him there. He said it would be fine if I did not want him there, he understood, but please let him know."

"Why in the world would he ask that?"

"I don't know."

"Where did he hear you don't want him?"

"I never said anything of the kind. I don't know if my mother told him that, maybe in the heat of an argument, or if he thinks that himself."

"So, what did you tell him?"

"I wrote to him and said that of course I wanted him there. I absolutely wanted him there."

"How odd."

"His birthday is the day after the wedding. It's his fiftieth birthday. I don't know what to think."

"Are you still spending your honeymoon at Windemere?"

"Yes, they offered it and I said yes."

"Ernie, have you thought about the different levels of meaning in that?"

Ernest cocked his head and looked at Katy.

"What do you mean?"

"It's a cottage your father built for the family; it's the cottage that your mother kicked you out of just last year; it's your parents marriage bed; didn't your mother give birth to one of your sisters in that very same bed that is now your honeymoon bed."

"It's been a summer home to me all of my life. It has deep meaning to me and now Hadley will be a part of that meaning. What is wrong with that?"

"Nothing, nothing is wrong with that," she said as she waved it off.

"Katy," Horne said, "I see your point but sometimes a bed is just a bed."

"Fine, that's okay. It just seems like you'd want something new and fresh to help make your new and fresh beginning."

Horne turned to Ernest.

"What is happening after the honeymoon? Are you going back to Ken's place or get a place of your own?"

"I already have a place. Ken told me in no uncertain terms that he does not want me back. He's still mad about the Doodles thing. But frankly I'd rather take my bride and stay in a backroom in a brothel in Seney than be roommates with Doodles."

2. Wedding II

September 3, 1921. It dawned with a bright clear sky. It remained that way the whole day. As it progressed everyone got ready for the wedding.

Ernest went swimming in the lake in the mid afternoon. When he got out he scampered up the slope barefoot to the Pinehurst Cottage and then to his room. He washed his feet in the basin. There was a knock on the door. When he opened it Dutch Pailthorp and Luman Ramsdell stood in the hallway. They were already dressed and ready. They drove down from Petoskey.

"Look at you," Dutch said, "don't you have somewhere to be pretty soon?"

Dutch was thin with reddish hair he combed down the middle of his head.

Ernest reached out and hugged each of them as they came in. Luman held up a bottle of whiskey as he came into the room.

"Glad you two could make it."

"Our man Stein getting married, we wouldn't miss it for the world."

"Yeah," Luman added, "who would have thought, our Kid Hemingway going down to the mat."

Ernest closed the door and then went over to the chest of drawers. He pulled out some clean underwear, clean silk socks, new sock garters, a white shirt, a white collar, and a tie. He took off his swimming suit and, standing in front of the full length swivel mirror, began to get dressed.

"Did you have any trouble driving down?"

"No, it was smooth sailing. We left early just in case."

"Did Marge come with you?"

In the mirror Ernest watched Dutch and Luman glance at each other.

"Ah, no; no. She said she couldn't come," Dutch said.

"Well," Ernest said. "We have some time."

"This is like being with a boxer in his locker room getting ready before the big fight," Dutch said.

"Or a football team before a big match," Luman said.

"Or a convict getting ready to be hanged," Ernest added.

"Oh, Stein," Dutch said as they both laughed. It was a nervous laugh. "Don't let him fool you Luman, he may talk big and tough but I know him, inside he's as soft as a meringue pie."

Ernest continued getting dressed: the underwear, the socks, the garter, the shirt, the collar. He watched his friends. They were nervous.

"Where is everybody?"

"In their rooms getting dressed I hope."

Dutch opened the bottle of whiskey. Ernest stood in front of the mirror tying his tie. Dutch held out the bottle.

"Take a good shot, Dutch."

"After you, Stein."

"No. What the hell. Go on and drink."

Dutch took a long drink. He handed the bottle to Ernest. Ernest handed it to Luman. He took a drink and handed it back to Ernest. Finally Ernest took a drink. He loved the way a shot of whiskey burned all the way down.

"All right Stein, now we are ready."

"First let me put my trousers on."

They all laughed.

Laura Charles sat in her rocking chair on the front porch of her cottage. Ruth Bradfield and Hadley's sister Fonnie were pacing the porch. They were both too nervous to sit down.

"Where is she, she is going to be so late." It was Fonnie.

"We are okay, we still have some time," Ruth said as she looked in through the window to the clock hanging on the wall, "although less than we had a few minutes ago."

"She's going to be late for her own wedding, isn't that so typical of my sister, so typical."

"There she is," Laura called out.

They all looked. They could see Hadley coming up the slope from the lake through the apple orchard. She walked as if there was nothing to be concerned about.

"Tell Helen and Katy she's here. We have to get this girl dressed in a hurry."

That morning Hadley wanted to take a swim in the lake alone. So she did. But lying on her blanket on the wooden dock in the bright and warm sunshine she fell asleep. When she woke up it was much later. The sun had moved across the sky. She did not know what time it was. It must be about time. She took one last dive, swam back and forth and then got out. Wrapping her towel around herself she climbed the slope to Mrs. Charles cottage.

Katy and Ruth spent the day flowering the church with small bouquets of goldenrod and swamp lilies wrapped in balsam boughs tied at the end of each pew.

"With all this goldenrod I hope no one has allergies," Katy giggle whispered to Ruth.

Mrs. Charles and Fonnie spent the day wondering if this wedding was in Hadley's best interest given that it was Ernest, and we both know how he is. He's going to be a difficult one that boy is, Mrs. Charles said. He is still such a boy at heart.

Once inside, in the bedroom, Hadley sat while they all buzzed around her like bees about a pollen rich flower. Katy and Ruth rubbed her wet hair with towels.

"This is never going to get dry," Fonnie announced. "Hadley, your hair is so long and thick you know it takes forever to get dry."

"Yes, Fonnie, I know."

"Why did you go swimming?"

"Calm down, Fonnie."

Helen clapped her hands.

"Outside everyone. Take a chair and sit in the direct sun and fan her hair out."

Like soldiers carrying out orders Hadley stood up, Katy grabbed the chair, Ruth grabbed some towels and they marched outside into the apple orchard. Fonnie and Mrs. Charles followed. Hadley sat in the chair in the sun and Katy and Ruth stood on either side fanning out her hair, a reddish sparkle in the sunlight.

Fonnie was concerned, she had brought it up before but now she would give it one last try.

"Hadley, I know we talked about this but I ask you one last time. For you and for all women, take out of the vows the part about 'obey,' cherish and obey. Why should women be commanded to obey?"

"Fonnie I don't think it is that big of a thing. You just don't understand, I don't want to be a separate person; I want to be him, a part of him, and isn't that a part of it?"

"No it is not. You are and will forever be a separate person."

Hadley held her head forward as they continued fanning out her hair. It was still damp and actually still wet near her skull.

"Actually," Katy spoke. "Actually you can obey but in your own way so it is what you want to do in the first place. He will never know. He'll think it was his idea."

"You agree with her?" Fonnie asked as if she was surprised that Katy of all people would not be on her side.

From the front porch Mrs. Charles called out.

"Let's go girls, wet hair or not we have to get dressed. We are late."

In the bedroom Hadley dressed in front of the full length swivel mirror. Ruth wrapped Hadley's hair around her head into a loose fitting bun. The wooden floors of the room creaked as they walked around. Everyone was talking. When there was a momentary lull Katy spoke up.

"You know I just thought about it, it's funny. Hadley, you are an Episcopalian and Hemingway was raised as a sort of Congregationalist but now you're being married in a Methodist church. All we need is the minister to be a Catholic priest and maybe a Jewish organist and we've about covered all of the bases."

Others laughed. Helen nodded.

"So it seems that all the heavens and the earth are wishing this marriage to be."

Soon it was done. She was dressed and ready. They all stood back in a semi circle around her and looked at her. Hadley smiled. She stood the goddess among them. Her red hair pulled back into a loose bun, a flowered wreath crowning her head holding a thin white lace veil cascading down her back, her long creamy white laced dress, her white stockings, her satin white soft slippers, and holding in her hands a large bouquet of baby's breath: Hadley stood happy.

Hadley looked at Katy, looked into her eyes. Katy smiled but there was a flicker of pain across her face. Hadley stepped forward and hugged her.

"Thank you ever so much," she said. "If it wasn't for you we would never have met."

"Yeah, well," Katy said shrugging her shoulders. "I wish you the best. I think you have quite a catch there."

"Yes, I think so too."

It was Helen who spoke up.

"Alright, let's get going. Fonnie, can you wake up George, I think he fell asleep in his chair."

Sitting in the back seat of the car Hadley quietly watched out the window. It was not that far of a drive and the road was lined on either side by tall elegant elm trees. She could see the distant lake shimmering; the sunlight on the meadows; the sky was a cloudless deep blue.

They drove up to the front entrance of the church. It was washed white and had a tall steeple. Almost everyone was already inside. Waiting. George got out of the car, opened the door for Hadley, and escorted her up the steps of the church with her hand on his arm.

As Mrs. Charles passed by them on her way into the church she mumbled that they were fifteen minutes late.

George Charles winked and whispered to Hadley.

"I don't know what the fuss is all about. Everyone is here today to see you so why wouldn't they want to wait and see you?"

Hadley smiled and patted his arm. She was glad she chose him to give her away.

Inside the organ began to play.

"Well," George said, "I think that's our cue. Nervous?"

She whispered "Please hold me up."

Grace was nervous. She stood in front of the full length swivel mirror braiding her hair. Ursula came in the room.

"Where are your ribbons?"

"There dear, in the top drawer."

Grace heard the single hit notes on the piano again and again. The man tuning the piano was taking his time. He was supposed to come the day before but he had to come today of all days. And he even got there late as it is. Grace wanted the piano freshly tuned for when Ernest and Hadley came to the cottage later this evening. Hadley had a good ear and she might want to play on their honeymoon.

"What on earth is taking that man so long?"

Ursula, pulling out some ribbon, shrugged her shoulders.

"Is Carol ready yet?"

"Almost."

"Well dear, can you help her along please?"

"Yes," Ursula mumbled as she turned to leave. Grace called her at the door and she stopped and looked back.

"You look very beautiful my dear, your mother is very proud of you."

Ursula shrugged her shoulders again and left.

Grace was done. She took a moment to look at herself in the mirror. Her hair was neatly braided. She wore a long pastel colored dress with an embroidered flowered tunic and a golden tasseled cord at her waist as a belt. Her new shoes were white. But they pinched a bit.

Grace went out into the living room. She admired the freshly varnished floorboards. It will be a wonderful honeymoon, she thought: freshly varnished floorboards, a freshly fixed roof over the patio, a freshly tuned piano, and freshly picked flowers in all the vases.

Les was sitting on the sofa.

"Let me see you, stand up."

Les stood up. He was six years old.

"Do I have to go?"

"Yes dear, you have to go," she said as she looked him over, his white shirt, his white pants, his white socks, his brown shoes, his combed hair.

"But I don't wanna."

"Want to, Les, it is I do not want to. Besides, it is your brother getting married, it is a very important day in you brother's life. You will remember this day all of your life."

"But I don't wanna."

Grace stood back. She was amazed. He was dressed and ready. "Now aren't you a handsome little man. So sit on the sofa until we are all ready."

She turned to the piano. The man had the piano closed and was closing his satchel. He wore a hat over his bald head and he had an enormously bushy moustache. He had the tinniest eyes she had ever seen.

"Want to try it out?"

"Certainly," she said as she sat on the bench. She played a few bars of her song "Lovely Walloona." But there was no time.

"Wonderful," she said. "We are in a bit of a hurry so how much do we owe you?"

The man handed her an invoice. "Oh my," she said and looked up at him. She got up and went outside.

"Clarence," she called. "Clarence."

"I'm up here."

She turned and looked up on the roof over the patio. Clarence, in his work clothes, stood on the roof. She was taken aback.

"You're not ready? Dear, you're not ready."

"You wanted this roof done before Ernie and Hadley get here so I had to finish it."

"Yes, I know, but you're not ready."

"My clothes are all laid out all I have to do is put them on. What did you need?"

"I need some money for the piano."

"In my wallet in the bedroom chest, left top drawer."

"Please get down and get dressed dear," she said as she went back inside. She paid the man and he thanked her.

"Are you folks going to that wedding over in Horton Bay?"

"Yes, we are."

"I figure that'll be a full house. Folks say they invited the whole town. This will be the biggest thing that happened around here for a long time."

"Really? And will you be there?"

"Nah, I ain't much for marrying, I done it four times already so I don't see much use in it anymore. But you folks have a good time."

"Thank you, I am sure that we will."

Clarence came in as the man left.

"Please hurry dear," Grace said as he came in.

Grace turned toward the piano. She picked up some sheet music on the table and placed it open on the music rack. It was her song, "Lovely Walloona." She then picked up a letter she had written to the newlyweds and placed it open on the music rack next to her song. If Hadley wanted to play she may as well play a song written by Grace Hemingway, her mother-in-law.

Grace followed Clarence into the bedroom. He stood in front of the full length swivel mirror and kicked off his shoes and took off his trousers. Grace handed him his clothes one by one as he dressed: grey trousers, white shirt, grey vest, starched white wing collar, black tie, grey socks, polished black shoes, grey jacket.

"I still don't see why you had Sunny stay at summer camp longer. She could have made it," he said.

"Yes, but, dear, Sunny is special. She has such a crush on her brother she was heart broken when he got engaged. It's hard for her to understand that he's leaving her for another."

"But she's his sister, and Hadley is his wife, the two are hardly the same."

"Yes, well, you know that and I know that but to her Ernie is almost like a boyfriend to her and she's hurt."

"Oh poppycock."

"Clarence."

"Well, it's true. She has to grow up at some point."

"I just felt it would have been too emotional for her. I was afraid that she might make a scene."

"Well, she will be home tomorrow night."

"And you will be there to pick her up at the train station?"

"Yes dear. The main luggage has already been sent on, you have at Grace Cottage what you and Carol need for your continued stay, and the car is packed. So, after the reception, I'll drive Ursula and Les up to Petoskey and tomorrow morning we ship out."

"You do think you will be home before Sunny gets there?"

"Yes, I think so."

"What if there is a delay?"

"Sunny is seventeen and she has a key to the house, I am sure everything will be all right. Stop worrying."

"I know; I am just so nervous. This is just too much, closing this down, packing everything, unpacking what I need, getting ready for the wedding, fixing this place up for their honeymoon, it is just too much."

"Relax, it will all turn out fine."

"I know."

"Marcelline, she could have come," Clarence said as he finished tying his black tie.

"Well, she and her brother don't see eye to eye anymore. There's that, but then she had to quit her camp councilor job and she's now in New Hampshire resting."

"So why doesn't she come?"

Grace watched Clarence for a moment. She sat down on the side of the bed.

"Clarence, I'm getting a little concerned for her. I see a lot of you in her, dear. She has these moods, like you; she says they can be very intense."

Clarence nodded but did not reply. He slipped his feet one by one into his shoes. He understood.

They were both quiet for a moment.

She looked up at him.

"You do think things will be all right don't you?"

Clarence stepped over to her and held her head in his hands.

"Yes, I do."

Suddenly there was a wave of pain. Tears filled her eyes and overflowed.

"It's our baby boy," she managed to say.

Clarence held her head against his chest.

"Yes, yes, I know, I know."

He felt her breathing against him. She took long deep breaths. Still holding her head in his hands he looked down at her. He smiled. He kissed her forehead.

"It will be alright," he whispered.

3. Wedding III

The church was filled with people. Every pew seemed to be full. Up in front, standing at the altar, was Ernest and next to him both Bill Smith and Bill Horne. They all wore white flannel trousers and dark blue coats. Ernest was nervous. He could feel his leg shaking. Streams of sweat crawled down his back.

In the front row sat his family: Clarence, Grace, Ursula, Carol and little Les. When he looked at his family his father winked, his mother smiled, Carol kept looking back to see if Hadley had come yet, and Les looked all around taking it all in.

You could smell the scent of the flowers clear. A small packet of flowers was attached at the end of each pew. But women as they walked by left a trail of their own perfume as well. It was after four in the afternoon and the sun came into the church through the western windows in long shafts of light.

But then the organ began to play. It was loud and filled the room. It was The Wedding March from "Lohengrin."

Those who were talking stopped. Those who were standing sat down. Everyone became quiet. Ernest closed his eyes for a moment and took a deep breath before he opened them again. Looking down the aisle he finally saw her. Hadley. Hadley slowly walked into the church holding the arm of George Breaker.

Ernest beamed a wide smile at the sight. She looked like a beautiful angel in white that had just then come down from the heavens to delicately walk the earth.

When the service was done everyone gathered outside in the grass. There were photographs to be taken. The sun was setting so they had to rush. Pictures were taken of Ernest and Hadley, again and again; Ernest and Hadley standing with his family, again and again; Ernest with all of his male friends standing as if in a chorus line, again and again; Hadley standing alone with her baby's breath and her smile. They all had to smile and look squinting into the setting sun.

There was a fried chicken dinner at Dilworth's across the road. People slowly migrated over there through the tall elm trees. Ernest directed traffic when a car came down the road and he held up the people walking across and waved the car through.

Outside as the shadows lengthened and gradually disappeared into darkness, inside the restaurant there was eating and laughing and drinking and dancing and the evening wore on. A cake was cut and dessert served.

When it grew late Bill Smith and Katy drove to Mrs. Charles' cottage and picked up Hadley's suitcase and brought it back to Pinehurst. Ernest brought his down from upstairs. John Kotesky loaded them into the back of his Ford.

Ernest and Hadley shook hands, waved good bye, and got into the car. John drove down the narrow sandy road bumping across the four miles to Lake Walloona. Ernest and Hadley in the back seat held hands and kissed as they bounced back and forth. John drove past Grace Cottage and drove down as far to the lake as he could.

When he stopped he left the car running and the lights on so they could see. Ernest and John carried the suitcases down and put them into the boat pulled up onto the shore. Ernest searched around behind some trees where his father said he hid the oars. It was dark and hard to see but he finally found them and pulled them out.

John shook hands with both of the newlyweds and said good bye. Ernest gave him five dollars. They watched as he turned the car around and drove away. It left them in the dark.

There was no moon; they only had the stars. It was very dark. They felt their way to the boat and he helped her in. He then pushed off and jumped aboard. He took one of the oars and began rowing. It was very quiet. There was only the splash of the oars. It was very dark. They moved out toward the center of the lake. The full canopy of stars glistened over them.

Hadley, staring up into the heavens, saw a few fast streaks of falling stars, quiet in the dark.

"Do you know the stars?" she asked.

"I know Orion and the Big Dipper," he said. He looked up and around. "I don't think Orion is out but look, up there, see, that's the Big Dipper. The other stars all come and go but the Big Dipper is always there."

She lay back in the boat and looked up.

"You know," Ernest said, "I never understood those star charts where they draw in the constellations. They show it to be a bear where the dipper part is the body and the handle part is its tail. But bears don't have tails that long. So I see it the other way where the dipper part is the body and the handle is the neck and head. That makes it more true."

"Yes, I see it."

She gazed at it for a moment.

"Beautiful isn't it," she said.

"Yeah."

She reached over the side and dragged her finger in the water. It was cold to the touch. It seemed like life could end here, that life could end now, and it would still be eternal.

"Ernie."

"Yes."

"Do you know that painting, I don't know the painter, but it is of the Lady of Shalott sitting splendid in her boat going down the river?"

"Yes."

"I feel like her. But you were able to break the spell."

"Are we on our way to many towered Camelot?"

"I think so," she said.

Then, after a moment, "I hope so," she said.

4. Honeymoon

The honeymoon turned out to be a disaster. Ernest did not want to sleep in the bedroom of his parents so he took each mattress from their twin beds and dragged them out onto the living room floor. He built a fire in the fireplace.

But the weather turned cool. The cabin was not insulated. The family only used it in the summertime so there was no need. A draft came in under the front door.

For the first few days they both came down with bad colds. They spent their time either sleeping or sitting with runny noses and hacking and coughing. They ate the food that was there. Clarence had made a deal with Ernest; he would leave enough food for them in exchange for Ernest's Marlin .22.

It took days but they gradually improved. Sitting on the covered front porch in the evenings drinking hot tea and hot chocolates they could occasionally hear Grace on her piano in Grace Cottage as the music floated across the lake.

"Let's go inside," Ernest said, not wanting to listen.

Toward the end of the first week Ernest left to hitchhike into Petoskey. He was going to buy some provisions. He made it to Petoskey but instead of buying provisions he met with two old drunks he knew and they spent the afternoon and the money in a bar celebrating him getting married.

By the time they left he could barely walk. He still had enough money to buy four pounds of steaks and he did get a ride back but only as far as the lake. He started walking home with his four pounds of steaks in his hand. It was then that he saw a motorboat tied to a dock. Surely they would not mind if he used it to get the meat home and then he could return the boat. It sure beat carrying the meat the whole way.

So he climbed aboard and started the engine and took off. But he forgot to untie the boat from the piling it was secured to and the boat had such a thrust it tore the piling out. He zoomed off into the lake pulling the piling behind him flapping and splashing like a water skier in trouble.

Meanwhile Hadley, wondering why it was taking him so long, walked up the side of the lake to see if she could find him. She found him. Looking through the trees she saw the motorboat coming down the lake, she saw him at the wheel trying to manage the boat, and she saw the flapping wood splashing in the water in his wake.

She waved her arms and shouted. He happened to see her and waved.

He shouted something but she could not make out what it was and he kept pointing toward the cabin. She ran as best she could back to the cabin. He circled around and brought the boat in toward the pier in front of the cabin. Massive waves from its wake splashed in. He cut the motor and the boat splashed into the pier with the waves. He threw a package onto the pier and again waved and shouted to her but she could not make it out. Then he started the engine again and roared off. She watched the splashing bouncing piling follow him up the lake. She waited until the waves had died down and then went out onto the pier and picked up the package.

It was more than an hour later when he got home. He walked up to the cabin singing. Once inside he sat down and promptly fell asleep.

Ernest and Hadley went into Petoskey. He wanted to take her to dinner at the Perry Hotel.

"I used to eat there when I lived in Petoskey. You'll love it."

But before that he wanted to introduce her to a couple of his old friends. When the older woman opened the door she was surprised to see Ernest.

"Why Ernest, what a surprise."

"Hello Mrs. Quinlan. Is Grace here?"

Mrs. Quinlan showed Ernest and Hadley into the kitchen. A young girl sat there doing her homework. She had long dark hair, glasses, and wore a checkerboard woolen sweater. When Ernest came in she stood. She took off her glasses. She was shocked to see him.

"Hello there Sister Luke, how are you doing?"

The girl was in too much shock to reply.

"Hadley, this is Sister Luke. This is Hadley."

They nodded to each other. Hadley thought it was strange that he did not say 'my wife Hadley' but just 'Hadley' as though the 'my wife' part did not really matter.

"It was Sister Luke here who got us the organist and the minister, what was his name?"

Grace cleared her throat.

"Dr. W. J. Dotson of Emanuel Episcopal Church."

"You did good kid. Hash, when I asked her if she could line somebody up I said we didn't really care what breed of priest he was just so long as he doesn't wear a celluloid collar or chaw tobacco, he can read and be dignified, and was not an evangelist that's liable to shout out 'Praise the Lord' and start rolling on the floor during a critical part of the ceremony."

Grace smiled. Hadley noticed that she found him funny.

Ernest smiled his big wide grin. "You did good kid," he repeated.

Grace smiled sweetly and cast her eyes down. Hadley felt sorry for her, she looked scared and hurt and embarrassed.

There was a knock on the kitchen door leading outside. Grace turned her head slightly but did not answer it. She stood still for a moment and then there was another knock.

"Did you need to get that?" Ernest asked.

"Well, it's just, you know."

Ernest made a face to her toward the door. She sighed and then opened the back door. Marjorie Bump walked in carrying some books. She froze when she saw Ernest.

"Hello Red," he said.

"Ernie," she stumbled. "What are you doing here?"

"I'm visiting Sister Luke. I was going to look you up next but, wow, here you are in the flesh."

Marjorie looked at Hadley.

"Hello," Hadley said.

"Hello," said Marjorie.

"This is Hadley, and this is Marge."

"Nice to meet you," Hadley said.

"Yes, it is; Ernie's talked a lot about you."

"Missed you at the wedding," Ernest said.

Marjorie shrugged her shoulder. "Yeah, well, I just, I didn't make it down."

On their way to the Hotel Hadley was very quiet. Ernest was afraid to ask but then he finally did.

"Is there something wrong?"

Hadley turned her head and stared at him as they walked.

"What was all of that about?"

"What?"

"Why did we visit Grace and Marge?"

"I wanted you to met them and for them to met you."

"It's obvious that Grace has a major crush on you, still, and she's terribly hurt that you got married."

"We're friends, she'll get over it."

"But Ernie: yes, she is young and she will get over it but in the mean time you have hurt her terribly. So why on earth are you rubbing her nose in it?"

"I'm not doing that, I just wanted you two to meet."

"Let the poor girl recover on her own time and in her own way. I can't believe how insensitive you were."

"I want to show you around to my friends and now we're having our first argument."

"Yes we are, you were so insensitive, and Marge, poor girl, she was your girlfriend and I think it's obvious that she loves you and still cares for you a great deal. What were you trying to do, show them who they lost to?"

"Well, actually I wanted you to see who you won over. I wanted you to see all of the women who pine over me but now can't have me because I picked you."

Hadley stopped in her tracks. Ernest took several steps before he realized that she stopped.

"I cannot believe this. You are so selfish and immature and your vanity, oh your vanity."

Ernest stepped over to her.

"Hash, Hash, come on," he said as he held her hand. "We're going to a nice dinner in a nice hotel, lets not spoil the evening."

"Was this just a contest for you, a contest of who is going to be the winner? Let me see is the winner going to be Marge or is the winner going to be Hash or is the winner going to be Katy. Let me see; spin the wheel."

"No, it wasn't like that."

"Darling when I chose you it was my heart that chose. Was it not the same for you?"

"It was," he said.

5. Anniversary

Hadley heard the knock on the door and wondered whom it might be. She was doing laundry and had dirty clothes piled on the living room sofa. When she opened the door she was surprised to find Grace Hemingway standing in the hall. She was panting and waving her hand in the air to get some breeze against her face.

"Mrs. Hemingway, what on earth?"

"My, Hadley, I was near here and thought I would stop in for a visit," she took a deep breath, "but little did I know it was five flights of stairs up." She took another deep breath. "That was so exhausting."

"Here please come in. Here, sit on the sofa."

Hadley moved some of the clothes out of the way.

"Thank you dear, I just have to catch my breath. There were so many stairs."

Grace's face was flushed rosy pink. Hadley smelled a strong scent of violets as Grace sat down.

"Let me get you some tea," Hadley said.

"Oh yes dear that would be lovely."

Hadley and Grace talked over tea.

She came by to make sure they were still going to attend the party that night. It was their twenty-fifth wedding anniversary. Hard to imagine isn't it. They invited many friends. Clarence invited many of his patients.

"But we want to also present the lovely newlyweds. It will be a night celebrating the joys of marriage, both as new young love as well as old and well seasoned love."

Hadley said yes they intended to attend.

"Excellent, excellent," Grace said as she tightly held Hadley's hands in hers. "I am so glad that Ernest found you. I know that my son and I do not see eye to eye on many things, such as responsibility and the values of love and sentiment. It causes me stress to think that a mother and her son can be at times at such odds. But I now feel very relieved, and with your positive influence I think he will turn out alright."

"I'm sure he will as well."

Grace looked around the apartment. It was very small. It was very cramped. The furniture was very old. Hadley felt embarrassed.

"Were you not going to move in where Ernest lived before, with the Kenley and Doodles Smith couple?"

"Yes," Hadley said.

But when Doodles complained to Ken about how mean Ernest treated her then Ken specifically told Ernest that he was no longer welcome under their roof.

"We were but then decided we wanted to have our own place."

"I see," Grace said as she continued looking around. "I invited some of Ernest's friends to the party and I included them."

"That was kind of you."

"Well, dear, please give my regards to my son. He's at work now, at that advertising place?"

"The Co-operative Commonwealth."

But he was seldom in the apartment at all. He worked and then in the evenings he took walks. Hadley sensed he was depressed with the apartment and wanted to spend as little time there as possible. Everything was on hold until they had enough money to leave for Italy. He was counting the days. Hadley spent time alone. When she shopped at the corner grocery she took her time. She wanted to avoid the apartment as well. The owner of the store, an older balding man who wore a white apron all day, talked with her and made her laugh with his jokes. Italian. Hadley figured he could smell a lonely woman.

They parted and Grace began the long descent down the stairs. She shook her head as she walked. These children, she expected it from Ernest but she hoped something more from Hadley. After the honeymoon ended and the couple left for Chicago Grace and Clarence went by Windemere cottage in order to close it up for the winter.

They were shocked when they entered.

The mattresses from both beds were on the living room floor. The bed sheets were still there. Dirty dishes were in the sink. There was dirt on the floor. No one had swept. And Clarence, she still pictured him sitting in the other room with Ernest's Marlin .22 in his lap. Clarence agreed to pay for their honeymoon food in exchange for the rifle.

"Look at this," he said, looking up at her with a forlorn look in his eyes. He held up the barrel of the gun.

"I taught Ernest how to take care of this. But he let something get into the bore and then tried to shoot it out. It is ruined. It will have to be completely rebored. He ruined a fine weapon like this."

Clarence shook his head.

"This is what he leaves me?"

As Grace descended the stairs she thought that having just seen their apartment perhaps she hoped for too much.

When Grace left Hadley called Ernest at his office and told him about the visit.

"Glad I was at work," he chuckled.

Then Hadley told him Grace invited Ken and Doodles. Ernest was furious. He instantly wrote a letter to Ken. His mother invited you to their party and "there is no chance, of course, that you and Doodles would go", he wrote, but just in case he was writing to "rescind it personally." Then he added he would come by to get "the residue of my clothes and my probably well thumbed correspondence." Ernest sent it in the afternoon post.

That evening the house was filled with people. Ernest was dressed in a suit and Hadley wore her white wedding dress. Everyone smiled and was proud. Marcelline and Hadley talked a great while. She told Hadley how radiant Hadley looked and how beautifully her shiny red hair glowed in the light. And Hadley listened and politely laughed. Many of the women commented on her having such a young husband. It made her wonder, she was older than Ernest but exactly how old did they think she was?

Ernest talked with his parents' friends. Yes, he was still writing. Yes, he worked for The Cooperative Commonwealth. Yes, she was a lovely bride. Yes, they plan to leave for Italy as soon as they could. Duke Hill, working for Montgomery Ward Company, talked about when they met at Kansas city Union Station when Ernest was a reporter down there. Clarence's brother George, real estate agent, and his wife Anna remembered when Ernest shot the blue heron and took refuge from the law at their house.

Grace and Hadley shared playing the piano. Grace sang as Hadley played. Grace smiled down at her with joy.

Ernest talked with his father in the waiting room of his office. Clarence was proud of him, he said, and he was proud that everyone matured past that unfortunate incident the summer before last.

As his father talked with others Ernest noticed the framed picture on the shelf of his grandfather Anson standing in his Civil War uniform at some Memorial Day with all the children lined up next to him. In the cabinet was the pistol he used in the war. It was clean and freshly oiled. Clarence kept it in perfect working order.

Ernest smiled. His father was like that.

Chapter Fifteen

Agnes traded and took the night shift. None of the other nurses wanted the night shift. Everyone was asleep. There was no one around. But you had to be there in case a patient needed something. You had to be awake in case something happened.

But she liked the night shift. It was dark. There were small lanterns in the hallway but not in the rooms. She could spend the time sitting with Ernest. She sat on the side of his bed. They talked for hours together. They held hands. They had to whisper so no one else could hear but to do so they had to sit close and lean their heads in close to each other and it enveloped their exchange with a veil of intimacy it might not have had in the bright sunlight of day.

He reached up and unhooked from her hair her starched white hat. He ran his fingers through her hair and took out the hairpins holding it in place. Her hair tumbled down. She leaned over him and pressed against him. He felt the press of her breasts against his chest. Her hair was like a soft warm tent enclosing their faces together. In the darkness they could see the glow of their eyes. They listened to each others breath. Their lips touched. Their lips explored.

"You are my sweet boy," she whispered.

"And you are my Angel," he replied.

When the next morning the day nurse discovered a hairpin on his pillow the whispered rumors flew out in all directions like a flock of pigeons frightened by a fox.

1. Medals

They stood in the drizzling rain and watched the parade. Clarence, Grace, Marcelline and Hadley all stood under opened umbrellas. There were hundreds of people lined along the street watching the parade. Most of them were Italian. There were bugles and fanfare, and large flags both American and Italian flapped in the drizzling rain.

In front, leading the parade, marched Captain Nickolas Neroni dressed in his uniform with a chest full of medals. He was the Vice Consul at the Italian Consulate of Chicago. Nick Neroni, friend and boxing partner to Ernest Hemingway, was from Abruzzi and had fought in the battles of Gorizia, Isonzo, Caporetto, Piave River, and the final battle of Vittorio Veneto: along the way he was wounded three times and was awarded four silver crosses and the Croce de Guerra.

Nick marched stiff and formal and kept his eyes to the front. He was very proud. Behind him was the band and behind them a group of soldiers. Some of them were dressed in their uniforms and some dressed in civilian clothes. All had seen service on the Italian front during the war. Clarence was the first to see Ernest walking in the group. Ernest was dressed in his suit. Clarence pointed him out and they shouted and waved. Ernest saw them out of the corner of his eye but he did not acknowledge them. The occasion was too formal for silliness.

It was a good day.

General Armando Vittorio Diaz, the Italian Chief of General Staff, arrived in Chicago and the Consulate had organized a welcoming parade. General Diaz stood on a raised platform under a canopy and watched as the parade passed him by. He wore his uniform. He wore a heavy woolen coat but held it open with his hands at his waist. It exposed his chest full of medals and his wide thick belt. He wore his hat. He smiled and nodded and talked with the others on the platform standing with him. He stroked his full but graying moustache.

General Armando Vittorio Diaz was the hero of the Italian nation. Born in Naples but of Spanish descent, after the disastrous defeat in the battle of Caporetto in October of 1917 Diaz succeed Marshal Luigi Cadorna as Chief of General Staff. He managed to stabilize the Italian Army and held the Austrian offensive at Monte Grappa and the Piave River. Then, in the summer of 1918, he was victorious at the Battle of the Piave River and later at the Battle of Vittorio Veneto. He was honored by delivering the Victory Address, the Bollettino della Vittoria, announcing the final victory of Italy, the defeat of the Austrians, and the conclusion of the war.

General Diaz was on a good will tour of the United States. Earlier in October he landed in New York and was met with bands and parades and thousands of cheering Italian-Americans. Then it was on to Washington D.C. where he was met with the same. Then on November the first he attended the dedication ceremony for the "Liberty Memorial" in Kansas City with General John Pershing and others. Now he was visiting Chicago.

It was Nick who helped organize the parade down Michigan Avenue and, afterword, in the early evening, the banquet at Congress Hotel.

In the banquet hall at the hotel there was a huge crowd. Everyone mixed and chit chatted and ate small hors d'oeuvres and sipped their wine. Clarence and Grace stood off to one side. Several young and handsomely dressed officers in the General's party entertained Marcelline. They stumbled with the language and laughed but she eventually understood them to ask if she would care to accompany them on the rest of the trip around America. She smiled and wondered for several delicious moments what the adventure would be like and seriously entertained the idea until she glanced at Clarence and Grace standing awkwardly in the corner and she knew she had to decline.

Ernest and Hadley in her new black satin dress with Bulgarian embroidery mingled in the crowd. Ernest spoke what Italian he remembered and everyone was overjoyed.

Then the moment came.

Nick rushed over to Ernest and pulled him by the sleeve. They stood at attention with another man by a table at the head of the room. Someone called out in Italian, got everyone's attention, and continued speaking in Italian until many in the room clapped and the General smiled and bowed to the group. He walked over to the table, was handed a medal, and he pinned the medal on the chest of the first man and shook his hand. Then he did the same to Nick and many in the crowd cheered. Then the General pinned a Silver Medal of Military Valor on Ernest. The General shook his hand and thanked him.

Ernest beamed to the crowd.

2. Anderson III

The four of them sat at the table eating. Sherwood Anderson was telling Ernest and Hadley about his trip to Paris with his wife Tennessee Mitchell.

"Paris is so wonderfully beautiful and the French people were all so kind to us. You can live there quite cheaply and the Left Bank is full of writers and artists."

"Where did you stay?" Hadley asked, looking back and forth at Sherwood and Tennessee.

"The Hotel Jacob," he replied.

"It was a small hotel but it was very inexpensive and it was very clean and friendly," Tennessee continued.

"And it is right in the center of things. You can walk almost anywhere from there."

"Sherwood liked to walk in the gardens; they have beautiful gardens all around the city."

"I like to sit in the Luxemburg Gardens on a bench under these large trees and watch the people going by with the breeze overhead tangled up in the trees. I found that to be very relaxing and interesting. But in addition to finding wonderful gardens there were several wonderful people that I was fortunate enough to meet. I was walking one day looking into bookstore windows, and I must say the bookstores in Paris are as frequent as there were bars in Chicago before Prohibition, and as I looked into the windows of one called 'Shakespeare and Company' I saw copies of my own book "Winesburg, Ohio" right there in a window display. I was startled and of course I had to go in and inside it was a warm cheerful place with tables and shelves of books and a big stove with chairs and photographs of different writers on the walls. The owner is a woman named Sylvia Beach with this very wavy brown hair she combs straight back from her forehead and wearing a brown velvet jacket with pockets and a large white tie tied about her neck. We talked and I told her who I was and that I was the author of the book. She was most glad to see me, she told me, and I told her what a surprise it was to see my book because I had not seen a single copy of my book anywhere else in Paris. I am not surprised, she said, because she had searched for it herself and only at one location did they seem to know when the owner said, 'Anderson, Anderson? Oh, sorry, we have only the Fairy Tales.'"

Ernest took another helping of the mashed potatoes. Hadley handed him the gravy boat.

"Sylvia Beach is currently publishing on her own the book "Ulysses" by James Joyce because apparently no one else wanted to touch it. It is an enormous undertaking and I myself subscribed for a copy when it finally appears. It is interesting that over here Ben Huebsch has come out with both of Joyce's other works "Dubliners" and "A Portrait of the Artist as a Young Man" but did not take up "Ulysses." Wanting to meet Joyce, and now friends with his publisher, I wrote a letter to him asking for the privilege of calling on him but instead he himself came to the hotel to meet me. As Miss Beach explained he still saw himself as the struggling artist but I had already become the established artist so I must say that I felt especially honored. He proved to be a misty gloomy Irishman, a long handsome man with the most delicately lovely hands I have ever seen on a human being. He is very witty in conversation and with a smile that lights up his face as when a light enters a dark room. We all liked him at once. And I dare say that his book "Ulysses" will be the most important book that will be published in this generation. I do say Ernest that you will be well served to heed him."

Anderson stopped and drank from his glass.

"You have given us some very interesting stories and observations," Hadley added.

Anderson smiled and nodded.

"It was Sylvia Beach who came with me and introduced me to the one person that I wanted most to see in Paris, and that was Gertrude Stein. I asked her if she could introduce us and she said that I was an accomplished writer and therefore needed no introduction but that she would do the honors so we went around to their apartment. Gertrude is a very large woman and a strong woman with legs like stone pillars sitting in a room hung with Picassos. I told her how much I admired her use of words in "Tender Buttons" and "Three Lives" and the tremendous influence she had on my own writing. It reminds me of Saturday mornings in Clyde when I went around collecting for the newspapers that I delivered the week before, and as standing on the porches women came out from their kitchens filled with the aroma of jarred fruits and jellies and preserves and handmade goodies so too she as the cook in her great kitchen of words creates and brings forth such delights. She was visibly touched by praise and she said that I was really the only person who understands what her writing is all about."

Anderson stopped and then smiled to himself.

"To dine is to west," he said as if remembering something but he did not share what it was.

As the pot of water on the stove heated for coffee Tennessee took Hadley into her studio.

"We'll let the boys have a moment," she said, "while we do too."

As they walked into the studio Hadley felt the cold. There were several half formed statues of clay on a waist high table. Sunlight through the window streaked the room. One of the windows was open and the cold air from outside came in. Tennessee, tall, thin and sleek, seemed to flow as she walked over to her statues and ran her fingers around the still unshaped forms.

"I sculpt," she said. "In an ideal world I would sculpt for a living. Sherwood tells me you wanted to play piano professionally, is that true?"

Hadley moved into the shaft of the sun.

"Oh, well, yes that was a dream I had at one time. Several of my teachers told me that I should try."

"Dreams are wonderful things to have, Hadley. I teach piano as a living. At one time I even tuned pianos as a living. One does what one needs to do to survive."

"Did you ever think of playing yourself?"

The sun felt warm on her. She could feel the warmth on her face and through her blouse. It counteracted the cold from the outside.

"No, I teach music but don't really play. I prefer sculpture; I like to feel the form with my fingers and I like to be immersed in the sensual. Music to me seems a little too intellectual, a little too much formal structure. That is why I like Sherwood, actually, because he is an artist that writes of the sensual life of people, of what they feel and live rather than what they intellectually ponder. And his books are a little formless and free. The sun feels good doesn't it, I can feel it on my back."

"Yes it does. But why do you have the window open on such a chilly day?"

"If all of the windows are closed then the afternoon sun can heat up this room fiercely and it gets hot and stuffy so I keep ajar a window to let the coolness of the air outside counter the sun's heat. It keeps the air fresh."

"I see."

Hadley walked around the room looking at the different statues in various stages of being complete. Tennessee watched her.

"Sherwood said that your mother recently passed away."

"Yes, well, that was just over a year ago."

"Still, something like that does not go away. If you don't mind the question, were you there when it happened?"

"Yes, yes I was. I was holding her hand."

Tennessee sighed.

"You see my sister Amber died of scarlet fever. It was just the two of

319

us and we were very poor at the time. I walked up and down the streets trying to find a hospital that would take her in but they all said no. No. So I took care of her myself in our small room. She died in my arms."

"That must have been awful. I am so sorry."

"I just hugged her and hugged her long after she was gone. I couldn't let go. I could not function at all for months. I just wanted to end."

Hadley felt cold. She moved back into the shaft of the suns setting sunlight.

"So we have some things in common," Tennessee said as if searching, asking.

"Yes, it seems that we do. Music. And with your sculpture too, in a small way, because I actually modeled for the sculptor Marguerite Schullyer in St. Louis."

"Oh really, I've heard of her. Well, see, there you are."

They both laughed.

"You know that Gertrude Stein is strange. When we went there Sherwood sat down and they started a conversation and I tried to sit down with them to hear but Gertrude's companion, Alice, she kept talking with me and calling me away to see something, she wanted to show me something, and she never let me sit down with Sherwood and Gertrude. It became very annoying. But then Sylvia told me that was the strategy. Gertrude wants unhindered access to the man so if he happens to bring his wife along then it is up to Alice to keep them away. Can you believe that?"

"You are right; it does sound a little bit strange."

"So if your husband ever goes there keep that in mind. Alice likes to talk about gardening and cooking."

"Gardening and cooking; I'll remember that."

"You know, it's good that you have your music. Unless you are an artist yourself you will never understand the force that drives them. I pity the woman who is married to an artist and does not have something else in her life. Art is like a mistress. It is a mistress that you have to live with."

They said goodnight and Ernest and Hadley left. It was dark by the time they left. The night was cold. The evening breeze chilled them through. They hugged their coats. Hadley had her arm in his. They walked in unison.

"He really says that Paris is the place for any writer," Ernest said.

"Yes, I know. He so wants you to go to Paris because he believes in you and that is where he thinks you will succeed."

They walked on in the cold together. Ernest stared in front of him as he thought about it. As they walked Hadley looked at the stark leafless trees. December cold: spring in Paris?

"But we've been planning Italy all along, and we bought all of the lira for the trip, and I can speak enough Italian to get by and I know parts of Italy and I wanted to show you were I was and what happened there."

They were walking fast. She did not know if it was because they were cold or excited.

"But we can exchange the lira, and I studied French in school for years so it should come back to me. We have to consider what is best for you and your writing."

"So what, do you think it should be Paris too?"

"Ernest, you've already had that experience in Italy, you need something fresh. There should be something new and fresh for us, something we share together. We can build something together, something that is ours rather than try to build onto the foundations of something that used to be. What I want is what is best for you. It seems being surrounded by other artists would be better than working alone in Italy."

They walked on in the chilly December evening. Ernest stared ahead thinking; thinking.

"Anderson said he could write me letters of introduction. I could meet James Joyce, Joyce, I mean I hear that he's like a god. The face of literature is changing and it is changing there."

"Well then?" she asked.

Ernest stopped and turned toward her. She looked at him. He held her close and kissed her long and hard. Then he turned and started walking again. She held onto his arm.

"Does that mean we are going to Paris?"

3. Money

Hadley sat at the small kitchen table. Papers were spread out in front of her. The morning dishes sat on the counter by the sink unwashed. Ernest had gone for a walk. He had to get out, he said, he was depressed and his anger was boiling over.

Hadley used the time to figure things out.

Ernest was writing and writing but did not sell a single story. At first he kept the rejection slips as a badge of honor but now, with so many, he simply threw them away when they came. So there was no income from that.

He no longer worked for the Toronto Star. It's managing editor, John Bone, wrote to Ernest in February offering him a job as a European correspondent. Ernest checked with his friend Greg Clark at the Star. He said yes, but ask for no less than $70 a week. In March Ernest wrote back to John Bone and said that he made $75 a week at the Co-operative (when he actually made $50) but he was willing to come back to the Star as European correspondent for $85 a week. He could start April first. Ernest never received a reply. So there was no income from that.

And now his job at the Co-operative Society of America had collapsed. The Society was a financial bubble. On October first the President, Harrison Parker, filed for bankruptcy. By October 7 Judge Evans put the company into receivership. The Judge called for a Grand Jury for criminal indictments against Harrison Parker, his wife Edith S. Parker, and several of their associates.

There had been fourteen million dollars worth of beneficial interest certificates sold to thousands of small investors, thousands of small working class men and women who believed in all of the advertising and believed in the intentions of the company. Eleven million of that capital Parker put into a company he set up called Great Western Securities Company. His wife Edith was the treasurer. The other three million dollars was given to Edith to buy Liberty Bonds.

But there were no Liberty Bonds to be found. And all of the money was gone. Ernest wrote the October 8 issue of the newsletter but that was the last one. His final check for September, with a week taken out for his honeymoon, was for $150. So now there was no income left from there.

Ernest, newly wed, was unemployed and without prospect. The loss of his job threw all of their plans to the winds. A trip to Europe, whether it was to be Italy or Paris, now seemed out of the question. Ernest now had to find work, any work, so how could he write?

Hadley had to figure it out. She was not going to let their dreams die so soon.

She took out the budget she had made and looked for where they could cut it down. Then she took out the folder where she kept all of her trust papers. On a blank sheet of paper she began tabulating.

Maybe, she thought, just maybe.

James Richardson Sr., her paternal grandfather, was very successful. In his will in 1893 he left Hadley a small trust fund of about $12,000. She had not touched the money and the interest accrued until it was now worth about $30,000.

Hadley tabulated the figures on her sheet of paper.

She set those trust papers aside.

Her mother Florence died August 19, 1920. The estate was not yet final but would be soon. The full estate was worth around $75,000. According to the will the estate was to be distributed to her children Hadley, Fonnie, Jaime, and Dorothea's two sons. Hadley would receive a trust of $15,636. There was also set aside a trust of $5,357 for any children that Hadley might have.

Ernest knew about the trust fund from her grandfather. And Ernest knew that she would inherit something from her mother although he did not know the final amount. Hadley kept that a secret.

Hadley tabulated the figures on her sheet of paper.

She set those trust papers aside.

But there was another secret that Ernest did not know. There was a reason Hadley picked September 3 as their wedding day. It could not be sooner.

There was a codicil her mother added to her will. She never believed Hadley would marry. She thought Hadley too weak and delicate and she was already almost twenty nine without any prospects. Fonnie was already married to a university professor. So her mother reasoned that Hadley would need a bit more than Fonnie. So her mother wrote in the codicil that if Hadley "be single one year after the date of my death, I give and bequeath. . .the sum of five thousand dollars, to be added to and become a part of the trust therein created for my said daughter."

If Hadley married before the year anniversary of her mother's death the five thousand dollars would go back into the general fund for everyone. But if Hadley were still single then the five thousand came to her.

Her mother died on August 19, 1920. Hadley intentionally made her wedding for September 3, 1921. The extra money was hers.

Hadley tabulated the figures on her sheet of paper.

She set those trust papers aside.

Hadley pulled out a letter from her trust papers folder. It was from a law office. Her Uncle on her mother's side, Arthur Wyman, had just that month passed away. Upon reading the will it was stipulated that he left Hadley the sum of $8,000. The lawyer requested the address and account number of her bank in order to transfer the funds. Attached to the letter was a copy of her response.

Ernest knew he had died but that was all.

Hadley tabulated the figures on her sheet of paper.

She set the letter back into her folder.

We can do it, she thought. She would be giving it everything she had but she felt good. All she wanted now was for him to be successful, for him to be happy, for him to have all that he wants.

She thought a strange thought. We will be totally living off of my income. That is not unlike when Ernest's parents were first married Clarence was just starting his practice as a doctor and they had to live off of Grace's income for a long while.

I better not point that out.

When Ernest came home he came up to her sitting at the kitchen table. He saw all of the papers.

"I've been thinking," he said.

"So have I," she said.

"I'm going to write to John Bone at the Toronto Star again. He offered me a job as a reporter in Europe but I think I scared him with my price. I just have to ask if he is still interested but this time let him set the pay."

She nodded and kept nodding, a growing smile creeping across her face.

"What?" he asked, knowing that something was up.

"I think that is exactly the right thing to do."

"And?"

"I've been going over everything, our budget, the money from my trust, and I think we can make it. As a matter of fact I know we can make it."

"How?"

"Well, I won't bore you with all of the details but we can do it, I mean we have to live cheaply, we can't be extravagant, we have to watch every penny, but we can do it just on the money from the trust, especially when my mothers kicks in. You can totally focus on your writing and I know that will break through at some point. But if you get newspaper work with the Toronto Star then that is even better."

"But all I have coming in now is from my medal, it pays fifty lira a year for life."

They both broke out laughing.

"Oh, we can live on that just fine," Hadley said as she tried to control her laughter.

"Gee, I thought so too."

When they calmed down Hadley stood up and held out her hands. He took her hands into his.

"What is important, Mr. Ernest Hemingway, is that we are going to Paris and you are going to be a famous writer."

Ernest sat down and wrote his letter to John Bone. He was reluctant at first. Greg Clark wrote to him that there were rumors about John Bone. As managing editor he was taking articles written by junior reporters, and especially articles without a by line, and reselling them to other papers but with his name in the by line. He personally pocketed the money.

Ernest was burned by the Co-operative experience. Why is there so much corruption, cheating, stealing, lying? And Ernest wrote for them, wrote advertisements for people to invest their money, Ernest helped promote their cause, their corrupt cause. And now with John Bone; if he is doing what Clark says then he will be stealing what Ernest writes and cheating him out of the republishing revenue. No matter how much you want to be true and clean how can you not get dirty in a dirty world?

But Ernest wrote the letter. He needed the money.

Several weeks later John Bone replied. He wanted Ernest as a roving reporter in Europe and will pay regular space rates for all stories they print as well as legitimate traveling expenses. He will also pay $75 a week for assignments such as the upcoming conferences at Genoa and Lausanne. But he had to work out of the Toronto Star's headquarters in Paris.

When Ernest read the letter to Hadley she was puzzled.

"Does that mean we have to go to Paris?"

4. Anderson IV

Ernest climbed the stairs to Sherwood Anderson's apartment on East Division Street. His heavy steps boomed and echoed in the narrow stairway. It was late in the evening. Everything was quiet except for his footfalls. He carried a heavy knapsack on his back.

At the door he reached up to knock but the door opened. Anderson, when he saw who it was, smiled and reached out his hand.

"Ernest, what brings you here this late?"

"How did you know it was me?"

"I didn't but I heard someone coming up the stairs. Please, come in, come in."

"I brought these for you," Ernest said as he pulled off his knapsack.

"And what do we have?"

Ernest walked into the small kitchen and snapped on the light. Anderson followed. Ernest swung the knapsack down onto the kitchen table with a clatter. He opened it and started taking out cans of food and putting them onto the table.

"We're leaving tomorrow and we have all this food left that we can't take so I wanted to give them to you."

Anderson stood speechless. He held up his hands, palms together, and touched his lips with his fingertips as if in prayer.

"How nice," he was finally able to whisper.

"If you can't use them then just give them to someone else."

"No, I will certainly use them. I thank you, I truly thank you."

"It's the least I can do for you. I should pay you back something for all that you have done for me."

"How touching it is for a gift of food from one scribbler to another."

When he finished stacking the cans Ernest strapped the empty knapsack on his back. They stood together for a moment.

"So," Anderson finally broke the silence. "So it is off for Paris then."

"Yes, I've had my heart set on Italy for so long it was a tough decision."

"But you have been to Italy. It represents an important part of your life that you will have in your heart forever."

"Yes, and that's why I wanted to show Hadley, show her where I was stationed and where I was wounded."

"She cannot share that, Ernest. It belongs to you and you alone. What did she say when you told her that?"

"She said that she would rather not see it so I asked her why, I was a little hurt that she didn't want to share that part of my life."

"And what was her reason?"

"She said that it's a painful hurtful place and why do I want to go back there because it is all changed by now. So I said no, I'll show you; something like that does not change."

"But it does, Ernest. Believe me when I say this. You left a part of yourself there and you cannot go back thinking you can find it. It is gone. You can only go forward."

"I guess I understand that now. I thought about it and you are right, if I want to really be a writer then Paris it is."

"And speaking of that, follow me into the front room."

Anderson walked over to a desk by the window. He picked up several envelopes.

"I sent a letter to Louis Galantiere telling him about you and Hadley so when you get there look him up. He lives at the Hotel Jacob. I wrote saying that you are a young fellow of extraordinary talent who will get somewhere and that Hadley is charming and the two of you are great playmates. He will take care of you."

Anderson handed Ernest the envelopes.

"These are letters of introduction that you should mail out like launching a flock of ships when you get to Paris. There is one to Sylvia Beach, one to Gertrude Stein and one to James Joyce. Each note says that you are an American writer instinctively in touch with everything worth while going on here and that you and Hadley are delightful people to know."

"Thank you for all you've done. You've been invaluable to me. As it turns out I've been hired by the Toronto Star."

"Really?"

"The editor is John Bone, I knew him when I worked there before. I wrote to him and we agreed that I could be a foreign correspondent based out of Paris. He'll pay me by the word with travel expenses."

"So you won't have to live as frugally as before."

"No, no we won't."

"Well that is excellent. I do hope you have as rewarding an experience in Europe as I did. I feel energized."

"I'm sure that I will."

"While we were there we visited the cathedral of Chartres. It was a gray morning, a little misty, and I sat on a wooden bench in the open space facing the cathedral. I sat for a long time, most of the day, just sitting and looking, looking, trying to absorb the whole thing. Sitting there, myself no longer young, I thought back over my life thinking of how I had spent most of my life striving to get all of the things that I believed I wanted, striving to get money and be a rich man, striving to get power, striving to be successful in all things, but then I found in the end I was perfectly content to just sit and look, to look and listen, and to absorb everything around me and then, in a small corner away from everyone, write it all down, put into words everything around me."

Anderson tapped Ernest on the arm.

"Who was it, I think it was Joseph Conrad who said that a writer only begins to live after he begins to write. I finally, after most of my life, found a way to be alive. I looked at the cathedral and thought of the men who built it, the twelfth and thirteenth century men who built it with their hands, craftsmen, helping to build the beauty that they felt in their hearts. There were many visitors there that day, all in a hurry, walking by the cathedral reading their brochures getting wet in the mist and then looking up and glancing back and forth for a moment and then moving on. Cathedral seen: what is next on the tour? They were in a hurry, they had a dinner engagement perhaps, or they were getting tired from too much walking, too much to see, why is there so much to see?"

Anderson stopped and cleared his throat. Ernest glanced at the clock on the wall.

"An American man came with two women, one woman appeared to be American and the other was French. They stood by the large open wooden carved cathedral doors and talked. The man and the French woman were flirting with each other, laughing and giggling, but the American woman pretended not to notice. She pretended to be most interested in the doors. I realized that before my eyes a woman was losing her man and she did not know how to stop it. The three of them went inside but then after a moment the American woman came back outside alone. She stood and faced toward the door, the thirteenth century door so beautifully carved and so lovingly created, she stood facing the door with a handkerchief in her hand, and what had been in the hearts of the workers as they carved the door, what loss, what hope, what love, what loneliness, and facing the door with her back turned toward me so no one would see with her handkerchief she quietly dabbed the tears in her eyes."

Anderson stopped for a moment as if to reflect, as if to remember. Ernest wondered if that was all to the story.

"After a moment or two the young woman went back inside the cathedral. I looked up and filled my eyes with the cathedral beauty. I wondered what the cathedral does, why was the beautiful art of it built, for what purpose. I thought that it makes us aware; it reminds us, here and now, of the presence of an eternal God. Does art do no more than that? It makes us aware. It catches a moment and allows us to see the eternal flow of life. See this moment, it seems to say, see this moment that was just here and now is gone, but here it is captured so we can forever be aware of that moment's sacred beauty."

Anderson stopped again. He smiled looking at Ernest. Ernest smiled in return.

"The man and the two women came out of the cathedral and walked off down the lane together. They left. They were gone. Sitting on my wooden bench in the gray mist of the day I watched. I had been touched. There was something there. What had happened, why did it happen, is it the end of something that was, is it the beginning of something that will be, what does each of them feel, what did they feel before, and how will they feel after now? I see a small face in the crowd and a story unfolds, a story that must be told, for it is the story of them, but it is also the story of everyone. If I am an artist, if I am a writer, then it is my task to take that moment and make it stop, make it stand still for all to see and for all to feel. And everyone will be touched, for some will say yes, that is me, now, while others will smile and say yes that was me ten years ago, while others will sigh and wonder if that will be them tomorrow. But everyone will be touched, yes, now everyone will see the face in the crowd that I saw, and everyone will experience the fleeting moment that was just here but is now gone, and everyone will then be made aware and come to touch again the eternity of the human heart."

Anderson stopped for a fourth time. He moved a pencil on his desk as if it had been in the wrong place.

"Is that the whole purpose of art?" Ernest asked.

"To touch the eternal and through the artist let others touch it too? I do not know," Anderson replied. "But it reminds me of a painting that I saw while I was in Europe. It was a painting by Vincent Van Gogh. It was a painting of an old pair of shoes. That is it: an old pair of worn and torn shoes. Now there are those who will ask, a pair of old shoes, but where is the art in that? Surely he should just discard those old shoes and wear some new shoes as if the purpose of the painting was about shoes at all. No: it is just a pair of old shoes, a simple pair of old and worn and torn shoes but what a story they tell. We only have to see the shoes to know the history of who wore the shoes, we know all of the toil and the hardships and the suffering and the loneliness of the man to which they belonged. The story is there, hidden, but brought forth in the golden moment of seeing the old worn out pair of shoes sitting in disarray on the wooden floor."

Anderson stopped. Ernest put the envelopes in his hand into his pocket. He wanted to ask.

"Do you see everything that way?"

Anderson was a little taken by the question.

"Don't you?"

5. Gone

They sat on the small sofa. Their packed luggage was sitting in the center of the small room. They were waiting for the movers to come and load the crates and luggage and take them to the train station.

"We'll come back won't we?" Hadley asked. She sat very stiff with her hands in her lap.

"To here?"

Hadley laughed as she looked around the small bare apartment.

"No, not here, but here, in the United States."

"Of course."

It was cold and it was raining. Ernest listened to the rain against the closed window. He could hear the rainwater flowing down the spouts.

He turned and faced her.

"You believe in me?"

"Yes; absolutely."

"You think I can be a great writer?"

"I think you already are one."

Ernest leaned in and kissed her. She watched his eyes as he pulled away.

"I'll make you proud," he whispered. "I'll make you proud of me."

"But I already am proud of you."

"No, I really mean it. You are the world to me."

She smiled but did not reply.

The door bell rang.

It was Clarence. He was wearing his oiled raincoat and a large slouch hat. He was wet from the rain.

There were several crates Ernest wanted to leave behind and Clarence said he could store them up in the attic. Ernest put on his heavy coat and then they carried the crates down the stairs. There was a box of wedding gifts, kitchenware, a box of his war souvenirs including his bloodied and shredded uniform, a box of clippings from the Kansas City Star, the Toronto Star and the Commonwealth. And there was a crate with his old unsold manuscripts.

Ernest was leaving behind all that he had been.

Leicester was in the front seat of car. He waved at Ernest through the rain washed windows.

Once the crates were loaded into the back of the car Clarence shut the back door and he and Ernest stood for a moment. The rain dripped from the rim of his father's hat. Ernest's hair was getting wet. It was a cold chilly rain.

"So long son," Clarence said. "I wish you the best."

"Thank you," Ernest said.

They stood for a moment but then they hugged each other.

"Well," Clarence finally said. "Write to me from Paris."

Ernest nodded.

When Clarence got into the car he sat for a moment shaking his head.

"Those young people," he muttered. He turned his head toward Les as he cranked the key. "Do you know what they were cooking their eggs in?" He chuckled and turned his head away. "Well, I won't say it."

Clarence drove off in the rain.

The next morning it was a freezing cold early morning. At the train station passengers and their friends saying goodbye stood with heavy coats and long woolen scarves. A large bulletin board announced the arrivals and the departures of trains. The rain from the day before stopped in the night but the platform was still wet. It was cold enough that if it started to rain now it could come down as snow. The four friends stood on the platform near the rear of the train. Ernest said good bye to each of them one by one.

He shook hands with Howell Jenkins.

"Goodbye Fever, don't howl at the moon."

"Ernie, best of luck," Jenkins said. His red moustache seemed to curl around the base of his nose. He held up his thumb and said: "For all the beer in Schio."

They were in Italy waiting to go to the front. Bill Horne called themselves the Schio Country Club after his fraternity Princeton school days. They were in uniform sitting in the checkerboard shade of the trattoria patio. Trellised wisteria hung down. Jenkins held up his half empty glass of beer and said to them all, 'to us, for all the beer in Schio.'

Ernest nodded at the memory.

It was Jenkins who told him that he should not get married. 'Don't do this, don't get married Ernie. Being tied to a woman is not good for a writer.' But yet he was there at the wedding and he was here to see them off.

"Don't get too rich being a stockbroker," Ernest said.

"There is no such thing as being too rich."

Ernest turned to his sister Marcelline.

"Well, so long Mazaween."

"Oh Ernie," she said as she in a rush wrapped her arms around him. "We all love you so much. You take care of yourself. Okay? Promise?"

He started to pull away but she seemed to cling to him for a moment in silence.

Ernest kissed her cheek. She pulled away. There were tears in her eyes. They had grown distant, different. Maybe one day it could be as it was, before they both grew up. Ernest laughed a little in order to keep control. He nodded to her and then turned to Bill Horne.

Bill stepped up to Ernest and hugged him and then quickly pulled away. There was pain in his eyes.

"Well, Mr. Horney."

"You're a good man Ernie; I'm going to miss you. I'm going to miss you a lot."

"Thanks for all you've done for me Horney, and I swear I'm going to pay you back the National Debt I owe you."

Bill waved him off.

"Don't worry. You can forget about that until you're on your feet. I told you before, I'm backing you in a marathon not a fifty yard dash."

Seeing him there, thin, his face drawn, his large black eyeglasses swallowing his eyes, his brown scarf wrapped around his neck, Ernest felt sorry for Bill Horne. He was so attached to Ernest, desperately attached, that this must be a great blow. Ernest was moving so far away that they would not see each other, they would not fish together, they would not camp and hike together, and they would not simply sit and drink wine and be with each other.

Ernest began to feel what it was he was leaving behind. He left behind a life lived; he left behind a world gone. Steam from the waiting train rolled by thick like a fog through a forest.

"We have to move on, Old Man," Ernest said not knowing why, as if trying to explain, trying to make amends.

Bill nodded.

Ernest moved on to the last in line.

Katy Smith stood silent: her tangled hair uncombed, her green eyes staring and absorbing every last detail of every last moment. She had her head turned to one side like she did; it was one of the things he liked about her.

"Well Wemedge," she said as she held out her hand. They shook hands in silence. They stood for a moment. But then Ernest put his arms around her and she put her arms around him. He held her close.

She whispered to him. "For what could have been." He held her close. "And for what is," she again whispered. Ernest took a long deep breath.

The train whistle blew a chilling call. They both jumped at the sound. Ernest let go and turned away. Hadley, watching, waited by the steps of the train.

When they went up the stairs onto the train Marc noticed Hadley's naked hand taking hold of the icy cold iron railing on the Pullman steps.

"Do put on your gloves, Hadley."

"I don't have any gloves."

"But your hands will freeze."

"It's fine, we'll be in New York soon."

Marc stripped off her own grey woolen gloves.

"Here, Hash, take mine," she said as she threw them up at Hadley who, surprised, managed to reach out and catch the gloves. She smiled down at Marc and then slipped the gloves on.

"Thanks, Marc. That's a real going away present."

The train gave out a long loud shrill.

The train jolted and began to move. Ernest stood next to Hadley and waved. The cold air played with his hair. Horne unwrapped his woolen scarf around his neck, rolled it into a ball, and then shouted out to Ernest as he threw the scarf at him. Ernest caught it with both hands.

"That's a going away present for you, Ernie."

"Thanks."

The train picked up speed.

Katy cupped her hands around her mouth and shouted out: "Write to us from Paris."

They all stood silent and watched as the train pulled away. Ernest had his hand around Hadley's waist and they stood on the back platform waving for as long as they could still see their disappearing friends.

Marc had to wipe away tears. She held a white handkerchief in one hand. She looked over at Bill Horne. He had taken off his eyeglasses and wiped his eyes with his sleeve.

The last they saw of Ernest Hemingway was of him standing on the back of the train waving to them as he disappeared into his future.

He was gone.

L'Envoi

Lieutenant Colter was admitted to the hospital. He was an aviator. He was sick with the influenza. Agnes cared for him. He had a bad fever. He could not keep any food down. He was constantly hot and sweating. She rubbed him down with cool wet cloths.

He was very nice, she said later. He was so sweet. He did not want me to worry. Is there anyone here I can call, I asked. No, he said. Everyone he knew lived so far away.

He got worse. She tried to make him as comfortable as possible. She told Cavie about him and even though her shift was over she stayed on to help.

He was so much worse that night. But both Agnes and Cavie thought they could pull him through. Ernest, wondering why Agnes had not come to him went looking for her. I'll be there soon, she said. Dr. Jardine came at ten forty five and examined the Lieutenant so sick so far away from home. The doctor told Agnes that these cases were liable to go very quickly.

Agnes and Cavie became desperate. They gave him his medications, they took his pulse, his blood pressure, and they had a constant supply of wet cool towels to wipe over him, to wipe away the fever.

It was no use.

Agnes hugged him in her arms feeling the heat of his burning body when he suddenly just stopped breathing. They pumped his chest. They blew into his mouth.

Nothing.

Agnes sat on the side of the bed and held him in her arms. It seemed so dreadful to die off in a strange land with none of his people near. She held him so he would know that there was someone here.

"He was such a sweet man," she said to Cavie.

Tears streamed down her face.

It was the first time she cried at the loss of a patient.

Ernest appeared at the door. He was impatient.

"Not now," she said. "Ernie, please not now."

335

NOTE TO READER

This is a historical novel. It is a fictional account about a real person and real events. Therein is the problem a writer of historical fiction faces. You want to make it up in your own words but you also want to be as historically accurate as possible. That creates a thin red line between fiction and plagiarism. There are parts where I use the actual words spoken, the actual words written, or the actual scene as it happened. In other places I put into fiction what biographers suggest may have happened.

Is this plagiarism? Short of filling the novel with footnotes how can you distinguish between what flows from my pen and what flowed from another? Should the fiction writer never use the actual words spoken? When the real Hadley said "the world's a jail and we're going to break it together" should the fictional Hadley be barred from saying it? Would you not diminish the passion and the drive and the style of speech of the real Hadley? You would, on purpose, divert from historical accuracy.

My solution is this. As you read keep in mind that not all of this is me. I do not claim that every word or every scene flowed from my pen. The novel is a close interwoven fabric of fiction and non fiction. A Hemingway aficionado can easily pick out where I used the actual words of others as well as scenes first suggested by biographers.

Many sources were consulted in the writing of this novel. I include a bibliography of the most consulted and the most suggestive. I invite the reader a place to begin your own journey toward being a Hemingway aficionado so you too can unravel the fabric between the real and my fiction of the real.

BIBLIOGRAPHY

1. Baker, Carlos, ERNEST HEMINGWAY: A LIFE STORY, New York, New York: Avon Books, 1968

2. Brian, Denis, THE TRUE GEN, New York, New York: Dell Publishing, 1988

3. Burrill, William, HEMINGWAY: THE TORONTO YEARS, Toronto, Ontario, Canada: Doubleday Canada Limited, 1994

4. Cappel (Montgomery), Constance, HEMINGWAY IN MICHIGAN, Waitsfield, Vermont: Vermont Crossroads Press, 1977

5. Diliberto, Gioia, HADLEY, New York, New York: Ticknor & Fields, 1992

6. Fanning, Michael, FRANCE AND SHERWOOD ANDERSON: PARIS NOTEBOOK, 1921, Baton Rouge, Louisiana: Louisiana State University Press, 1976

7. Federspiel, Michael R., PICTURING HEMINGWAY'S MICHIGAN, Detroit, Michigan: Wayne State University Press, 2010

8. Fenton, Charles A., THE APPRENTICESHIP OF ERNEST HEMINGWAY: THE EARLY YEARS, New York, New York: Compass Books, 1954

9. Griffin, Peter, ALONG WITH YOUTH: HEMINGWAY, THE EARLY YEARS, New York, New York: Oxford University Press, 1985

10. Hemingway, Ernest, IN OUR TIME, New York, New York: Charles Scribner's Sons, 1925

11. Hemingway, Ernest, THE COMPLETE SHORT STORIES OF ERNEST HEMINGWAY, New York, New York: Charles Scribner's Sons, 1987

12. Hemingway, Ernest, THE NICK ADAMS STORIES, New York, New York: Charles Scribner's Sons, 1972

13. Hemingway, Ernest, THE TORRENTS OF SPRING, New York, New York: Charles Scribner's Sons, 1926

14. Hemingway, Leicester, MY BROTHER, ERNEST HEMINGWAY, Cleveland, Ohio: The World Publishing Company, 1961

15. Hemingway, Marcelline, AT THE HEMINGWAYS, Moscow, Idaho: University of Idaho Press, 1998

16. Lynn, Kenneth S., HEMINGWAY, New York, New York: Fawcett Columbine, 1987

17. Main, Georgianna, PIP PIP to Hemingway in Something from Marge, Bloomington, Indiana: iUniverse, 2010

18. Mellow, James R., HEMINGWAY: A LIFE WITHOUT CONSEQUENCES, Cambridge, Massachusetts: Perseus Publishing, 1992

19. Meyers, Jeffrey, HEMINGWAY: A BIOGRAPHY, Cambridge, Massachusetts: Da Capo Press, Inc., 1985

20. Reynolds, Michael, THE YOUNG HEMINGWAY, New York, New York: W. W. Norton & Company, 1986

21. Rideout, Walter B., SHERWOOD ANDERSON: A WRITER IN AMERICA, VOLUME ONE, Madison, Wisconsin: The University of Wisconsin Press, 2006

22. Sokoloff, Alice Hunt, HADLEY: THE FIRST MRS. HEMINGWAY, New York, New York: Dodd, Mead & Company, 1973

23. Spanier, Sandra and Trogdon, Robert w., THE LETTERS OF ERNEST HEMINGWAY: VOLUME 1 1907-1922, New York, New York: Cambridge University Press, 2011

24. Townsend, Kim, SHERWOOD ANDERSON, Boston, Massachusetts: Houghton Mifflin Company, 1987

25. Villard, Henry S. and Nagel, James, HEMINGWAY IN LOVE AND WAR: THE LOST DIARY OF AGNES VON KUROWSKY, New York, New York: Hyperion, 1989

26. Westbrook, Max, "Grace under Pressure: Hemingway and the Summer of 1920," Wagner, Linda W. (editor), ERNEST HEMINGWAY: SIX DECADES OF CRITICISM, East Lansing, Michigan: Michigan State University Press, 1987

ABOUT THE AUTHOR

With a Masters Degree in Philosophy, John is a writer, owns an accounting firm, is married to an accomplished photographer and performing musician, has a best friend who is the daughter of a famous abstract painter, and also has an artistic photographer as a friend.

He lives in and experiences multiple worlds. This gives him a unique blend of practical and artistic insight that carries over into his novels and stories.

John is a highly eclectic writer. His short story collection *Pillar of Stories* ranges from the literary to horror to travel to comedy. His historical novels, like *J.P.*, his novel of the banker J. P. Morgan, are fast paced and plot driven narratives. However his more literary novels, such as his four volume *Fire in Winter*, are very character driven, slower paced, and richly dense symbolic works.

In his output there is something for everyone.